THE HISTORY OF BEES

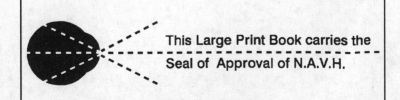

This Large Print Book carries the
Seal of Approval of N.A.V.H.

THE HISTORY OF BEES

MAJA LUNDE

THORNDIKE PRESS
A part of Gale, a Cengage Company

Farmington Hills, Mich • San Francisco • New York • Waterville, Maine
Meriden, Conn • Mason, Ohio • Chicago

Copyright© 2015 by H. Aschehoug & Co. (W Nygaard), AS
Originally published in Norwegian in 2015 as *Bienes historie* by
Aschehoug, Oslo
Translation copyright © 2015 by Diane Oatley
Thorndike Press, a part of Gale, a Cengage Company.

LIBRARY OF CONGRESS CIP DATA ON FILE.
CATALOGUING IN PUBLICATION FOR THIS BOOK
IS AVAILABLE FROM THE LIBRARY OF CONGRESS

ISBN-13: 978-1-4328-4576-6 (hardcover)
ISBN-10: 1-4328-4576-4 (hardcover)

Published in 2017 by arrangement with Touchstone, an imprint of
Simon & Schuster, Inc.

Printed in the United States of America
1 2 3 4 5 6 7 21 20 19 18 17

To Linus, Jens and Jesper

Tao

District 242, Shirong, Sichuan, 2098

Like oversize birds, we balanced on our respective branches, each of us with a plastic container in one hand and a feather brush in the other.

I climbed upwards, very slowly, as carefully as I could. I was not cut out for this, wasn't like many of the other women on the crew, my movements were often too heavy-handed. I lacked the subtle motor skills and precision required. This wasn't what I was made for, but all the same I had to be here, every single day, twelve hours a day.

The trees were as old as a lifetime. The branches were as fragile as thin glass, they cracked beneath our weight. I twisted myself carefully, mustn't damage the tree. I placed my right foot on a branch even further up, and carefully pulled the left up behind it. And finally I found a secure working position, uncomfortable but stable. From here I could reach the uppermost flowers.

The little plastic container was full of the gossamer gold, carefully weighed out. I tried to transfer invisible portions lightly out of the container and over into the trees. Each individual blossom was to be dusted with the tiny brush of hen feathers, from hens scientifically cultivated for precisely this purpose. No feathers of artificial fibers had proven nearly as effective. It had been tested, and then tested again, because we had had plenty of time — in my district the tradition of hand pollination was more than a hundred years old. The bees here had disappeared back in the 1980s, long before The Collapse; pesticides had done away with them. A few years later, when the pesticides were no longer in use, the bees returned, but by then hand pollination had already been implemented. The results were better, even though an incredible number of people, an incredible number of hands were required. And so, when The Collapse came, my district had a competitive edge. It had paid off to be the ones who polluted the most. We were a pioneer nation in pollution and so we became a pioneer nation in pollination. A paradox had saved us.

I stretched as far as I could, but couldn't quite reach the blossom at the very top. I was about to give up, but knew I might be punished, so I tried once more. Our pay was docked if we used up the pollen too quickly. And our pay was docked if we used too little. The work was invisible. When at the end of the day we climbed down from the trees, there was no evidence of our work except for the red chalk *X*'s on the tree trunks, ideally up to forty trees each day. It wasn't until autumn came and the trees were laden with fruit that we would know who among us had actually succeeded in their work. And by then we had usually forgotten which trees had been dusted by whom.

I was assigned to Field 748 today. Out of how many? I didn't know. My group was one of hundreds. In our beige work uniforms we were just as anonymous as the trees. And just as close together as the flowers. Never alone, always together in a flock, up here in the trees, or wandering down the tire ruts from one field to the next. Only behind the walls of our own small flats could we be alone, a few short hours a day. Our whole lives were out here.

It was quiet. We weren't allowed to speak while we worked. The only sound to be heard was that of our careful movements in the trees, a faint clearing of the throat, some

9

yawns and the material of our uniforms against the tree trunks. And sometimes the sound we had all learned to dislike — a branch creaking and in the worst case breaking. A broken branch meant less fruit, and yet another reason to dock our pay.

Otherwise only the wind was audible, passing through branches, brushing across the blossoms, slipping through the grass on the ground.

A fly buzzed through the air, a rare sight. It had been several days since I had seen a bird, there were fewer of them as well. They hunted the few insects to be found, and starved, like the rest of the world.

But then an earsplitting sound broke the silence. It was the whistle from the management's barracks, the signal for the second and final break of the day. I noticed immediately how parched my tongue was.

I climbed down with awkward caution. My workmates and I crept down from the trees to the ground. The other women had already begun chatting, as if their cacophonic prattle was flipped on like a switch the split second they knew that they could.

I said nothing, concentrating on getting down without breaking a branch. I managed it. Pure luck. I was infinitely clumsy, had been working out here long enough to know that I would never be really good at the job.

On the ground beside the tree was a beat-up metal water bottle. I grabbed it and drank quickly. The water was lukewarm and tasted of aluminum, the taste made me drink less than I needed.

Two young boys dressed in white from the Trade Commission rapidly distributed the reusable tin boxes containing the second meal of the day. I sat down by myself with my back against the tree trunk and opened mine. The rice was mixed with corn today. I ate quickly. As usual, a bit too salty, and seasoned with artificially manufactured chili pepper and soy. It had been a long time since I had tasted meat. Animal feed required too much arable land. And a lot of the traditional animal feed required pollination. The animals weren't worth our painstaking handiwork.

The tin box was empty before I was full. I stood up and put it back in the return basket from the Trade Commission. Then I jogged in place. My legs were tired, but nonetheless stiff from standing still in locked positions up there in the trees. My blood tingled; I couldn't stand still.

But it didn't help. I took a quick look around me. Nobody from management was

11

paying attention. I quickly lay down on the ground, just to stretch out my back. It was aching after having been bent over in the same position for a long time.

I closed my eyes for a moment, tried to shut out the conversation of the other women of the crew, instead listening to how the chatter rose and fell in volume. This need to talk, all of them at the same time, where did it come from? The other women had started when they were little girls. Hour after hour of group conversations where the subject was always of the lowest common denominator and one could never really go into depth about anything. Perhaps with the exception of when the one being talked about wasn't there.

Personally I preferred one-on-one conversations. Or my own company, for that matter. At work, often the latter. At home I had Kuan, my husband. Not that we had the longest conversations, either, conversation wasn't what held us together. Kuan's references were here and now, he was concrete, didn't crave knowledge, something more. But in his arms I found peace. And then we had Wei-Wen, our three-year-old. *Him* we could talk about.

Just as the cacophony had almost sung me to sleep, it suddenly fell silent. Everyone was quiet.

I sat up. The others on the crew were facing the road.

The entourage was walking down the tire ruts and towards us.

They were no more than eight or nine years old. I recognized several of them from Wei-Wen's school. All of them had been given identical work clothes, the same synthetic beige uniforms that we were wearing, and they walked towards us as quickly as their short legs could carry them. Two adult leaders kept them in line. One in front, one behind. Both of them were equipped with powerful voices that corrected the children without cease, but they did not reprimand them, giving instructions with warmth and compassion, because even though the children had not yet fully taken in where they were headed, the adults knew.

The children walked hand in hand, in mismatched pairs, the tallest with the shortest, the older children taking care of the younger. An uneven gait, disorganized, but the hands held on tight as if they were glued together. Perhaps they had been given strict instructions not to let go.

Their eyes were on us, on the trees. Curious, wrinkling their noses a bit, cocking their heads. As if they were here for the first time, even though all of them had grown up in the district and didn't know of any kind of nature other than the endless rows of fruit trees, against the shadow of the overgrown forest in the south. A short girl looked at me for a long time, with big, slightly close-set eyes. She blinked a few times, then sniffed loudly. She held a skinny boy by the hand. He yawned loudly and unabashedly, didn't lift his free hand to his mouth, wasn't even aware that his face stretched open into a gaping hole. He wasn't yawning as an expression of boredom; he was too young for that. It was the shortage of food that caused his fatigue. A tall, frail girl held a little boy by the hand. He was breathing heavily through a stuffed-up nose, with his mouth open, missing both front teeth. The tall girl pulled him behind her while she turned her face towards the sun, squinted and wrinkled her nose, but kept her head in the same position, as if to get some color, or perhaps glean strength.

They arrived every spring, the new children. But were they usually so small? Were they younger this time?

No. They were eight. As they always were. Finished with their schooling. Or . . . well, they learned numbers and some characters, but beyond that school was only a kind of regulated storage system. Storage and preparation for life out here. Exercises in sitting quietly for a long time. *Sit still. Completely still, that's right.* And exercises to develop fine motor skills. They wove carpets from the age of three. Their small fingers were ideally suited for work with complex patterns. Just as they were perfect for the work out here.

The children passed us, turned their faces to the front, towards other trees. Then they walked on, towards another field. The boy without teeth stumbled a bit, but the tall girl held his hand tightly, so he didn't fall. The parents were not here, but they took care of one another.

The children disappeared down along the tire rut, drowned between the trees.

"Where are they going?" a woman from my crew asked.

"I don't know," another replied.

"Probably towards forty-nine or fifty," a third said. "Nobody has started there yet."

My stomach twisted into a knot. Where they were going, which field they were headed for, made no difference. It was *what* they were going to do that —

The whistle sounded from the barracks. We climbed up again. My heart pounded, even though I wasn't out of breath. For the children had not grown smaller. It was Wei-Wen . . . In five years he would be eight. In just five years. Then it would be his turn. The hardworking hands were worth more out here than anywhere else. The small fingers, already accustomed to weaving carpets, trained in fine motor skills every single day at school, already fine-tuned for this type of work.

Eight-year-olds out here, day in and day out, stiffened small bodies in the trees. Not even an excuse for a childhood, as my peers and I had had. We had gone to school until we were fifteen.

A non-life.

My hands shook as I lifted the hand holding the precious dust. We all had to work to acquire food, it was said, to make the food we would eat ourselves. Everyone had to contribute, even the children. Because who needs an education when the wheat stores are diminishing? When the rations become smaller and smaller with each passing month? When one must go to bed hungry in the evenings?

I turned around to reach the blossoms behind me, but this time my movements were too abrupt. I hit a branch that I had not noticed, suddenly lost my balance and leaned heavily over to the other side.

And that did it. The cracking sound we had come to hate. The sound of a branch breaking.

The supervisor came quickly towards me. She looked up into the tree and assessed the damage without saying anything. Quickly she wrote something down on a pad of paper before leaving again.

The branch was neither large nor strong, but I knew all the same that my entire surplus for this month would vanish. The money that was supposed to go into the tin box in the kitchen cupboard where we saved every single yuan we could spare.

I drew a breath. I couldn't think about it. I couldn't do anything but keep going. Lift my hand, dip the brush into the pollen, move it carefully towards the blossoms, brush across them as if I were a bee.

I avoided looking at my watch. Knew it wouldn't help. I only knew that with each flower I moved the brush across, the evening came a bit closer. And the one hour I had every day with my child. That tiny hour was all we had, and in that tiny hour perhaps I could make a difference. Sow a seed that would give him the opportunity that I myself never had.

WILLIAM

Maryville, Hertfordshire, England, 1851

Everything around me was yellow. Endlessly yellow. It was over me, under me, around me. Blinding me. The yellow color was completely real, nothing I was imagining. It came from the brocade tapestry my wife, Thilda, had stuck up on the walls when we moved in a few years ago. We'd had a lot of space at that time. My little seed shop on Maryville's main street was thriving. I was still inspired, still thought I would manage to combine the business with that which really meant something, my natural science research. But that was a long time ago. Long before we became the parents of an inordinate number of daughters. And a very long time before the final conversation with Professor Rahm.

Had I known the kind of anguish the yellow tapestry would cause, I would never have gone along with it. The yellow color

18

did not settle for remaining on the tapestry. If I closed my eyes, or kept them open, it was there, every bit as furious. It followed me into my sleep and never let me get away, it was like the sun's highlights from foliage in the forest. The color kept forcing me to return there, to the forest of my childhood. In there I became blind to the rest of the world.

I forced my eyes open, did not want to go in there again. Compelled myself to be present. To listen.

It was late afternoon; from the kitchen the sound of the rattling of pots and the burner rings being moved about on the stove could be heard. Perhaps it was the sound of food being prepared that awakened my stomach, twisting it into knots. I collapsed into a fetal position.

I looked around. An untouched piece of bread and a dried slice of cured ham lay on a plate beside the half-empty water glass. When had I last eaten?

I sat up halfway, grabbed the glass of water. Let it run through my mouth and down my throat, washing away the taste of old age.

The saltiness of the ham was rancid on my tongue; the bread dark and heavy. The

19

food found its way to my stomach, which settled.

But I still could not find a comfortable position in bed. My back was one large blister, my hips worn to the bone from lying on my side.

An agitation in my legs, a prickling.

The house was all of a sudden silent. Had they all left? Nothing but the crackling of coke burning in the hearth. But then, suddenly, singing. Clear voices from the garden.

Hark! the herald angels sing
Glory to the newborn King

Would it be Christmas soon?

In recent years, the region's different choirs had begun singing at people's doors during Advent, not for money or gifts, but in the spirit of Christmas, solely to bring joy to others. There was a time when I'd found it beautiful, when these small performances could ignite a light in me that I was no longer certain existed. It felt ever so long ago.

The bright voices flowed towards me like meltwater:

Peace on earth and mercy mild
God and sinners reconciled

I placed my feet on the floor. Beneath the soles of my feet it felt unusually hard. I myself was the infant, the newborn, whose feet were not yet accustomed to the ground, but instead still shaped for dancing on my toes. That's how I remembered Edmund's feet, with a high instep and just as soft and arched underneath as on top. I could stand with them in my hands, just look and feel, as one did with one's firstborn. I thought that I would become something else for him, *be something else for you,* something else entirely, than my father had been for me. That's how I stood with him until Thilda snatched him away from me under the pretext of a feeding or diaper change. The infant feet moved slowly towards the window. Every step hurt. The window grew before me, huge and white.

Then I saw them.

All seven of them. For it wasn't a choir of strangers from the village. It was my own daughters.

The four tallest in the back, the three shorter ones in the front. Dressed in their dark winter clothes. Wool coats, too tight and too short, or too big and with ever more patches, the threadbare quality disguised behind cheap ribbons and pockets in odd places. Brown, dark blue or black wool bonnets with white lace trim framed narrow, winter-pale faces. The song became frost in the air before them.

21

How thin they had grown, all of them.

A path showed where they had walked, footsteps through deep snow. They must have waded through it far above the knees and had certainly gotten wet. I could feel the sensation of damp wool stockings against bare skin, and the frost penetrating up from the ground through the thin soles of their shoes — none of them had more than this one pair of boots. I walked closer to the window. I half expected to see others in the garden, an audience for the choir, Thilda, or perhaps some of the neighbors. But the garden was empty. They weren't singing for anyone. They were singing for me.

Light and life to all He brings
Risen with healing in His wings

All of their gazes were focused intently on my window, but they had not yet discovered me. I stood in the shadows, at the back of the room, and the sun shone on the window-pane. They probably could only see the reflection of the sky and the trees.

Born to raise the sons of earth
Born to give them second birth

I took one step closer.

Fourteen-year-old Charlotte, my eldest daughter, was standing at the far end. Her eyes were on the window, but she was singing with all of her body. Her chest rose and fell in time with the melody. Perhaps it was her idea, all of it. She had always sung, hummed her way through childhood, with her head in her schoolwork or bent over the dishes, a melodious murmuring, as if the soft notes were a part of her movements.

She was the one who discovered me first. A light slid across her face. She nudged Dorothea, the precocious twelve-year-old. She quickly nodded to eleven-year-old Olivia, who turned her wide-open eyes towards her twin sister, Elizabeth. The two did not in any sense resemble each other in appearance, only in temperament. Both gentle and kind, and dumb as posts — they couldn't understand arithmetic even if you were to nail the numbers onto their foreheads. In front of them a restlessness had begun in the ranks. The young ones were also about to discover me. Nine-year-old Martha squeezed seven-year-old Caroline's arm. And Caroline, who always sulked because she really wanted to be the youngest, gave little Georgiana, who would have liked to have escaped being the youngest, a hard shove. No great cheer to the heavens above, they didn't allow themselves that, not yet. Only the slightest irregularity in the singing betrayed that they had seen me.

That, and weak smiles, to the extent that their singing, O-shaped mouths would allow.

A childish lump pushed forward in my chest. They did not sing badly. Not at all. Their narrow faces glowed, their eyes shone. They had arranged it all just for me. And now they thought that they had succeeded. That they had pulled it off — they had gotten father out of bed. When the song was over they would release the cheer. They would run jubilantly light-footed through the freshly fallen snow into the house and tell me about their own homespun miracle. We sang him well again, they would crow. We sang father well!

A cacophony of enthusiastic girls' voices would echo in the hallways, bouncing back at them from the walls: *Soon he will return. Soon he will be with us again. We showed him God, Jesus — the born-again. Hark, the herald angels sing, glory to the newborn king. What a brilliant, yes, truly dazzling idea it was to sing for him, to remind him of beauty, of the message of Christmas, of everything he had forgotten while bedridden, with the thing we call illness, but which everyone knows is something else entirely, although mother forbids us to speak about it. Poor Father, he is not well, he is as thin as a ghost, we have seen it, through the cracked-open door as we have crept past, yes, like a ghost, just skin and bones, and the beard he has let grow, like the crucified Jesus. He is beyond recognition. But now he will soon be among us once more, soon he will be able to work again. And we will once more have butter on our bread and new winter coats. That is in truth a real Christmas present. Christ is born in Bethlehem!* But it was a lie. I couldn't give them that gift. I did not deserve their cheers. The bed drew me towards it. My legs trembled, my new-born legs were unable to hold me upright any longer. My stomach knotted again. I gritted my teeth, wanted to crush the pressure in my throat. So I slowly pulled away from the window.

And outside the singing subsided. There would be no miracle today.

GEORGE

Autumn Hill, Ohio, USA, 2007
I picked Tom up at the station in Autumn. He hadn't been home since last summer. I didn't know why, hadn't asked. Maybe I couldn't bear to hear the answer.

It was a half-hour drive up to the farm. We didn't say much. His hands just lay in his lap while we drove home. Pale, thin and silent. His bag lay beside his legs. It had gotten dirty. The floor of the pickup hadn't been clean since I bought it. Dirt from last year, or the year before that, became dust on the floor in the winter. And the moisture from the snow melting on Tom's boots trickled down and mixed into it.

The bag was new, the material stiff. Definitely bought in the city. And it was heavy. I was startled when I lifted it up from the ground at the bus station. Tom wanted to take it himself but I grabbed it before he had the chance — he didn't exactly look as

26

if he'd been working out a lot since the last time I'd seen him. You wouldn't think he'd need anything but clothes. He was only going to be home on vacation for a week. And most of his things were already hanging on a hook in the hallway. His coveralls, boots, the hat with the earflaps. But he had clearly brought a load of books with him. Apparently he thought there would be a lot of time for that kind of thing.

He was standing waiting for me when I came. The bus had been early, or maybe I was late. I had to shovel snow in the yard before leaving.

"It doesn't matter, George. He has his head in the clouds anyway," said Emma, who stood and watched me, shivering with her arms hugging her chest.

I didn't answer. Had to shovel snow. The snow collapsed like an accordion, light and new. I didn't even break a sweat on my back.

She kept looking at me.

"You'd think it was Bush coming to visit."

"Someone has to shovel here. You don't do it."

I looked up from the snow. There were white specks before my eyes. She smiled her crooked smile. I couldn't help but grin back. We had known each other since school, and I don't think one day had passed without our having exchanged exactly that smile.

But she was right. I was exaggerating with the shoveling. The snow wouldn't stay, we'd had many warm days already, the sun came out and it melted away everywhere. This snowfall was merely the final gasp of winter and it would melt away in the course of a few days. I got carried away when I cleaned the john today, too. Behind the toilet, to be more exact. It wasn't exactly normal behavior on my part. I just wanted everything to be spick-and-span, now that he was finally coming home. That he would see only the recently shoveled yard, and the clean john, and not notice how the paint was peeling on the south wall where the sun beat down, or that the gutter had come loose in the wind.

When we took him to college he was tan and strong, eager. For once he hugged me for a long time, and I could feel the strength of his upper arms as he embraced me. I thought of others who talked about how their children just got bigger and bigger every time they saw them, how you're sort of startled when you see your offspring again after some time has passed. But that wasn't the case with Tom. Now he had shrunk. His nose was red, his cheeks white, his shoulders narrow. And it didn't exactly help that he shivered and hunched over, so he looked like a shriveled pear. His shaking did subside as we drove towards the farm, but he still sat like a weakling in the seat next to me.

"How's the food?" I asked.

"The food? You mean at college?"

"No, on Mars."

"Huh?"

"Of course at a college. Have you been anywhere else recently?"

He ducked down between his shoulders again.

"I just mean that . . . you look a bit undernourished," I said.

"Undernourished? Dad, do you even know what that means?"

"Last I checked I was the one paying your tuition, so there's no need to answer back like that."

He fell silent. For a good while.

"But everything's fine, then," I said finally.

"Yes, everything's fine."

"So I'm getting my money's worth?" I tried to grin, but from the corner of my eye saw that he wasn't laughing. Why didn't he laugh? He could have tried to go along with the joke, so we could have laughed off the awkward words, and maybe had a nice chat for the rest of the ride.

"Since your meals are paid for you could maybe make sure to eat a bit more," I ventured.

"Yes," was all he said. My temper flared up inside me. I only wanted for him to smile, but he just sat there with this stone-faced gravity. Better not say anything. Hold my tongue. But something compelled me.

"You couldn't wait to get away, could you?"

Was he angry now? Would we get into that again?

No. He just sighed.

"Dad."

"Yes. Just kidding. Again."

I swallowed the rest of my words. Knew that I might possibly say a whole lot of things I would regret if I continued now. It wasn't supposed to start like this, not when he had finally arrived.

"I just mean . . . ," I said, trying to soften my voice, "you seemed happier when you left than you do now."

"I am happy. OK?"

"OK."

End of story. He was happy. Very happy. So happy that he was jumping up and down. Couldn't wait to see us, see the farm again. Hadn't thought of anything else for weeks. Obviously.

I cleared my throat, even though it wasn't scratchy. Tom just sat there, with those quiet hands of his. I swallowed a lump, but something lay there, squeezing. What had I been hoping for? That a few months apart would turn us into buddies?

Emma held Tom in her arms for a long time. As before, she could still squeeze and nuzzle him without him minding.

He didn't notice the freshly shoveled yard. Emma had been right about that. But he didn't care about the paint that was peeling off the wall, either, and that was a good thing . . .

No. Because really I wanted him to notice both. And that he would pitch in, now that he was finally home. Take responsibility.

Emma served meat loaf and corn, large portions on the green plates. The yellow corn shone brightly and steam rose from the cream sauce. There was nothing wrong with the food, but Tom ate only half of his helping, didn't touch the meat. Apparently he had no appetite for anything. Not enough fresh air, that was the problem. We would do something about that now.

Emma asked and pried. About school. Teachers. His classes. Friends. Girls . . . Didn't get much of an answer to the last question, not exactly. But the talk between them flowed smoothly nonetheless, the way it always had. Even though she asked more than he answered.

They had always had something special, those two. The words didn't get stuck between them. Their closeness didn't seem to require any effort. But of course, she was his mother.

She was enjoying this, had rosy-red cheeks, kept her eyes on Tom the whole time, was unable to keep her fingers off of him, had months of missing him in her hands.

I was quiet for the most part, tried to smile when they smiled, laugh when they laughed. After the flop of a conversation in the car, it wasn't worth taking any chances. I would have to look for the right occasion to initiate the so-called father-son talk instead. It would come. He was going to be here for a week.

I just enjoyed the meal, emptied my plate, at least *someone* here knew how to appreciate good food. I sopped up the sauce with a piece of bread, laid my silverware across the plate and stood up.

But then Tom wanted to stand up, too. Even though his plate was still half-full. "Thank you."

"You have to eat the food your mother has prepared," I said. I tried to sound breezy, but it might have come out a little sharp.

"He's eaten a lot already," Emma said.

"She's been at it for hours, getting dinner ready." That was strictly speaking an exaggeration.

Tom sat down again. Lifted his fork.

"It's only meat loaf, George," Emma said. "It didn't take *that* long."

I wanted to object. She had worked hard, no doubt about it, and she was so excited about having Tom home again. She deserved for him to know that.

"I had a sandwich on the bus," Tom said to his plate.

"You filled up right before coming home to your mother's cooking? Haven't you missed it? Have you had better meat loaf anywhere else?"

"Sure, Dad, it's just that . . ." He fell silent.

I avoided looking in Emma's direction, knew that she was staring at me with pinched lips and eyes signaling to stop.

"It's just that what?" Tom pushed his food around a bit on his plate.

"I've stopped eating meat."

"What!"

"Now, now," Emma said quickly and

33

started to clear the table.

I remained seated. It fell into place. "No wonder you're scrawny."

"If everybody were a vegetarian, there would be more than enough food for the entire world's population," Tom said.

"If everyone were a vegetarian," I mimicked and stared at him over the rim of my water glass. "Human beings have always eaten meat."

Emma had stacked the plates and serving dish into a tall pile. It rattled perilously.

"Please. I'm sure Tom has thought this through carefully," she said.

"I don't believe it."

"I'm not exactly the only vegetarian," Tom said.

"We eat meat on this farm," I said and stood up so abruptly that the chair fell to the floor.

"Now, now," Emma said again and cleared the table with jerky movements. She sent me another one of her looks. It didn't say *Stop* this time. It said *Shut up.*

"It's not as if you're in pork production," Tom said.

"What does that have to do with it?"

"What difference does it make to you if I don't eat meat? As long as I keep eating honey."

He sniggered. Amiably? No. A bit cheek-ily.

"Had I known that going to college would make you like this I never would've sent you." The words grew as I talked, but I was unable to hold them inside all the same.

"Of course the boy has to go to school," Emma said.

Of course, that was apparently as clear as the first night of frost. Everyone had to go to school.

"I got all the education I needed out there," I said and waved my hand vaguely, trying to indicate the east where the field with some of the hives lay, but discovered too late that I was waving to the west.

Tom couldn't even be bothered to reply.

"Thank you." He cleared his plate quickly and turned towards Emma. "I'll take care of the rest, too. Just go ahead and sit down."

She smiled at him. Nobody said anything to me. They both avoided me: she crept out to the living room with the newspaper, and he put on an apron, he actually did that, and started scrubbing the pots.

My tongue had dried up. I took a sip of water, but it didn't help much.

They walked around me. I was the ele-phant in the room. Except that I wasn't an elephant, I was a mammoth. An extinct species.

Tao

"If I have three grains of rice, and you have two, and we put them together, how many does that make?"

I took two grains of rice from my plate and placed them on Wei-Wen's plate, which was already empty.

The faces of the children were still with me: the tall girl tilting her face towards the sun and the boy whose mouth stretched open in an unwitting yawn. They were so tiny. And Wei-Wen was so big all of a sudden. He would soon be just as old as they were. In other parts of the country there were schools for a select few. Those who would become leaders, those who would assume responsibility. And who were spared having to work out there. If only he excelled enough, stood out as one of the best at a young age . . .

"Why are there three for you and only two for me?" Wei-Wen looked down at the grains of rice and pouted.

"I have two, then, and you have three. There." I switched the grains of rice on our plates. "How many does that make when we put them together?"

Wei-Wen placed his whole stubby fist on the plate, moved it around as if he were finger painting.

"I want more ketchup."

"Oh, Wei-Wen." I firmly removed his hand, it was sticky after the meal. "It's *may I have more ketchup.*" I sighed, pointed at the rice grains once more. "Two for me. And three for you. Then we can count. One, two, three, four, five."

Wei-Wen wiped one hand across his face, leaving behind a streak of ketchup on his cheek. Then he reached for the bottle. "May I have more ketchup?"

I should have started earlier. This one hour was all we had together every day. But I often squandered it, spending the time on eating and cozy pastimes. He should have made more progress by now.

"Five grains of rice," I said. "Five grains of rice. Right?"

He gave up trying to get hold of the bottle and threw himself back into his chair with such force that the chair legs hit against the floor. He often acted like this, with large, dramatic movements. He'd been robust ever since he was born. And content. He'd started walking late, not having the necessary restlessness inside of him. He was content to remain seated on his bum, smiling at everyone who talked to him. And there were many who wanted to, because Wei-Wen was the kind of baby who smiled easily.

I took the bottle containing the red substitute and poured some out onto his plate. Maybe he would cooperate now. "There. Help yourself."

"Yeah! Ketchup!"

I took two more dried grains of rice from the bowl on the table.

"Look here. Now we have two more. How many does that make?"

But Wei-Wen was busy eating. There was ketchup all around his mouth now.

"Wei-Wen? How many does that make?"

He emptied his plate again, looked at it a bit and lifted it up. He started making rumbling sounds, as if it were an old-fashioned airplane. He loved old vehicles. Was obsessed with helicopters, cars, buses, could crawl around on the floor for hours on end and create roads, airports, landscapes for transport vehicles.

"Wei-Wen, please." I swiftly took the plate

away from him and put it down, out of his reach. Then I continued pointing at the cold, dried grains of rice.

"Look here. Five plus two. How many does that make, then?"

My voice trembled slightly. I covered it up with a smile, which Wei-Wen didn't notice, because he was reaching for the plate.

"I want it! I want the airplane! It's mine!"

Kuan cleared his throat. He was in the sitting room having a cup of tea with his legs on the table and he stared at me over his teacup, demonstratively relaxed.

I ignored both of them and started to count. "One, two, three, four, five, six, and . . . seven!" I smiled at Wei-Wen, as if there were something extraordinary about these seven grains of rice. "Altogether that makes seven. Right? Do you see? One, two, three, four, five, six, seven."

Just this, if he understood this, I'd let up, then he could play. Baby steps, every day.

"I want it!"

He reached out his chubby hand as far as he could.

"Little one, it has to stay over there," my voice rose. "We're going to count now, right?"

Kuan let out an audible sigh, stood up and came in to join us. He laid a hand on my shoulder. "It's eight o'clock."

I twisted out of his grasp. "It won't hurt him to stay up another fifteen minutes," I said and looked up at him.

"Tao . . ."

"He can manage fifteen minutes." I continued staring at him.

He looked perplexed. "But why?"

I looked away, couldn't bring myself to explain, to tell him about the children. I knew what he'd say anyway. *They haven't become younger. They're just as little as they've always been. They were eight years old last year, too. That's how it is. That's how it has been for many years.* And if he continued, words would be spoken that were so big that they didn't belong to him: *We must be happy that we live here. It could have been worse. We could have lived in Beijing. Or Europe. We must make the best of it. Live in the here and now. Make the best of every second.* Phrases, unlike those he otherwise used, like something he had read, but spoken with conviction. He really believed these words.

Kuan stroked Wei-Wen's bristly hair. "I'd like to play with him," he said softly and gently.

Wei-Wen squirmed in his seat, a high chair he was really too big for, but where he sat securely buckled in and couldn't run away from my home school. He reached for the plate. "I want it, it's mine!"

Kuan didn't look at me, just said in the same controlled tone of voice: "You can't have it, but you know what, a toothbrush can also be an airplane." Then he lifted up Wei-Wen and walked towards the bathroom.

"Kuan . . . But . . ."

He heaved Wei-Wen easily from one arm to the other as he walked towards the bathroom, pretending not to have heard me, continuing to chat with Wei-Wen. He carried his son as if he weighed nothing. Personally, I felt that the child's body was already growing heavy.

I remained seated. Wanted to say something, to protest, but the words didn't come. He was right. Wei-Wen was exhausted. It was late. He should be put to bed before he became overtired and refused to sleep. Then we were in for it, I knew that. Then he could keep it up until long after our own bedtime. First foolishness, the door to the bedroom being opened and shut, then he would come into our room again and again, peals of laughter, *come and get me.* This would be followed by frustration and anger, howling, wild protests. That's how he was. That's how three-year-olds are.

Although . . . I couldn't remember that I'd behaved like that. I learned to read when I was three. I picked up the characters on my own, surprising the teacher when I skillfully read fairy tales for myself, but never for the other children. I stayed away from them. My parents were amazed spectators on the sidelines, letting me read fairy tales, simple stories for children, but never daring to challenge me with other texts. But at school they noticed. The teachers gave me the opportunity to read books when the others were outside, presented me with what they had of teaching programs, texts and choppy films. Much of it stemmed from the time before The Collapse, from the time before the democracies fell, before the world war that followed, when food became a commodity bestowed upon only a select few. At that time, the production of information was so enormous that nobody had full oversight any longer. Trails of words stretched as far as the Milky Way. Expanses the size of the sun's surface, made up of pictures, maps, illustrations. Time attached to film, time equivalent to millions of human lives. And technology had made everything available. Availability was the mantra of that period. Human beings were at all times logged on to all of this information

43

with increasingly more advanced communication tools.

But The Collapse also affected the digital networks. In the course of three years they had completely disintegrated. All human beings had left were the books, choppy-quality DVDs, worn-out videotapes, scratched compact discs containing outdated software and the ancient, deteriorating landline network.

I devoured the dog-eared old books and choppy films. Read and remembered everything, as if the books and films made a precise imprint in my memory.

I was ashamed of my knowledge because it made me different. Several of the teachers tried to speak with my parents about how I was a gifted child, had abilities, but during these conversations they smiled shyly, would rather hear about normal things, like whether I had any friends, was good at running, climbing, arts and crafts. All of the areas in which I was not successful. But my shame was gradually consumed by my hunger for learning. I studied the language in depth, learned that every single thing and feeling did not have a single word or description, but many. And I learned about our history. About the mass death of pollinating insects, about the rising of the ocean, the temperature increase, about nuclear power accidents and about the former superpowers, the US and Europe, who had lost everything in the course of a few years, who had not managed to adapt and were now living in the most abject poverty, with a population reduced to a fraction and food production consisting only of wheat and corn. While here, in China, we had coped. The Committee, the Party's highest council, our country's efficient government, had led us through The Collapse with a hard hand and a series of decisions that the people often didn't understand, but had no opportunity to question. All of this I learned. And I just wanted to keep going. To have more and more. I wanted to fill up on knowledge, but without reflecting upon what I learned. It wasn't until I came upon a tattered printout of *The History of Bees* that I stopped. The translation from English was clumsy and artless, but the book nonetheless intrigued me. It was published in 2037, a few years before The Collapse became a fact and pollinating insects were no longer to be found on earth. I brought it to show my teacher, shared with her the pictures of beehives and detailed drawings of bees. It was the bees I was most interested in. The queen bee and her children, the latter no more than tiny larvae in the cells of the hive, and all of the golden honey with which they surrounded themselves.

The teacher had never seen the book before, but was, like myself, fascinated. She stopped at passages of rich text to read out loud to me. She read about knowledge. About acting against one's instincts, because one knows better, about how in order to live in nature, *with* nature, we must detach ourselves from the nature in ourselves. And about the value of education. Because this was what education was actually about, defying the nature in oneself.

I was eight years old and only understood a small portion. But I understood my teacher's reverence, that the book had moved her. And I understood the part about education. Without knowledge we are nothing. Without knowledge we are animals.

After that I became more focused. I did not want to learn solely for the sake of learning, I wanted to learn to understand. I soon advanced far beyond the level of the others in my class and was the youngest in the school to become a Young Pioneer in the Party and was allowed to wear the Scarf. There was a banal kind of pride in this. Even my parents smiled when the red piece of cloth was tied around my neck. But first and foremost the knowledge made me richer. Richer than the other children. I was not beautiful, not athletic, not good with my hands or strong. I could not excel in any other fields. In the mirror an awkward girl stared back at me. The eyes were a little too small, the nose a little too big. That ordinary face revealed nothing about what she was carrying — something golden, something that made every single day worth living. And that could be a means of getting away. By the age of ten I had already outlined the possibilities. There were schools in other parts of the country, one day's journey away, which would accept me when I turned fifteen, the age when I was actually supposed to start working out in the fields. The school supervisor helped me to find out how to apply. She thought I'd have a good chance of being accepted. But it would be expensive. I spoke with my parents but got nowhere; they grew anxious, looked at me as if I were a strange creature they didn't understand and didn't even like. The school supervisor also tried talking to them, I never found out what she said, but the only effect it had was to make my parents even more resolved. They had no money, and they weren't willing to save. I was the one who would have to give in, they felt, I was the one who would have to settle down, stop "dreaming foolish dreams." But I was unable to. Because this was who I was. And always would be.

I started at the sound of Wei-Wen's laughter. He laughed a loud, warbling laugh in the bathroom and the acoustics in there amplified the sound. "No, Daddy! No!"

He laughed as Kuan tickled him and gave his soft tummy a raspberry kiss.

I stood up. Put the plate in the sink. Walked towards the bathroom door and stood there listening. When I heard Wei-Wen's laughter I felt the urge to record it, so I could play it back for him when he grew up and acquired a deep voice.

All the same it didn't make me smile.

I put my hand on the latch, pushed the door open. Wei-Wen was lying on the floor while Kuan yanked and pulled at one of his trouser legs. He pretended that the trousers were fighting against him, did not want to come off.

"Can you hurry up a bit?" I said to Kuan.

"Hurry up? That's impossible with these obstinate trousers!" Kuan said and Wei-Wen laughed.

"Now you're just winding him up."

"Listen here, trousers, now you have to

stop fooling around!"

Wei-Wen laughed even more.

"He's getting too wild," I said. "It will be impossible to put him to bed."

Kuan did not reply, looked away, but followed my instructions. I went out and closed the door behind me. In the kitchen I quickly did the dishes.

Then I took out my pen and paper. A brief fifteen minutes more, that much he could stand.

WILLIAM

She often sat there, beside my bed, with her head bowed over a book, turning the pages slowly, reading with concentration. My daughter Charlotte was fourteen years old and should have many other things to keep her busy besides seeking out my mute company. Still she came more and more frequently. I distinguished day from night through her presence, and her perpetual reading.

Thilda had not come by today. She came to see me more seldom now, didn't even drag the family doctor here anymore. Perhaps the money had now really come to an end.

Thilda had never said a word about Rahm. I would have known, even if she were to speak about him while I lay in the deepest of slumbers. His name could awaken me from the beyond. She probably had never put it together, never understood that our conversation the last time we met, his laughter, had led me right here, to this room, to this bed.

He was the one who had asked me to come. I didn't know why he wanted to meet me. I hadn't been to see him for several years, and made only compulsory, polite conversation on the rare occasions that we happened to meet in the city — conversation that he always brought to an end.

The autumn was at its peak when I went to visit him. The leaves were an intense play of colors, clear yellow, warm brown, blood red, before the wind had succeeded in tearing them off, forcing them down to the ground and decay. Nature was brimming with fruit, trees laden with apples, juicy plums, dripping sugary pears, and the soil, not yet fully harvested but full of crunchy, crisp carrots, pumpkins, onions, fragrant herbs alongside the field, everything ripe for the picking, for eating. One could live just as carefree as in the Garden of Eden. My feet stepped lightly across the ground as I walked through a grove overgrown with dark green ivy, towards Rahm's house. I was looking forward to meeting him again, to having time to converse with him properly, as we had done so long ago, before I became the father of so many children, before the

51

seed shop took all of my time.

He met me at the door. He still wore his hair cut close, was still thin, wiry, strong. He flashed a smile, his smiles never lasted long, but warmed nonetheless, and then he let me into his study, which was full of plants and glass tanks. In several of them I caught a glimpse of amphibians, full-grown frogs and toads, bred from the tadpole stage I presumed. It was towards this field of the natural sciences that all his attention was directed. When I came to see him after completing my exams eighteen years ago, I hoped to study insects, particularly the eusocial species, the individual insects that functioned together virtually as *one* organism — a superorganism. That was where my passion lay, with the bumblebees, wasps, hornets, termites, bees. And ants. But he held that this would have to come later and soon *I* was also busily occupied with these inbetween creatures that his study was full of, creatures that were neither insects, nor fish, nor mammals. I was only his research assistant, so I could not object. It was an honor working for him, I knew that and was therefore concerned about showing reverent gratitude rather than imposing demands. I attempted to adopt his fascination and expected that when the time was ripe, when

I was ready, he would allow me to reserve time for my own projects. That day never came, however, and quite soon it became clear to me that I would instead have to carry out my own research during my time off, start with the fundamentals and slowly work my way forward. But there was never any time for this, either, before or after Thilda.

The housekeeper served biscuits and tea. We drank from delicate, thin cups that almost disappeared between our fingers, a tea set he had bought himself on one of his many trips to the Far East in the years before he settled down out here in the village.

As we sipped the tea, he told me about his work. About the research he was doing, about his most recent scientific lectures, about his next article. As I listened I nodded, asked questions, taking care to formulate my words in a qualified fashion and then listened once again. I fixed my gaze on him, wanted him to meet it. But he did not look at me much, instead his eyes slid across the room, across the artifacts, as if they were the ones he was talking to.

Then he fell silent, no sound other than that of the wind tearing the yellowing leaves off the trees out there. I took a sip of tea;

the slurping sound was heightened in the quiet room. Heat rose to my cheeks and I quickly put the cup down. But he did not appear to have noticed anything, just sat there quietly without dedicating any more attention to me.

"Today is my birthday," he said, finally.

"I'm sorry. I had no idea . . . but I extend to you my heartfelt best wishes!"

"Do you know how old I am?" He turned his eyes towards me.

I hesitated. How old could he be? Very old. Well over fifty. Perhaps closer to sixty? I fidgeted, noticing suddenly how warm it was in the room, cleared my throat. How should I answer?

When I said nothing, he looked down. "It's not important."

Was he disappointed? Had I disappointed him? Again? His face, however, expressed nothing. He put down his teacup, took a biscuit, how mundane, a biscuit, even though the conversation we were about to embark on was anything but mundane and he put it down on the saucer.

He didn't eat it, just let it lie there. The room was uncomfortably quiet. I had to say something, it was my turn now.

"Are you going to celebrate?" I asked and regretted it immediately. What a foolish question, as if he were a child.

Neither did he deign to answer. He sat there with the saucer in his hand, but did not eat, just looked down at the tiny, dry biscuit. He moved his fingers, the biscuit slid towards the edge of the saucer, but he quickly straightened it, saving the biscuit at the last second and put the saucer down.

"You were a promising student," he said suddenly.

He drew a breath, as if he were about to say something more, but no words came.

I cleared my throat. "Yes?"

He shifted his position. "When you came to me I had great expectations." He let his hands hang at his sides, just sat like that, straight up and down. "It was your powerful enthusiasm and passion that convinced me. I had otherwise not planned to hire an assistant."

"Thank you, Professor. Those are immensely flattering words."

He straightened his back, sat very erect as if he were a student himself, glanced at me quickly. "But something happened to you."

My chest tightened. A question. It was a question. But how should I answer?

"Had it happened already by the time you gave the Swammerdam presentation?" Again he looked quickly at me. His gaze, which was usually so steady, wavered.

"Swammerdam? But that was so many years ago," I said quickly.

"Yes. Exactly. So many years ago. And it was there that you met her?"

"You mean my wife?"

His silence confirmed my question. Yes, I met Thilda there, after the lecture. Or, rather: the circumstances led me to her. The circumstances . . . no, *Rahm* led me to her. It was his laughter, his derision that caused me to look in another direction, to look in *her* direction.

I wanted to say something about this, but couldn't find the words. He leaned forward abruptly, cleared his throat faintly. "And now?"

"Now?"

"Why have you brought children into the world?"

He made the last comment in a louder voice, a voice that almost broke and now he was staring at me, unwavering, a frost had emerged inside of him.

"Why?" I looked away quickly, unable to meet his gaze, the hardness in his eyes. "Well, it's what one does."

He rested his arms on his knees, simultaneously inhibited and demanding. "It's what one does? Well, it is perhaps what one does.

But why you? What do you have to give them?"

"To give them? Food, clothing."

He abruptly raised his voice. "Don't bring up that confounded seed business of yours!"

He sat back again abruptly, as if he wanted to distance himself from me, and wrung his hands in his lap.

"No . . ." I struggled against the cowed ten-year-old inside of me, tried to remain calm, but noticed that I was shaking. When I finally managed to speak again my voice was high-pitched and forced. "I would very much like to continue with my research. But it's just that . . . as you, professor, can probably understand . . . there isn't enough time."

"What do you want me to say? That it's completely acceptable?" He stood up. "Acceptable that you can't find the time?" He stood there on the floor in front of me, moved a few steps closer, grew, became large and dark. "Acceptable that you still haven't finished writing a single research article? Acceptable that your bookshelves are full of unread books? Acceptable that I've spent all this time on you and you still haven't achieved more in life than a mediocre boar?"

The last word hung quivering in the air

between us.

A boar. That's what I was to him. A boar.

A weak protest rose inside me. Had he really spent that much time on me, or had I first and foremost been a henchman for his projects? Because that was perhaps what he actually wanted, that I should inherit his research, keep it alive. Keep *him* alive. But I swallowed my words.

"That's what you want to hear? Right?" he said, with eyes as empty as the amphibians' who were staring at us from the glass tanks. "That that's how life is? One reproduces, has offspring, one instinctively puts their needs first, they are mouths to feed, one becomes a provider, the intellect steps aside to make way for nature. It's not your fault. And it's still not too late." He stared at me until it hurt. "That's what you want to hear? That it's still not too late? That your time will come?" Then he laughed suddenly. A small, hard laugh without joy, but full of scorn. It was brief, but it remained inside me. He fell silent, but did not wait for my answer, knew that I wouldn't have the strength to say anything. He just walked to the door and opened it. "Unfortunately I must ask you to leave. I have work to do."

He left me without saying good-bye, let the housekeeper show me out. I wandered back to my books but didn't take any out. I couldn't even bear to look at them, just crept into bed and stayed there, stayed here, while my books accumulated dust. All of the texts I'd once wanted to read and understand.

They were still there, in disarray on the shelves, some with the spine further out than others, like an uneven row of teeth on the shelf. I wrenched myself away from them, could not stand seeing them. Charlotte lifted her head, became aware that I was awake and quickly put down the book.

"Are you thirsty?"

She got up, found a mug of water and held it out to me.

I turned my head away.

"No." I heard the severity in my voice and hastened to add, "Thank you."

"Do you want anything else? The doctor said —"

"Nothing."

She looked at me closely, as if she were studying me.

"You look better. More alert."

"Don't be ridiculous."

"Really. I mean it." She smiled. "At least you answer."

I refrained from saying anything else, as any further speech on my part would only reinforce the impression of restored health. Instead I let the silence confirm the opposite, and my gaze slide away, as if I no longer noticed her.

But she did not give up, just remained standing by my bedside, holding one hand in the other, wringing them a little and releasing them again, until she finally came out with what was clearly weighing on her heart.

"Has God abandoned you, Father?"

Imagine if it were that simple, if it had something to do with Our Lord. To lose one's faith, for that there was a simple remedy: find it again. When I was a student I had immersed myself in the Bible. I always had it at my side, and I took it to bed with me every evening. I kept searching for the connection between it and my field, between the small wonders in nature and the big words on paper. I lingered especially over the writings of Paul the Apostle. I can't count the number of hours I'd sat studying Paul's Epistle to the Romans, because so many of his fundamental ideas are found in this, it was the closest one that came to a theology according to St. Paul. *And having been freed from sin, you became slaves of righteousness.* What did that mean? That he who is captive is perhaps the only one who is truly free? Doing the right thing can be a prison, a form of captivity, but we had been shown the way. Why didn't we manage it, then? Not even in meeting with His creation did human beings succeed in doing the right thing.

I never found the answer and I took out the little black volume more and more seldom. It gathered dust on the shelf, along with the others. What was I going to say now? That this, my so-called sickbed, was far too banal and vile to have anything to do with Him? That its core was to be found solely within me, in my choices, in the life I had lived?

No. Perhaps another day, but not now. So I refrained from answering her, only shook my head feebly and pretended to fall asleep.

She sat with me until peace descended upon the house below us. I listened to the pages being turned, she read quickly, the soft sound of muslin moving when she now and then changed position. She was apparently chained to the books, just as I was chained to the bed, even though she was wise enough to know better. Book learning was a waste of time for her; she would never have use for the knowledge anyway, simply because she was a daughter and not a son.

But all of a sudden she was interrupted.

The door opened. Rapid footsteps stomped across the floor.

"Is this where you're sitting?" Thilda's stern voice, and without a doubt her equally stern gaze upon Charlotte. "It's bedtime," she continued, as if the information in itself were a command. "You have to do the dishes from supper. And Edmund has a headache, so I want you to put on some tea water for him."

"Yes, Mother."

I could hear Charlotte's feet against the floor as she stood up and the sound of the book being put down on the sideboard. Her light footsteps moving towards the door.

"Good night, Father."

Then she disappeared. Her serenity was replaced by Thilda's brisk steps. She walked over to the stove and with loud, brusque movements she put in more coal. She did it herself now; the maidservant had long since been obliged to find other work, and now Thilda suffered daily over having to take care of the heating herself, a suffering she did very little to conceal. She emphasized it rather, by accompanying all of her movements with sighs and groans.

When she finally finished, she just stood there. But I had only a moment of silence before her perpetual orchestra started up. I didn't need to open my eyes to know that she was standing down by the warmth of the stove, allowing her tears to flow freely. I had seen it a number of times before and there was no mistaking the sound. The crackling of the coal accompanied her tirade. I squirmed, laid my ear against the pillow in an effort to muffle the sound, but without any particular success.

A minute passed. Two. Three.

Then she finally relented and concluded her lamentation with a powerful blowing of her nose. She probably understood that she wasn't getting anywhere today, either. The mucus warmed by her body flowed out of her, with loud, almost mechanical snorting sounds. She was always like this, so well lubricated, whether she cried or not. Except for down there. There it was woefully dry and cold. And all the same she had given me eight children.

I pulled the blanket over my head, wanted to shut out the sound.

"William," she said sharply. "I can see that you're not sleeping."

I tried to keep my breathing quiet.

"I *can* see it."

Louder now, but no reason to move.

"You have to hear this." She took an extra deep sniff. "I've been forced to let Alberta go. Now the shop is empty. I've been obliged to close."

What? I couldn't keep myself from turning over. The shop closed? Empty. Dark. The shop that was supposed to provide for all of my children?

She must have noticed my movement, because now she drew closer. "I had to ask the shopkeeper for credit today." Her voice still choked with tears, as if she might at any minute start honking again. "The entire purchase was put on credit. And he stared at me so, with pity. But said nothing. He is a gentleman, after all."

The last words were swallowed by a whimper.

A gentleman. Unlike yours truly. Who probably did not incite any great admiration from the surrounding world, and especially not from my wife, where I lay, without a hat and cane, monocle or manners. Yes, imagine; I had such bad manners that I was leaving my entire family high and dry. And now the circumstances had grown dramatically worse. The shop was closed, my family would not manage without me for long, although it was wholly necessary for them all that the daily operations continued. Because it was the seeds, the spices and the flower bulbs that put food on the table for all of them.

I ought to get up, but could not manage it, no longer knew how. The bed paralyzed me.

And Thilda, too, gave up on me today. She inhaled vigorously, a deep, trembling sigh. Then she blew her nose one last time, probably to make sure that every single little drop of mucus had left the ear, nose and throat region.

The mattress complained when she lay down. That she could bear to share a bed with my sweaty, unwashed limbs was more than I could fathom. It essentially said everything about how headstrong she was.

Slowly her respiration grew calmer; finally it was heavy and deep, a credible sleep-induced breathing, wholly unlike my own.

I turned over. The light from the masonry stove rippled across her face, her long braids lay on the pillow, released from the tight intricate bun on the back of her head, her upper lip covered her lower lip and gave her a dogged look, like an old toothless woman. I lay there and observed her, tried to find my way back to what I had once loved, and what I had once desired, but sleep overcame me before it happened.

George

Emma was right about the snow. By the next day it was already melting all over the place, running and trickling so you couldn't hear anything else. And the hot sun beat down on the boards of the house, bleaching out the color on the south wall a little more. The temperature crept steadily upwards, growing warm enough for the bees' mass defecation flight. They are clean creatures and won't relieve themselves in the hive. But when the sun is finally beating down, they fly out and empty their bowels. I had actually hoped for this, that the winter would release its grip now while Tom was home. Because then he could come along out to the hives and clean the bottom boards. I had even given Jimmy and Rick the day off, so Tom and I could have the chance to work alone. But as it turned out we didn't go until Thursday, just three days before he had to go back.

It had been a quiet week. We walked in circles around each other, he and I. Emma stayed between us, laughing and chatting as usual. She was clearly putting her heart into finding food that suited Tom, because there was no end to the number of fish meals she conjured up, how much "exciting" and "delicious" fish they had suddenly acquired in the frozen goods section at the store. And Tom, he bowed and scraped in thanks, was so pleased about "all the good food."

When yet another fish meal had been consumed, he usually remained seated at the kitchen table. He read alarmingly thick books, tapped away feverishly on the computer or was completely consumed by some Japanese crossword puzzle thing he called sudoku. It apparently didn't occur to him that he could move somewhere else, that outside the day was suddenly flooded with sunshine, as if somebody had put in a more powerful lightbulb.

I found things to do, of course, I knew how to stay busy, too. One day I even drove to Autumn and bought house paint. As I stood there painting the south wall, I could feel how the sun scorched the back of my head. And I knew that we could take the chance on a trip out to the hives. I didn't really need to clean the bottom boards just yet, but it was the last chance for Tom, so it wouldn't hurt to start with a few hives. The bees had already been out for a while; they gathered pollen when the sun was shining. He used to enjoy this. He always used to go out with me. Jimmy and I cleaned the flight holes a few times in the course of the winter, but apart from that we left the bees alone, so it was always a special occasion when we were out among the hives for the first time. Seeing the bees again, the familiar buzzing, *that* was a joyful get-together, like a real reunion celebration.

"I need help with the bottom boards," I said.

I was already dressed to go out; I stood there in my rubber boots and overalls, in the middle of the room. My legs were restless, I was looking forward to this. I had folded the veil up, I could see better like that. I had taken out extra gear, too, held it out with both hands.

"Already?" he asked and didn't look up. He was slower than molasses. Just sat there all pale in the glow of the laptop with his fingers on the keyboard.

I suddenly noticed how I was holding the suit and veil out a bit too far, as if I was going to give him a gift he didn't want. I pushed both under my arm and put my other hand on my hip.

"It's rotting underneath them. You know that. Nobody likes living in muck. You wouldn't, either, even though student dorm rooms aren't exactly known for being the cleanest."

I tried to laugh, but it came out more like a croak. One of my hands was also at an odd angle. I removed it from my hip. It remained dangling idly at my side. I scratched my forehead just to give it something to do.

"But you usually wait a couple more weeks," he said.

He looked up now. My boy's eyes stared at me.

"No. I don't."

"Dad . . ."

He saw that I was lying. Looked at me with one eyebrow raised.

"It's warm enough," I hastened to say. "And we'll only take a few. You'll be spared the rest. I'll take care of them with Jimmy and Rick next week."

I tried handing him the suit and hat again, but he didn't accept them. He basically gave no sign of moving, just nodded at his computer.

"I'm in the middle of an assignment for school."

"Aren't you on vacation?" I put the gear in front of him on the table. Tried to stare at him firmly, let my eyes say that he'd better help out now that he had finally decided he could be bothered to pay us a visit. "See you outside in five minutes."

We had 324 hives. 324 queens, each with her own colony, located throughout the area in different places, rarely more than 20 in each place. If we'd lived in another state, we could have had up to 70 hives in one site. I knew a beekeeper in Montana, he had gathered close to 100 in the same place. The region was so fertile that the bees only had to fly a few yards to find everything they needed. But here, in Ohio, the agriculture wasn't diversified enough. Mile after mile of corn and soybeans. Too little access to nectar, not enough for the bees to live on.

Emma had painted the hives, all of them, over the years, the color of candies. Pink, turquoise, light yellow and a kind of greenish pistachio color, as artificial as sweets full of additives. She thought it looked festive. For my own part they could just as well have been white, like before. My father had always painted them white and his father and grandfather before him. They used to say that it was the inside that counted — not the color. But Emma thought the bees

70

liked them this way, that it made it more personal. Who knows, maybe she was right. And I had to admit that the sight of the colored hives scattered across the landscape, as if a giant had dropped his sweets, always gave me a warm feeling inside.

We started on the meadow between the Menton farm, the main road and the narrow Alabast River, which, despite its fancy name, this far south wasn't much more than a riverbed. Here I had assembled the majority. Twenty-six bee colonies. We started on a shocking-pink hive. It was helpful that there were two of us. Tom lifted the box while I changed the board. Removed the old one, which was full of debris and dead bees from the winter, and put in a new, clean one. We had invested in modern bottom boards with screens and removable ventilated pollen trays last year. It had been expensive, but it was worth it. The air circulation improved and the cleaning was simpler. Most bee-keepers operating on this scale had dropped changing the bottom boards at this time, but I didn't believe in letting things take their own course. My bees were going to thrive.

A lot of debris had collected on the bottom board in the course of the winter, but otherwise everything looked good. We were fortunate, the bees stayed calm, few flew up. It was good to see Tom out here. He worked skillfully and quickly, was back where he belonged. Sometimes he wanted to bend his back, but I stopped him.

"Lift with your legs." I knew several people who had ended up with slipped discs and spasms and no end of back troubles because they had been lifting wrong. And Tom's back would have to last for many years, withstand thousands of lifts. We kept working without a break until lunchtime. We didn't say much, just a few words, and only about the work. "Hold on here, like that, good." I kept waiting for him to ask for a break, but he didn't mention it. And as the hour approached 11:30, my stomach was growling, so I was the one who suggested a bite to eat.

We sat on the edge of the flatbed and dangled our legs. I had brought along a thermos full of coffee and some sandwiches. The peanut butter had been absorbed by the spongy bread and the slices were sticky but it's incredible how good everything tastes when the air is fresh and you're working outdoors. Tom said nothing. He was definitely not one for small talk, this son of mine. But if that was his preference, it was fine by me. I'd gotten him out here, that was the most important thing. I just hoped that he was enjoying it a little and felt it was good to be here again.

I finished eating and jumped down onto the ground to work again, but Tom was still toiling away. He took baby-size bites and stared intently at the sandwich, as if there were something wrong with it.

And then suddenly he came out with it.

"I have a very good English teacher."

"Is that right," I said and stopped. I tried to smile, even though there was something about the way he said this completely ordinary thing that gave me a lump in my stomach. "That's good."

He took another bite. He chewed and chewed, apparently unable to swallow.

"He's encouraging me to write more."

"More? More of what?"

"He says that . . ."

He fell silent. Put the sandwich down, gripped around his coffee cup, but didn't drink. That was when I first noticed that his hand was shaking a little.

"He says that I have a voice."

A voice? Academic nonsense. I forced a grin, I couldn't be bothered to take this seriously.

"I could have told you that a long time ago," I said. "Especially when you were little. Loud and cutting it was. Thank God your voice changed. It didn't happen one day too soon."

He didn't smile at the joke. He just sat there in silence.

The grin slid off my face. He wanted to say something, no doubt about that. He was sitting there with some burning issue on his mind, and I had a strong suspicion that it was something that I absolutely did not want to hear.

"It's good the teachers are satisfied with you," I said finally.

"He really thinks I should write more," Tom said softly, with an emphasis on *really.* "He said I can apply for scholarships, too, and maybe continue with it."

"Continue?"

"A Ph.D."

My chest tightened, my throat grew constricted, I could taste the raw flavor of peanut butter in my mouth, but was unable to swallow.

"Is that right. So he said that."

Tom nodded.

I tried to keep my voice calm. "How many years does one of those Ph.D.s take?"

He just stared down at the toes of his shoes, without answering.

"I'm not exactly getting any younger," I

continued. "Things don't run by themselves up here."

"No, I know that," he said quietly. "But you do have help?"

"Jimmy and Rick come and go as they please. It's not their farm. Besides, they don't work for free."

I started working again, lifted the dirty boards over onto the flatbed. The woodwork in the frames hit the metal on the flatbed with a rude clang. Yes indeed, we had heard from teachers before about how Tom was good with words. He'd always gotten As in English, there was obviously nothing wrong with his head. But it wasn't English we had in mind when we sent him to college. He was supposed to learn economics and marketing, prepare the farm for the future. Expand, modernize, make operations more efficient. And maybe make a proper website. Those were the kinds of things he was supposed to learn. That was why we had scrimped and saved for his tuition, ever since he was a little boy. We hadn't treated ourselves to a single real vacation in all those years, not once. Everything had gone into the college account.

What did an English teacher know? Probably sat there in his dusty college office full of books he pretended to have read and slurped tea and wore a scarf while he was inside, trimming his beard with embroidery scissors. While he gave "good" advice to young boys who happened to be good at writing, without knowing shit about what he was starting.

"We can talk more about that later," I said. We never had that talk. He left before we had the chance. I decided that "later" was a long way off. Or maybe he was the one who decided that. Or maybe Emma. Because we were never alone in the same room, Tom and I, not on one single occasion, the rest of the time that he was home. Emma cooed around us like a wood pigeon on speed, served, cleared, talked and talked about absolutely nothing.

I was so tired during those days. Fell asleep on the couch all the time. Had a long list of jobs I was supposed to do, old hives that needed maintenance, orders I needed to follow up on. But I didn't have the gumption. It was like I was going around with a mild fever all the time. But I didn't have a fever. I even took my temperature. Snuck into the bathroom and found a thermometer at the bottom of the first-aid kit. Light blue with teddy bears on it, Emma had bought it for Tom when he was a baby. It was supposed to be especially quick, the instructions said, so as not to disturb the child any longer than necessary. But it sure had to stay in long enough. Somewhere or other in the house I could hear Emma cooing and Tom answering from time to time. And there I was, with the cold metal tip in my butt, that had been in the backside of my son hundreds of times. Emma was not the kind to think twice about checking his temperature, and yet again I felt my eyes fall shut while I was waiting for the digital peep that told me my body was as it should be, even though it felt as if I had run a marathon, or how I figured that had to feel.

Once I had finally confirmed that I didn't have a fever, I just went and lay down anyway, without saying anything. Let them carry on.

The cooing continued until he was sitting on the bus. Then, with Tom inside, his face plastered against the back window and relief painted all over his mug, she was finally silent.

We stood there and waved, as automatically as if we were full of batteries, hands up and down, up and down, completely in sync. Emma's eyes became shiny, or perhaps it was just the wind, but luckily she didn't cry.

The bus pulled out onto the road, Tom's

face shone faintly at us, smaller and smaller. It suddenly reminded me of another time when he drove away from me on a bus. Then, too, his face had shimmered faintly at me with relief. But also with fear.

I shook my head, wanted to get rid of the memory.

Finally the bus disappeared around the corner. We lowered our hands in unison, stood there watching the point where it disappeared, as if we were stupid enough to believe it would suddenly come back.

"Well, well," Emma said. "That was that."

"That was that? What do you mean?"

"We just have them on loan." She dried a tear that the wind had nudged out of her left eye. I had a good mind to unleash a sharp retort, but let it go. I had too much respect for that tear. So I turned and walked towards the car.

She plodded behind me. It seemed she'd grown smaller as well.

I got in behind the wheel, but was incapable of starting the engine. My hands were so limp, as if worn out by all of the waving.

Emma put on her seat belt, she was always so particular about that, and turned towards me.

"Aren't you going to drive?"

I wanted to lift my hand, but it didn't work.

"Did he talk to you about it?" I said to the steering wheel.

"What?" Emma asked.

"About what he's planning? For the future?"

She was quiet for a moment. Then it came, softly.

"You do know he loves to write. He always has."

"I love Star Wars. Haven't become no Jedi, though."

"He clearly has a special talent."

"So you support him? You think his plan is wise? Real smart? A good choice of direction?" I turned to face her now, straightened my neck, tried to seem severe.

"I just want him to be happy," she said meekly.

"You do."

"Yes. I do."

"You haven't thought about how he has to live as well? Earn money eventually?"

"The teacher has said that he has something to offer."

She sat there with that large, open gaze of hers, completely sincere. She wasn't angry, just had such an unshakable belief that she was right.

I squeezed the car keys in my hand, suddenly noticed that it hurt, but couldn't let go.

"Have you thought about what we'll do with the farm then?"

She was silent. For a long while. Looked away, fiddled a bit with her wedding ring, pulled it up over the first joint in her finger. The white band on her skin below was revealed, the mark from the ring that had been there for twenty-five years.

"Nellie called last week," she said finally, into space, not to me. "They have summer temperatures in Gulf Harbors now. Seventy degrees in the water."

There it was again. Gulf Harbors. Floating, even though the name of the housing development hit me like a shingle in the head every time she said it. Nellie and Rob were childhood friends of ours. Unfortunately, they had moved to Florida. Ever since that happened, they had been pestering us something fierce, not just to visit this so-called oasis on the outskirts of Tampa, but also that we should move there ourselves. Emma kept showing me new ads for houses in Gulf Harbors. Real cheap. On the market for a long time. We could find a bargain. A pier and a swimming pool, recently renovated, a common beach and tennis courts, as if we would need that, yes, it seems they even had dolphins, and manatees, carrying on and splashing around, right outside their front door. Who needed it? Manatees? Ugly beasts.

Nellie and Rob bragged like crazy. They'd made lots of new friends, they said, listing random names: Laurie, Mark, Randy, Steven. There was no end to it. Every week they had Sunday brunch together at the community center, a full brunch for only five dollars, with pancakes, bacon, eggs and fried potatoes. And now they were trying to get us to come down, all of us, yes indeed, they were nagging more people than just us, apparently wanted all of Autumn to come south. But I knew what it was really all about. They were lonely down there on their deep-water canal. It was wretched living so far away from family and friends, to have run away from everything they'd had around them their whole lives. Besides, summer in Florida, you can't get closer to hell, sticky and hot and horrible, with insane thunderstorms several times a day. And even though the winter is probably just fine, with summer temperatures and not much rain, who wants to live without a real winter? Without snow and the cold? I'd told Emma this many times, but she still wouldn't give up.

Thought we had to start making proper plans, plans for our old age. She didn't understand that I'd done just that. I wanted to leave behind something substantial, a legacy, instead of sitting there with a rundown vacation home that was impossible to sell. Yes indeed. I'd done a little reading about how things were on the housing market in Florida these days. There were good reasons why these houses weren't sold the first weekend they were shown, to put it that way.

But I had another plan. Some new investments. More hives, many more. Trucks. Trailers. Full-time employees. Plans for agreements with farms in California, Georgia, maybe Florida.

And Tom.

It was a good plan. Realistic. Levelheaded. Before Tom knew it, he'd have a wife and children. Then it would be a good thing that his father had made proper plans, that the farm was in working order, well maintained, that the enterprise was adapted to the modern world, that Tom had worked here long enough so he knew the craft from the inside out. And that maybe there was a little money in the bank. These were uncertain times. I created security. I *alone* created security for this family. A future. But it didn't seem like anyone understood that.

I got tired just thinking about it, about the plan. Before it had given me the energy to work extra, but now the road ahead seemed as long and twisted as a muddy wheel rut in the autumn rain.

I couldn't bring myself to answer Emma. Stuck the car keys in the ignition, the key was slick with sweat and had created a red mark on the palm of my hand. I had to drive now, before I fell asleep. She didn't look up, had taken off her wedding ring and was rubbing her fingers against the white band on the skin. She couldn't fool me, but all the same she wanted to put our whole life in jeopardy.

TAO

"Will you turn off the light?" Kuan turned around to face me, pale with sleepiness.

"Just want to finish reading this."

I continued with the old book about early-childhood education. My eyes were sore, but I didn't want to go to sleep yet. Didn't want to sleep, wake up and then have to go out into a new day.

He sighed beside me. Pulled the blanket over his head to shut out the light. A minute passed. Two.

"Tao . . . please. In six hours we have to get up."

I didn't answer, merely did as he asked.

"Good night," he said softly.

"Good night," I said and turned to face the wall.

Sleep was just taking me away when I felt his hands creeping under my camisole. I reacted to them instinctively, unable to refrain from taking pleasure in his caresses, but I tried to push them away all the same. Wasn't he tired? Why had he asked me to turn off the light if this was what he wanted?

His hands disappeared, but his breathing was still shallow. Then he cleared his throat, as if he had something on his mind. "How . . . How did things go today?"

"What do you mean?"

"You've forgotten what day it is."

"No. I haven't forgotten."

I didn't say that I'd hoped *he* had forgotten so I wouldn't have to have this conversation.

He stroked my hair, tenderly now, not seductively. "Have you been OK?"

"Every year it gets a little easier," I said, because that was certainly what he wanted to hear.

"Good."

He stroked my hair one more time, then his hand disappeared back under his own blanket.

The mattress undulated slightly when he turned over, perhaps onto his stomach, that's how he liked to sleep. Then he mumbled good night again. Judging from how it sounded, he had turned over with his back to me. Soon he was sleeping deeply. But I lay awake in bed.

Five years.

Five years had passed since my mother left.

No. Not left. Was sent away.

My father died when I was nineteen. He was just a little over fifty, but his body was much older. Shoulders, back, joints, all of him was worn out from all of the years in the trees. He moved more heavily with each passing day. Perhaps his blood circulated more poorly as well, because one day when he got a splinter in his palm, the cut wouldn't heal.

He put off seeking help for too long, being the man that he was. And when the doctor had finally received approval to give him antibiotics, even though my father was actually too old to be given priority for this type of expensive treatment, it was already too late.

My mother recovered surprisingly quickly after his death. Said all the right things, was optimistic. She was still young, she said, and smiled bravely, had a long life ahead of her. Perhaps she would even meet another man one day.

But they were just words. Because she fluttered away, the way petals blow away when the blossoming season is over. There was wind in her gaze, impossible to capture.

Soon she failed to show up for work in

the fields. She just stayed home. She had been thin before, and now she ate almost nothing. Began sniffling, coughing, grew more and more lethargic, and soon she developed pneumonia.

One day when I came to look in on her she didn't open the door. I rang the bell several times, but nothing happened. I had an extra key that I took out and unlocked the door with.

The flat was neat and clean, all that remained were the old furnishings that belonged to the household. All of her things were gone; the pillow she used to lean her back against on the couch, the bonsai tree she tended with such diligence, the embroidered blanket she liked to fold up and spread across her thighs, as if she felt a particular chill right there.

The same afternoon I found out that she'd been sent north. She was fine, the district's health supervisor assured me, and gave me the name of the nursing home. I was shown a choppy presentation film from there. Bright and beautiful, large rooms, high ceilings, smiling personnel. But when I asked about leave so I could go and visit her, I was told that I would have to wait until the blossoming season was over.

A few weeks later word came that she had

departed.

Departed. That was the word they used, as if she had in fact gotten out of bed and left. I tried not to think about how her final days had been. A rasping cough, feverish, frightened and alone. To think she had to die like that.

But there was nothing I could have done. Kuan said so as well. There was nothing I could have done. He said it again and again, and I continued saying it to myself.

Until I almost believed it.

WILLIAM

"Edmund?"

"Good afternoon, Father."

He stood alone beside my bed. I had no idea how long he'd been in the room. He had become somebody else, taller, and his nose . . . The last time I saw him, it was far too big. Noses often grow at their own pace in young people, leaping ahead of the rest of the body, but now it suited his face, his features had grown into place around it. He had become handsome, a beauty that had always lain latent in him, elegant, but dressed a bit rakishly, a bottle-green scarf hung loosely around his neck, his fringe just a bit too long, it was becoming, but made it difficult to see his eyes. On top of it all he was pale. Wasn't he getting enough sleep?

Edmund, my only son. *Thilda's* only son. It hadn't been long before I understood that he was hers, wholly and completely. From the day we met, she let it be known that her greatest wish was to have a boy and when he arrived the following year, her vocation was fulfilled. Dorothea and Charlotte, and later the five other little girls, became mere shadows of him. In a sense I understood her. The seven girls gave me a constant headache. Their fierce and unceasing howling, shouting, whining, crying, giggling, running, coughing, sniffling, not to mention chattering — the way such young girls could chatter, they were relentless chatterboxes — all of these sounds surrounded me from the minute I got up until I went to bed, and not just that — they continued all through the night as well. There was always a child who cried over a dream, always one who came tiptoeing in wearing only a nightgown and had kicked off her stockings in her sleep, so that bare feet slapped lightly against the cold floorboards, and then crept up into the bed making some sound or other, some woebegone whimpers, or an almost aggressive demand to be allowed to squeeze in between us in our bed.

It seemed impossible for them to be quiet and it was therefore impossible for me to work, impossible to write. I had really tried, I had not given up right away, as Rahm believed. But it was no use. Even though I closed the door to my room after having clearly informed the entire family that Father had to work, they had to show consideration, even though I tied a scarf around my head to shut out the noise, or stuffed my ears full of wool, even then I could hear them. It was no use. Over the years there was increasingly less time for my own work, and soon I was no more than a simple merchant who struggled to feed the eternally voracious little-girl stomachs. They were bottomless. The promising naturalist had to step aside for a weary, middle-aged seed merchant, with tired feet from hours spent behind the counter, rusty vocal cords from the eternal small talk with the customers, and the fingers, endlessly counting the money that there was never quite enough of. All of it due to the noise made by the young girls.

Edmund stood completely still, frozen. Before his body had been like the sea by a peninsula, winds and waves met and collided with one another, chaotic, unruly. The restlessness was not only in his body, it was also in his soul. One minute he would show his good-natured side, and fetch a bucket of water just to be nice, the next minute he emptied the bucket across the floor in order, as he explained it himself, to create a lake. Reprimands had no impact on him. If we raised our voices, he just laughed and ran away. Always running, that was how I remembered him, the small feet, never at rest, always running away from some catastrophe or other that he had instigated, from the capsized bucket, a broken porcelain cup, knitting unraveled. When that happened, and it happened often, I had no choice but to catch him, and hold him tightly while I pulled the belt out of the loops on my trousers. I had come to despise the hissing sound of the leather against fabric and the jangling of the buckle as it struck the floorboards. The anguish over what was to come was almost worse than the actual blows. The sensation of the leather against my hand and the belt buckle, I clung to it — I never hit with that end, not like my father, who always slung the buckle through the air so it hit the back hard. I clutched it tightly, so it dug into my palm and left behind welts. The leather against the bare back, the red marks that blossomed out of the white skin, like twisting vines. In other children, these red welts helped to settle them down, and the memory of the punishment remained in the child's consciousness, so the next time they would avoid making the same mistake. But it didn't have that effect on Edmund. It was as if he didn't understand that all of his impetuous actions led him back to the belt, that there was a connection between the lake on the kitchen floor and the subsequent blows. But it was nonetheless my responsibility to continue and I hoped that deep down he also noticed my love, understood that I had no choice. I disciplined him, therefore I was a father. I hit him as the tears swelled in my chest, while the sweat ran and my hands shook, I wanted to beat the restlessness out of him, but it never helped.

"Where are the others?" I asked, because the house was so oddly quiet.

I regretted it right away. I shouldn't have asked about them. Not when he had finally come in to see me. Not when it was finally just him and me.

Edmund swayed slightly as he stood there, as if he were struggling to keep his balance, didn't know on which leg he should rest his weight.

"In church." So it was Sunday.

I tried to sit up in bed. I lifted the blanket a bit. The stench of my own body hit me. When had I last bathed?

But if he noticed anything, he didn't show it.

"And you?" I said. "Why have you stayed home?"

It sounded like an accusation when it should have been a thank-you.

He didn't look at me, stared into the wall above the headboard.

"I . . . I was hoping to have a chance to talk to you," he said finally.

I nodded slowly, while I strove to keep my face from disclosing how exceedingly pleased I was about his visit.

"Good," I said. "I appreciate seeing you very much . . . and have been hoping you would come for a long time."

I tried to sit up, but it was as if my skeleton could no longer hold me upright, so I supported myself on a pillow. *That* in itself was an enormous effort. I resisted the urge to pull the blanket all the way up to my shoulders to shut in the odor. I could barely stand the smell of myself. How had I not noticed it before, how badly I needed a bath? I lifted my hand to my face. The stubble, which had never been especially thick, had now managed to grow into a shaggy beard several centimeters long. I must have looked like a caveman.

He stared at my toes, which were sticking out from under the blanket. The toenails were long and dirty. I quickly pulled my feet out of sight and sat up in bed.

"Edmund. Tell me. What's on your mind?"

His eyes did not meet mine, but there was no shyness about him when he delivered his message.

"Perhaps Father can get out of bed soon?"

A blush of shame rose to my cheeks. Thilda had asked. The girls had asked. The doctor had asked. But Edmund had never come to my bedside before.

"I am so infinitely pleased about your coming," I said in a voice that was on the verge of breaking. "I would like very much to explain."

"Explain?" He pulled one hand through his fringe. "I don't need any explanation. I just want you to get up."

What was I supposed to say? What did he expect from me? I tapped my hand against the mattress, a small inviting gesture. "Sit down, Edmund. Let's talk a bit. What have you been doing lately?"

He didn't move.

"Tell me about your schoolwork. With the good head you have on your shoulders I assume it's all smooth sailing?"

He was preparing for the autumn, when he would be attending school in the capital. We had scrimped and saved for his schooling and now he was finally almost ready. I felt a sudden stab in my chest. His tuition, could it be that Thilda was spending it, now that I was lying here like this?

"I presume that nothing has changed. The plans for school are as before?" I asked quickly.

He nodded without any evident enthusiasm. "I work when I find the inspiration."

"Good. Inspiration is an important incentive."

I reached out my hand to him. "Come and sit down. Let's have a proper conversation now. It's been such a long time."

But he just stood there. "I . . . . have to go downstairs."

"Just a few minutes?" I tried to keep my voice light.

He tossed his fringe, did not look at me. "I'm going to study."

I was glad he was working, but still, he could certainly sacrifice a little more time, now that he had finally come.

"I just want to hold you," I said. "Just for a minute."

An almost inaudible sigh escaped from his lips, but all the same he came over to me. Finally he sat down beside me, hesitated a moment and gave me his hand.

"Thank you," I said softly.

His hand was warm and smooth. It radiated with life, became a bond between us, as if his healthy blood ran through me. I just wanted to sit like this, but there was no mistaking his ever present restlessness. He couldn't manage to hold his arms still, changed position, his feet twitched.

"Sorry, Father." He stood up abruptly.

"No," I said. "You needn't apologize. I understand. Of course you have to work."

He nodded. His eyes were fixed on the door. He just wanted to get away, leave me lying here alone again.

He took a few steps, then stopped himself, as if he remembered something, and turned around again.

"But Father . . . can't you at least try to find the will to get out of bed?"

I swallowed. I owed him a proper response.

"It's not that I lack the will . . . it's . . . the passion, Edmund."

"The passion?" He lifted his head, the word had apparently stirred something inside him. "Then you have to find it once more," he said quickly. "And allow it to move you."

I had to smile. Such big words from that ungainly body.

"We are nothing without passion," he concluded with a gravity I had never heard from him before.

He said nothing more. Just left the room

— the last impression I had of him was the sound of his footsteps against the floorboards out there. They disappeared towards the stairway and then down and away. But I still felt I had never been so close to him before.

Rahm was right; I had forgotten my passion and allowed myself to be consumed by trivialities. I demonstrated no enthusiasm in my work, which is why I lost Rahm. But Edmund was still there, I could still show *him,* make *him* proud. That way we could grow closer. Through the honor I would bring to the family name, our relationship would blossom and bear fruit. That way I would perhaps also find my way back to Rahm, so it could be the three of us after all: father, son and mentor.

I rolled over onto my side. I threw the blanket off my foul-smelling body, and then I got out of bed. This time it was for good.

GEORGE

I was building hives in the barn. That's what I often did this time of year. While spring was gearing up, nature about to explode with greenery and everyone talked about how nice it was, while everyone just wanted to be outside and enjoy it, I stayed inside under crackling fluorescent lights and hammered away as if possessed. This year more than ever. Emma and I hadn't talked very much since Tom left. For the most part I stayed in the barn. To be honest, I was afraid to start a conversation with her. She was better with words than I was, that's often the case with women and more often than not she got her own way. She was also often right, once I had a chance to think about it. But not this time. That much I knew.

So that's why I was in the barn. From morning till night. I repaired old hives, constructed new ones. Not standard hives, not in this family. We had our own design.

The drawings hung on the wall of the dining room — framed. It was Emma who had done it. She had found the drawings in a clothes chest in the attic, where they lay because everyone in my family knew the dimensions by heart anyway. The chest, a real going-to-America trunk, could easily have been sold to an antique shop for a nice lump of cash. But it was nice to have it up there, I thought. Reminded me of where I came from. The chest had traveled across the pond from Europe, when the first person in my family put her feet on American soil. One solitary woman. Everything stemmed from her, from this chest, from the drawings.

The yellowed, brittle paper was about to crumble into pieces, but Emma rescued it with glass and heavy gold frames. She even made sure the drawings were hung in a place without direct sunlight.

I didn't need them anyway. Had built these hives so many times I could do it blindfolded. People laughed at us because we built them ourselves. I didn't know any other beekeepers who built their own hives. It took too long. But we had always done it that way. These were our hives. I didn't speak about it out loud, didn't want to brag, but I was sure the bees were happier in our hives than in the mass-produced standard boxes. So people could just go ahead and laugh.

The equipment was ready and waiting in the barn along with thick, fragrant planks of wood.

I started with the boxes. Cut out slots with the electric saw and pounded the planks together with a rubber hammer. It went quickly; it was work that had visible results. The frames took longer. Ten frames per box. The only thing we bought prefabricated was the metal queen excluder, with 4.2-millimeter openings to ensure that the queen stayed inside the hive and the smaller worker bees could come and go freely. There were limits.

The work kept me from falling asleep. Out here in the cold barn where the sawdust flew like snowflakes through the air, drowsiness didn't overcome me the way it did indoors. Besides, it was impossible to sleep to the angry sound of the electric saw. I usually wore earmuffs but now I took them off, let the sound fill my head. Then there wasn't room for much of anything else.

I didn't notice Emma come in. She could have been standing there watching me for a long time, had at least had time enough to put on safety earmuffs. When I turned around to get more wood moldings I discovered her. She just stood there with the big, yellow plastic earmuffs over her ears. She smiled.

I turned off the saw.

"Hello?"

She pointed at the earmuffs and shook her head slightly. Fine. She couldn't hear what I said. We stood there like that. She continued to smile. No mistaking it, that smile. Menopause was a big topic these days, the women whispered when they thought we weren't listening, about hot flashes, urination, night sweats and, yes indeed, we also picked up on that: reduced libido. But Emma was as she had always been. And now she stood there wearing earmuffs and it wasn't hard to understand what she wanted.

It had been a long time, long for us. Not since before Tom was home. We became shy with him in the house, afraid he would hear, just as if he were still a toddler sleeping in our bedroom with us. We started whispering every time we got into bed. Moved carefully, lay right down under the duvet and quietly turned the pages of our respective books. And afterwards, after he had left, it simply hadn't come up. I hadn't even thought about it.

She put her arms around me, kissed me on the mouth, with her eyes closed.

"I don't know," I said. My body was stiff and slow, no pep in me. "I'm a little tired."

She just smiled and pointed at the earmuffs again.

I tried to take them off, but she removed my hand.

We stood there like that. I held her hand. The smile remained plastered across her face.

"OK."

I pulled out a pair of earmuffs, too. "Is this how you want it?" For some reason or other I came to life. It wasn't quiet, it was never quiet when you shut everything out, the hissing of the brain, of my own breath, the heart pounding, all of it invaded you.

We kissed, her tongue was soft, her mouth open and warm. I pulled her up on the carpenter's bench. Her head was level with mine. The air was cold, my fingers were like icicles against her skin. She winced, but did not pull away. I tried to blow on my hands, don't think it helped much, because she trembled when I tried to push them under her sweater. She lay back on the table, with her legs dangling towards the floor. I kissed her on the stomach but she pushed my head down. Her body jerked when my tongue hit

103

the spot. Perhaps she moaned, but if she did I couldn't hear it.

Then we both lay on the table. She was on top. It didn't take long, it was too cold for that. And the boards of the table were too hard against my shoulder blades.

Afterwards she took off the earmuffs, pulled up her pants and tucked in her shirt. Before I could say anything she had gone.

She left behind the warmth of her body, suspended in the air above the carpenter's bench.

Gulf Harbors. There it was again. *Gulf Harbors.* The words wouldn't go away, kept messing around in my head, *Gulf Harbors,* kneaded, like dough, *Gulf Harbors, Harb Gulfors, Bors Gulf-harb,* I shook my head hard, wanted to get rid of them, but they were damn well there all the same, *Gulf Borsharb, Bors Harbgulf, Harb Forsgulf.*

It was hot there now. I checked the weather report yesterday, without Emma noticing. Don't know why, I just happened to find a national weather forecast on TV and sat there waiting for Tampa to show up. I could see that there wasn't much precipitation this time of year. There was still a raw chill here, but the dream summer had already arrived there. The nightlife. Barbecuing. Dolphins. Manatees.

Gulf Harbors.

The words were permanently stuck, it was impossible to get rid of them. So they would have to stay.

She was something, Emma. I was lucky to have her. No matter what happened. That wouldn't change, even if we did move to Florida.

Tao

The Day of Rest finally arrived. Unannounced, like every year. We were not notified until the evening before that the Committee had decided the citizens had finally earned the right to a day off. The official announcement was made by Li Xiara, the Committee's leader, a woman who always presented the Committee's most recent decisions to us, on the radio, and on battered information screens. Her chanting, dispassionate voice was the same, regardless of whether the message was good or bad. The pollination was finished, she now reported, the blossoming season was almost over. They could treat us to this, she said, we, the community, could treat ourselves.

We had been waiting for this day for weeks. More than two months had passed since we'd last had time off. While the tendons in our lower arms grew more and more inflamed from the repetitive brushing movement, while our arms and shoulders grew stiffer and stiffer and our feet perpetually tired from standing, we worked and waited.

For once I was awakened not by the alarm, but by the light. The sun warmed my face, I lay in bed with my eyes closed, feeling how the temperature slowly rose in the room. Then I finally managed to open my eyes and look around. The bed was empty. Kuan was already up.

I went to him in the kitchen. He was having a cup of tea and looking out at the fields, while Wei-Wen played on the floor. It was so quiet, a day of rest for all of us, as had been decided. Even Wei-Wen was playing more calmly than usual. He drove a red toy car around the floor while making a soft rumbling sound.

His soft neck, the close-cropped hair, the short fingers clutching the car, the mouth buzzing so intensely that a little spit was pressed out between his lips. His enthusiasm. He could probably sit like this for hours, create roads down there on the floor with all of the vehicles he had, cities full of life.

I sat down beside Kuan, took a sip of his tea. It was almost cold; he must have been sitting here for a long time.

"What do you want to do?" I said finally. "How do you want to spend our day?"

He took yet another sip of tea, just a little sip, as if he were saving it.

"Well . . . I don't know . . . what do you want?"

I stood up. He knew what he wanted to do. I'd already heard him speaking with some of his workmates about everything that would be taking place in the center of the little place we called the town, an eatery was being set up on the square, long tables and entertainment.

"I want to spend the day with Wei-Wen," I said lightly.

He laughed softly. "So do I."

But his eyes didn't meet mine.

"We have many hours, we can get a lot done. I would really like to teach him numbers," I said.

"Mm." The still evasive gaze, as if he acquiesced, even though I knew that he was doing the opposite.

"You asked what I wanted to do," I said. "That's what I want."

He got to his feet, then he walked over to me and put his hand on my shoulder, massaged it lightly. A persuasive massage, trying to hit my weak spot; he knew that even if I could resist him verbally, I seldom managed

108

it physically.

I gently twisted out of his grasp, he was not going to win. "Kuan . . ."

But he just smiled at me, took hold of my hand. Then he pulled me towards the window, stood behind me while letting his hands slide from my shoulders and all the way down towards my hands.

"Look outside," he said softly and intertwined his fingers with mine. I gently tried to pull free, but he held me tight. "Look outside."

"Why?"

He held me calmly against him, and I did as he asked. The sun was shining. It was snowing white petals out there. The ground was covered. The petals floated through the air, turning a luminescent white from the sun. The rows of pear trees were endless. The amount of blossoms made me dizzy. I saw them every single day, every individual tree. But I didn't see them the way I did today. Together.

"I think we should go to town. Dress up, go out and get something good to eat." His voice was mild, as if he had made up his mind not to get angry.

I tried to smile, meet him halfway, couldn't start this day with an argument. "Not the town, please."

"But that's where everyone is."

He wanted to join the queue, the way we did every single day. I took a breath.

"Can't we do something, just the three of us?"

He lifted the corners of his mouth in an attempt at a smile. "Makes no difference to me. As long as we go outside."

I turned towards the window again, towards the flowers, the white sea. We were never alone out there.

"Maybe we can just walk over there?"

"Over where? To the fields?"

"That's outside." I tried to smile, but he did not return it.

"I don't know . . ."

"It will be nice. Just the three of us. And then we won't have to walk that long distance with Wei-Wen. It will be good for him to be spared that, just this once?"

I lay my hand on his upper arm, an affectionate gesture, refrained from saying anything more about the lesson. But he saw through me.

"And the books?"

"We can bring some with us? And I needn't keep at it all day."

His eyes finally met mine. Resigned, but with a little smile.

WILLIAM

I stood beside the desk. It was placed by the window, where the light was the best, the most suitable place in the room and absolutely the most pleasant. But I hadn't sat here in months.

One lone book lay on the table. Was it Edmund who had placed it there while I was sleeping?

The pages were yellowed, a thin layer of dust covered the top and the brown leather cover was dry and brittle against my fingers. Now I recognized the work, I'd purchased it in the capital during the years when I'd been a student. At that time I happily sacrificed my midday meal for a week in exchange for a new book. But this book in particular I'd never got around to reading, probably it had been purchased towards the end of my time as a student. It was written by François Huber, published in Edinburgh in 1806, almost forty-five years ago and the title read: *New Observations on the Natural History of Bees.*

It was a book about bees, about the beehive, the superorganism, where each individual, each tiny insect was subordinate to the greater whole.

Why had Edmund picked out this book? This book in particular?

I took out my spectacles, had to wipe off the dust on my shirt, then I sat down. The feeling of the desk chair against my back was like meeting an old friend.

The cover creaked in protest when I opened the book. I carefully turned the title page and then I began to read.

I knew of François Huber's story from my student days, but had never really studied his theories in depth. He was born into an extremely well-to-do Swiss family in 1750. The father had ensured the wealth of the family, and unlike himself, little François had never been obliged to work, but there were clear expectations on the part of his family that he should immerse himself in intellectual pursuits and in this way justify his position on this earth. He had to create something, something that put both his name and the family name on everybody's lips; he was supposed to write them into the history books. François did his utmost to please his father. He was an intelligent child and read difficult works even as a young boy. He stayed awake into the wee hours, hidden behind a stack of exceedingly thick books, reading until his eyes burned and ran, until they were gleaming with pain. Finally it was too much for him, the pressure too great, and his eyes couldn't take anymore. For the books did not lead him into an era of enlightenment, they led him into darkness.

As a fifteen-year-old he was almost blind. He was sent to the countryside, told to rest and not exert himself, he could help out with simple farm work, that was all.

But young François couldn't rest, because he hadn't forgotten the expectations which once had rested on him, and his mind was designed in such a way that he viewed his blindness not as a hindrance, but as an opportunity, because even though he could no longer see, he could still hear, and around him, on all sides, was life itself. Birds sang, squirrels chattered, the wind blew through the trees and the bees hummed.

The latter in particular caught his attention.

He slowly commenced his scientific work, which became the foundation for the book I held between my hands. With the valuable assistance of his faithful apprentice and namesake François Burnens, he started mapping out the honeybees' different life phases.

The first important discovery the two of them made was in connection with fertilization itself. Nobody had formerly understood how the queen was impregnated; the process had never been witnessed before, although various scientists in different periods had carried out enthusiastic observational studies of life in the hive. But Huber and Burnens understood what was crucial, that fertilization did not take place on the inside, but rather, outside. Newborn queens left the hive, flew away and it was there, on these flights, that it happened. The queen came back, full of the sperm of the drones but also covered with their reproductive organs, which had been torn off in the act. How nature could demand such a ludicrous sacrifice on the part of the drone was a question to which Huber never found an answer. That nature actually demanded the greatest sacrifice of all, death, was not discovered until later, and perhaps it was just as well that Huber never understood precisely this. Perhaps it would have been too much for the blind Huber to take, that the drone's only duty in life was to reproduce, and in so doing, to die.

Huber not only studied the bees, he also did what he could to improve their lot. He set about constructing a new type of beehive.

For many years, people's contact with bees was limited to the harvest of natural hives, crescent-shaped honeycombs, built by the bees themselves on branches or in hollows. But with time, some people became so obsessed with the bees' gold that they wanted to keep them like domestic animals. Attempts were made to build ceramic beehives, but with little success, and then the straw hive was developed, which was the most common in Europe in Huber's day. In my district they still predominated, they blended in like part of the wildlife in the fields and on the roadsides. I had never before reflected upon these hives, not before now, reading Huber's book, but they had their shortcomings. It was difficult to inspect the inside of the straw hive and when the honey was to be harvested, it had to be pressed out of the honeycombs, destroying eggs and larvae in the process, so that the honey was impure. Not to mention that the honeycombs themselves were destroyed. The bees' home.

To harvest the honey it was, in other

words, necessary to deprive the bees of their basis for survival.

Huber set out to change this. He developed a hive that was easier to harvest. It opened up like a book where each leaf of the book was a frame for larvae and honey: the movable-frame hive.

I studied the pictures of Huber's hive in the book, the frames, the visually beautiful but patently inexpedient design of the leaves. It had to be possible to develop this further, to work out a solution that was better, so the harvesting could be done without hurting the bees and the beekeeper could more effectively inspect and keep an eye on the queen, larvae and production. Suddenly I noticed that I was trembling with excitement. This was what I wanted, this was where my passion lay. I was unable to take my eyes off the drawings, off the bees. I wanted to go in there. Into the hive!

TAO

"One, two, three — jump!"

We followed the tire ruts inwards across the fields. Wei-Wen walked between Kuan and me. He was wearing my old red scarf around his throat. He loved it, wanted to wear it every day, but was only allowed when nobody else could see. It was awarded as a kind of badge of honor, not a dress-up garment. But I liked that he wore it, perhaps it would inspire him, make him want to have one of his own someday.

Wei-Wen was holding each of us by the hand and demanded that we pull him up through the air in long jumps forward. "More. More." The scarf was blown upwards into his face, almost covering it, hiding it and without thinking he pushed it aside.

"Look!" he shouted again and again and pointed. "Look!" At the trees, the sky and the flowers. Being out here was new for him, the fields were usually a place he observed from the window, before he was forced out the door to get to school on time or lifted into bed in the evening.

We were going to walk to a hilltop not far from the forest and eat there. We could see it from our house, it was located no more than three hundred meters away, so it was not a long walk for Wei-Wen, and we knew that up there we would have a nice view of both the city and the fields. We had packed fried rice, tea, a blanket and a tin of plums we had been saving for a very special day. We would then take out the pen and paper, and sit in the shade and work. I hoped I'd manage to teach him the numbers up to ten. It would be easier today. Wei-Wen was well rested. So was I.

"One, two, three — jump!"

We pulled him up into the air again, this had to be for the fifth or sixth time.

"Higher!" he shouted.

Our slightly defeated gazes met above his head. Then we lifted him, yet another time. He would never tire of it, we knew that. It was in the nature of a three-year-old never to tire. And he was used to getting his way.

"Imagine when he doesn't have us all to himself any longer," I said to Kuan.

"That will be tough on him," he said and smiled.

We were very close now, just a few more months, and then we would have enough money. All the extra money we had went to the battered tin box in the refrigerator. When we could demonstrate a sufficient amount of savings, we would receive the permit. 36,000 yuan was the requirement. We had 32,476. And it was urgent, because soon we would be too old. The age limit was thirty years old and we were both twenty-eight.

Wei-Wen was to have a sibling. It would presumably be a shock, having to share.

I tried to release his hand.

"Now you can walk by yourself a little, Wei-Wen."

"Nooo!"

"Yes. Just a bit. To that tree there." I pointed to a tree fifty meters away.

"Which one?"

"That one over there."

"But they're all the same."

I was unable to keep from smiling, he was right. I looked at Kuan. He grinned at me, his face open and happy. He was not angry because we were here, but in fact seemed satisfied with the compromise. He was, like me, determined for this to be a good day.

"Carry me!" Wei-Wen squealed and attached himself to my leg.

I shook myself free.

"Look. Take my hand."

But he kept whining.

"Carry me!"

Then suddenly he was flying through the air, as Kuan hoisted him easily up onto his shoulders.

"There. Now I can be a camel and you can be the rider."

"What is a camel?"

"A horse, then."

He neighed and Wei-Wen laughed. "You have to run, horse."

Kuan took a couple of steps, but stopped. "No, not this horse. This is an old and tired horse who also wants to walk together with the mommy horse."

"The mare," I said. "It's not called a mommy horse, it's a mare."

"Fine. The mare."

He continued walking with Wei-Wen on his shoulders. He reached for my hand and we walked hand in hand for a few meters, but Wei-Wen swayed precariously up there, so he hastened to take hold of him again. Wei-Wen's entire body bobbed with each step he took, he held his head high, looked around and discovered suddenly that he had acquired a wholly new stature.

"I'm the tallest!" He smiled to himself, as happy as only a three-year-old knows how to be.

We reached the top of the hill. The landscape was spread out before us. Rows of trees, as if drawn using a ruler, blossoming, symmetric cotton balls, against brown soil where the grass had only just begun to sprout through last year's rotting leaves.

The wide and shady forest lay just a hundred meters away. Dark and overgrown. There was nothing for us there, and now these areas, too, were going to be planted.

I turned around. To the north there were fruit trees from here to the horizon. Long, planted lines, tree after tree after tree after tree. I had read about trips people made, in former times, tourists. They traveled to see areas like this in the spring, making the trip solely to see the blossoming fruit trees. Was it beautiful? I didn't know. It was work. Every single tree was a dozen hours of labor. I couldn't look at them without thinking that soon they would be full of fruit and we would have to climb up them again. Pick with hands just as attentive as when we pollinated, pack every single pear in paper with extreme care, as if it were made of gold. An overwhelming amount of pears, trees, hours, years.

But all the same, we were out here today. Because I'd wanted to be.

Kuan spread a blanket on the ground. We took out the boxes of food. Wei-Wen ate quickly and spilled his food. He was always in a hurry at mealtimes, thought food was boring, was picky, ate little, even though we always sat there waiting with our portions, ready to give him more if he should want it.

But when we opened the tin of plums, he calmed down, perhaps because both Kuan and I were quiet. We put it between us. The tin opener made a scraping sound against the metal as Kuan twisted it around. He tilted the lid to the side and we looked down at the yellow fruit. It smelled sweet. I carefully took a plum with a fork and put it on Wei-Wen's plate.

"What is it?" he asked.

"A plum," I said.

"I don't like plums."

"You don't know that until you've tasted it."

He leaned over the plate and stuck his tongue into it, tasting the flavor for a second. And smiled. Then he snapped it up like a hungry dog, the entire plum went in his mouth at once, the juice ran out of the

122

corners of his mouth.

"Is there more?" he asked, still with his mouth full.

I showed him the tin. It was empty. One for each of us, that was all.

"But you can have mine, too," I said and passed the plum to him.

Kuan gave me a defeated look. "You need your vitamin C, too," he said softly. I shrugged my shoulders. "It just makes me want more. Just as well not to have any."

Kuan smiled at me. "All right." Then he also let his plum slide onto Wei-Wen's plate.

In just two minutes Wei-Wen had eaten all of them. He was on his feet again, wanted to climb the trees. And we had to stop him.

"The branches can break."

"I want to!"

I opened the bag looking for the pen and paper.

"I thought instead that we could sit here and play with arithmetic a little."

Kuan rolled his eyes, and Wei-Wen didn't seem to have heard what I'd said.

"Look! A boat!" He held up a stick.

"That's nice," Kuan said. "And there's a lake." He pointed towards a mud puddle a short distance away.

"Yeah!" Wei-Wen said and ran away.

I put the pen and paper back into the bag

without saying anything, turned my back to Kuan. He ruffled my hair. "The day is long."

"It's already half over."

"Come here." He pulled me down onto the blanket. "Feel how lovely it is, just lying here like this. To relax."

I smiled in spite of myself. "OK."

He took my hand and squeezed it. I squeezed his back. He squeezed mine in return. We both laughed. The usual discord was nowhere to be found.

I turned over onto my back. Stretched out completely, without any fear that someone would come and order me up from a break. The sunlight blinded me. I closed one eye, the world lost its depth. The bright blue sky merged with the white blossoms on the tree above us. They became the same surface. The sky peeked through between each individual petal. If I looked at it long enough, the foreground and background changed places. As if the sky were a blue crocheted blanket with holes against a white backdrop.

I closed both eyes. I could feel Kuan's hand resting in mine, completely still. We could have talked. We could have made love. But neither of us wanted to do anything but lie like this. Down by the mud puddle we could hear Wei-Wen put-putting, the boat sailing back and forth.

After a while I had to change positions. My shoulder blades were digging sharply down into the ground. The small of my back started aching a bit. I turned over onto my side and supported my head against my arm. Kuan had of course fallen asleep, and was snoring lightly. He could probably have slept for a whole week, if given the chance. He was always a little too thin, a little too pale, his body at all times running on a deficit. He got less sleep than he needed, less food than his metabolism consumed. Still, he kept himself going, worked longer days than I did, but was never dissatisfied. He rarely complained.

How quiet it was out here . . . Without the workers around me it was even more obvious. Even Wei-Wen's noises had stopped. No wind in the trees, just the absence of sound, emptiness.

I sat up. Where was he? I turned towards the mud puddle. It lay alone in the sunlight. The muddy-brown water glittered.

I stood up.

"Wei-Wen?"

Nobody answered.

"Wei-Wen, where are you?"

My voice didn't carry for more than a few meters, was swallowed up by the silence.

I walked a few steps away from the blanket, gaining a full view of the landscape.

He was nowhere to be seen.

"Wei-Wen?"

Kuan was awakened by my shouting, got to his feet and also began scanning the landscape.

"Can you see him?"

He shook his head.

It was only then that it struck me how infinitely large the area was. And that everything looked the same. Field after field of pear trees. Nothing else by which to navigate except the sun and the forest. And a three-year-old alone out here . . .

We hurried down to the puddle. The stick lay bobbing on the surface of the water.

"If you walk over there, I'll go here?" Kuan's voice was matter-of-fact and undramatic.

I nodded.

"He's probably just wandered off somewhere without thinking," Kuan said. "He can't have gone very far."

I hurried across the field, trotting across the uneven ground, along the tire ruts heading north. Yes, surely he had just wandered off. He had probably found something or other that was so exciting that he didn't notice us calling.

"Wei-Wen? Wei-Wen?" Perhaps he had been very lucky and discovered a small animal, an insect. Or perhaps a tree stump that looked like a dragon. Something that stopped him, made him start daydreaming, forget everything around him, learn something. An earthworm. A bird's nest. An ant-hill.

"Wei-Wen? Where are you? Wei-Wen!"

I tried to keep my voice light and breezy, but heard how piercing it sounded.

In the distance, I could hear Kuan's calls. "Wei-Wen? Hello?"

His voice was calm. Not like mine. I tried to call with the same calm. He was here, of course he was here. He was sitting and playing and lost in his own world.

"Wei-Wen?"

The sun scorched my back.

"Wei-Wen? Little one?"

It was as if the temperature had risen dramatically.

"Wei-Wen! Answer me, sweetie!"

My own breathing. It was uneven. Jagged. I turned around and discovered that I had already run several hundred meters away from the hill. It was impossible that he'd gone this far. I started running back, but changed course, moving in relation to the tire rut that was a few meters away.

I remembered that he'd been wearing the red scarf. Wei-Wen had been wearing the red scarf. That should be easy to see. Between the brown earth, the green grass and the white blossoms the scarf should stand out brightly.

"Tao! Tao! Come here!" Kuan's voice. Unfamiliar and sharp.

"Have you found him?"

"Come here!"

I changed directions and ran towards him. Something was squeezing my larynx, with every breath I took it became more difficult to breathe, as if the air didn't reach my lungs.

I caught a glimpse of Kuan between the trees. He ran towards me from the forest. It lay huge and dark behind him. Had he come from there? Had Wei-Wen disappeared in there?

"Is something wrong? Did something happen?" My voice forced its way out, was constricted, strained.

And now I could see him properly. Kuan ran towards me. His face was frozen, eyes open wide. He was carrying something in his arms.

The red scarf.

One shoe that flapped in time with his steps as he ran, a black, dangling child's

head. I ran over to Kuan.

A weak sound escaped me. I squelched a scream.

Because Wei-Wen was fighting for his breath. His face was white under his black hair. The eyes that looked at me, pleading for help. Had he broken something? Was he injured? Was he bleeding? No. It was like he was paralyzed.

Kuan said something, but I didn't hear the words, saw his lips moving, but no sounds reached me.

Kuan didn't stop, but kept running.

I shouted something. *The things. Our things!* As if they were important. But Kuan didn't stop. He just ran with Wei-Wen in his arms.

I followed him. Followed him and the child towards the houses, towards help.

The shoe flapping. The wind that caught hold of the red scarf.

We ran all the way back to the development. I kept my eyes on my child, on Wei-Wen, his eyes were huge and frightened. But I couldn't do anything but run.

I said his name again and again.

But now he no longer reacted.

Less resistance in his body. His face was even paler, the sweat beading on his forehead.

His eyes closed.

What a long way it seemed. How far we had walked. Was it really this far?

Finally the first of the houses came into view before us. But we came from the other side, opposite from where we'd gone in. The carriage road was so similar that we hadn't seen the difference.

Silence. Where was everyone?

Finally we saw a person. An older woman. On her way out. She was dressed up. I noticed that. That the woman was wearing lipstick and a dress. "Stop," Kuan shouted. "Stop. Help, help us." The woman looked confused. Then she discovered the child.

An ambulance arrived in a few minutes. As they came driving up the dust swirled up from the dry road and settled into Wei-Wen's hair, on his shoes, in his eyelashes. The personnel dressed in white came running out. Carefully they lifted him out of Kuan's arms and took him with them. His arm hung limply, slung out of the grasp of one of the personnel in white. That was the last thing we saw. Kuan and I were led into the car, but not in the back with him, they put us up front. Somebody reminded us to put on our seat belts.

Seat belts. What did we need those for?

GEORGE

I woke up an hour and twenty-two minutes before the alarm went off. The bedclothes were sweaty. I threw off the duvet, but knew that it was impossible to fall asleep again. It was the day for the quality control of the hives, the first inspection after the winter. I often slept poorly before this day, my head was way inside the hives. Beeswax, boards and larvae occupied my thoughts. I had no idea what I'd find when I opened them, had experienced winter death of close to 50 percent. And that feeling, when you discover that there are neither larvae nor queen bees in almost half of the hives, it's horrible. But the winter had been normal, nothing worth mentioning there. Not especially cold or warm, no reason anything should be out of the ordinary.

Nonetheless, I was shaking as I stood waiting for Rick and Jimmy. I had asked them to get here by seven thirty. I just wanted to get started. I would have preferred to have started already, but it was a tradition we had, the three of us, that the first quality control day we met here in the yard, we talked, we drank.

Rick arrived first, as always. He was tall and skinny, not properly put together — he looked a little like James Stewart, just without the winning face. Long, sharp nose, eyes that were set deep into his skull, thinning hair, even though he wasn't even thirty years old. He struggled out of the car. Rick always moved ten times more than he needed to, regardless of what he was doing, his whole body was badly organized. But he was eager. Had taken a mail-order agricultural course, and read a lot, all the time. No matter what we were going to do Rick could give us the background on it. And the history. And the theories. It was like dropping a coin in a machine. The man was a regular anecdote vending machine. He dreamed about a farm of his own, but truth be told, he should have been dreaming about sitting behind a desk and using his head.

He stood there swinging his arms; as usual he couldn't stand still.

"So," he said.

"So," I said.

"Do you have any thoughts about how

things are?"

"No. Good? Just fine. No reason to think otherwise."

"No. No reason."

He wrinkled his forehead, tugged at his thinning hair. ". . . Well." He was scratching himself with both hands now, you'd think he had lice. "You never know."

"No. You never know. But with the past winter . . ."

"Yes. Clearly . . ."

"Yes."

"But then there's those disappearances."

"Ah. Those."

I acted as if I hadn't thought about it. But of course I had. I kept myself informed. Even *The Autumn Tribune* had mentioned the mysterious colony collapses that a number of beekeepers down south had experienced. In November a guy in Florida reported beehives that were suddenly empty. David Hackenberg was his name. Suddenly everyone was talking about what happened on his farm. And since then, new reports kept coming in all the time from Florida, California, Oklahoma and Texas.

It was the same story every time. Healthy beehives one minute, enough food, larvae, everything perfectly fine. Then, in a matter of days, in a matter of hours, the hive was as good as empty. The bees were gone, abandoning their own larvae, leaving everything. And they never came back.

Bees are clean animals. They fly away to die, not wanting to leave their remains behind to contaminate the hive. Perhaps that was what they'd done. But the queen always stayed behind with a small cluster of young bees. The worker bees left the mother and her young, left them to die alone in the hive. It was contrary to the laws of nature.

Nobody really knew why. The first time I heard about it, I thought it was because of poor beekeeping. That this Hackenberg hadn't taken proper care of his bees. I'd met many keepers over the years who blamed others when they themselves were actually to blame. Too little sugar, too warm, too cold. It wasn't exactly quantum physics we were working with. But after a while there were too many stories, too similar and too sudden. This was something else.

"That's only in the south," I said.

"Yes. They run more intensive operations down there," Rick said.

At that moment Jimmy's green pickup skidded into the yard. He got out of the truck wearing a big grin. While Rick was worried, thought too much, Jimmy was the cheerful, simple, opposite. Not a single extra movement, not one turn of the wheels in his head that wasn't absolutely necessary. But he worked hard; you had to give him that.

What Jimmy lacked on the inside he made up for on the outside. He was handsome in a high school kind of way. Blond, thick bangs, a cleft chin, powerful jaw, the right proportions. He should have worn a football uniform around the clock. And he took good care of his appearance, too. Always freshly ironed and groomed. But it was unclear who he was dressing up for — there were never any women in the picture.

In his hand he held a thermos. A new one for the occasion, I noticed. The shiny steel reflected the sunlight for a second, blinded me momentarily, until he held it at another angle.

Each of us took out our cups. Jimmy had bought them a few years ago. Small, green hunter's cups from the outdoor living department at Kmart that could be squeezed flat. Rick and I pressed out the cups at the same time and held them out to Jimmy. Without a word he opened the thermos.

"Fresh-ground beans," he said and poured.

I was first.

"Colombia. Dark, roasted flavor."

Could have just as well been instant for all I cared. Coffee was coffee. But for Jimmy coffee was probably the closest he came to art. He bought beans over the Internet. The beans had to be fresh. In his opinion, pre-ground coffee was considered the work of the devil. And then the coffee had to drip at the right temperature. To achieve this, he had invested in a European coffeemaker, a drip-brew machine that was stuck in customs for weeks before he could finally bring it home.

We raised and knocked the three cups together. Soft plastic hit soft plastic, almost without a sound. We each took a sip.

Then came the moment when we were supposed to praise the coffee, say something intelligent. It was a part of the routine. For appearances' sake I squinted, while I swirled the coffee around in my mouth, like some wine expert.

". . . rich . . . full."

"Mm," Rick said. "I can taste the roast, yes."

Jimmy looked at us expectantly, like a child on the Fourth of July. Waiting for more.

"Yes, sir, nothing like instant," I said.

"Best coffee this year," Rick said.

Again Jimmy nodded. "Just buy yourself a grinder and be sure to get good beans. Even you two can manage it at home."

He always said that and knew perfectly well that we would never drag a coffee grinder over our doorsteps. At home it was Emma who made the coffee. And she went for freeze-dried. Lately she had tried out some dull-as-dishwater stuff with powdered milk and sugar added, but I stuck to black.

"Did you know that the earliest reference to coffee is from a fifteen-hundred-year-old story from Ethiopia?" Rick said.

"No kidding, you don't say," Jimmy said.

"That's right. Kaldi the shepherd. He discovered that the goats behaved oddly after having eaten some red berries. They couldn't sleep. He told a monk about it."

"Were there monks in Ethiopia fifteen hundred years ago?" I said.

"Yes?" He looked at me in confusion, his gaze wavering slightly.

Jimmy waved his hands from the sidelines. "Of course there were monks."

"They weren't exactly Christians? I mean, Ethiopia, isn't that in Africa, at that time?"

"Regardless. The monk became interested. He was struggling to stay awake during his prayers, so now he poured hot water over the berries and drank it. Voilà! Coffee."

Jimmy nodded in satisfaction. Rick had done research, it was in honor of his coffee.

We drank up. The coffee quickly turned cold in the spring wind. The last sip was sour and lukewarm. Then we each walked towards our own cars and set out in the direction of the hives.

It was when I rested my hands against the steering wheel that I noticed how much I was sweating. They stuck to the leather, I had to dry them off on my work pants to get a good grip, in the same way that my shirt was sticking to my back. I didn't know what was coming. Was dreading it.

It was just a few hundred yards down a bumpy dirt road. The car shook along with my hands, then we arrived at the meadow by Alabast River.

I climbed out, putting my hands behind my back to hide the trembling.

Rick was already standing there. Jumping a little. Wanted to get started.

Jimmy got out of his car. Pointed his nose at the sun, sniffing.

"How warm is it?" He closed his eyes, looked like he wasn't planning to move one inch and especially not get started on the task at hand.

"Warm enough." I walked quickly towards the hives. It was important to set an example. "May as well get started."

I checked the flight board, the entrance to the first, a pistachio-colored hive. The color clashed garishly with the grass sprouting from the ground below it. It was full of bees, the way it was supposed to be. I lifted the cover. Took off the cloth on top. I expected the worst, but everything was fine down there. I didn't see the queen, but there were plenty of eggs and larvae in all stages. Six full frames. The hive could remain as it was, there was enough life and there was no need to combine it with another one.

I turned to face Jimmy. He nodded towards the hive he had opened "All's well here."

"Here, too," Rick said.

We moved on.

As the sun beat down and hive after hive was opened and checked, I could feel how my body began to loosen up. My hands became dry and warm, my clothing detached itself from my back. In some places there were problems, of course. Some bee colonies had to be combined, some places we found no queen. But nothing out of the ordinary. It seemed as if the winter had been kind to them. As if the stench from the widespread annihilation further south hadn't reached us up here. And it was only fitting. They were well taken care of. They hadn't wanted for a thing.

We gathered for lunch. We perched on our creaky lawn chairs and ate sweaty sandwiches in the sun. All three of us were, for some reason or other, as silent as the grave. Until Rick could no longer contain himself.

"Have you heard about Cupid and the bees?"

Neither of us answered. Yet another story.

"Have you?" he asked again.

"No," I said. "You know perfectly well that we haven't heard about Cupid and the bees."

Jimmy snickered.

"Cupid was a kind of love god," Rick said. "According to the ancient Romans."

"The guy with the arrows," I said.

"Yeah, that's him. Son of Venus. He looked like a big baby and went around with a bow and arrow. When the arrows hit people, passion was awakened."

"Yuck, isn't a love god who looks like a baby a little perverse?" Jimmy said.

I laughed, but Rick gave me a dirty look.

"Did you know that he dipped the arrows in honey?"

"Can't say that I did, no."

"I haven't even heard of Cupid," Jimmy said. "Before now."

"Yes indeed, he dipped them in honey, which he stole," Rick said and stretched his body so the chair suddenly shrieked.

We had to chuckle about the loud noise. But not Rick. He wanted to continue.

"So this baby went around stealing honey from the bees. He took entire hives. Until one day . . ." He paused dramatically. "Until one day the bees had had enough and attacked him." He let the words hang in the air. "And Cupid was stark naked, of course, the gods usually were in those days. He was stung everywhere. And I mean *everywhere.*"

"He sort of deserved it," I said.

"Maybe so, but remember that he was just a little boy. He ran to his mother, Venus, for consolation. He screamed and was surprised that something as tiny as a bee could cause him so much pain. But do you think his mother consoled him? No. She just laughed."

"Laughed?" I said.

"Yup. 'You're little, too,' she said. 'But your arrows can cause even more pain than a bee sting.' "

"Wow," I said. "And then what? What happened?"

"That's it. Nothing more," Rick said.

Jimmy and I stared at him.

"That was the whole story?" Jimmy said.

141

Rick shrugged his shoulders. "Yes. But lots of paintings were done of it. Venus just stands there. She's beautiful, right, porcelain skin and lovely curves. And she's naked, too. Her baby is standing beside her and crying, with wax plates in his hands, while the bees are stinging him."

I shuddered.

"Some mother," Jimmy said.

"You can say that again," Rick said.

Finally it was silent again. I blinked, tried to get the image of the howling baby, swollen from bee stings, out of my head.

The sun warmed my neck. It was what Emma called a lovely day. I tried to feel exactly how lovely it was. And how great it was, that the sun was shining like this. Because sun meant honey. It looked like it would be a good year. A good year meant some money in the bank. And money in the bank could be invested in the farm. That's how it should be. Who needed Florida anyway? I'd tell her so this evening.

Tao

It was nighttime, but we weren't asleep. Of course we weren't sleeping.

We thought we were headed to the small local hospital in our town, but instead we were sent to the big hospital in Shirong. It covered the entire district. Nobody had told us why we were sent here. The ambulance without a driver changed directions when we were halfway there and since we were sitting alone up front, there was nobody we could ask.

We were put in a room for family members. From time to time we heard people passing by in the corridor, but they never opened the door; it appeared that we would have the room to ourselves.

I stood by the window. We had a view of the emergency arrival zone. It was located in the middle between the buildings; five low, white arms stretched out on all sides. There was light in some of the windows, but not in all of them. An entire wing dark. The hospital was built for another time, a time when there were many more people living in the district than were to be found here now.

Sometimes cars arrived, even a helicopter. I couldn't remember the last time I'd seen a helicopter. It had to have been several years ago, they weren't used much any longer, they consumed so much fuel. The shuddering rotor blades stirred up the air, causing the personnel's white coats to lift, as if they were about to take off.

Sometimes an alarm sounded when a car drove up, loud and droning. Then many more personnel appeared, standing by in a receiving line. And the patient was rapidly carried out of the car and into the hospital while nurses and doctors worked on him. We hadn't seen how it was when Wei-Wen arrived. It happened so quickly. He had already been carried away when we were allowed to get out of the ambulance. We saw the backs of the health personnel disappear with a stretcher. He was probably lying on it, but I was unable to catch sight of him, the backs in white coats were in the way. I tried to run after them, just wanted to see him. But the door was shut and locked.

We remained standing there outside the

144

entrance. I stretched out my hand to Kuan but he was standing too far away. I couldn't reach him. Or perhaps he didn't want to be reached.

Then the door opened and two men dressed in white came out. Doctors? Nurses?

They took each of us compassionately by the arm and asked that we accompany them. I followed them with all of my questions. Where was Wei-Wen? What was wrong with him? Was he injured? Would we soon be allowed to see him? But they had no answers. Said only that our son, they said *son,* perhaps they didn't even know his name, was in good hands. It would be fine. Then they just put us in here, and vanished.

I had been standing like this for hours when the door finally opened and a doctor came in. She introduced herself as Dr. Hio and closed the door behind her, without meeting our gazes.

"Where is he? Where is Wei-Wen?" I asked. My voice came from somewhere far away.

"They are still working on your son," the woman said, and moved further into the room.

Her hair was gray, but her face was smooth, expressionless.

"His name is Wei-Wen," I said. "Can I see him?"

I took a step towards the door. She had to take me to him. It had to be possible. I didn't have to be at his side, behind a glass window would do, as long as I could see him.

"Working on him. What do you mean?" Kuan said.

She lifted her head and looked at him, while avoiding my eyes.

"We're doing everything we can."

"He will survive, right?" Kuan asked.

"We're doing everything we can," she repeated mildly.

Kuan lifted his hand to his mouth. Bit his knuckles. I felt the jolt of a sudden chill.

"We must be allowed to see him," I said, but the words were so faint that they almost disappeared.

She didn't answer me, merely shook her head gently.

That couldn't be right. It had to be a mistake. Everything that had happened was a mistake. It wasn't him lying in there. Not Wei-Wen. He was at school, or at home. It was another child, a misunderstanding.

"You have to trust us," Dr. Hio said quietly and sat down. "And in the meantime, I need you to answer some questions."

Kuan nodded and sat down on a chair.

She picked up a pen and paper and prepared to take notes.

"Has your son ever been ill before?"

"No," Kuan answered obediently and turned to face me. "Has he? Can you remember whether he has?"

"No. Just an ear infection," I said. "And the flu."

She wrote down a few words on the pad of paper. "Nothing out of the ordinary?"

"No."

"Other respiratory infections? Asthma?"

"Nothing," I said firmly.

Dr. Hio turned to face Kuan again.

"Where, exactly, was he when you found him?" Kuan leaned forward, doubled up, as if he wanted to shield himself from her questions.

"Between the trees, near Field 458, or maybe 457. Right by the forest."

"And what was he doing?"

"He was sitting there. Slumped over. Pale. Sweating."

"And you were the one who found him?"

"Yes. It was me."

"He was so frightened," I said. "He was so unbelievably frightened."

She nodded.

"We ate plums," I continued. "We had

147

brought plums. He ate the entire tin."

"Thank you." She wrote something down again on her little pad.

Then she turned to Kuan again, as if he were the one who had the answers. "Do you think he was in the forest?"

"I don't know."

She hesitated. "What were you doing out there?"

Kuan leaned forward again. Sent me a look, blank, a look that didn't disclose what he was thinking.

The tension mounted, it became difficult to breathe. I was unable to answer. Kept my eyes on him, tried to plead, get him to cover up the truth. Say that it was our idea to go there, perhaps even his, when in reality it was mine alone.

My fault that we were out there.

Kuan didn't respond to my gaze, just turned towards the doctor and took a deep breath. "We were on an outing," he said. "We wanted to spend our day off doing something pleasant."

Perhaps he didn't hold me responsible, perhaps he didn't blame me. I kept watching him, but he didn't look in my direction. Revealed nothing, no answers, but neither did he make any accusations. And perhaps that's how it was. Perhaps that was the truth. We were together in this, together in being out there. It was a decision we both made and an agreement, a compromise, not just my idea.

Dr. Hio didn't seem to notice everything that lay between us — she just looked from one to the other, compassionate, more than merely professional. "I promise to come back as soon as I have more information."

I took a step forward. "But what happened? What's the matter with him?" My voice was shaking now. "You must know something more?"

The woman just shook her head slowly. She had no answers.

"Try to get some rest. I'll see if I can have some food sent in."

She disappeared out the door and we were left standing there.

There was a clock hanging on the wall. The time passed in erratic jumps. Sometimes when I looked at the clock, twenty minutes had passed, other times, only twenty seconds.

Kuan stayed at all times on the opposite side of the room. Regardless of where I stood, he was far away. It was not just his wish, equally so my own. It was impossible to get past the big thing between us. In the face of this, we were both transformed into thin ice, like the first thin sheets that formed on ponds in the autumn, which shattered at the lightest touch.

I took a sip of water. It was sour, water from a tank, water that had always been stagnant.

It had become dark. Neither of us turned on the light. What did we need light for? An hour had passed since the doctor had been here.

I checked the hallway once more. But nobody was at the counter.

I kept walking, but found only locked doors. Leaned my ear against one of them, but heard nothing. An intense humming from the air conditioner drowned out everything else.

Back again. Just stay here. Wait.

GEORGE

We had reached the hives by the Satis farm. I took those closest to the main road. I caught a glimpse of Jimmy and Rick, who were working their way across the field. I was tired, but not worn out, knew I was going to sleep as if somebody had pulled out the plug on me that night.

I was just about to lift the lid off the last hive when Gareth Green showed up.

His semitrailer truck thundered through the landscape. Three more followed behind him. When he saw me, he stopped. He actually stopped. And the semitrailer trucks behind him had to wait in line, stand there with the engines running and the sun beating down on the windshields and just wait for Gareth. It probably wasn't the first time.

He got out of the cab with a huge smirk on his face, sporting mirror sunglasses and a suntan. And a bright green cap with the words CLEARWATER BEACH, SPRING BREAK

2006. Bought on sale down south, maybe. Gareth liked doing things on the cheap, but preferably in a way so people wouldn't notice, because he also liked it if people were impressed. He left the door open and the engine running.

"So. Everything good up here?"

He nodded towards me and my hives, which were placed at irregular distances across the field. There weren't many of them so they looked pretty sparse.

"Looking good," I said. "A good winter. Didn't lose many."

"Good. Good. Happy to hear it. Us too. Not much waste." Gareth always used the word *waste* about the bees. Made it sound as if they were plants. Farm crops.

He nodded towards the landscape. "We're going to stop here for a round now. Pears."

"Not apples?"

"Nope. It's pears this year. Got a bigger farm. Have more bees now, you know. The Hudson farm is too small for us."

I didn't answer. Just nodded again.

He nodded, too.

We stood there nodding, while our gazes slid away in opposite directions. Like two figurines, the kind we had when I was little, where the head is loose and just needs a tiny push to set it into motion, nodding and nodding while staring out into space.

He concluded with a final nod towards the trucks. "Been on the road a long time now. It'll be good to get everything in place up here."

I followed his gaze. Hive after hive, all prefabricated, gray expanded polystyrene, were securely strapped to the semitrailers and covered with a green, fine-mesh netting material. The rumbling of the engines drowned out the buzzing of all the bees inside.

"California, is that where you're coming from?" I said. "How many miles is it from there?"

"You're out of touch." He laughed. "California was in February. Almonds. The season ended a long time ago. Now we're on our way back from Florida. Lemons."

"Lemons, right."

"And blood oranges."

"Right."

Blood oranges. Nope, ordinary oranges weren't good enough for Gareth.

"Been driving for twenty-four hours," he continued. "Small potatoes compared to the trip we took before that. California to Florida. That's some serious driving. Just getting across Texas takes almost twenty-four hours. Do you have any idea how wide that state actually is?"

"No. Can't say I've ever thought about it."

"Wide. The widest state we have. Except for Alaska, that is."

"Right."

Gareth's four thousand beehives were on the road year-round, never at rest. Winter in the southern states, peppers in Florida, almonds in California, back to lemons and oranges — or blood oranges, which were apparently new this year — in Florida, then north for three or four stops in the course of the summer. Apples or pears, blueberries, pumpkins. The bees were only at home here in June. Then Gareth took stock, as he put it, calculated his losses, combined hives, did repairs.

"By the way, I met Rob and Nellie down there," he said.

"That right?"

"What's the place called — Gulf Village?"

Well, well. So he'd been there. To the so-called paradise.

"Gulf Harbors."

"Well, I'll be! You've heard of it, too! Gulf Harbors, yes. Got to see the new house. Right out on the canal. They've got themselves a water scooter. Rob took me out for a ride. Believe it or not we saw dolphins."

"Dolphins, you say. Not manatees?"

"No. Manatees? What're those?"

"Rob and Nellie have been bragging about it. That they have manatees right outside their house."

"Wow. No. I didn't see any manatees. Anyway. They've got a good setup there. Nice place."

"So I've heard."

Someone in one of the trucks behind him gunned the engine. Impatient. But Gareth ignored it. That's how he was. My legs were itching. But he just stood there calmly, it seemed like he'd never finish.

"And you." He took off his glasses and looked at me. "Any trips planned?"

"Yes," I said. "More than enough trips. Going out in a few weeks. Maine."

"Blueberries, as usual?"

"Yeah, blueberries."

"Then we'll see you, maybe. I've got Maine this year, too."

"You don't say. Yeah, well, be seeing you, then." I tried to twist a smile out of my lips.

"White Hill Farm, know where that is?" He scratched under his cap. His hand turned green under the sunlight shining through the fabric.

"No," I said. It was the biggest farm for miles around. Everyone, even the youngest toddler, yes, even every single dog, knew where it was.

He grinned, didn't answer, knew for sure I was lying. Then he finally turned around to face the truck again, gave a salute with his hand against his cap, winked cheekily at me and got in.

The cloud of dust blocked the sunlight as they disappeared.

We went to school together, Gareth and I. He was a sluggish guy. Ate too much, worked out too little, afflicted with eczema. The girls weren't interested. Not us guys, either. For some reason or other he took a shine to me. Maybe because I couldn't bring myself to bad-mouth him all the time. Could see there was a person in there. And my mom was on my case all the time. *You should be nice to everyone, especially those who don't have many friends.* Gareth was without a doubt in that category, the one for people without many friends. That's how my mom was. It was impossible to be really cruel when you had her voice in your head all the time. Mom even made me invite him home a couple of times. Gareth thought it was out of this world to be invited to dinner on the farm. My dad took us out to the bees. Gareth asked questions, poking and prying. He was a lot more interested than

I'd ever been, or at least had given the impression of being so. And my father was happy to explain, of course.

Luckily, in high school we lost touch. Or else, it was just easier to stay away. I got the impression that Gareth buried himself in school and work. He had a part-time job at the hardware store, already started saving money back then. With time the extra pounds disappeared and he apparently got one of those sunlamps that helped the eczema, and as a result his skin was always slightly golden. Had to admit, it didn't look half bad.

He also managed to find himself a pretty nice girl. After finishing school, he bought a piece of land, and wouldn't you know he started with bees. Operations boomed, Gareth apparently had a knack for it. He expanded, got more hives. The girl had children, more attractive than Gareth had been, no eczema on any of them. And now he'd become a big shot. One of the biggest in town. Cruised around on Sundays with his family securely seat-belted into a huge German SUV. Was a member of the country club, paid $850 a year so the whole family could stand out there in the meadow and hit balls in all kinds of weather. Sure, I'd checked what it cost.

He'd also invested in the new library. A shiny brass plaque informed everyone who cared to read it, and there were many who did, that the local community was deeply grateful to Green's Apiaries for its generosity when the library was built.

Revenge of the nerds, that's what it was. And the rest of us, those of us who hadn't been particularly nerdy, but popular enough in school, had to sit on the sidelines and watch how Gareth wallowed in increasingly more dough with every passing year.

Everyone who worked with bees knew that the real money didn't lie in honey; Gareth's assets didn't come from honey. The real money was in pollination. Agriculture didn't have a chance without bees. Mile after mile of blossoming almond trees or blueberry bushes; they weren't worth a dime unless the bees carried the pollen from one flower to another. The bees could travel more than several miles a day. Many thousands of flowers. Without them the flowers were just as useless as the contestants of a beauty pageant. Nice to look at, while they lasted, of absolutely no value in the long run. The flowers wilted, died, without bearing fruit.

Gareth had invested in pollination from day one. His bees had always been traveling colonies. Always on the road. I'd read that it made the bees stressed, that it wasn't good for them, but Gareth claimed the bees didn't notice anything, they were thriving just like mine.

Maybe it was exactly because Gareth had come to the trade from the outside that he'd invested in that field. He'd understood where things were headed — that small honey farms, like mine, run more or less in the same way for generations, didn't exactly put money in the bank, hadn't done so before and certainly didn't do so now. Every single small investment was an effort, and we lived at the mercy of the friendly local bank, which wasn't always a stickler when it came to making loan payments on time and trusted that the bees would do the job this year as well, trusted me when I said that the watered-down cheap stuff from China, which was sold as honey and came in greater quantities with every passing year, didn't make a difference, that honey prices would remain exactly where they'd always been, that the prospects for a steady revenue were good, that the ever more unpredictable weather had no impact on us, that we could guarantee good sales in the fall. That the money would pour in, just as always.

It was all lies. And that was why I had to reorganize. Become like Gareth.

WILLIAM

"Do you want me to do it?" Thilda asked. She stood at the door with the shaving things and a mirror in her hands.

"You could cut yourself on the razor," I replied.

She nodded. She knew, as I did, that she'd never been particularly steady-handed.

A bit later she came in with a bowl of water, some soap and a brush. She put all of it on the bedside table, which she then shoved up against the bed, so that I had a good working angle. Finally she put the mirror there. She stood waiting while I lifted it up. Was she worried about how I would react?

It was another man who stared back at me. I should have been frightened, but I felt only a sense of wonder. Gone was the feeble chubbiness. Gone was the pleasant shop-keeper. The man who stared back at me was someone else, someone who had experienced something. A paradoxical idea, in that I'd been lying in bed for months and had not experienced anything besides my own vile thoughts. Still, the reflection in the mirror said nothing about this. The man staring back at me reminded me of an ocean voyager who had returned after months at sea, or perhaps a miner who came up after a long shift, or a scientist on the way home from a long and dramatic research trip in the jungle. His features were clearly defined, he was slender, hardened into elegance. He was life lived.

"Do you have a pair of scissors?" I said.

Thilda looked at me in confusion.

"I can't start with the razor, there's too much."

She nodded and understood.

Soon she was back with the sewing scissors. They were awkwardly small, made for dainty women's fingers, but I was able to cut away the worst of the shaggy growth.

Slowly I dipped the brush in the water and rubbed it against the soap. It foamed with the fresh scent of juniper.

"Where is the razor?" I looked around. She just stood there with her hands folded in front of her apron and her eyes fixed on the floor. "Thilda?"

Finally she handed me a razor that she'd

had in her pocket. Her hand trembled slightly, as if she didn't quite want to surrender it. I took it and started shaving. The razor scraped against my skin; the blade needed sharpening.

Thilda stood watching me.

"Thank you. You can leave now," I said to her.

But she stayed. Her eyes were on my hand, on the razor. And suddenly I understood what she was standing there and worrying about. I let my hand drop.

"Isn't it a healthy sign that I'm shaving?"

She had to think, as usual.

"I am so very grateful that you have the energy for this," she replied finally, but remained standing there all the same.

If one was going to do something like that, it was a matter of finding a method that would give the impression of death by wholly natural causes. That way I would spare Edmund. I had several procedures in mind — I'd had a lot of time to plan them — but of course Thilda didn't know that. She just assumed that if she left me alone in a room with a sharp instrument, I would take advantage of the opportunity, as if it were the only one. That's how simple she was.

If I wanted to put an end to it all, I would

have long since walked out into the snow, wearing only a nightshirt. Then I would be found frozen to death the next day, with ice in my beard and eyelashes, and my death would be just that: the seed merchant lost his way in the dark and froze to death, poor wretched soul.

Or a mushroom. The woods were full of them and some of them had last autumn found their way down into a top drawer of the bureau furthest to the left in the shop, duly locked, with a key to which I alone had access. The effect of the mushroom was quick, in the course of a few hours one grew lethargic and dull, then unconscious, followed by a few days during which the body was quickly broken down before it collapsed. A doctor would hold that the cause of death was organ failure. Nobody would know that it was self-inflicted.

Or drowning. There was a strong current in the river behind our property even in the winter.

Or Blake's dog farm, with seven savage mutts snapping against the fence.

Or the steep cliff in the woods.

There were many possibilities, but now here I was, shaving off my beard and did not have the slightest intention of implementing any of these methods, including the razor I held in my hand. Because I had gotten out of bed, and I would never consider such a course of action again.

"Don't let me keep you," I said to Thilda. "I'm sure you have work to do out there." I pointed towards the door, in reference to the rest of the house, with its relentless demands for dusting, cooking and scrubbing of clothing and floors and everything else that women at all times maintain must be cleaned.

She nodded and finally she left.

There were times when I had the impression that Thilda would have been more than grateful if I took a razor blade or perhaps preferably a carving knife, put it against my throat and let the blood pump out of the main artery until there was nothing left of me but an empty shell, an abandoned cocoon, on the floor. She had never said as much, but she and I had both come to curse the sunlight that found its way to precisely her nose in the assembly hall more than seventeen years ago. It could have found its way to so many others, or no one at all.

I was twenty-five years old; about a year had passed since I'd arrived in the village. I don't know if there was something about the weather that month, perhaps a dry wind had long been blowing across the region, so her lips were red and dry and she continually moistened them with saliva, or she had been secretly chewing on them, the way young girls do to produce alluring mouths, but on that particular day I didn't in any sense notice that she was virtually without lips. I only remember that I was in the middle of my lecture when I saw her.

I was extremely well prepared. First and foremost because of Rahm. I wanted nothing more than to make a stunning impression on him. I knew I was fortunate; many of my classmates had received far less interesting tasks. As a recent graduate I could make few demands, to be taken under the wing of a well-recognized scientist was the greatest possible opportunity for success. At this time in my life, Rahm was the only person who meant something to me. From the moment I stepped over the threshold to his study, my mind was made up: he would be my most important relationship. He would not be just my soul mate and mentor, but also my father. I no longer had contact with my own and didn't wish to have any, at least that was what I told myself over and over again. But under the professor's guidance I could grow and flourish. He would turn me into what I actually was. I had never given a lecture before so I had prepared well. When Rahm asked me to make a contribution at his modest zoological evening for the residents of Maryville, I first regarded it as unimportant. But as the days went by, it built up inside me, grew into something almost uncontrollable. How would it feel? To stand there in front of so many people, everyone listening to my voice, everyone's attention directed at me? Although the people of the village were of a simpler sort, to put it tactfully, than my peers at the university, it was nonetheless a scientific lecture. Would I be equal to carrying out such a task?

It wasn't just the fact that I would be giving a lecture for the first time in my life, but also the meaning it could have for others that filled me with awe. The natural sciences were an unfamiliar subject for the village population; their view of the world was based on the Bible, which was the only book they had faith in. It struck me that I would have the opportunity to show them something more, to present connections between the small and the large, between the power of creation and creation itself, that I now had the opportunity to open their eyes and change their view of the world, yes, even of existence itself.

But how to best demonstrate this? Choosing a topic became an immense task, one that had me going in circles. Just about any topic was of interest when viewed from the perspective of the natural sciences. The earth's crops, the discovery of America, the seasons. So many options!

In the end it was Rahm who made the decision. He put his cool hand on top of my clammy one, and smiled at my confused enthusiasm. "Tell them about the microscope," he said. "The possibilities it has given us. Most of them don't even know what such a device is."

It was a brilliant idea; I would never have come up with it myself, so of course that decided it.

The day arrived, with this dry wind and sun from a towering sky. We were uncertain about how many would come. Several of the older villagers pointed out that what we were doing was ungodly, that one didn't need any books other than the Bible. But curiosity had apparently titillated the majority, because the assembly hall was soon so crowded that it heated up to a summer temperature, despite the chilly April weather outdoors. It was out of the ordinary that little Maryville hosted events such as this.

I would be presenting my work first; that was what Rahm wanted. Perhaps he wanted to show me off, as if I were his own newborn child, perhaps he was still proud of me at this time. After a few long minutes, my voice trembling in time with my knees, I found my confidence. I leaned on the words that were so thoroughly prepared, discovered that they carried, that they absolutely did not lose their credibility as they left the paper and were dispersed into the air between the audience and me, but instead made it all the way to their destination.

I began by quickly summarizing the history, spoke briefly of the condenser lens that came into use all the way back in the sixteenth century, about the compound optical microscope, described by Galileo Galilei in 1610. To demonstrate the microscope's significance in practice I had decided to tell them about one specific individual. I had chosen the Dutch zoologist Jan Swammerdam. He had lived in the seventeenth century and was never properly recognized by his contemporaries, was poor and lonely, but for posterity he was a true monument in natural history, perhaps precisely because he made a connection between creation and creativity at such an early stage.

"Swammerdam," I said and allowed my gaze to sweep across the assembly. "Never

168

forget his name. His work has shown us that the different stages in the life of an insect, the egg, larvae and pupae, are in fact different forms of the same insect. Swammerdam developed a microscope which enabled him to study the insects in detail. During these studies he produced drawings unlike anything else we have seen."

With a dramatic hand gesture, which was well rehearsed, I pulled down a chart I had hung up behind me.

"Here you can see Swammerdam's illustration of the anatomy of the bee, as he has drawn it in his work *Biblia Naturae.*"

I allowed myself a dramatic pause, let my gaze come to rest on the assembly, while they took in the extraordinarily detailed drawings. At that exact moment the spring sun in its passage over the roof of the assembly hall hit the window on my left, a lone ray of sunshine fell through, spread out towards the rows of benches and fell upon the person sitting furthest to the left, beside two female friends: Thilda.

Afterwards I've understood that it hadn't been as much a surprise for her as for me. I was of course on the minds of many young women; the young natural scientist, educated in the capital, dressed in modern garments, well spoken, a bit short, perhaps, not the most athletic — to tell the truth I had already begun struggling with weight gain, but what I lacked in physical attributes, I made up for intellectually. The eyeglasses on my nose alone were testimony of this. I usually wore them pushed down a bit, so I could gaze sagely over the frames. When I got them, I had spent an entire evening working out the perfect position for the glasses, finding the precise spot on my nose where they were securely in place and which simultaneously made it possible to look people right in the eye, without having to look through the small oval lenses, well aware as I was that the concave lenses made my eyes look smaller. I also knew that many women found my lush mane of hair attractive. I kept my hair at medium length, which showed it off to its best advantage. Perhaps Thilda had already observed me for a long time, assessing me, comparing me with other young men in the village. Perhaps she had seen the kind of respect I was treated with, deep bows and humble looks, wholly different from the other young men she had in her circle, who were probably always coarse in both their dress and conduct and were treated accordingly.

Thilda was wearing her Sunday best, something blue, a dress, or perhaps a blouse, that was nicely fitted across her bosom. On either side of her round face corkscrew curls descended towards her shoulders, the virtually uniformlike hairstyle she had in common with all of her female companions, and which was also to be seen on many married women — even though one might think they should be past the need for that kind of tomfoolery with their appearances. It was, however, neither the curls nor the clothing that made such an impression on me. What the lone ray of sunshine wormed its way forward to, through the heavy air of the assembly hall, was an unusually straight and well-proportioned nose, like an illustration in a textbook on anatomy. It was a classical nose; I immediately got the urge to draw it, study it, a nose with a shape corresponding exactly with its function. Or so I thought. The function of her nose was regrettably not in keeping with its form, as I would later find out, in that it was always red and runny from an eternal cold. But on this day it beamed in my direction, neither shiny nor red, just extremely interested in me and my words, and I was unable to take my eyes off of it.

The dramatic pause grew too long. The audience began to move restlessly, and I became aware of the sound of a long and affected clearing of the throat from Rahm, who was standing behind me. The chart still hung there, dangling and neglected.

I hastened to point at it. "Swammerdam spent five whole years studying the life found in a beehive. All of this was done through the microscope, which gave him the possibility to include every single tiny detail . . . so here . . . here you can see the queen bee's ovaries. Through his studies Swammerdam determined that a single queen bee in fact lays the eggs for all three of the different types of bees — drones, worker bees and new queens."

The members of the audience stared at me, some squirmed a little, nobody appeared to understand. "This was groundbreaking in its time, in that many until then had believed that it was a king bee, in other words, a male bee, that led the hive. But with genuine fascination, truly great enthusiasm, Swammerdam undertook studies of the *male bee's* organs. And here you can see the results." I pulled out another chart.

"This is the genitalia of the male bee."

Blank faces out there.

The audience moved restlessly. Some directed their gazes towards their laps to study a loose thread in the fabric of their dresses carefully, while others showed a sudden interest in the irregular cloud formations in the sky outside.

It suddenly occurred to me that they probably didn't know what either ovaries or genitalia were, and I felt a compelling urge to help them understand. Now came the part of the lecture that never became a part of the story that Thilda told our children, and neither had it ever once been mentioned between her and me. For years the thought of what happened afflicted me with a burning sense of shame.

"Ovaries are the same as . . . I mean to say, that is, the reproductive system, where the eggs are produced . . . which become larvae."

When the words came out, I suddenly understood what I'd embarked upon, but I couldn't stop now. "And genitalia are thus the same as umm . . . the male bee's reproductive organs. These are wholly necessary in the process of ahem . . . producing new bees."

A gasp went through the room as they understood what the drawings they were looking at depicted. Why had I not understood it myself, the effect the subject would have on them? For me it was a given part of the natural sciences, but for them this was something sinful, something one kept to

173

oneself, something one never talked about. In their eyes, my passion for this was dirty.

But nobody left, nobody stopped me, had only somebody done so, just soft noises told of how badly this was going, bottoms shifting upon the wooden benches, boots scraping against the floor, the soft sound of throats being cleared. Thilda bowed her head. Was she blushing? The mutual gazes of her female companions froze as they stared at one another in shock and I, simpleton that I am, I continued, in hopes that the rest of the lecture would move the focus away from the words I had just said and over to what was really important.

"He has dedicated three whole pages to these in his life's work, *Biblia Naturae,* or *Nature's Bible,* if you will. Here we see some of his incredibly detailed illustrations of the male bee's, the drone's . . . geni . . . genitalia." The word was heavy in my mouth. "The different stages, how they open, unfold and ahem . . . expand to their full potential." Had I really said that? A fleeting glance at the assembly informed me that that was precisely what I had done. I forced my eyes down into the lecture again, continued reading, even though it just got worse and worse.

"Swammerdam himself described them

as . . . exotic sea monsters."

They giggled now, the ladies.

I didn't dare look at them. Instead I took out Swammerdam's work and quoted the fabulous words that I personally had pondered so much over, clung to the book, hoped the audience would finally understand and recognize the true passion.

"If the reader looks at the admirable structure of these organs, he will discover exquisite art, and he will understand that God, even in the smallest insect, even in its tiny organs, has hidden overwhelming miracles." I ventured to look up and it was extremely clear that I'd lost, because the faces that stared back at me were at best upset, some even angry, and finally I understood, took in fully what I'd had done. I had not succeeded in any sense in telling them about the wonders of nature; I had stood here and spoken about the vilest of the vile, and on top of that had mixed God up in all of it.

I didn't tell the rest of the story; that poor Swammerdam never managed to do anything else after this, that his career was over, the studies of the bee chased him into a maelstrom of religious musings, because the bees' perfection frightened him and he had to remind himself all the time that only

God, and not these small creatures, was worthy of his investigations, love and attention. Confronted with the bee it was difficult to believe that something else existed out there that was more perfect, not even God. The five years he virtually lived inside a beehive destroyed him forever.

But I realized there and then that if I told them this, I would not only be ridiculed, I would become somebody they hated, because one does not question the Almighty.

I folded up my manuscript, while the blush rose in my face and I stumbled like a little boy as I stepped off the podium. Rahm, whom I wanted to impress more than anybody else, was clearly struggling to contain his laughter, because his face was frozen in a strange smile. He reminded me of my father, my real father.

I shook hands with several of those who'd attended after the lecture was over. Many of them didn't know what to say and I noticed how people were whispering around me, some snickering in disbelief, others reacting in anger and shock. The blush spread from my face, slid down my spine, planted itself in my shins and found expression in an uncontrollable trembling, which I vainly sought to hide from my surroundings. Rahm must have seen it, because he rested a hand on my shoulder and said softly: "You must understand that they are imprisoned by trivialities. They will never become like us."

The consolation didn't help, it just emphasized the difference between him and me; he would never have chosen examples that offended his listeners. He understood what they could stand, held sway over the balance between us and them, understood that the world of science and the world of human beings were two different places. As if to stress what he'd said and my obvious lack of understanding of my audience, he suddenly laughed. It was the first time I heard his laughter, it was short and low, but it startled me all the same. I turned away, was unable to look at him, his laughter weighed too heavily upon me, it took all the importance away from his consolation, stung so intensely that I had to turn away and take a step away from him. And there she was.

Perhaps it was weakness, the poorly concealed vulnerability in me on this day; I was no longer simply the mysterious visitor who worked with something grand and incomprehensible out there with the professor, and this enabled Thilda to become forward. Because she didn't laugh. She proffered a gloved hand, curtsied and thanked me for the "ahem . . . marvelous" lecture. In the background her female companions were still giggling. But the sound faded away, *they* faded away, and I didn't notice Rahm, either, just the hand. I held it in my own for a long time, felt the warmth of her skin emanate through the glove, how my strength came back through this hand. She didn't mock me, she didn't laugh at me, and I was so infinitely grateful to her. Her eyes sparkled above the beautiful nose; they were wide-set, so open to the world and life, but first and foremost, to me. Imagine, to me! Never before had a young woman looked at me like that, it was a gaze that allowed me to understand that she was willing to surrender herself completely, to give me everything, and just me, because she didn't look at any of the others around us in the same way. This thought caused my knees to start wobbling again and I finally looked down. It was like cutting a cord; it was physically painful and I wanted nothing more than to resume this eye contact and forget about the world around me.

It took months for people in the village to stop talking about my performance. While I had previously been met exclusively with respect and deference, there were now several people who grasped my hand harder, pounded me on the back, the men in particular, and spoke to me with a half smile and poorly disguised sarcasm. And the words *expand to their full potential, Nature's Bible* and *exotic sea monsters* pursued me for years. Nobody ever forgot Swammerdam, either, and his name was later used in many and extremely diverse contexts. When the horses mated on the meadow, it was described as "Swammerdam-like activity." Drunk men who had to relieve themselves at the tavern in the evening said that they were going out to "air the Swammerdam," and the local bakery's signature dish, an oblong meat-filled pie, was suddenly only called "Swammer pie."

It bothered me astonishingly little. In a way my decline in status was worth it. At least that's what I thought when a few months later Mathilda Tucker and I were wed. I had long since had the opportunity to notice her narrow, typically British lips, by the time we walked down the aisle of the church. I had ventured to steal a kiss during the proposal and discovered to my dismay that they did not have the ability to open up like a large, secret, sticky flower, or perhaps a Swammerdam sea monster, as I had fantasized about in the late-night hours. They were just as dry and stiff as they ap-

179

peared. And the nose was, truth to be told, a smidgen too big. But nonetheless, my cheeks were flushed when our marriage was blessed by the priest. I was, after all, getting married, and truly becoming part of adult life, without understanding then that adulthood contained features that made most of my dreams impossible, that forced me away from the world of science. Because Rahm was right — although I continued with some half-hearted research projects, I had opted out, abandoning my passion for the discipline.

But I was so certain, so completely convinced that Thilda was the one for me. Her sedateness fascinated me enormously, she always thought carefully before she answered a question. Her pride as well; I was filled with admiration for how she truly stood behind what she believed, a quality one seldom found in young women. It was only later, though not much later, only a few months into our marriage, that I understood she actually considered each answer for so long because she was not especially bright and I recognized the pride for what it actually was: an indomitable stubbornness. She never gave in, as it would turn out. Never.

But the most important reason of all for

why I wanted to marry her was one I wouldn't even admit to myself, but which I only now, in my sickbed, could bear to take in, a recognition that was about my still being just as primitive and greedy as a ten-year-old child: the fact that she was a living, soft body. That she was mine, that she would be accessible to me. That very soon I would have the chance to squeeze up against this body, lay it down beneath me, pound my body against it, as if it were raw, moist earth.

Unfortunately, that part didn't turn out as I had imagined, either, but was instead a dry and hurried affair with far too many buttons and ribbons, corset wires, prickly wool stockings and a sour smell of armpits. I was nonetheless drawn to her with the instinct of an animal, a drone. Again and again, ripe for procreation, even though the last thing I wanted were descendants. Like the drone, I sacrificed my life for procreation.

Tao

"They're doing what they can. They've said they are doing what they can." Kuan filled a teapot a nurse had just given us with tea leaves. With calm hands he poured tea into a cup. As if we were at home, as if it were an ordinary day.

A day. Another evening. Had I eaten? I didn't know. They brought in food and drink for us on a regular basis. Yes, I had managed to get something down, a few spoonfuls of rice, a little water, to stop the gnawing of my stomach. The leftovers had hardened into a cold, rubbery lump in the aluminum bowl. But I hadn't slept. Hadn't showered. I was wearing the same clothes as yesterday, before everything happened. I had dressed up, put on the nicest outfit I owned, a yellow blouse and a skirt that went down to my knees. Now I hated the feeling of the synthetic fabric against my body, the blouse was too tight under the arms and the sleeves were too short, so I went around constantly stretching them.

"But why don't they tell us anything?"

I was standing. I never sat down. Stood and walked, running a marathon in captivity. My hands were sticky, with a constant cold sweat. My clothes stuck to me. There was an odor around me, a scent I had never smelled before.

"They know more about this than we do. We just have to trust them."

Kuan took a sip of tea. It filled me with rage. The way he drank, the steam from the cup, how it floated up under his nose, the faint slurping sound. It was something he had done thousands of times before. He couldn't be doing it now.

He could scream, shout, scold, blame me. That he just sat there like that, with the cup between his hands, warming himself on it, his completely calm hands.

"Tao?" He put the cup down suddenly, as if he understood what I was thinking. "Please."

"What do you want me to say?" I stared hard at him. "Drinking tea doesn't help, that's for sure!"

"What?"

"It was an example."

"I understood that." His eyes were shiny now.

It's our child, I wanted to scream. *Wei-Wen!* But I just turned away, couldn't bring myself to look at him. The sound of the teapot being lifted and hot tea being poured. He stood up and came towards me.

I turned around. There he was, holding a steaming cup of tea out to me, in a steady hand.

"Maybe it will help," he said softly. "You need to get something down."

A cup of tea was supposed to help matters . . . drinking a cup of tea. Was *that* his plan? Do nothing, just sit here. So passive, without any will for change, for control, to do something.

Once again I turned my face away. I couldn't say all of this. He had too much on me.

The weight between us was not equally balanced. But nonetheless, he didn't blame me, didn't put the responsibility on me. He just stood there, holding out the teacup, his arm sticking straight out from his body, almost unnaturally rigid. He drew a breath, was perhaps about to say something else.

At that moment the door opened. Dr. Hio came in. Her facial expression was impossible to read. Regret? Dismissal?

She didn't say hello, merely nodded to us in the direction of the hallway. "Please accompany me to my office."

I followed her right away. Kuan stood there with the cup in his hand, as if he didn't know what to do with it.

Then he finally collected himself, quickly put it down on the table; a little tea splashed over the rim. He noticed it and hesitated.

Was he going to waste time wiping it up? No. He straightened up quickly and followed after us.

She went first, Kuan and I did not look at each other, the huge thing would have to remain unsaid. We just kept our eyes on her. Her back was erect in the white coat. She moved quickly and lightly. Her hair was put up in a ponytail and it swung like a young girl's.

She opened a door and we entered a gray room. A room without personality. No pictures of children adorned the walls, just a telephone on the desk.

"Have a seat, please."

She indicated two chairs and rolled her own to the other side of the desk, so it didn't separate us. Perhaps that was something they had learned during their studies, that the desk gave them authority and when they were going to speak about serious matters, it was best to come across as much like a fellow human being as possible. She was going to say something serious. Suddenly I wished that she were seated elsewhere, not so close. I leaned back, away from her.

"Can we see him?" I asked quickly. Suddenly I didn't dare ask the other questions. *How is it going, what's happening to him, what has happened to our son?*

She looked at me. "I'm afraid you can't see him yet . . . and I have unfortunately been relieved of responsibility for your son."

"Relieved of responsibility? But why?"

"We have worked with a number of hypotheses in connection with the diagnosis. But it is still unclear." Her gaze wavered. "Anyway, the case is so complicated that it lies outside of my field."

I felt a weak sense of relief. The worst words were not used. She didn't say *departed, dead, passed away.* She said it was complicated, that they had hypotheses. That meant that they hadn't given up on him.

"OK. Fine. Who has taken over?"

"A team was flown in from Beijing yesterday evening. I will give you their names as soon as I receive word myself."

"Beijing?!"

"They are the best."

"And in the meantime?"

186

"I've been asked to tell you that you must wait. That you can go home."

"What? No!"

I turned towards Kuan. Wasn't he going to say something?

Dr. Hio fidgeted in her chair. "He's in the best hands."

"We will not leave here. This is our child."

"I've been asked to say that it will take time before they know any more. And there's nothing you can do here now. Wei-Wen's case was very special."

I stiffened. *Was.*

The words could scarcely be heard when I finally opened my mouth.

"What are you trying to say?"

I turned to Kuan again for help, but he sat without moving. His hands lay motionless in his lap. He was not going to ask any questions. I turned to face her again.

The words came from deep inside me: "Is he alive? Is Wei-Wen alive?" She leaned forward slightly, ducked her neck and lifted her head towards us, like a turtle peeking out of its shell. Her eyes were round, pleading, as if she were begging us not to pester her anymore and she showed no signs of answering.

"Is he alive?"

She hesitated. "The last time I saw him,

he was being kept alive through artificial means."

Beside me Kuan gasped. I saw that his cheeks were wet, but it didn't concern me.

"What does that mean? That he's still alive, that means that he's still alive?"

She nodded slowly.

Alive. I held on to the word. *Alive.* He was alive.

"But not without help," she said in a low voice.

It wasn't important. I forced myself to think that it wasn't important. The most important thing was that he was alive.

"I want to see him," I said loudly. "I am not leaving until I've seen him."

"I'm afraid that's not possible."

"He's my son."

"As I told you, I'm no longer responsible for him."

"But you know where he is."

"I'm truly sorry."

I got to my feet abruptly. Kuan raised his head, looked at me in astonishment. My eyes did not meet his. I turned to face the doctor.

"Show me where he is."

George

I sent Rick and Jimmy home around five o'clock. Just one-third of the hives were left. I could manage the rest by myself. Couldn't afford to pay them for hours that weren't necessary.

Around sunset I'd almost finished. At about the same time, the field was attacked by some extremely tenacious flies. Where they went during the daytime, I had no idea. But at dusk they appeared, huge clouds of them, impossible to get rid of. It seemed as if they liked people, because they were all over me, following my every step.

There was nothing to do but go home. I was on my way to the car when Tom called. I hadn't saved his number, honestly didn't know how, but I recognized it.

"Hi, Dad."

"Hi."

"Where are you?"

"Why do you ask?" I said and chuckled.

"I don't know."

"Used to be people started conversations with *how are you.* Now, since cell phones, people ask where you are," I tried to explain.

"Yes."

"I'm out in the fields. Doing quality control."

"Oh. Does it look good?"

"Terrific."

"Good. Good to hear. That makes me happy."

That makes me happy? The words sounded awkward in his mouth. Was that how he'd started talking?

"What do you think that means, by the way?" I asked.

"Means?"

"About society? That we ask each other where we are, instead of how it's going?"

"Dad."

"I'm kidding, Tom." I tried to laugh. As usual, he didn't laugh back. We were silent for a couple of seconds. I laughed louder, hoping it would help, but just when I was standing there with my mouth open like the church doors on Sunday, a fly flew right into my trap, all the way in. I could swear that it hit my uvula. It tickled something fierce. I didn't know what I should do, whether I should try to cough it up or swallow, so I tried doing both at the same time. It didn't work.

"Dad," Tom said suddenly. "You know that thing we talked about the last time I was home?"

The fly wriggled and tickled in the back of my throat.

"Are you there?"

I coughed again. "Yes, last time I checked."

He was silent for a moment.

"I got a scholarship."

I could hear him inhale. The line between us crackled, as if the phone signals were objecting to the entire conversation.

"It won't cost you a cent, Dad. John has taken care of everything."

"John?" My voice was husky, the fly was good and stuck in my throat.

"Yes. Professor Smith."

I cleared my throat, coughed violently, but neither the fly nor words came out.

"Are you crying, Dad?"

"I'm sure as hell not crying!"

I coughed again. Finally the fly came loose, sliding across my tongue, but it was still in my mouth.

"No," he said.

Another silence.

"I just wanted to tell you."

"Now you've told me."

I couldn't spit now. He would hear it.

"Yes."

"Yes."

"So long, then."

"So long."

One solid spit gob and the fly vanished, didn't see where, I wasn't very interested in studying it anymore, either. I stood there with the telephone in my hand. Had a strong hankering to chuck it right down onto the ground, see the cheap, trashy electronics that made it possible to receive such bad news even way out here in the fields shatter in all directions. But I knew that getting a new one would be one hell of a headache. And it would cost money. Besides, it wasn't for sure that the cell phone would even be damaged; the grass was already tall, as soft as a quilt. So I just stood there, with my hand clutching the phone and a pitchfork in my heart.

WILLIAM

I was on my way out of the blindness, was eating well and had slowly but surely started to exercise. I bathed every day, asked for freshly laundered clothes often and shaved frequently, up to twice a day. After all of these months spent like a bearded chimpanzee I had come to like the smoothness of my face, feeling the air directly against my skin.

And I read until my eyes smarted. I could stand more all the time, increasingly more words a day, spent entire days at my desk, surrounded by all of my books, opened on the table, on the bed, on the floor.

I reread Swammerdam; his research remained solid. I studied Huber's hive in detail, his practical framework, and also ordered what I came across in the way of pamphlets and journals on the practice of beekeeping. There were many of them, it turned out. For the upper class beekeeping had become a leisurely pastime in recent years, something with which one filled the long hours between lunch and tea. But most of these small manuals were naturally written for the common man, in a simple language, with simple line drawings. For someone like me it didn't take long to get through them. Some described experiments with hives made of wood, some even held that they had discovered what would have to be the new standard, but none of them had so far managed to come up with a hive that truly gave the keeper complete access and oversight. Not like the hive I knew I would create.

Dorothea visited me daily now. She showed up with apple-red cheeks and small dishes she had prepared herself. It had to be Thilda who asked her to do so, in the hopes that I would eat more when I knew that my child had prepared the meal with her own hands. An assumption I had to acknowledge she was right about. The food tasted surprisingly good and Dorothea was clearly in the process of evolving into a proper housewife. Georgiana also came now and then. Like a wave she washed in across the room with her penetrating little-girl voice and wiped out everything I was pondering over, until she was suddenly gone again. Charlotte was the least bothersome, stuck her sharp nose in the door and usually asked if she might borrow a book, one I didn't need myself at the moment. She picked out new books all the time; soon she would certainly have finished everything I had, so quickly did she read.

But Edmund never came. In the afternoons I could hear his voice from below sometimes, or from the garden, or even from the hallway outside my room, but he never gave me the pleasure of his presence.

Finally I went in to see him. It was early evening. Peace and quiet had been restored in the house following afternoon tea. It would soon be shattered by noise when the evening meal was served, but for now all was silent.

I knocked gently on his door. Nobody answered. I lifted my hand towards the latch, but hesitated, wanting to give him time. Instead I put my hand against my face, stroking the smoothly shaved cheek. I had prepared myself before I went in, changed into clean trousers, washed. I so fervently wished that he would see this version of me, and forget the one he had met last.

He still didn't come to the door and I tried knocking again.

No answer.

Could I walk in all the same? It was his room, his private one. But still, I was his father, and the house, and thus also his room, were mine.

Yes, I could. It was my right.

I carefully pushed the latch down. The door slid open, remained ajar, inviting. The room was in semidarkness, the only light came from the sunset-washed landscape outside. But the room faced east and the rays of the evening sun did not reach here.

I walked in and discovered a key on the inside of the door. Did he usually lock the door? The air was stuffy, with a scent of musk, and something else a bit rank that I was unable to define. Clothes lay carelessly scattered everywhere, a jacket over the chair, a pair of trousers and a shirt on the bed. Above the mirror was a scarf, the same bottle-green scarf he'd been wearing when he'd paid me his visit. On his night table there were dirty cups and dishes and there was a pair of unpolished shoes thrown onto the middle of the floor.

I just stood there. An uneasiness came over me. There was something wrong with this room. Something or other that wasn't right.

Was it the disorder?

No. He was young. He was a man. Of course his room was like this. I should get one of the younger girls to help him keep it tidy.

It wasn't the mess, but something else.

I looked around. Clothes, plates, shoes, a mug.

Something was missing.

Suddenly I knew what it was.

His desk. It was empty. The shelf by the wall. Empty.

Where were all of his books? Where were his writing materials? Everything he needed to prepare for his studies.

"Father?"

I spun around. Again he had appeared without my having heard him.

"Edmund." I hedged. Should I get out? No. Because I had every right to be here. Every right.

"I forgot something." He was breathing hard and his cheeks were rosy, he had clearly been outdoors. He was handsomely but somewhat haphazardly dressed today, too, with a red velvet vest, open coat and a kerchief draped around his neck. He held a purse in his hand and walked quickly towards the sideboard up against the short wall by the bed. There was a small chest on it, which he opened and began rummaging around in. The sound of coins jingling could be heard. He opened his purse and dropped few coins into it. Then he finally turned towards me.

"Did you want something?"

He was not indignant about my having let myself into his room. It was apparently of no importance whatsoever.

"Where are you going?" I asked.

He nodded into space, towards nothing. "Out."

"Where is this 'out'?"

"Father." He smiled, a little resigned, it seemed. I couldn't remember the last time I had seen him smile and of course he owed me no explanation.

"You must forgive me." I smiled back. "I forget that you're no longer a child."

He walked towards the door again. I took a step forward. Was he leaving already? Couldn't he wait a little, so he had the chance to see me, look at me properly, notice how healthy I was, how well groomed, so different from the person I'd been the last time we'd spoken?

He hesitated and stopped. We stood on either side of the door, a darkness opened between us. Two steps and he would be gone.

"Can I ask you about something?" he said.

"Of course. You can ask about anything you might be mulling over."

I smiled agreeably. Now the good conversation would soon be under way; this could be the beginning for us, of something completely new.

He drew a breath. "Do you have any money?"

I started. "Money?"

He waved his purse and made a face. "Almost empty."

"I . . . No. I'm sorry."

He shrugged his shoulders. "I'll have to ask Mother."

Then he disappeared out the door.

I went into my own room, feeling oddly dejected. Was I merely a provider in his eyes? Was money all he wanted from me?

I sat down by the desk. No, it couldn't be so. But money — for him perhaps it represented everything we lacked. The poverty the family had lived in during recent months, it was completely understandable that it had an impact on him. For him the lack of money was the clearest indication that his father was ill. That I had gotten out of bed again was all well and good, but I still didn't manage to procure for him what he really needed. He was young. Of course this simple, precarious need was the most essential for him. But he had to give me time. Because my idea would potentially give him both what he knew he needed immediately and what in the long term he would understand was most important.

I dipped my pen in the inkwell and drew it across the paper. I had never been much of an illustrator, regrettably; as a zoologist, observational drawings are an important part of the work. But over the years I had nonetheless forced myself to work on my technique and now I could at least use the pen as a tool.

I had some vague thoughts that I had to get down before they disappeared. I envisioned a box of wood, with a sloping roof. The basket hives were organic in design, like a nest; they almost blended in with the waving hay in the meadows. I wanted to create something else, a construction based on civilization, a small house for the bees, with doors, openings, the possibility for inspection. It should be man-made, because only humans could construct proper buildings, a building it was possible to monitor, which gave humans, not nature, control.

I drew for several days, scale drawings of the different parts, envisioned how the hive could be put into production, and put all of my energy into the details. The family lived its own life in the house out there, I scarcely paid them any heed, but nonetheless I received daily visits from Georgiana and Thilda. And Charlotte.

One morning she came especially early. Knocked lightly on the door, as was her custom.

At first I didn't answer, I was too busy with the details on the roof of the hive.

Another knock.

"Yes," I sighed. The door opened. She stood there with one foot in front of the other, as if she were summoning her strength.

"Good morning, Father."

"Good morning."

"Can I come in?" The voice was calm, but her gaze wavered uncertainly towards the floor.

"I'm working."

"I won't disturb you. I just want to give this back to you."

She held out a book. Held it in both hands, as if it were something valuable. She took a couple of steps across the floor, lifted her head and looked at me.

"I was hoping perhaps we could talk about it a little?"

Her eyes were gray-green, a little close-set. Not like Thilda's. On the whole she bore very little resemblance to her mother.

"Put it there."

I nodded in the direction of the bookshelf. A telling gaze, one I hoped would be enough so I'd be spared rejecting her outright.

"Yes." She lowered her head again and went over to the shelf and stood there.

I thought better of it. I was indeed busy, but there was no cause to be sharp all the same. "I'm in the middle of something, but would be happy to speak with you later," I said in what I hoped was a gentle voice.

She didn't answer, just looked at the book that she still held in her hands. "Where does it go?"

"On the shelf, of course."

"Yes, but I mean, don't you have a system for them?"

"No. Just put it there."

She looked up, eager now.

"Maybe I can organize them for you?"

"What?"

"The books. I can organize them alphabetically by author, if you like."

She was apparently not giving up.

"Well, yes, why not."

She smiled slightly, bent down towards the shelf and sat down on the floor. Her neck was a nicely curved line, with her hair put up simply, no corkscrew curls over the ears. She didn't seem to care about that kind of thing. She squirmed, changed her position, clearly found a comfortable position that she could maintain for a while. She was apparently going to be here for some time.

Then she started to work. She worked quickly, her movements were precise. And the care with which she handled the books, as if they were baby sparrows she was helping back into the nest.

I bent over the drawing again, tried to continue, but was unable to refrain from watching her. The enthusiasm in her movements, the meticulousness, concentration, awe, every single book was lined up exactly with the next. She ran her finger along the spines to make sure that not a single one stuck out from the row. That is how I had handled them myself once upon a time. She must have noticed my gaze because suddenly she turned around and smiled. I smiled back fleetingly and quickly returned my attention to my work again, with an incomprehensible feeling of having been found out.

Soon she was finished. I could hear that she got to her feet, but pretended that it had no effect on me, as if I was far too immersed in my own work. But she didn't leave the room, just remained standing there.

I looked up. "Thank you."

She nodded in response. But wasn't she going to leave? It was impossible to work with this shadow of flesh and blood that stood there breathing.

"You're welcome to sit down," I said, finally, and pulled out a chair. I owed her that much.

"Thank you." She hastened to perch on the edge of the chair seat.

Again I resumed working.

"What's *that*?" she asked and pointed at the drawing.

I looked up. "What do you think?"

"A beehive," she replied quickly.

I looked at her in surprise. Then I realized that she'd of course seen all of the pamphlets I'd had sent.

"Are you going to build it?" she asked.

"I'm going to *have* it built."

"But . . . is that the first thing you're going to do?"

"The first? Don't you see all of the books I've already read?" I waved around me.

"Yes," was all she said. Then she stared down at her hands, which lay primly folded in her lap.

The irritation rose inside me. "Didn't you

say that you would be quiet?"

"Forgive me. I'm quiet now."

"I can hear the wheels grinding in your brain."

"It's just that . . ."

"What?"

"You've always said that one must start with the fundamentals."

"Now then, have I said that?"

Yes indeed, so I had. Many times. Not to Charlotte directly, but to Edmund, when he was sitting with his schoolwork and wanted to start straightaway with the most difficult calculations, even though he still didn't master simple multiplication.

She lifted her gaze.

"And you've spoken so much about how zoology always starts with observations."

"Is that right."

"You've always said that the foundation lies in the observations. And after the observations comes the reasoning."

A band formed around my forehead and tightened. My own words in Charlotte's mouth. I'll be damned if she wasn't right.

Tao

Dr. Hio took us with her. One lift going up, then a long corridor. Then a lift down. She walked quickly, glanced every now and then over her shoulder; perhaps she didn't want to be seen. She had received clear instructions, she said, nobody was to visit him. He was in the isolation ward. Nobody was allowed to enter.

"But," she continued, mostly to herself, "you are the mother." She glanced quickly at Kuan, as if discovering him for the first time and corrected herself. "You are the parents. You must be permitted to see him." Her voice trembled as she said this, the businesslike empathy was gone.

What awaited us? Wei-Wen in a sickbed. Pale. His eyes closed. The blood vessels on his eyelids, more visible than usual. The little body, previously so full of stubbornness and energy, now completely lifeless. His arms at his sides, a cannula with a plastic tube in one. The arms that wrapped themselves around my neck, the cheek, damp and smooth, that was pressed against my own: surrounded by machines, bleeping apparatuses, shimmering screens. Sterile. White. Alone?

It was a long walk. Or had she taken a detour? Every time we passed somebody, she nodded curtly and sped up her pace a bit more. We were swallowed up inside the building. As if we were on our way to a place with no exit.

Finally she stopped. We stood in front of a steel door. She looked quickly around her, as if to ensure that there was nobody nearby, before she pressed a button. The door opened with a suction sound. The door was framed by black rubber molding, making it completely airtight. We stepped over the threshold. A louder hissing could be heard here, an air-conditioning system in high gear. The air pressure changed. The door slid shut behind us, the suction pulling it into the frame.

I had been expecting health care personnel. Sterile staff members, dressed in white, who flocked around us. Stern voices, authorities, *you have to go, you have to get out, this zone is off-limits.* I had prepared the words I would say. Prepared myself to be tough with

Kuan. I could see from his eyes that he had already pulled out, he was on the defensive, didn't want to be here, in forbidden territory.

But the corridor in front of us was deserted. The ward was deserted. We walked in, turned a corner. I expected a counter, a reception, doctors hurrying past. But there wasn't a soul to be seen here, either. Dr. Hio led the way. I didn't see her face, but her steps were hesitant; she walked more and more slowly.

She stopped in front of a door. This one was also made of shiny steel, no fingerprints, no signs of life, as shiny as a mirror. A round window in the middle, a porthole, like on an old ship. I tried peeking in, but the ceiling lights shone too sharply, the greenish reflection made it impossible to see anything at all.

"It's here. This is where he is," she said.

She stood there, uncertainly. Then she retreated.

"You can go in alone."

I put my hand on the door. The metal was surprisingly cold against my skin, I pulled my hand back momentarily. The palm of my hand left behind a damp mark in the midst of all the sterility. Then I opened it.

I stepped into a dimly lit room. Scarcely

registered that Kuan followed behind me. It took time to get accustomed to the darkness. I almost butted into a pane of glass that ran from the floor to the ceiling just one meter away from the door. Behind it lay a simply furnished hospital room. A closet. A bed. A bedside table of steel. Bare walls. A bed.

Empty.

The bed was empty.

The room was empty. He wasn't there.

I stormed out into the corridor again, but then came to a sudden halt. There was Dr. Hio with another doctor. They were speaking quickly and whispering. The other doctor leaned towards her, rigid and fuming. Reprimanding.

Kuan followed behind me, remained standing there as well.

"Where is he?" I said loudly.

The doctor spun around towards us and suddenly fell silent. Tall, thin, pale. Restless hands that he pushed down into the pockets of his coat.

"Your son is unfortunately no longer here. He has been discharged."

"What?"

"Transferred."

"Transferred? To where?"

"To . . ." His eyes still didn't meet mine.

"Beijing."

"Beijing?!"

"As you have perhaps been told, we are still unsure of what has afflicted your son. It was therefore decided that he would be in better hands with a special team." Kuan said nothing, just nodded.

"No," I said.

"What?" Finally the doctor looked at me.

"No. You can't just send him away."

"We haven't sent him *away*. We have sent him to the best specialists. You should be grateful . . ."

"But why hasn't anyone told us anything? Why couldn't we go with him?"

The same thing all over again. First Mother. Now him. Taken away from me, without any explanation.

"Which hospital is he in?"

"You will be informed."

"Now!"

"If you will just go home, we will give you more information soon."

I had reached my limit. I no longer had the strength to be reasonable, controlled, sensible. My voice rose, became sharp. "Take me to my son now! Take me to him!"

In two steps I was beside the doctor and grabbed his shoulders. "I want to see my child. Do you understand?"

The blood rushed to my head, my cheeks became damp, I tried shaking him, and he just stood there, in disbelief.

Then somebody took hold of me and held me tightly, took hold around my arms, paralyzed me, making *me* just as incapacitated as he was himself. Kuan. Obedient, now like he always was.

We didn't speak on the train home. The trip took almost three hours. We had to change trains. And go through two checkpoints. A fingerprint check and many questions. Who were we? Where did we live? Where were we going? Where had we been? Kuan answered all of the questions calmly; I could not fathom how he managed it. As if he were himself. But at the same time, he wasn't. I met his gaze once; unfamiliar eyes stared back at me. I turned away.

We traveled the final stretch on foot. We were just a hundred meters from our house when we became aware of the helicopters circling above us. The loud clattering rose and descended. At first I thought they were right above our house, but when we came closer, I saw that they were flying over the fields, over the pear trees. Over the forest.

We turned the corner and stopped. There, in front of our house, where the fields began, stood all of our colleagues, all of them in work uniforms. They had been interrupted in their work and they stood around passively in a small group. Some still held pruning shears and baskets for debris in their hands. They were quiet, just stood there looking in astonishment at the area in front of us. In the distance I could make out the hill where we had eaten lunch. Behind it lay the wild forest. The air above the trees was full of different aircraft, and in front of us, a wall of silently moving tanks passed by, a wall between us and the field out there. Behind the tanks soldiers were working. They were in the process of putting up tall white tarpaulin fencing, several hundred meters long. They worked quickly and efficiently, said nothing. I heard only the thudding sounds as they pounded the poles down into the ground. Beyond the soldiers, behind the fence, I could discern figures wearing full-body suits with helmets. Protected from something out there.

GEORGE

I couldn't fall asleep. The pitchfork was still there vibrating in my heart after my conversation with Tom, his words rattled around in my head, again and again. *Received a scholarship, won't cost you a cent, John's taken care of everything.*

Emma lay quietly beside me, breathing almost without a sound. Her face was smooth. She looked younger when she was sleeping. It was almost rude, that she could lie there like that and just sleep while I lay beside her struggling.

A bulb out in the yard blinked. One of the floodlights was about to go out, or perhaps there was something wrong with the wiring. The flickering became a disco light. A strobe light flashing through the window penetrated my eyelids. I pulled the duvet over my head, but it didn't help, it just got even harder to get the air down into my lungs.

Finally I got up, tried to adjust the curtains, was able to cover up the crack on the side where the light came in.

But it wasn't enough. The light flickered through the curtain, too. Maybe Emma was right about how we should get some of those completely lightproof blackout things. She'd shown me some in a magazine, they looked like ordinary window shades. But that would have to be later. Now the light had to be repaired. Right now. It couldn't possibly take long, a simple and manageable job, something that could be fixed quickly. I actually needed to fix the light in order to sleep.

It was a warm night. I didn't put on my jacket, just went out wearing the T-shirt I'd worn to bed. Nobody saw me anyway.

The light was hung high up on the wall, I had to get a ladder. I went to the barn, lifted the longest one down off the wall, walked out, put it in place, checked that it was stable and climbed up.

The glass dome over the bulb was good and stuck. Couldn't be budged. It was hot, too. Just warm enough that I managed to hold on to it, but not for too long at a time. I tried with my T-shirt, held the dome inside the fabric while I twisted, but it didn't work. Finally I pulled off my T-shirt.

The bulb flickered at irregular intervals, erratically. Wouldn't surprise me if there was a problem with the switch. Emma objected every time I did electrical work myself, but honestly, electricians charge you just for looking at them. They must be raking it in — maybe that's what one should have become. Or maybe that was what Tom should have become. Would have been much better, a short education, well paid.

Scholarship. Won't cost you a cent. John's taken care of everything.

It was a disappointment, but not enough to scare me.

There I was, bare-chested, wearing boxer shorts, socks and shoes on my feet and twisting the dirty light dome. Finally it loosened. I held it and the T-shirt in my left hand while I tried to attack the bulb.

"Dammit!"

It was burning hot to the touch. I had to climb down again with the dome, put it on the ground and then go up again. Luckily the bulb was easily unscrewed. But it occurred to me that if the problem was with the voltage, perhaps the entire light should be taken down, the entire socket. Leaving it like this was a fire hazard. It could not possibly be all that difficult.

Back into the barn to find my tools. Up

the ladder again.

I hated cross-head screws. It didn't take more than a few turns before the cross-head had become a hole that the screwdriver just spun around in, unable to get a grip. And these four were of the extrastubborn, rusty variety. But I was even more stubborn. Wouldn't give up, not this guy, no sir.

I leaned in and screwed away with all of my might.

Finally all four were out. The light was still stuck to the wall, painted into place. But that much I would manage, a little resistance didn't scare me. So I grabbed hold and shook away.

It came loose. Just the wires dangled there in its wake, sticking out of the wall like earthworms. I poked at one with my finger.

"Hell!"

The shock wasn't strong enough to knock me off balance. Not by itself. But in the other hand I held the socket and screwdriver. And the ladder wasn't particularly stable, either.

I lay on the ground. Don't know if I'd passed out as I fell. Had an unclear image of the ladder swaying midair, with me on top, like some cartoon character. I became aware of pain in several parts of my body, it hurt like hell.

Way up there I could see the wires creeping along the wall, downwards, towards me. I focused. They came to rest.

Then Emma's face appeared. Pale with sleep and her hair tousled.

"Oh, George."

"It was the light."

She lifted her head and discovered the wires splaying out of the hole in the wall.

I sat up. Slowly. My body responded, luckily. Nothing broken. And the light was down. I'd done it.

She nodded towards the ladder.

"Did you have to take care of that in the middle of the night?" She extended her hand towards me, pulled me up. "Couldn't it wait?"

I took a couple of steps. My leg ached, but I tried not to show how much it hurt. Should be embarrassed, but was actually just relieved that I had fixed it. I was a stubborn devil. Not the kind to take off when the going got tough.

She handed me the T-shirt. I was about to pull it down over my head.

"Hold on a minute."

She started brushing off my back. Now I noticed for the first time how filthy I was. Covered with dust and gravel from my socks to my scalp, hands full of sticky, black muck from the light.

I twisted out of her hands and pulled on my T-shirt. I could feel how a number of pebbles still stuck to my back, caught now between my skin and washed-out Chinese cotton. It was going to be painful to sleep on, like walking with pebbles in your shoes. But what was done was done — the light was down, that was the most important thing.

I put up the ladder and walked towards the barn again. Had to finish what I'd started.

"Have to get the electrical tape," I said. "Can't leave the wires hanging and dangling like that."

"But can't you do *that* in the morning?"

I didn't answer.

She sighed. "At least let me turn off the power for you." Her voice was louder now.

I turned around. She attempted a smile. Was she being ironic? Because I'd forgotten the electrician's first commandment?

"Go on up to bed," I just said.

She shrugged her shoulders. Then she turned and walked towards the house.

"And listen, Emma," I said.

"Yes?" She stopped. Turned around.

I straightened up, summoned my strength.

"Florida is not gonna happen. Just so you

know. Not for me. You'll have to find yourself somebody else. I'm going to live here.
There'll be no Gulf Harbors."

WILLIAM

The straw hive I'd ordered arrived three days later and I had found a location for it in the semi-shade of an aspen on the lower part of the property, in the part of the garden we allowed to grow wild. It wouldn't be in anybody's way in this part, none of the children spent time down there, and I would really be allowed to work in peace, make my observations of the bee colony, take notes and draw without being disturbed. A farmer south of town sold me the hive without blinking; probably because I offered him a price, instead of asking what he wanted for it. He didn't even try to barter with me but accepted on the spot, which told me that I probably could have gotten the hive for half what I'd offered.

He explained to me about harvesting, but I waved him away. It was obviously not for the sake of honey that I had gone to the trouble of procuring the hive.

Thilda had sewn a suit, not unlike a fencer's, out of an old white sheet. She had to take it in three times in the process, apparently unable to comprehend that my former measurements no longer pertained. On my hands I wore a pair of discarded gloves that did indeed make the skin clammy, but were utterly necessary for protection.

There I stood, under the aspen tree. Now it was just me and the hive, me and the bees.

I picked up a notebook. Observational studies were a meticulous task, but they usually gave me pleasure, because it was there, in the observation, it all started. That was where my passion originated. How could I have forgotten that?

I was about to make notes when something else occurred to me. How out of practice I was after all the years that had passed: I needed a chair.

A little later I was back with a simple stool; out of breath, the sweat was running under the suit, which, now that I felt it on my body, was a tiny bit too small, tight under the arms and in the crotch.

I sat and slowly settled down.

There wasn't much to see. The bees left the hive and returned, there was nothing surprising about that. They were out gathering pollen and nectar — the latter they transformed into honey, while the pollen was feed for the larvae. It was meticulous and peaceful work, systematic, instinctive, hereditary. They were all siblings, because the queen was everyone's mother, they were produced by her, but not subjugated to her. They were subjugated to the whole. I would have liked to see the queen, but the basket covered the bees, and everything they did inside was hidden.

Carefully I lifted it and peeked in from underneath. The bees swarmed up and spread out into the air around me, they were not fond of being disturbed.

I observed brimming honeycombs, a drone or two, I saw eggs and larvae and leaned in even closer. My skin was prickling with expectation, because now I had begun, finally I had begun!

"Time to eat!"

Thilda's voice sliced through the buzzing of insects and chased the birds into hiding.

I leaned over the hive again. It did not concern me, the family meals were not a part of my life, I had not eaten with them for months. The children streamed towards the house behind me, one after the other they disappeared inside.

"Teatime!"

I peeked at Thilda from under my arm. She was standing in the middle of the garden staring at me, and now she even set out in my direction.

Little Georgiana's fork scraped against an empty plate.

"Hush!" Thilda said. "Put the fork down!"

"I'm hungry!"

Thilda, Charlotte and Dorothea put serving dishes on the table. One with vegetables, one with potatoes and a tureen with a watery dishwaterlike liquid that was supposed to resemble soup.

"Is that all?" I pointed at the dishes that were served.

Thilda nodded.

"Where's the meat?"

"There isn't any meat."

"And the pie?"

"We're out of butter and pastry flour." She stared at me resolutely. "Unless you want us to take some of the tuition money."

"No. No, we aren't touching Edmund's tuition."

Now I suddenly understood why she had insisted I take part in the family dinner. She was more cunning than I thought.

I looked around me. The thin faces of the children were all turned towards the three dismal dishes on the table. "So," I said finally. "Then we'll have to be grateful for the food we have received."

I bowed my head and prayed. The prayer felt amiss on my tongue, I spit it out quickly in order to finish.

"Amen."

"Amen," the family repeated softly.

Through the window I could glimpse the hive in the distance, down there in the garden. I served myself a small portion, so I would be able to get back as quickly as possible.

Thilda received the serving dishes after me, then the children, one after the other according to age. It pleased me that Edmund was the eldest and was allowed to help himself right after Thilda, because boys at that age need solid meals four times a day. But he took little, and just poked at his food. He was unusually pale and thin, as if he never saw daylight. His hands were trembling, too, and his forehead sweating. Was he not feeling well?

The girls, on the other hand, eagerly devoured the meal. But there was not enough for all of them. When little Georgiana finally received her portion, only scraps were left. Charlotte pushed one of her potatoes onto to her little sister's plate.

We ate in silence. The food disappeared

from the girls' plates in just a few minutes.

During the meal I could feel Thilda's eyes on me. She did not need to say a thing. I knew only too well what she wanted.

GEORGE

I left at first light. Took some sandwiches in a bag and a thermos full of coffee. Drove the whole way without stopping. Seven hours straight, without a single break. I hadn't seen Emma at all. After I'd fixed the light, I passed out for a couple of hours on the couch. She was up in the bedroom, maybe she was sleeping, maybe not. I couldn't bring myself to check. Didn't have time. No . . . didn't dare, to tell the truth.

My eyes itched, were slightly bloodshot, but I was nowhere close to falling asleep. It cost me nothing to drive all these miles. I was well over the speed limit the whole way, but there wasn't much traffic and no speed traps. Would have been just perfect if my driving had cost me my license.

At exactly 12:25 p.m., according to the clock on the dashboard, I pulled up with a skid in front of the college. Parked in a space bearing the sign RESERVED FOR

PROFESSOR STEPHENSON, but didn't give a damn. Stephenson, whoever he might be, would have to find himself another space.

The college buildings were of red brick — of course they were, all schools are made of red brick — and even though the college wasn't particularly old, it was built to seem venerable, tall and wide, paned windows with white frames, was probably supposed to remind you of Harvard, or one of those places. Command respect. But it didn't scare me.

I hadn't been to this place since we'd brought Tom here in the autumn of last year. Set him up in a tiny room he would share with a short, bespectacled Japanese boy. The room smelled of dirty socks and hormones. Poor guys, there wasn't anywhere you could be alone. But that was apparently part of the deal.

I hurried in, passing a long row of brass plaques for the college's benefactors. Green's Apiaries luckily wasn't among them. There were various display cases containing trophies the college's students had won in various senseless competitions, along with portraits of bad-tempered college deans. Men, all of them. There weren't that many — the college was built in the 1970s and couldn't boast of a particularly long history.

I came out into a large round room with a marble floor against which the sound of my footsteps echoed from wall to wall. I started tiptoeing, but then stopped myself. I had nothing to apologize for. I paid Tom's tuition, it wasn't exactly as if I didn't belong here. In a sense I was actually a co-owner of this college.

I asked for Tom. Loud and clear. Without any preamble. The guy at the counter was lean and had dreadlocks, sat with his head submerged in the computer screen. He checked a register without gracing me with so much as a glance.

"He has a free period now," he said.

He continued tapping away on the computer, playing some game, probably, in the middle of the working day.

"It's urgent," I said.

He grunted. Doing his job was apparently not at the top of his list of priorities.

"Try the library."

Tom sat bent over some books, speaking quietly with two others. A brunette, quite pretty, but wearing sad-looking clothes, and a guy with glasses. They were clearly deep in conversation, mumbling intensely, because he didn't notice me until I was standing almost right on top of him.

"Dad?"

He said it softly, apparently here in knowledge's stronghold using your voice was not allowed.

The other two also looked up. Both with expressions as if I were a buzzing fly that had flown in here by mistake.

I thought he'd be alone, for some reason, just sitting here and waiting for me, but he was living a life of his own, with people I knew nothing about.

I raised my hand in a feeble greeting.

"Howdy, partner."

I kicked myself immediately. Howdy, partner? Nobody says that.

"You're here?" he said.

"Darn tootin'." This was just getting worse. Darn tootin'? I couldn't think straight. Guess what I'd planned to say would have to wait.

"Is something wrong?" He jumped to his feet. "Is something wrong with Mom?"

"No, no. Mom is as fit as a fiddle. Ha-ha."

Good Lord. I'd better just keep my mouth shut.

He took me outside into the sunshine. We sat on a bench. Spring was further along here than at home, the air was heavy and warm. There were young people around us everywhere. College kids. A lot of eyeglasses and leather satchels.

I noticed that he was looking at me, but suddenly I didn't know where to begin.

"Have you driven all this way just to talk?"

"Seems so."

"What about the farm? The bees?"

"They won't go anywhere . . . I mean fly anywhere."

I tried to laugh, but the laughter came out wrong and ended up like a cough.

We sat a little longer in silence. I pulled myself together, remembered what I'd actually planned to say.

"I'm going to Hancock County next week. Blue Hill."

"Oh. Where's that?"

"Maine. Just ten minutes from the ocean. Do you remember that you went there with me?"

"Yeah . . . I don't know."

"When you were five, before school. We went just the two of us. Slept in a tent, you know."

"Oh yeah. That trip."

"Yes, that trip."

He fell silent.

"There were bears there," he said finally.

"But it was fine," I said, a little too loudly.

"Are there still?"

"What?"

"Bears?"

"No, not anymore."

I suddenly remembered those big eyes of his. Round as saucers in the darkness. When we heard the sound of the bear through the tent canvas.

"They're facing extinction, did you know?" he said suddenly, the swagger was back in his voice.

"They're not alone." I tried laughing again. "Your old man is, too."

He didn't laugh.

I drew a breath. Had to come out with it, now, that's what I was here for.

"I've come to ask you to go to Maine with me," I said.

"What?"

"Do you want me to say it one more time?"

"Now?"

"On Monday. Three trucks, one more than before."

"That's good. You're expanding?"

"*We're* expanding."

"I can't go with you, Dad. You know that."

"There's more work than before. About time you pitched in."

"I have finals soon."

"It doesn't have to be for very many days."

"I won't get it approved."

"One week, tops."

"Dad."

I swallowed. My speech had gone down the toilet. The speech with a capital S that I'd prepared the entire way here. All the big words I'd lined up, like brand-new tin soldiers, had turned to lead in my brain. Inheritance, I was going to say, this is your inheritance. This is who you are, Tom. The bees, I was going to say, with a telling pause, that's where your future lies. Just give it a chance. Give them a chance.

But none of those words reached my mouth.

"I can get you the time off, say the family business needs you," I tried.

"Nobody gets time off for stuff like that."

"How many sick days have you had this year? None?"

"Two, maybe three."

"You see? Almost none."

"I don't think that matters."

"Well, then, God Almighty, say you're sick. You can certainly do your studying anywhere."

"It's not just studying, Dad. We have to hand things in, papers."

"Can't you do that there?"

"No, I need books."

"Take them with you."

"Books from the library. Here."

"It's just one week, Tom. Just *one* week."

"But Dad. I don't want to!"

He'd raised his voice now. Two girls with short hair wearing outfits that should have been reserved for men, jeans and giant army boots, passed by us, staring in curiosity. "I don't want to." He said it more softly now. Looked at me with dog eyes, not all that different from Emma's. A look I usually gave in to.

I stood up abruptly. Couldn't sit still for one more second.

"It's his fault, isn't it?"

"What? Whose?"

I didn't wait for the answer. Just stormed back towards the redbrick hell.

The faculty wing was located behind the reception.

"Hey, where are you going?"

I walked quickly past the dreadlocks, couldn't be bothered to answer.

"Hello?" He got to his feet, but I was already a good stretch down the corridor, passed office after office, some with open doors. Professor Wilkinson, Clarke, Chang, Langsley. Caught glimpses of heavily laden bookshelves, deep window frames, thick drapes. Nothing personal, everything reeked of knowledge.

And Smith. There it was. A closed door with yet another brass plaque. Almost made me believe there was a future in brass. PROFESSOR JOHN SMITH.

The dreadlocks approached.

"It's here," I called to him, noticing that I was short of breath. "I found it."

He nodded, stopped and stood there, maybe he wasn't allowed to let strangers in, before he shrugged his shoulders and sauntered back to the reception.

Should I knock? Like some puny student with a textbook under my arm?

No. I would walk right in.

I stood up straight, swallowed hard. Put my hand on the handle and pushed down.

It was locked.

What the hell?

At that moment a young man came strolling down the corridor. Clean shaven, and with a new haircut, wearing a hoodie and Converse sneakers. A student.

"Can I help you?"

He smiled broadly. White teeth, adjusted into a straight line. Everyone got braces these days, looked exactly the same, all the charm of special teeth was gone.

"I'm looking for John Smith," I said.

"That's me."

"You?" I was a little taken aback. He clearly wasn't as I'd expected. Hard to make a scene with this guy. He looked downright innocent. Just a kid.

"And you are?" He smiled.

I lifted my head.

"I'm Tom's father."

"Right." He kept smiling, reached out his hand. "Nice to meet you."

I took his hand. Couldn't exactly turn it down.

"Nice, yes. Very."

"Shall we go in?" he said. "I expect you have something on your mind?"

"You bet I do." It came out way too harsh.

"What?"

"Never mind." I tried to smile it away.

"Never mind?"

"Yes. I mean . . . I have something on my mind."

He unlocked the door and let me in. The sun greeted us, pouring in through the windows and painting clear stripes in the air, shining on framed pictures behind glass. Mostly posters. Movie posters. *Back to the Future, E.T., Star Wars,* the first movie: *A long time ago in a galaxy far, far away . . .*

"Have a seat." He pointed at an armchair.

I sat down. So did he. On his desk chair. It made me shorter than him, I wasn't thrilled about that.

"Oh, sorry."

He stood up again, sat instead in the other armchair. We were the same height. Sat in our respective chairs and all that was missing was a drink.

"There." He smiled again. "Yes. What can I do for you? Tell me."

I squirmed. Looked away.

"Nice poster." I pointed my chin towards *Star Wars*. Tried to keep my voice calm.

"Isn't it? Original."

"You don't say."

"Bought it on eBay when I started working here."

"I was about to say — are you old enough for that movie?"

He laughed. "I saw it on video."

"That's what I thought."

"But I had all the figures. The spaceship, too. Are you a fan?"

"Damn straight." There I went again. Guess I'd have to watch my language.

He suddenly started singing the opening melody while he directed with one finger in the air. I had to chuckle.

He interrupted himself. "Movies will never be the same again."

"You're right about that."

We sat in silence for a bit. He just looked at me. Waited.

WILLIAM

I did as Thilda wished, as her gaze commanded, although every step towards the shop hurt. It was my Canossa. I was out early, already at the crack of dawn. A cock crowed hoarsely from a back garden. A metallic hammering could be heard from the saddler's workshop, but I didn't see anyone. All was still silent at the wainwright's, the watchmaker's and the dry goods shop. The tavern, a stuffy and stinking place in which I had never set foot, lay closed at the end of the road. An intoxicated guest, I recognized him as one of the most frequent regular patrons, had clearly not found his way home to his own bed, but was instead sleeping seated against the outside wall. I turned away; his fate awakened feelings of disgust in me. To lose control in that way, to let alcohol run one's life, take over.

Only the bakery was open, and the aroma

of freshly baked bread, buns and perhaps a Swammer pie or two seeped through every tiny crack in the building so it was virtually visible. Luckily the baker and his two sons were still deep inside beside the large, hot oven. There still wasn't time for a break, to come out here onto the street and enjoy a pipe of tobacco as the first customers of the day dropped in at the shop. Or to discover me.

I usually didn't open the shop for a few more hours yet, but I couldn't bear to be seen. Couldn't bear the questions of the audacious ones: *Well, now, if it isn't that chap. What do you know. So you're still alive? Been ill, we've heard? But all better now? Back to stay?*

The red, low brick building was dark and shut up, and the small stretch of the street in front covered with leaves from last year. I lifted a heavy arm and stuck the key in the lock. Metal against metal, the sound made me shudder. I didn't want to go in, knew what was in store. A dusty, filthy shop, days and days of work to make it presentable.

I pushed at the door. It was stuck, was usually reluctant to open, but when I put my shoulder against it, it slid open silently on well-oiled hinges, not with the ancient creak I'd become accustomed to over the years. I reminded myself that the girl I'd hired in a moment of weakness, the bosomy, loud, tittering niece of Thilda's, could have oiled the hinges. Alberta was a redundant pair of hands in a home a bit too full of children, and was at a long since marriageable, perhaps overripe, age, a pear just a bit too soft that would soon tumble to the ground under the weight of its own juices. Both her parents and Alberta herself were painfully aware of the precariousness of her situation, although it had not proven to be the simplest task to find a suitable and willing life companion for her. They hoped for something second-rate, but she came without a dowry and was not in possession of anything else that made her especially attractive, with the exception of said bosom. But she was to be commended for her efforts; she might just as easily have put herself in the display window. She was so ripe for the picking that she behaved as if every single person of the male persuasion that stepped into the shop was her intended. Apart from writhing invitingly along the counter and showing off the female-reeking, sweaty cleavage between her breasts to anyone who would look (and smell), she didn't lift a finger. And I couldn't imagine that she'd done much of anything except put on airs in the doorway of the shop after I fell ill and up until Thilda had been obliged to let her go. No matter what she did, she made a mess of it, and her constantly tittering presence rendered me half amused, half seething with irritation. Her desire, this lack of inhibition, that she could even permit herself to express it so blatantly . . .

The shop lay in semidarkness. I lit a few candles and was able to light a brass lamp. The interior was surprisingly clean and extremely tidy. The large counter was almost empty, with the exception of the inkwell, receipt pad and the heavy scale of brass situated neatly on the far end. The voluminous ceiling lamp had been polished till it shone, and the glass bulb was cleaned, it was full of oil and ready for use. Usually the floor was covered with a crunchy layer of peppercorns and grains of salt which made itself felt with every single step, but now it was scrubbed so clean that you could see all the scratches, the palest areas in the woodwork, where the floor was especially worn, like a path from the counter to the wall of drawers and out to the exit. Thilda had told me that she had allowed Alberta to take care of closing on the last day. She had not mentioned that anyone else had been in the shop since that time. Had somebody been here nonetheless?

I walked over to a window. The frame was free of dust. Not a single dead fly, as one would normally expect after all this time. And it was easy to breathe, not heavy and stuffy, but recently aired out. I moved towards the wall that was covered with small drawers, put my hand on a handle, pulled the drawer out and looked down into it. It was spotless.

I examined one more. This one turned out to be clean as well.

Somebody had dusted. Was it Alberta? To the best of my knowledge she'd been promoted to the fabrics department at the dry goods shop, and so I could not believe that she had either the time or the desire to assist me in the midst of all of her so-called important work over there.

Regardless of who it had been, all I could feel was relief. Everything was shining, the shop was not only prepared for opening — it was cleaner and tidier than ever before.

I went over to the storeroom, and *that* on the other hand was a sad story. It was about as abundant as the Sahara. We were out of wheat and seed corn, while the pepper, salt and spices were reduced by half. In the drawers for flower bulbs there were just a few odd leaves and solitary white roots. Alberta had closed when the first snow came. By that time she had clearly sold off everything we had in the way of autumn bulbs, even some rather dubious, dry narcissuses that had been lying there for many years. But there were still spring bulbs and tubers for greenhouse cultivation. In fact, the selection was not bad at all. It felt good holding them, like taking the hand of an old friend. But unfortunately, it was without a doubt too late in the year for these, too late for precultivation indoors, and if planted directly in the ground now, they would not have time to flower before the frost once again crept along the hill during the night hours.

Nonetheless I had to open and try to sell what little I had, show Thilda that at least I was trying and in that manner quell her incessant fretting, if only for a few days.

At exactly eight o'clock I opened the door and let the sunlight stretch into the shop.

I put two potted dahlias outside, which I had dug up from the bed at home. They nodded gently in the wind and lit up the entire stretch of street with red, pink and yellow.

I stood there, in the doorway. The shop lay bright and inviting behind me. I stood tall. I had been dreading so coming back here, to this shop which had been such a burden, had given me tense shoulders and dark circles under my eyes. But now it was clean and welcoming, scrubbed as clean as I felt. The shop was ready, I was ready, to once again meet the village, look the world in the eye.

A queue formed. The entire village had apparently discovered that I had returned from the dead and suddenly everyone wanted to buy my dusty spices and dried-up flower bulbs. I had taken care to send off a few orders already in the morning, but by the time the sun was at its zenith in the sky, it was impossible to get anything else done except wait on customers. Presumably it only took these few hours before everyone knew. It wasn't the first time I'd been shocked by how quickly gossip spread in this little place — it was as if it had the help of a near-gale, at least when something really big had happened. And clearly something had now. My return was apparently on a level with the resurrection of Christ, judging from the crowd.

I heard people whisper about me, but it was surprising how little it bothered me. Because they did not greet me with mocking smiles and sharp comments like after my lecture about Swammerdam, but rather with open gazes, bowed heads, hands extended with respectful curiosity. A glimpse of myself in the windowpane reminded me of why. My new appearance was really doing its part. I no longer resembled a phlegmatic shopkeeper. The chubby feebleness had disappeared. This clean-cut, slender man inspired respect. He was exciting, special, not one of them. Very few people knew with certainty what had ailed me and if they had suspicions, it was perhaps awe rather than derision that filled them. Because I had stood face-to-face with death, but had fought back and risen again.

I was in my element. The money poured through my fingers. I counted and calculated at a furious pace, while I chatted with anyone and everyone, making sure to ask how things were going with each of them. *Has the marriage of your daughter, Victoria, wasn't it, been blessed with little ones? How about the farm? How many foals did you say? Fantastic! And the crops? What do you think, does it look like it could be a plentiful harvest? But little Benjamin, is he already ten years old, and still smart as a whip? He will become something important, that boy.*

When I locked the door for the evening, it was with a light, precise movement. In my hand I held a bulging money purse. And although my feet were blessedly tired, it cost me nothing to walk the few miles home. My books awaited me there. I would work until midnight, because I wasn't the least bit tired, had even more energy. I thought I had to choose, but I could manage both — both life and passion.

Tao

It was nighttime and I was awake again. Sleep had no meaning; neither did anything else. I was in the sitting room with my back against the one wall. I bowed my head and looked down at my hands, put my fingertips against each other. The nails were too long, I pushed them under each other until it hurt. Wondered how long I would have to push until I drew blood.

I'd been able to handle Mom's disappearance. She was sick, old. It seemed like she'd come to a good place, it looked beautiful on the film, and safe. But Wei-Wen . . . The tears burned in my chest, tightened my throat, were so physically painful that I struggled to breathe. But I didn't release them.

Nobody required us to work. The supervisor of my work team showed up the day after we came home, together with Kuan's supervisor. They had both been informed.

By whom he didn't say, and I forgot to ask. They stood stammering outside the door, wouldn't come in, and said we must take all the time we needed.

We didn't know how long they would leave us in peace.

On the first few days gifts arrived at our door. Mostly food. Canned goods. A bottle of real ketchup. Even a kiwi. I didn't even know that anyone produced kiwis any longer. But it had no taste. Somebody had also gathered up our things and had them delivered to us. Everything was there, even the empty plum tin. The smell of it nauseated me.

In the beginning, Kuan just lay in the bedroom. He cried for both of us. Sobs filled the apartment, unfurling through the narrow rooms. But I was unable to go in and see him.

Then he got up. We walked around each other in silence. The days slipped by; we lived in a vacuum, just as stagnant and closed as the room where Wei-Wen had been lying. The only voice that spoke in our home was that of Li Xiara over the radio, giving a speech about national sacrifice. Kuan was still silent. And I was unable to say anything, because I didn't know how. Perhaps he didn't blame me, perhaps he hadn't even thought that thought.

Yes.

The vacant gaze. The distance he kept from me at all times. He had previously been so physically intimate, now our bodies were never in close proximity. But he was too passive to say anything. Perhaps he didn't dare. Or was it an attempt to protect me? I didn't know.

But this thing that was between us had grown to be so insurmountably large. *He* kept his distance from me, but neither did I manage to touch *him,* talk to him. It became almost unbearable to be in the same room. He stirred up the same thoughts again and again. The same two words. *My fault, my fault, my fault.* That was why everything about him was repulsive. His body disgusted me. I felt sick at the thought of him touching me, but hid it the best I could. We played house, but without the child. Cooked meals. Tidied up. Did laundry. Every day was the same. We got up, got dressed, ate a little. Drank tea. The eternal tea. And waited.

I kept trying to call the hospital. I was always the one who did it, as he didn't even have the initiative to do that much. I never spoke to Dr. Hio again and after a few weeks it was revealed that she had quit. The other doctors said nothing about why.

The answers were the same regardless of whom I talked to: *We don't know anything else. You will have to wait. Of course we will find you a name. Of course. Just wait a little longer. Just a few days. We will look into it. We will get back to you. You will just have to wait.*

In spite of the fact that we had been given all the time off we might need, Kuan came out one morning wearing his work clothes after his shower.

"Just as well," he said softly.

I was surprised, almost dumbfounded, not that he was going out, but over how relieved I was. This, to get rid of him, to be by myself — I experienced it as the first bright spot in all of these weeks.

"Is that all right?" he asked.

"Yes. Just go."

"If you think it's difficult to be alone, I don't have to."

"It's fine."

But he kept standing there. His clothes hung loosely on him; he was even thinner than before. He just looked at me. Perhaps he expected me to say something. Get angry, shout, explode at him. But why did he expect *me* to go into a rage? Had *that* also become my responsibility? His huge eyes stared at me, begging, his soft mouth slightly open. I turned away, was unable to look at him. That handsome man who formerly had caused me to forget myself. Now I just wanted to get him away from me as quickly as possible.

"Tao?"

"You have to go if you're going to make it in time for roll call."

I still didn't look at him. Heard how he took several breaths, wanted perhaps to say something, but couldn't find the words.

Then he disappeared — his steps across the floor, the door slamming shut — and finally left me alone in the empty apartment. I went into the bedroom. On Wei-Wen's bed lay his pajamas. I picked them up and sat there holding them in my arms. I hadn't wanted for us to wash them. They'd only been worn for two nights, and were lying ready for him on his bed. Until he came back. The fabric felt thin between my fingers, smiling moons against a background of blue. They still smelled faintly of child sweat.

I sat like that all day.

After this I began gradually to reverse my sleeping pattern. While Kuan slept his heavy manual-labor sleep, I was awake in the sitting room. I paced and stood still, and it was not until dawn that I collapsed into bed. I could not rest; if I sat down, if I relaxed, if I slept, then Wei-Wen would be gone forever.

I turned to face the window. We had a view directly facing the white fence that enclosed the fields. Guards were posted at one-hundred-meter intervals. I could make out the silhouette of the guard closest to me. He was staring out into space and did not move. I would have done anything to find out what he was guarding.

The fence was so high that we couldn't see inside, not even from the roof of the house. I'd been up there and tried. A net had been stretched on top of the fence, which the wind caught hold of constantly. During the initial weeks there had been workers up there several times to secure it better. Every day people appeared who were curious to see it, but they were all turned away. The area was heavily guarded. I had walked along the fence to see if there were any openings, places one could crawl through, but there were guards everywhere.

Kuan spoke of how people talked. The work team had to report to another field now. It was a mile's walk each way and people had plenty of time to talk. He heard them. The speculations ran wild. It had something to do with Wei-Wen, everything that happened, they thought. The fence, the closing off, the military. It must be so, because we were the last ones who'd been there. And Wei-Wen was in the hospital. But when they became aware that Kuan was listening, they fell silent. And the moment they felt confident that he wasn't listening, they continued. The jabbering was about us now and sensational in nature. We were the target of everyone's attention and there was nothing I could do.

We knew as little as they did. Something had happened to Wei-Wen out there, and now he was gone. That was all we knew.

All of a sudden I noticed the guard down there. He had collapsed by the fence, sat with his knees curled up beneath him and his head dipping gently forward. He was asleep.

WILLIAM

The eggs are no more than 1.5 millimeters in length. One in each cell, grayish against the yellow wax. After just three days the larva hatches, and she, because usually it's a she, is overfed like a spoiled child. Then the days of growth come, before the cells are covered by a wax lid. In there, she creates the cocoon, the larva spins it around itself, a protective garment against everything and everyone. Here, and only here, she's alone.

After twenty-one days the worker bee crawls out of the cell to the others, a newborn, but not ready for the world, an infant, can't fly, can't eat on its own, and barely manages to hang on to the boards, crawling, creeping, searching. On the first days she therefore receives simple tasks indoors and has a short radius. She cleans the brood box, first her own cell, subsequently others, and she's never alone. There are many hundreds of others, who at any given time are at the exact same phase of development as she is.

Then her work as a nursing bee begins, although she's still only a child. It's now her responsibility to feed those who are not yet born. At the same time she attempts her very first flights, testing out her wings, in the afternoon, days with good weather, careful, hesitant. She finds the way out of the flight hole; for a while she circles in front of the hive, before she slowly increases the distance from her home. But she's still not ready.

She still has tasks in the hive. She takes care of the pollen that comes in, produces wax and carries out her stint as a guard bee. And at the same time, the trips outside of the hive become longer. She's preparing herself. Will soon be ready. Soon.

And then, finally, she becomes a forager bee. She disappears outside on her own, is free, her wings carry her from plant to plant, she collects the flowery-sweet nectar, pollen and water, for mile after mile. She's alone out here, but still a part of the community. Alone she's nothing, a part so tiny that it's insignificant, but with the others she's everything. Because together they're the hive.

The idea began out of nowhere, but

developed like the bee itself. I started with sketches, light charcoal strokes on paper, imprecise dimensions, vague designs. Then I became more daring, I measured, calculated, the lines became clearer, I lay the full expanse of the paper out on the floor. In the end I took out a pen and ink and it finally took shape before my eyes, clearer, more precise lines, exact measurements. And finally, on the twenty-first day, the hive was ready. "Can you build this?"

I spread the drawings out across Conolly's worn tabletop. The table was full of nicks and scratches from many years back, and on top of this it was not completely steady. You would think that he, of all people, would insist on furniture in one piece. Everything in this little sitting room of his was crooked and lopsided: an unmade bed in the corner, a broken chair placed by the hearth. Perhaps he didn't have the energy to repair his own furnishings, and instead tossed them into the fire when they were beyond repair. The floor was full of sawdust, as if he brought his work in with him, even though he had a workshop in an adjacent room.

He picked up one of the drawings. They seemed fragile in that powerful hand. He held it up to the light in the cramped sitting room, moved a step closer to the peephole of a window, where one of the panes was broken and the opening boarded up with a knotty plank. He had been recommended to me, the best carpenter in the area, it was said, but his surroundings were not convincing.

"The box is fine, but why does it need a slanted roof?"

"Well, it is a house, after all. A building, a home."

"A home?" He hesitated. "It's bees you're talking about, right?"

I couldn't explain all of this to him, had to come up with a logical reason, speak his language. "It's because of water. Rain. When it rains, it will run off."

He nodded; that was an argument he could accept, because it was related to construction, not feelings.

"That makes it more complicated. But it should be fine."

Then he picked up the drawing of the interior.

"And frames?"

"They're supposed to hang from the top. It would be preferable with ten per hive, but we can make do with seven or eight. A piece of wax is to be attached to these."

He looked at me questioningly.

"Beeswax. So the bees can continue to build on it."

"Really?"

"The bees build diagonal honeycombs by nature, but I don't want to let them build as they like, which is why I am adapting the working conditions."

"Right," he said and scratched his ear, seeming on the whole completely uninterested.

"In this hive, the frames will help them build honeycombs in a line. I want to be able to have a complete overview of the working conditions through the door, and to be able to take the honeycombs out and put them in. That way it will be easier to take care of, observe and, not least, harvest the honey without hurting the bees."

He looked at me blankly for a moment, then he studied the drawing again.

"I have the cornices," he said. "But the walls and roof . . . I'm a little unsure about the materials."

"I will leave those assessments to you," I said with all the friendliness I was able to muster. "This is, after all, your field."

"You're right about that," he said. "And the um . . . the parallel honeycombs will be up to you."

He smiled for the first time, a broad and

easy smile, while he held out that powerful fist. I smiled back and grasped his hand. I could already envision crate after crate of Savage's Standard Hives being carried out of the carpenter's workshop and being sold at a good profit for both of us. Yes, this really had all the promise of a splendid collaboration.

GEORGE

Kenny's vehicles rolled into the yard with a resounding cough of exhaust fumes. The dust sprayed off the tires and settled in a thick layer on the empty flatbeds and the engines completely drowned out the small birds twittering at the approach of sunset. I had rented three trucks this year. Regular trucks, unfortunately, not semitrailer trucks like the kind Gareth used. These were old, rusty wrecks on the outside, nothing impressive, and in terms of space were not more than three hives high and four wide. But under the hood they were trusty workhorses, with engines so simple that you could fix them yourself if something happened, and something happened all the time.

We began loading hives in the twilight. This couldn't be done during the day while the bees were out, so we had to wait until they'd turned in for the night.

Darkness fell. We started the engines so

the headlights lit up the meadow while we were working. We were like Martians in white suits with hats and veils, in and out of the beams of light from the vehicles, as if we had come from a foreign planet to take with us biological material in the boxes. I had to chuckle to myself. He should have seen us now, Professor Hoodie.

The sweat trickled down under my suit. It was heavy work. Every single hive weighed many pounds.

But next year. Next year there would be a truck, perhaps a proper semitrailer truck. I'd been saving money, hoped it was enough for another bank loan. Hadn't talked to Emma about it. Knew what she thought. But to make money you have to spend money. That's how it is.

We left as soon as the hives were in the vehicles. Nothing to wait for and we had a long trip ahead of us. We drove two men in each vehicle, taking turns driving. I took my own car. Tom and I.

Maybe it was because of Star Wars, maybe because Tom himself had said that he would write about the trip, that it would give him inspiration. He had arrived, at least, the same afternoon. With full approval from John, the professor. Tom gave Emma a hug, pulled on his coveralls and went out. He had been with the bees ever since. Didn't say much. I couldn't see his face. It was in the shadow behind the veil. But he worked, did what we asked him to. Silently and quickly, even faster than Jimmy and Rick. I wanted to tell him so, praise him, but couldn't find the right moment. There was no chance for it in the car, either, because he just rolled up his sweater into a sausage, leaned his head against the window and closed his eyes.

He was handsome, my boy. A little thin, but handsome. The girls must like him. Did he have a girlfriend? I didn't know.

The engine hummed smoothly. Tom's breathing was just as smooth. There were few cars on the road, we passed someone only once in a great while. The road was dry, we maintained a fast speed, but not reckless.

Everything was going according to plan.

We slept and drove in shifts. Nobody said much. Morning came. The rolling hills of the landscape all around us. A machine drove past in a field a distance away. Like a gigantic insect. The body of the machine, the tank of pesticide, was huge and round, contained thousands of gallons. It had long, rotating wings that spread the material on the fields in a cloud of tiny drops.

I kept my bees far away from pesticides. It dulled them, always led to losses. But in recent years many had started using something new. The pesticide was no longer sprayed but spread in small pellets on the ground. It was safer and better, it was said. Lay in the soil and was absorbed by plant roots, lasted longer, worked longer. It was shit all the same. I would have liked to have seen the farmers manage the old way, that the crops in the fields had to survive on their own, without the help of pesticides. But it seemed that wasn't possible. Insect pests could eat a ripe field down to the ground in one night. There were too many of us, the food prices too low, and everything else too expensive for anyone to take the chance.

Tom woke up beside me. Opened the thermos, poured out the last dregs and suddenly thought of me.

"Sorry, did you want some?"

"Help yourself."

He drank it down in two gulps. Said nothing more.

"Well, well," I said. Mostly to fill the silence.

He didn't answer. There wasn't much to say.

"So," I said. "Yeah." And cleared my

throat. "Any girls in the picture? At school."

"No. Not really," he said.

"None who are pretty?"

"None who think I'm pretty." He laughed and I registered that he was in a talkative mood.

"Just you wait," I said.

"Hope I won't have to wait as long as you and Mom."

Emma and I got married when we were thirty. My father had long since given up on me.

"You should be grateful for that," I said. "So you were spared noisy little siblings. Don't know how good you've got it being an only child."

"Siblings could have been nice, too," Tom said.

"On paper," I said. "In reality it's hell. And I know what I'm talking about."

I had three brothers. Arguing and fighting from morning to night. I was the eldest and was a mini-dad from the age of six. Had always been happy that Tom was an only child.

"Anyway. First you have to start by finding yourself a lady. And then you can have kids, one at a time. You know how it works. Birds and bees. Or maybe we never had that talk."

"No, maybe we can have it now?" He chuckled. "Let's hear it, Dad. What's the story with the birds and the bees?"

I laughed.

He did, too.

WILLIAM

"Edmund?" I knocked on the door to his room.

The past few days, while I was waiting for the new hive, I had spent outside getting to know the bees, first with trembling hands, then with more and more certainty. I had found the queen, she was larger than the workers and drones, and I marked her with a tiny spot of white paint on her carapace. I observed the queen cells that had been built, but destroyed them right away, couldn't take the chance of swarming — the old queen taking parts of the colony with her to make room for a younger queen and her progeny. Beyond this the hive didn't provide much knowledge. I opened it with great care and caution; the bees became agitated every single time. I still didn't understand how it could be that the queen laid two types of eggs, both for worker bees and drones. But the working conditions for observations weren't the best. I presumed that as soon as the new hive was in place, this would be much easier to study.

One thing was certain, at least: it was a hardworking bee colony I was dealing with. The hive was increasingly heavier, the bees brought in nectar and pollen, the honey was glistening in there already, dark golden, sugary-sweet and tempting.

Charlotte often kept me company. She observed the bees with great enthusiasm, picked up the hive in her hands, weighed it, made wagers on the amount of honey. She lifted it with skill, checked for queen cells, found the queen, took it out with her hand — yes, she dared to do it without gloves — and I saw how the bees swirled up, searching for her, as they always do with their queen. Charlotte had grown this summer, her ungainly body acquired curves, her pale cheeks color, her skirts became almost indecently short and had crept up to the middle of her shin. A new dress, I thought, she deserved that, but it would have to be later, because now other things were more important.

On some days I had to go in to the shop. Then she would help me there as well, cleared, washed, kept the stock organized, did figures so the nib of the pen scratched, added, subtracted, assessed profits.

But Edmund never participated. The preparations for his studies in the autumn were not going as they should. That was clear, even to me, although I seldom spent time with the family. The books he kept in a dark corner of the parlor were in the process of becoming just as dusty as mine had been. He was always so tired, off color, often shut himself in his room. The restlessness had been replaced by something sedate, something slow, a sluggishness one rarely saw in young people.

I hoped nonetheless that he would come along and sit with me, so I could explain to him about the straw hive and subsequently show him how much more brilliant my own invention was. I wanted to show him what he and his book had initiated in me, and hoped I could manage to awaken the same passion in him.

"Edmund?" I knocked again.

He didn't answer.

"Edmund?"

Nothing happened.

I hesitated, then I carefully pushed down on the door handle.

Locked. Of course.

I bent over, peeked through the keyhole and glimpsed the key that was in the hole from the inside. He was not out, then; he had locked himself in.

I pounded on the door. "Edmund!"

Finally footsteps could be heard on the floor inside and the door was pulled open a tiny crack. He blinked at me and the light. His fringe was longer, he had grown a wispy moustache on his upper lip, and was dressed in a wrinkled shirt and nothing else. His feet were bare against the plank floor and above them were some astonishingly hairy legs.

"Father?"

"I'm sorry I had to wake you."

He shrugged his shoulders, stifled a yawn.

"I was hoping you might come out with me," I said. "There's something I want to show you."

He stared at me from slitted, drowsy eyes. Rubbed one of his feet against his shin, as if to warm himself, but didn't respond.

"I'd very much like for you to understand the straw hive," I continued, while I tried to keep my eagerness under control.

"The straw hive?" Still this urbane, somewhat listless tone of voice.

"Yes. You've seen it, furthest down in the garden."

"Oh. That." He swayed and swallowed.

"So that you understand the difference

between it and the new hive. When it gets here."

"All right." He said it through pinched lips, and swallowed again, as if choking back vomit.

"And how much better-constructed the new one is."

"Yes."

His eyes were still as if drugged with sleep, not a hint of interest.

"Perhaps you'd like to get dressed?"

"Can we do it another day?"

"Now is a good time." I noticed suddenly that I was standing there with my head ducked, as if I were begging. But he didn't appear to have noticed.

"I'm so tired," was all he said. "Maybe later."

I straightened up then, tried to make my voice sound authoritative. "As your father I demand that you come with me now."

Finally his gaze met mine. His eyes were bloodshot, but still oddly clear. He tossed his fringe back, raised his chin. "Or what?"

Or what? I was unable to reply, noticed that I was blinking rapidly.

"Or I'll get a taste of the belt?" he continued. "Is that what you mean, Father? Or you'll take out the belt and whip it across my back until I bleed and have no other choice but to say yes?"

This hadn't gone the way I'd hoped, not at all.

He stared at me, I stared at him. Nobody said anything.

All of a sudden Thilda was there. She hurried towards me through the hallway, her skirt brushing against the floorboards.

"William?"

"It's almost two o'clock," I said.

Her voice rose. "He needs sleep. He's not well. Go on and go to bed, Edmund."

She stopped beside me, laying a hand on my elbow.

"You don't do anything but sleep," I said to Edmund. It came out loudly, sounded too desperate.

He didn't answer, merely shrugged his shoulders. Thilda tried shoving me away, while she looked kindly at Edmund.

"Go to bed, my dear. You need rest."

"Rest from what?" I asked.

"You're not exactly one to talk," Edmund said suddenly.

"What?!"

"You went to bed for several months."

"Edmund," Thilda said. "*That* has nothing to do with it."

"Why?" he asked.

I could feel the desperation paralyze me.

"I'm sorry, Edmund. I'm going to make things right. I'm in the process of making things right now. That's why I would so like to show you . . ."

But Thilda shoved me away. "Poor Edmund," she said in a sugary-sweet voice. "It's too much for him. He must rest now, he needs it."

Edmund stared at me without expression. Then he closed the door and left us standing there.

Thilda was still holding on to my arm, as if to hold me in place and her gaze was still just as insistent. I wanted to object, but suddenly it hit me. Was he ill? Was Edmund ill?

"Is there something you're not telling me?" I asked Thilda.

Her gaze was like flint against my own and almost frightened me.

"I'm his mother and can see that he needs rest," she said slowly and clearly, and had apparently no intention of explaining anything at all to me.

"And I'm his father and can see that he needs fresh air," I said and heard immediately how foolish the words sounded.

She lifted the corners of her mouth in a mocking smile. Neither of us said anything more, we just stood like that facing each other. She offered neither answers nor compliance. Because he wasn't sick, of course he wasn't; she was just protecting him, from schoolwork and everything that demanded something of him. But she had no idea what had transpired between us, the fire he had lit inside me, how important it was that I had the chance to share it with him.

But I wasn't up to the task of trying to explain; I knew how meaningless it was to fight with her, all logical arguments were just swept aside. She was a windmill.

Perhaps instead I would have to grab him before evening came, before he went out, as he often did. This indefinable "out." I wished, hoped, that he was in the forest, doing his own observation studies, inspired by me, as I myself had been at his age. Yes, perhaps that was in fact the case.

And as far as I was concerned, he probably wanted to wait until I really had something to show him. But that increased my excitement. I would make him proud.

TAO

I rounded the corner of the house. The fence lay in front of me. Impenetrable, tall, it shone white in the darkness, reflecting the rays of the half-moon. The soil was fragrant, the weather warm and humid, the grass flourished along the side of the road.

I tiptoed past the guard. His face lay in darkness, but his head was bowed, and I could hear him breathing deeply and calmly.

Something buzzed in the air, a low sound, perhaps ten meters directly above me. An insect? No, far too large. But the sound moved quickly away and again all was silent.

Carefully I reached out a hand and touched the fence. I expected an alarm, a howling sound. But nothing happened.

I walked a few meters along the fence, allowing my hand to trace the smooth, tightly woven material. And there, between my fingers, I suddenly felt a splice. The canvas was taut, but nonetheless I managed to get my fingers between the two layers. I tugged a little. With a faint sound, the layers separated. Soon I had managed to create a hole that was big enough to allow me to slip through.

I threw one final glance towards the soldier, he was still sleeping deeply. Then I forced my way through.

It was darker here. I knew that there were searchlights; from time to time we had seen the sweeping light in the evening, but now they were all turned off.

Did they have guards on the inside? I didn't know. I just stood there, trying to accustom my eyes to the darkness. Slowly the trees became visible before me. They were without blossoms now, but heavy with leaves.

Everything was quiet, just the light breeze that slid through the leaves and the grass, but nonetheless I was shaking with excitement. It was prohibited, what I was doing. What would happen if I got caught?

I slowly moved forward. A distance away I could just make out the rut we had followed to the hill. I walked there.

I had never in my life felt apprehension out here. Many other feelings — resignation, boredom and also joy — but never fear. Now I moved as quietly as I could, while the sound of my own heart rose into my ears and my back became drenched with sweat.

The ruts led me forward between the trees. All of a sudden there was something moving at the far edge of my field of vision, a shadow. Was somebody there? I spun around, but saw nothing. Nothing. The world out here was empty and hushed. It was only my own fear playing tricks on me.

I took a few more steps forward.

One, two, three — jump. One, two, three — jump.

We had walked here.

Wei-Wen between us. Healthy, determined, warm, soft. My child.

My child.

I had to stop, bend over, a physical pain in my midriff hit me with such force that I was unable to move.

Breathe calmly. Think about something else. Straighten up. Be rational. Look around. How much further was it now? To the hill, where we had eaten lunch.

Keep going.

I hadn't walked much further when I discovered it. Light. A yellow light shimmered in the air above an area a distance away.

I walked closer. More slowly now, putting

my feet down one in front of the other with increasing caution.

And then I saw the tent. It was located on the border against the forest, with a back-drop of bushes and trees growing wild. Round, as big as a small house, with a peaked roof, lit up from all sides. It was made of the same canvas as the fence, the same sterile whiteness. Outside I could see the silhouettes of several soldiers on patrol. The tent was far more heavily guarded than the fence. They walked calmly back and forth, throwing sharp shadows against the tent canvas, a strange shadow-puppet show on a circus tent somebody had forgotten to color. Were they a threat or protection?

I couldn't see an entrance. There were no windows, either. I didn't dare move any closer, kept going instead, around a hundred meters away, parallel with the tent, to see it from the other side. I passed the hill, and at that moment it struck me that the tent was in approximately the same place where Kuan must have found Wei-Wen. With that realization, my fear intensified. My legs were shaking so much they could scarcely carry me forward. I understood that I'd hoped there wasn't a connection, that the fence and the military people had nothing to do with Wei-Wen.

But now. The telephone call I went around waiting for, the message that Wei-Wen had just fallen and hit his head, that he'd suffered a completely ordinary concussion and was now recovering, that the two of us could visit him and soon take him home with us, these thoughts now appeared even more to be helpless, desperate fantasies. Right between myself and the tent I glimpsed a stack of cardboard boxes. I approached quietly; behind the boxes I was hidden from the guards.

Some of the boxes were folded up, others were still intact. I peeked into one, ran my hand along the bottom, removed the contents. Soil and remains of plant roots. A name was printed on the side of the box, postal code and city. Beijing.

I put it down and moved on slowly. I was afraid my usual clumsiness would give me away, that I would once again break branches, and I concentrated every muscle in my body on moving as quietly as possible.

The front of the tent became visible. Just as white and impermeable, but with an opening on the side, closed by a tight, broad zipper. I crouched down. Waited. Sooner or later somebody would certainly come or go.

I sat crouched down like that until the

lactic acid built up in my legs and I had to change positions. The ground was damp, but I sat all the way down nonetheless; the raw chill of the earth penetrated my clothing. It was only now that I noticed the piles of branches outside. They had chopped down a dozen fruit trees to make room for the tent. Dry branches stood out stiffly against the tent canvas.

Nothing happened. From time to time low voices could be heard from inside, but I was unable to distinguish any words.

I just sat like that for a long time, surrounded by darkness. The minutes passed, became an hour. The stagnant air was starting to make me drowsy.

Then: the rasping sound of a zipper. The tent was opened and two figures came out, both wearing white safety clothing, their heads bent together, discussing intensely in low voices. I leaned forward, squinting to see. The tent was opened just for a moment, but nonetheless I had time to make out something of what it was hiding. A transparent inner tent full of plants. Glass walls. Flowers. A greenhouse? Shiny green leaves, pink, orange, white and red flowers surrounded by golden light. Like a fairy-tale landscape in an illustration, richly colorful and warm, another world, living plants, blossoming plants, plants I had never seen before, not to be found among the uniform rows of fruit trees.

All at once one of the figures began walking in my direction. I remained seated. But the figure came closer.

I stood up and silently moved backwards.

The figure stopped. Listened, as if sniffing me out. I didn't dare to move any more, stood completely still, in hopes of blending in with the tree trunks.

He remained motionless for another moment, but then he turned around and walked back to the tent. I hurried away.

I increased my pace, ran as quietly as I could back towards the fence.

I'd seen something. But I didn't know what. The fences, the boxes, the tent. It made no sense.

Neither here nor at the hospital would anyone give me what I needed. Nobody would give me answers. And they wouldn't give me my child.

I reached the fence, crept through the same place, passed the guard. He was still sleeping at his post.

I stood there outside in the warm night. The fence towered over me. But Wei-Wen wasn't here. He wasn't even in this part of the country. He was where the plants came from. In Beijing.

GEORGE

Blueberry bushes in bloom are beautiful things. I'd forgotten in the course of the winter, but every time Maine greeted me with its white and pink knolls in May, I just had to stop and look.

It was so beautiful that books should be written about it. But without bees, the flowers were just flowers, not blueberries, not bread and butter. Guess that's why Lee breathed a sigh of relief every time we showed up. He walked around and kept an eye on his bushes, looked at the blossoms, probably wishing they could pollinate themselves, that he wasn't so damn dependent on a sweaty farmer from another state and his equally sweaty men.

We were supposed to be here for three weeks. Lee paid $80 a hive. An expense that stung, for sure, but I knew of many who charged more. Gareth, for instance. I was cheap compared to Gareth.

Besides, Lee also really got his money's worth. In every hive fifty thousand bees worked from sunrise until it was dark. Happy bees. Every single hive buzzing with health. He'd never had anything to complain about. I'd been at his place every spring since he took over the farm and the bees produced a lot of berries, every single year.

Lee almost stormed towards me when I got out of the car, sharp angles of his arms and legs, giant shoes against the ground, trousers a bit too short and a dirty cotton sun hat on his head, held out a slim hand and took mine, shook it and didn't let go, as if he wanted to hold me in place and make sure I hadn't left before the bees and I had done the job.

His hand was thinner than I remembered. His hair, too.

I smiled at his long horse face. "Look at you. Even more wrinkles."

He smiled back. "Not as many as you."

Actually, Maine was way too far for us, I should have found something closer to home. But Lee had become kind of a friend over the course of all these years, I made the trip just as much because of him. We talked a lot while I was here. He probed away, asking questions. About the bees, about our operation. Never tired of it. I teased Lee about being a university farmer. After many years of education and with great enthusiasm he bought a broken-down wreck of a farm in the 1990s. Started out with strong opinions about everything that worked in theory. Had to be organic. Yes, sir. Since then he'd no doubt made every mistake in the book and some not in the book, too. Practice turned out to be something else entirely. The last few years he'd completely reorganized everything. Now he ran a standard farm — the huge spraying machines rolled around in these fields, too. I'd probably do the same thing if I were him.

I nodded towards Tom, who was standing a few feet behind me.

"You remember Tom."

Tom stepped forward, obediently reaching out his hand.

"Well, look at that," Lee said. "You're twice as big as last time."

Tom laughed politely.

"So you came along this year."

"Looks like it."

"What about school?"

"Got time off."

"This is school, too," I said.

Kenny's vehicles rolled away. It grew quiet. We were done putting out the hives. Only Lee, Tom and I were left. Tom was in the car. Reading, or sleeping, maybe. It'd been hard to get anything out of him again the last few hours. But he worked hard today, too, when he was asked. I had to give him that.

Lee took off his gloves, pulled up the veil and lit a cigarette.

"There. Nothing to do now but wait. I've checked the weather. It looks good," he said.

"Good."

"A few showers in the long-term forecast, but not much."

"We can take a little rain."

"And I've put up new fences, too."

"Great."

"That should keep them away."

"We'll count on that."

We fell silent again. I was unable to get rid of the image of huge bear paws tearing the hives to pieces.

"Anyway, they're your expenses," I said.

"Thanks. I know."

He inhaled heavily.

"So he's going to take over?" He nodded towards Tom, who was sitting in the car.

"That's the idea."

"Does he want to?"

"He's getting there."

"Does he need college, then? Can't he just get started?"

"You went to college."

"That's what I mean."

He looked at me with a crooked smile.

The bees are calm the first couple of days in a new place, staying mostly indoors, at home. After a while, they take short trips out of the hives, check out the conditions and get to know the place. And slowly the trips get longer and longer.

On the third day they were really up and running, buzzing away on all sides. Lee sat among the bushes, fifty or sixty yards away.

Head bowed. He was counting, didn't see me.

I snuck up on him.

"Boo!"

He was so startled that he jumped. "Ah shit!"

I laughed.

He threw his arms up in defeat. "You interrupted me!"

"Relax, I'll give you a hand."

"I don't trust that counting of yours. You're not objective."

I squatted down next to him.

"You're chasing them away." He smiled. "There's no room for bees here anymore."

"Fine, fine."

I got up, walked ten yards away, tried to pick out an area of about three square feet.

Looked around.

Oh yeah, they were here.

A bee had just flown away from a flower. Another came to rest simultaneously. And by gosh, a third one, too.

"How's it going?" I looked up.

"So-so. Two here. And you?"

"Three."

"Sure about that?" he asked. "You're just making up bees."

"You're the one who's bad at counting," I said.

He sat there awhile.

"Fine. Here are some more."

I stood up, smiled at him. 2.5 bees per square yard is good pollination. That's why Lee often sat like this and counted, almost like he was obsessed. Because the number of bees per square yard determined the amount of berries he could pick when summer was over.

Two for him. Three for me. It was going to work out.

But then came the rain.

WILLIAM

It was finally here. Conolly jumped from the coachman's seat and over into the wagon; there it was, new and bright against the dirty, scratched wagon floor. I stepped up to him, reached out my hand, and touched it, the hive. The woodworking was soft and smooth beneath my fingers, polished with the finest artistry, the roof carved out of wooden boards, almost seamlessly joined and the doors had been given small doorknobs. I stroked them with my hand, not a trace of a splinter to be found. I opened one of them; it slid open without a sound, and peeked in. The frames hung in straight rows, ready to be filled. The hive had a strong scent of fresh woodwork; the smell enveloped me, almost made me dizzy. I walked around it. The detailing work was impressive, every corner perfectly rounded, he had even gone so far as to add some beautiful carvings on the one side. Yes, all of the words of praise I had heard about Conolly were true. He had really delivered a marvelous piece of handiwork.

"So?" Conolly smiled proudly like a child. "Satisfied?"

I couldn't even answer, merely nodded and hoped he noticed how broadly I was smiling.

Together we lifted the hive onto the dusty courtyard.

It was so bright and clean, it felt almost sacrilege to put it down on the dirty ground.

"Where do you want it?" Conolly asked.

"There."

I pointed towards the aspen.

"Do you already have bees?" he asked.

"They're going to move into this one. When we've built more, we'll breed them.

He assessed me with his eyes.

"When *you* have built more," I corrected myself, and attempted a smile.

"But that is the only thing I'm going to take credit for," he said with a grin.

Then he turned towards the straw hive down there. Thousands of bees were buzzing around it, hard at work. At the same moment, one of them zipped straight towards us. Conolly jumped away.

"I believe you'll have to carry it there yourself."

"They're not dangerous."

"You want me to believe that."

He took another step away, as if to emphasize his point. I gave him a little smile, tried to seem both understanding and indulgent at the same time.

"Then you will be spared," I said.

Together we lifted the hive onto a wheelbarrow and bid each other farewell for the time being. But we both assumed that we would be seeing each other again soon.

And the hive was waiting for me. It was ready.

It was with considerably greater gravity that I dressed in the white suit today, the hat, the gloves, the veil; as ceremoniously as a bride I hung it over my face before I pushed the wheelbarrow down through the garden. A path of flattened grass had formed on the way to the hive, like a narrow church aisle, it suddenly occurred to me. I had to chuckle at the thought of myself as the bride-to-be, on the way to the altar, flushed with excitement. That's how important this day was for me; it sealed my fate.

I pushed the old hive a bit and set the new hive in its place. Then I stood there looking at it. The golden material shone in the sun. The old straw hive was faded and bedraggled in comparison.

Carefully, with slow movements, I started the work of moving the bees. I found the queen and put her in the new hive; she quickly made herself at home. The others followed her lead.

My calmness infected them. I felt completely safe, so safe that I removed my gloves and worked with bare hands. The bees accepted it; they could be controlled, tamed.

I looked forward to all the hours I would be spending out here, just the bees and I in undisturbed tranquility, shared contemplation, with an increasing bond of mutual trust.

But then something happened. I felt something along my shin, the quick movement of wings beating, then a stinging pain.

I jumped, and a high, female shriek escaped me. Luckily nobody heard me. My hand went instinctively towards my shin to slay what was hiding there.

I shook the leg of my trousers. The bee fell out and onto its back in the grass, with a furry torso and a lustrous tail section, the skinny insect legs sprawling helplessly in the air.

My shin stung fiercely. To think something so small could cause such severe pain. Step on it, I wanted to step on it, squash it, even though it was already dead. But one glance towards the hive, towards all of its sisters, kept me from doing so. You could never be certain.

I hastened to shove my trouser leg down into my boots, pulled on my gloves, made sure to batten down all the hatches, and then, with swift hands and firm shoulders, continued working. Perhaps I couldn't trust them yet; I hadn't really given them many reasons to trust me. But with time, the trust would come. I was convinced of that. I would not give them any reason to sting me, and one day we would be as one.

Finally, many arduous minutes later, the bees were in place.

I took one step back to observe them. They were the judges, at the end of the day; they were the ones who determined whether the hive would be their home. Many were still whirring around the old straw hive, homeless, in search of the queen. I lifted it onto the wheelbarrow. It was to be taken away to be burned, and then I would finally find out whether I had succeeded.

TAO

Sweaters, trousers, underwear. For how many days? A week? Two?

I packed everything I had room for. I'd taken out a beat-up bag of my father's; now I was throwing clothes into it quickly, with the urgency of someone who has already waited too long.

When I came home again after I'd been behind the white fence, it was impossible to go to bed. I trotted back and forth across the floor. Not because I was restless, but because I was finally on my way. I wouldn't have to stay here and wait, hoping for the one phone call that would explain everything, wait and fret over the two simple words I had never said to Kuan. Those two little words: *forgive me.* I was unable to. Because if I said forgive me, it was true. Then I was to blame.

This was the only thing I could do.

I closed the bag. The zipper made a loud

rasping noise. The sound must have covered up his footsteps, because when I turned around, he was there. Blinking his eyes a little, rumpled, barely awake.

"I'm going to Beijing."

"What?"

His jaw dropped. Perhaps because of what I said, perhaps because I didn't ask him to come with me. At that moment it hit me that I should have said we. *We're* going. But it had never occurred to me that he'd come along.

"But how . . . ?"

"I have to find him."

"You have no idea where he is. Which hospital he's in."

"I have to go."

"But Beijing . . . Where will you start?"

He was so thin. Sharp shadows. Thinner than ever before. Far too gaunt.

"I found addresses. I have to search the hospitals."

His voice rose: "Alone? But is the city safe?"

"It's our son."

The words sounded unreasonably harsh. I lifted the bag down onto the floor without looking at him anymore. Noticed only how he stood uneasily behind me, the words as if stuck inside him. Was he thinking about offering to come along?

"But how will you pay for it? The ticket, hotel?"

My hands stopped in midair. I knew it had to come, the question of money.

"I'll just take a little," I said softly.

He walked quickly to the kitchen cupboard, opened it, searching. His face hardened as he turned to face me. Suddenly there was something cold in his eyes. With an abrupt movement he tore the bag out of my hands, opened it and looked straight at the tin that lay on top.

"No." It came out loudly, with a force I seldom heard from him.

He dropped the bag with a thud on the floor and took one step towards me.

"You won't find him, Tao," he said. "You'll spend everything we have, but you won't find him."

"I won't spend it all. I said I won't spend it all."

I took out yet another sweater, even though I didn't need any others. Started to fold it. Tried to work calmly. The synthetic material rustled between my fingers.

"I have to try." I looked down at the floor. Tried not to look at the bag, which I wanted to snatch up. Fixed my gaze on a crack; Wei-Wen had dropped a toy there once last winter, a yellow wooden horse. I was angry when it happened, we didn't have many toys. And he screamed, because his horse broke, one of the legs snapped off.

"But if the money disappears . . . We've been saving for three years. We'll be too old. If the money disappears, we . . ."

He didn't finish, just stood there. The bag between us, the tin box on top of it.

"It won't help," he said finally. "Going there won't help."

"As if sitting here does."

He didn't answer, perhaps didn't want to contradict my accusation. Just stood there, unable to speak of what he was carrying, what was troubling him — not just that Wei-Wen was gone, lost to us, but that it was my fault. And now I was going to take away from him the chance for another child, too.

I looked away, couldn't look at him, couldn't think about it. *My fault. My fault.* No. I knew that wasn't right. The fault was just as much his. We could have just stayed home that day. Stayed home with the numbers, the books. He was the one who had wanted to go out. He was just as much to blame. We were both at fault.

"Come with me."

He didn't answer.

"You can come with me, we can go together."

I ventured a look at him. Was he furious? His eyes met mine. No. Just infinitely sad.

Then he shook his head feebly.

"It's better if I stay here. Available. Besides, it will be more expensive if there are two of us."

"I won't spend all of it," I said softly. "I promise I won't spend all of it."

Quickly I pulled the bag towards me. Tossed the sweater on top so it covered the box. Then I pulled the zipper closed. He didn't stop me.

I carried the bag out into the hallway and found my jacket. He followed me.

"Do you have to leave right away?"

"The train only leaves once a day."

We stood there. His gaze lingered on me. Did he expect me to say it now? Would that make everything easier? If I shouted it?

I was incapable. Because the moment I asked him for forgiveness, I would have to take in precisely this: that if he'd had his way, we wouldn't have been standing here now. We wouldn't have been out there that day, and Wei-Wen would still . . .

I put on my jacket. My shoes. Then I picked up the bag and walked towards the door.

"Bye, then."

He took a step forward. Was he going to tear the bag away from me? No. He wanted to give me a hug. I turned away, put my hand on the doorknob, couldn't bear his body against mine. Couldn't bear his cheek against my own, his lips against my throat, that he might awaken the same feelings as before, against my will. Or maybe *that* would stir up the nausea in me as well. And even more . . . would I stir up the same feeling in him? Would he still want me? I didn't know and didn't want to know.

I didn't breathe easily again until I'd found my seat, sat down and felt the chair beneath me. I rested my spine against the seat's worn plastic. I lay my head back and found the headrest. I stayed seated like that, watching the houses, the people, the trees and the fields outside. They didn't concern me. The train slid through the landscape so quickly that the trees we passed became mere shadows. The 1,800 kilometers were supposed to be behind us by evening, according to the timetable, but that depended on the number of checkpoints along the way.

My own world vanished behind me. The landscape changed, gradually, as we eventually got further north and higher up. From the mild fruit orchards of my home district, the tree-covered hills, the terraced gardens, to the wide flatlands of rice fields, and further, as the train climbed upwards into the mountains, to more barren, more fallow areas. When we came down again, a deserted landscape met me. Dry, barren, almost no trees. Mile after mile of the same monotony. I turned my face away from the window, there was nothing to see.

I had been in Beijing only once before, when I was little. My parents had friends there. We went to visit them. I remember only some images. A large and lively street, dusty, intense. Deafening noise, people everywhere, many more than I'd ever seen before. And the train trip, I remembered it well, exactly the same as now. The train, too. The technology hadn't changed throughout my entire lifetime. Nobody had time for innovation anymore.

I nodded off. Dozed in and out of dreams that resembled one another, that I came to Beijing and searched, that I found someone who would lead me to him. On one occasion it was a hotel employee. He knew where Wei-Wen was, he said, and took me through narrow alleyways and busy streets. We ran, him first, me behind him. I bumped into people all the time, almost lost sight of him. I caught him, but he tore loose. I woke up out of breath. The next time I fell asleep, it was a woman in a store. The same thing happened. She said she would bring me to him. She led me out into the jungle of streets, where the skyscrapers blocked the sun and the street vendors kept trying to stop us. She ran so fast that I lost sight of her, and sobbing, I had to stop and realize that my only chance to see him again was gone.

And then I was immediately somewhere else. A garden party. A dream, a memory? I was wearing a summer dress, it was hot. I was a child and attending an end-of-term party. We ate cakes, dry cakes made with artificial low-fat lard and an egg substitute. And a watery Popsicle, artificial, but good nonetheless. I was sweaty; the ice slid coolly down my throat.

Some of the girls were doing a circle dance, the sound of their singing rose through the garden, growing louder and louder, some voices clear and pure, others a little off-beat and off-key, the way children often sing. I stood quietly in the shade and observed them.

The cake table was being emptied. Some children went to take an extra serving. Daiyu was one of them. She was wearing a light blue jumpsuit with short trouser legs, and her hair was put up with clips. Her shoes were tight and shone brightly in the sun; they looked hot. She stood at the cake table and took a piece. Put a piece of cake on her plate. One of the very biggest. Then she found a fork and went to sit with the parents.

Another child came forward to the table. A boy. Wei-Wen. My Wei-Wen. What was he doing here? He took a piece of cake as well. A big piece, even bigger than Daiyu's.

And then he left.

No, I thought, not the cake. Don't take it.

But he slipped away from me, always with the cake in his hand, slipped away among the people, then he appeared again. I had to reach him before he took a bite. He must not eat any of the cake. Must not. I was an adult now, following after him, jogging, clearing the way in front of me, caught a glimpse of him anew, but then he dis-appeared again, turned up, disappeared. The party grew around me, there were more and more people.

His red scarf in the crowd, a patch, in the distance.

And yet again he slipped away.

I was awakened by the train driving into a large, dark and run-down railway station. Beijing.

301

GEORGE

We were in the motel room. The walls of
the room were a pale yellow and the wall-
to-wall carpeting was stained. We sat there
immersed in the smell of mothballs and
mildew.

Outside the window was a wall of water.
Not the kind of light, cozy rain shower that
left behind a sweet fragrance and twittering
birds. No. This was rainy weather of biblical
proportions, as it's called. Even on the fifth
day. I began to wonder whether there was
somebody out there who had it in for me, if
maybe I should be building an ark.

Tom was leaving the next day. He had his
nose in a book, highlighting with a neon-
yellow marker. The sound of the marker was
the only sound in the room. Over and over.
You'd think he needed to highlight every
single word in the book.

There was nowhere to go. The room had
seemed large when we got it, I'd asked for a

suite, since both of us were staying here, but it had shrunk dramatically over the past few days. Just one window and a view of the back alley. The two queen-size beds took up way too much space. I sat on one of them, the one closest to the wall, the bedspread with a large floral pattern rolled up underneath me. I was already tired of looking at the two pictures on the wall, a field of flowers and a lady in one, a boat in the other, the glass not quite clean, plenty of fingerprints in the middle of the lady's face. Tom had taken the group of chairs by the window. His books covered the entire table, and next to him was his bag full of things for school.

Come to think of it, he'd been sitting like that most of the time. Not that there was much of anything else to do, but still. There wasn't a trace of interest. Not in the bees, not in the rain, either. He could have allowed himself to get worked up — get irritated, yell, but he just read. Read and highlighted with fat neon-colored markers. Pink, yellow, green. It seemed as if he had a kind of system, because the markers were lined up in a tidy row in front of him on the table and he alternated between them.

I jumped when the telephone rang. I stood up. Lee's number lit up on the screen.

"Yes?"

"Anything new?"

"Not in the last half hour, no."

"I checked another weather report," Lee said. "They predicted good weather starting this afternoon."

"And the other five you checked?"

"More rain." His voice was flat.

"Guess there's some things we can't control," I said.

"Is there . . . ?" He hesitated. "Is there any chance you could stay a few more days?"

We'd been through this before, but he'd never asked so directly.

"I've booked the cars for the way back already. And the crew."

"Yes."

He didn't say anything else, knew that it wasn't possible.

"It'll let up soon," I said, trying to sound like my mother.

"Yes."

"And a day or two, give or take, won't make a big difference."

"No."

We were silent. Just heard the rain tumbling down out there, and car tires splashing through the puddles.

"I think I'll go out there now," he said

suddenly.

"Really?"

"Just to check."

"I was out there this morning. They're inside. Nothing's happening."

"No, but still."

"Do as you like, they're your bees."

He laughed softly, but there wasn't much joy to be heard in his laughter.

Then we hung up.

Tom looked up from his book.

"Why don't you just tell it like it is?"

"What do you mean?"

"It's obvious that this will have an impact on his crop."

"Yeah, well."

"He's an adult, he can handle hearing the truth."

He put the cap on the marker with a decided click. The click, the way he did it, made me itch inside. And his words — he expressed himself like a fifty-year-old professor.

"I thought you were studying," I said.

"I'm done now."

"Like you weren't listening to my phone calls."

"Jesus, Dad. We're ten feet away from each other."

"And how come you have so many opinions all of a sudden?"

"Excuse me?"

The itch was horrible. I couldn't sit still.

"Excuse me?" I mimicked. "After having loafed around for a week, you're suddenly getting involved?"

He stood up. He was taller than me.

"I haven't been loafing around. I've been working. Every time I've had the chance, I've been lifting and sweating more than you have. And you know it."

"But you didn't want to."

I took a step towards him. He backed up automatically, but maybe he noticed it himself, because all of a sudden he stood up straight and placed his feet soundly on the floor.

"I never claimed to be very interested. You were the one who asked me to come with you, remember?"

"Kind of hard to forget."

He fell silent. Just looked at me. A penny for his thoughts.

Then all of a sudden he came out with it: "Can you describe Jimmy and Rick for me, Dad?"

"Huh?"

"What are they like? Describe them for me."

"Jimmy and Rick? When did you get so

interested in them?"

"I'm not that interested in them. But if I ask you to describe them, you'd have a lot to say, right?"

I just looked at him.

"I know lots about them, too," he continued. "Just because I've heard you talk about them. And about Lee, too. I know what they like, what they do in their free time, even what they're afraid of. Because you've told me." His voice was gentler now, softer. "That Rick doesn't have a girlfriend, for instance. And Jimmy, I've heard enough about him to know that you actually wonder whether he's playing for the other team."

I was about to answer, say something about Jimmy, but didn't know exactly what to say. Because strictly speaking this had nothing to do with either Jimmy or Rick. I understood that Tom was going somewhere with all of this, but I didn't know where. It was as if he'd pushed my brain into a can and was shaking it hard.

"How would you describe me, then?" he asked.

"You?"

"Yes. What do I like? What am I good at? What am I afraid of?"

"You're my son," I said.

He sighed. Smiled, almost scornfully.

We just stood there looking at each other. The itchiness was getting intense.

Then his gaze broke away from mine. He walked towards the bag of books.

"If we're not going to do anything anyway, I'll get started on my history."

He picked up a thick, dark blue book. I could just make out Big Ben on the cover.

Then he sat down, turning the chair around so that the back faced me.

I wished I had a really thick book to read myself. And a chair to turn around. Or most of all a really smart comeback at the ready. But he'd gotten me now. I was speechless.

An hour passed, maybe an hour and a half, before the rain let up. The sky cleared up into something that wasn't exactly blue, but at least a little less intensely gray than what we'd seen the last few days. Lee's seventh weather report had clearly been onto something.

Tom finally put his book down. Got up and pulled on a jacket. "I'm going out for a walk."

"You can't take the car."

"No, that's fine."

"I might need it."

"I know. I won't take the car."

"Fine."

He was about to open the door when the

telephone rang again. It was Lee. He asked us to come right away.

TAO

I found a hotel that was open right by the railway station. Run-down and empty, but cheap. Across the street there was a restaurant that served simple, inexpensive food. I went in and treated myself to a hot meal today, knew that I couldn't afford one every day, at least not if the money was going to last for more than a week. And I had no idea how long I would have to stay here. Until I found him. I wasn't leaving until I found him.

A young boy put a plate down in front of me. Fried rice — that was all they had at this family-run place. It was the father who did the cooking, the boy told me while serving me. Nobody but the two of them worked here.

I was the only customer in the large restaurant. I hadn't seen many people on the street, either. Everything was different from what I remembered. The noisy, intense city was gone. Most of the houses were vacated now, the roads quiet. There was no basis for survival here anymore. I knew that many had been forced to move away to other parts of the country, where more hands were needed for agriculture, but the complete silence surprised me all the same. The city had grown and developed to a certain point, then everything had come to a halt, and was now deteriorating. Like an old person approaching death. More and more alone, more and more quiet, at a pace that slowed with every passing day. The only place with the lights on was the little restaurant right across the street from the hotel; otherwise the street was deserted.

I pulled the chair closer to the table. The sound of the legs against the floor sounded hollow and strident in the empty establishment. The waiter stood by the table waiting as I ate. He was young, no more than eighteen, and skinny. His hair was longish; it looked as if it had been a long time since his last haircut. He wore his uniform with a youthful negligence, and moved lightly and casually. In a schoolyard he would have been someone you'd want to be seen with. Someone who didn't need to try, someone whom nature had given that little something extra. He was the kind of adolescent who should have had a group of friends around him.

He noticed that I was observing him. Suddenly he didn't know what to do with his hands, and he stuck them quickly behind his back.

"Is the food to your liking?" he asked.

"Yes. Thank you."

"Sorry we don't have any of the dishes on the menu."

"That's fine. I wouldn't be able to afford them anyway," I said, smiling. He smiled back and seemed relieved; perhaps he understood that we were in the same situation.

"Is it usually so empty here?" I asked.

He nodded. "The past few years that's how it's been."

"What do you live on?"

He shrugged his shoulders. "Some people come in from time to time. And we've sold some of the utensils and equipment." He nodded towards the kitchen, where his father was doing the dishes. "All of the good knives, a meat grinder, some pots, the big stove. That will do for a while. We have worked out that we have enough money to manage until November."

He fell silent, thinking no doubt the same thing I was. What would they do after that?

"Why are you still here?" I said.

He started to wipe invisible dust off a table.

"When everyone we knew was forced to leave, we were allowed to stay because we run a restaurant with a long history. Father struggled for months to get permission." He rolled up the rag, squeezed it. "I remember how happy he was when he came home and had finally gotten confirmation that we didn't have to move. And wouldn't have to leave our home."

"But what about now?"

He looked away.

"Now it's too late. Now we're here."

He tugged a little at his bristly hair. Reminded me suddenly of Wei-Wen. He was so young, this boy, perhaps even younger that I'd first thought, just fourteen or fifteen years old. At the growing age.

I pushed the plate towards him.

"You take the rest. I've had enough."

"No." He looked at me in confusion. "You've paid for it."

"I'm full."

I handed him the chopsticks.

"Go ahead. Sit down."

He stole a glance at his father in the kitchen, but he wasn't paying attention to us out here. Then the boy quickly pulled out the chair, sat down and grabbed the chopsticks. As quickly as a dog, he ate the rice, like Wei-Wen when he had wolfed down the plums. But all of a sudden he stopped and looked up, as if embarrassed by my attention. I smiled at him in encouragement. He began eating again, clearly trying to slow down. I stood up to leave, wanting to leave him alone.

But then he stood up as well.

"Just sit," I said and walked towards the door.

"Yes." He stood there, hesitating. "No."

He came towards me.

I put my hand on the door handle and was about to open it. I looked at him, didn't quite understand.

"Where are you staying?" he asked.

"There." I pointed across the street at the hotel.

He came over to me, looked out at the street. Not a vehicle in sight, no people, no life of any kind.

"I'll stand here until you're inside."

"What?"

"I'll stand here, the whole time."

He spoke with a conscientious gravity on his young face.

"Thank you."

I opened the door and left. The street was

deserted. There was a smell of damp brick, dust and something slightly spoiled. A husk of a city. Dilapidated facades. There was a battered information screen hanging on a wall. The first ten seconds of a film played over and over. Li Xiara, the leader of the Committee, intoning about community and moderation, perhaps. The message was gone because the soundtrack had stopped working long ago but her moderated voice was ingrained in my head after all of these years. The shops were all closed and had bars in front of the doors. Broken windows. Only shades of brown and gray. No colors left, as if everything was covered by fog. And a huge, heavy silence.

I turned around when I'd crossed the street. Yes, he was still standing there. He nodded towards the hotel, as if he wanted me to hurry inside.

GEORGE

Lee was hanging over the hives trying to tidy up. Even though he was hidden by coveralls, a hat and veil, I could see he was upset. Four hives were turned upside down on the ground. A big cloud of bees, confused, homeless, angry, hovered above the hives in the humid air following the rain.

"Ouch!"

He suddenly screamed out loud, grabbed his neck.

"Watch out for the openings," I said and pushed his veil better into place. He could remove the dead bee later.

He cursed; I could see tears in his eyes. Maybe because of the sting, or maybe they'd been there all along.

"I thought the fence would be enough," he said quietly.

"Once it's got a whiff of honey, there's not much that can stop it."

That was when I first noticed Tom's

eyes on me.

"Didn't you say there weren't bears here anymore?"

I couldn't look him in the eyes, didn't want to hear that question. Picked up a box. Checked it out. No damage.

"Give me that." I pointed at a frame further away.

He walked over, kept looking at me. Picked up the frame and gave it to me. I noticed then that his hands were shaking. I looked up. His eyes were as big as they'd been the last time. Nothing of the professor left; in front of me was a little boy.

"Is it close by?" he said softly.

I accepted the frame and held his gaze.

"No, they take off immediately."

He stood there, watching me, his eyes doubtful.

I put my hand on him, something that I seldom did.

"Tom. This isn't like that time. This happens every year and I've never, not once, actually seen them. It's just the bees that take a beating, not us. And it's hardest for Lee, who has to pay for it."

He nodded, didn't pull away from my hand.

"That's why we're staying in a motel, right? Not in a tent," I said. He nodded again. I squeezed his shoulder. Mostly I wanted to hug him. For once, I could tell that he needed me. He still needed me. But just then Lee came back over.

"Three hives," he said. "That's $240?"

I let go of Tom and nodded to Lee. But I stopped when I saw the look of despair behind his veil. "Two hundred forty? No. Let's make it two hundred."

"But George . . ."

"Nothing more to talk about. You can consider it a loan."

Lee turned away, swallowed hard. But Tom kept looking at me. He didn't say anything, but his eyes said everything. And remembered everything.

It had happened the first time I'd been at Lee's place, the first time I'd ever been on a trip with the bees. We hadn't taken many hives with us, only the ones I had room for in the back of the pickup. I thought of it as an experiment, if the venture worked, I could expand and start with pollination on a small scale, mostly like a vacation. Because Tom, who was five, was going with me. Just the two of us, out in the middle of nature. Far away from people. Fishing, drinking water from the stream, a campfire burning. We'd been talking about it for weeks.

We found a hill a ways away from the

hives. There we had a good view, on all sides, the ground was nice and flat. I put up the tent, took my time, making sure to push all of the pegs deep into the ground, that the canvas was taut. This would be our home for three weeks, so it had to be done right.

Tom got the task of unrolling the sleeping bags. He, too, went to work diligently, arranging them to perfection. I guess he'd seen what Emma did when she made the beds at home. He was enthusiastic, talking up a storm, hadn't yet had the time to notice that he missed his mom. And anyway it would be fine, I thought. The two of us would have a fantastic time up here on the hill, the weeks would go by in a flash and be something he would remember for the rest of his life.

We lit a fire. Huddled together and toasted marshmallows. He shivered a little, so I held him close. His narrow shoulders almost disappeared under my arm. We looked at the stars, I pointed out the constellations I knew. That wasn't a lot — only the Big Dipper and Orion — so I made up a couple more.

"Can you see the snake there?"

"Where?"

"There."

His eyes followed my finger as I pointed out a suitably wavy line of stars. "Why is it called the snake?"

"It's not *called* the snake. It *is* a snake."

And then I told him about the snake. Usually I wasn't very good at making up stories, but now it poured out of me. Maybe because Tom was sitting there in the crook of my arm, maybe because we were so far away from everything like television and entertainment that the caveman inside of me suddenly emerged, or maybe knowing that this was gonna be our life for three whole weeks gave me special powers.

"The snake lived in a rock crevice outside a small village," I began, "and was such a devil, more evil than evil itself, hungrier than the hungriest. It ate everything, absolutely everything it could find. First it took the forest, then it took the crops. Then the kitchen gardens, the fruit, the vegetables, the berries, while it grew larger and larger. When it had eaten every single bush, every single tiny potato, yes, every single scruffy blade of grass in the field, it started eating people. Little kids for breakfast, grandmothers for lunch. It grew and grew; in the end it was so long and fat that it lay down in a circle around the village. And it lay there and gobbled up one person after the other.

People ran into their houses, hid in the closets, under the beds and in the basements. But the snake found them, wriggled its way into every nook and ate them one after the other."

I noticed that Tom was trembling in the crook of my arm and it wasn't just from the cold. I held him tighter; he huddled up against me, as if he wanted to get inside me, reveling in horror and joy.

"Nobody knew what to do, the people were powerless. *Now we're going to die,* they thought, *now we're going to be eaten.* Everyone hid the best they could. Everyone except for one little boy."

"Who was that?" His voice was low and excited.

"It was . . . It wasn't just any little boy."

"No?"

"He was actually a beekeeper."

"Oh," Tom said quickly, as if he were afraid to say anything else, afraid I would stop telling the story.

"He had a nice, big hive. With the best bee colony you've ever seen — loyal, hardworking, they never swarmed. The queen was living her third year, laying eggs like never before. And now he went out to the hive and opened it. And then he whispered inside and asked for their help."

I took a dramatic pause. I knew the ending now and was quite pleased with it.

Tom waited. I let him wait. Noticed his eyes on me, round as saucers with expectation. I wanted to let him hold on to that feeling for a bit.

Finally he couldn't take it anymore. "And then what?"

Slowly I continued.

"The bees listened, and the bees contemplated, while the hissing serpent drew closer to the boy." Tom looked at me with his mouth open. "And just as the snake was about to gobble up the little boy, the bees appeared! A gigantic swarm flew straight at the snake. And they stung and stung, on its head, on its throat, on its tail, in the eyes, they stung it everywhere, until the snake couldn't take anymore and crawled away as fast as it could."

All the muscles in Tom's body were still tense; he sat silent as the grave in the crook of my arm.

"And then everyone was saved?" he asked, almost inaudibly, afraid maybe to hear the answer.

I waited again, felt him tremble beneath me.

"Yes," I said.

Tom exhaled.

"But the bees weren't satisfied with that," I continued.

"They weren't?" He laughed a little now.

"They chased the snake further and further away."

"Until it was gone?"

"Yes, completely gone."

Finally Tom relaxed, his little body softened against my own.

"All the way up into the sky they chased it," I said. "And there you can see the snake. To this day."

Tom nodded, I could feel his head moving up and down against my arm.

"There it is," I said. "And there" — I pointed a distance away — "there you have the hives."

"There?"

"Yes, you see. There and there and there." I drew three squares in the sky.

"What about the bees?"

"The bees?" I thought about it and then the answer came and I felt pretty darn brilliant. "They are the rest of the stars."

This is how it's gonna be, I thought. *This is how we'll pass the time for three full weeks.* We went to bed and Tom fell asleep right away. I lay awake listening to his breath in the dark. He snored lightly, his nose was a little stuffed up. And he rolled over a few times in his sleeping bag before he settled down. And then I fell asleep, too.

But then the bear came. The first sound woke us up, a sharp bang when the pot over the fire fell to the ground. A hard shadow against the bees glittering in the sky. The sound of its paws trampling through the bushes, so close we could hear its fur bristling.

I hugged Tom, but my arm gave him no support now. His eyes were wide open, staring into the darkness.

We could hear the bear raiding the campsite. The plastic bag of marshmallows was torn to pieces. The wood I'd stacked so neatly was knocked over and we heard a hollow thumping against Styrofoam when its huge paws hit the cooler.

Then there was complete silence.

We just sat there. For a long time. I ruffled Tom's hair, hoped he would turn his face towards me, look at me, but he just kept staring in front of him, into space. What could I say? What would Emma say? I had no idea, so I didn't open my mouth. I pulled him even closer, but his body was stiff.

Finally I ventured outside.

The campsite was turned upside down. The marshmallows had been eaten, but the bear was gone.

It was only then that I dared to breathe properly.

I peeked into the tent.

"All clear."

But Tom didn't answer. Just sat there with that dark gaze, his mouth shut and his whole body immobilized. I picked him up and carried him to the car. The next day I put him on the bus home. There was no other option. Emma would meet him at the station. He didn't complain about having to make the long trip alone. Until then that would have been out of the question.

Her voice became stern when I told her what had happened. I knew what she was thinking, although she didn't say much more than yes and oh. *You should have checked better,* she thought, *you should have looked into it properly, you should have known there were bears in the area. Just a tent canvas between the two of you and death, luckier than you deserved.*

I saw his white face in the rear window when the bus drove away. The relief painted across his face, and his eyes, large and scared. He never came to Maine with me again.

Not until now.

The weather was still dry when we got into the car. Lee went his own way, said he was going home to send a letter of complaint about the electric fences.

Tom didn't say a single word on the way back. Maybe he was looking for the bear, expecting it to storm out into the road in front of the car, slam its paw on the hood and maul the car body in two, plucking us out as if we were mice in a hole.

Once we were in the motel room, he quickly began packing his things, swept up his markers, tossed the book with Big Ben on the cover into his bag. I watched him.

"There's no rush."

"Might as well finish up," he mumbled, again with his back to me.

It was only after he'd closed his bag that he looked at me. I'd sat down, pretended to be reading the newspaper.

He stood tall in the middle of the room, his hands dangling at his sides. He put them into his pockets, but took them out again. There was something in his eyes I couldn't put my finger on.

"Yes?" I said finally.

He didn't answer. Was definitely wrestling with something.

"All right, then." I leaned over the newspaper again, tipped my head a little to the side, made a face, as if what I was reading was of particular interest.

"Why do you do it?" he asked suddenly.

I looked up.

"What? Do what?"

"Why do you drag them around with you like this?"

"Huh?"

"The bees." He drew a breath. "You just lost three hives. Three bee colonies lost their homes." His voice rose, his eyes widened, he crossed his arms over his chest as if he had to hang on to himself. "And just the business of carrying them back and forth in trucks. Do you really know what that does to them?"

The extreme seriousness in his young body. It was too much, made me want to laugh. And that's just what I did. A grin spread across my lips, a coughing sound escaped my throat, but the laughter didn't come out as genuine as I'd expected.

"Don't you like blueberries?" I asked.

Something in him wavered. "Blueberries?"

I tried to hold my head high, preserve the grin, protect myself behind it. "There wouldn't be many blueberries in Maine without bees."

He swallowed. "I know that, Dad. But why are you taking part in the whole system? Farming, the way it's become . . ."

I folded up the newspaper with broad gestures. Laid it on the table. Tried to keep my voice calm, not yell.

"If you were Gareth's son, I could understand what you're talking about. But I don't operate the way *he* does."

"I thought you wanted to be like him?"

"Be like Gareth?"

"I know you want to expand."

He said it simply, not like a question. Not an accusation, although that's what it was.

I laughed again. A hollow laugh. "And I've signed us up for the golf club. And invested in a brass manufacturer."

"What?"

"No. Nothing."

He sighed from his stomach. Then he turned his gaze away from me, towards the window. The weather was still good out there.

"Think I'll take that walk now," he said without giving me another look.

Then he left.

My entire plan walked out the banged-up door of the motel room.

WILLIAM

"But, where is he?"

Thilda and all the girls were lined up in front of me in the kitchen. Now they would finally see what I had been working on. I planned to lead them down to the hive, but keep them far enough away so they wouldn't be stung. I would subsequently open it with care and explain it all to them. So that they, so that Edmund, would understand the kind of invention that would come to change our lives. That would bring us honor, put our name in the history books.

The sun was hovering just above the far edge of the fields behind the garden, where it fought with the horizon and a few gloomy clouds that had gathered in the west. Before long it would inexorably set, and perhaps it would rain tonight. I wanted to show my family the hive at this moment, as the sun was going down, because this was when the bees were gathered inside.

"He left word he wouldn't be home for supper," Thilda said.

"Well, then, why not?"

"I didn't ask."

"But you did tell him I had something to show you all today?"

"He's a young man with his own life. Who knows where he might be."

"He should be here!"

"He's exhausted," Thilda said. She talked about him as if he were still an infant, with a soft, whimpering voice, even though he wasn't even present.

"And how will he manage in the autumn, do you think, if he's unable to fulfill his obligations?"

She waited a long time before answering. Thinking, sniffling.

"Does he need to?"

"I beg your pardon?"

"I think it's sensible for him to wait another year. Live at home, have a proper rest."

Her nostrils flared as she spoke; it nauseated me and I turned away.

"Find him," I said, without looking at her.

Eight pairs of eyes stared at me, but none of the family members showed the slightest sign of moving an inch.

"Go find him!" Finally someone understood who the head of the family was. She took a step back towards the door and lifted her bonnet from a peg. "I'll go."

Charlotte.

We waited in the kitchen while the darkness spread from the corners and enveloped us. Nobody lit any lamps. Every time one of the young girls said something, Thilda hushed them. I caught a glimpse of the sky through a window. The clouds had long since crowded out the sun, but soon one would not even see them, because the darkness swallowed the outlines. Soon we were blinded by the night and it was too late to show them anything.

Where was he?

I walked outside, remained standing on the doorstep. A humid low-pressure system had descended upon the landscape. The air was sticky and close, without a single breath of wind. Everything was silent. The bees had retreated into the hive now, and I could no longer hear them.

Where was he all the time? What could be more important than what I was about to show him?

Thilda concealed a yawn when I came inside again. Georgiana had fallen asleep with her head in Dorothea's lap; the twins leaned against one another, their eyelids drooping.

It was far too late for them. They should have been in bed a long time ago.

Suddenly I didn't know what to do with myself and took two steps to the side. On the table was a mug; I picked it up and poured myself some water. I became aware of a hollow sensation in my abdomen, a faint rumbling accumulating. Quickly I pulled the chair away from the table, hoped the scraping sound would distract their attention from my stomach. Then I sat down, put both hands over my midriff, leaned a bit forward and the rumbling remained inside of me.

Suddenly the door opened.

I stood up quickly.

Charlotte came first. She stared at the floor.

And a dark figure followed behind her. Edmund. She had found him.

"But sweetheart!" Thilda quickly got to her feet.

He was dripping. He took a few unsteady steps across the floor. His hair and clothing were wet, but his trousers were dry, as if somebody had thrown water at him.

"Charlotte?" Thilda said.

"Edmund, he . . ."

"I fell into the brook," Edmund said slowly.

Then he staggered past us.

I took a step forward and lay a hand on his shoulder, perhaps it was still not too late to take him with me outdoors, show him and make him understand.

But now I could feel how he was shaking beneath his wet clothes and noticed that his teeth were chattering in his mouth.

"Edmund?"

"I have to sleep," he murmured without turning around.

Then he squirmed out of my grasp and with shuffling steps he walked towards the stairs to the second floor.

Thilda skipped after him; her feet sounded like hen's claws against the floor, the chattering, like nervous clucking. "My dear boy. Come, I'll help you. Look here, walk carefully. Your bed is turned down. Take my arm . . . like that, yes. Like that."

His heavy back disappeared up the stairs. I looked down at my hand, it was still damp from having held on to him, and I rubbed it quickly against my trouser leg.

The melancholy that had attacked me so brutally, could it be that it also resided in my son? From my bloodstream to his? Hereditary? Perhaps that was why he never let me in?

My chest tightened. No, not him. Not Edmund.

All of a sudden I became aware of the children; the girls stood in a circle around me. Silent, swaying with drowsiness. Looking at me, awaiting my next move. All except for Charlotte. She did not meet my gaze, but she, too, was pale from lack of sleep.

I drew a breath. "Tomorrow," I said to them softly. "It will have to wait until tomorrow."

TAO

"Do you know how to get there?"

I stood in the hotel's worn, nondescript lobby and pointed at the map I had unfolded. The hospital was one of the last on the list. I had worked my way down, crossing out, eliminating one by one.

"There used to be a subway line from here to here," the receptionist said and pointed, "so you could change there." She put her finger on the map, not far from the creased edge of a fold.

She was a tall, erect woman, who laughed surprisingly loud and long every time the opportunity presented itself. She was always at work. The others had been relocated, she explained. Now she clung to the hotel, which paid less and less, to provide food for herself and her daughter. The ten-year-old came by every day after school and did her homework in the lobby. It was the only way that mother and daughter could see one another.

"But that's the part of the subway system the City Council recommends that one should no longer use," she continued.

I looked at her inquisitively.

"The areas are rough. Occupied. No. *Occupied* is not the word. But those who still live there have nothing. And nobody controls them anymore," she said.

"What kind of people are they?"

"The ones who don't want to move. The ones who were left behind. The ones who hid. It happened so fast and afterwards, if you had regrets, you were told that it was already too late."

She swallowed and looked away. Perhaps the same was true for her as for the boy and his father in the restaurant. But I couldn't ask, I couldn't cope with yet another of these stories.

I just wanted to get going, search, as I'd done every single day since I'd arrived here. He had to be somewhere. Every morning I went out at daybreak, with money and a few dry biscuits wrapped in paper in my purse. Every day I visited a new neighborhood, a new hospital. Many of them I had contacted ahead of time, called both from home and from the hotel. I had the names of units, the names of doctors. Now I sought out the same people, thought that if they knew something, it would be harder to brush me off if I showed up in person, when they saw me, saw the mother, face-to-face. Some of them remembered me and felt bad for me. Some even dared to look me in the eyes and say that they understood my desperation.

But the message was the same everywhere. They couldn't find any record of him. They had never heard of Wei-Wen. And I was referred elsewhere again and again, to other hospitals. *Have you tried in Fengtai, have you tried the Central Hospital in Chaoyang, have you been to the Haidian Center for Respiratory Ailments?*

I always asked to speak with a supervisor, seldom gave up with the first person they referred me to. And then I waited. Entire days. Sitting, standing, wandering. By windows, in dark rooms, across cold stone floors, in cheerlessly lit rooms, with a glass of water in my hand, a cup of tea from the vending machine, usually alone, sometimes in drafty waiting rooms. It was never crowded, never busy, nonetheless it seemed as though I was continually bumped down on a list; often I didn't speak to the right person until it approached closing time. Sometimes I encountered rolling eyes: *can't she give up, there are many desperate people, many ill, undernourished, a single child, she has to calm down, understand that we don't have time.* But I stayed. Did nothing, was simply visible, until I got my way.

On several occasions the waiting led me all the way to the director's office. Large rooms with heavy furniture, rooms which had once been elegant, but which now spoke of deterioration. I presented my business, got them talking, experienced compassion. Some of them double-checked, called others. They actually tried. But nobody was able to help. Wei-Wen was gone.

In the beginning I called Kuan every evening. But the words between us were few. I let him know that I hadn't come any closer. He informed me that he hadn't heard anything, either. Businesslike and more terse with every passing evening. And then he asked about the money, how much I had spent, how much was left. I lied. I couldn't tell him that the train ticket here alone had cost 5,500 yuan. One evening I didn't call. He didn't call me, either. We both knew that neither of us had anything to report. An unspoken agreement had been formed that the one who learned something first would be in touch.

At night I slept heavily and without

dreaming, as if somebody had laid a black carpet over my consciousness as soon as my head hit the pillow. Knowing there was nothing more I could do gave me equilibrium. I was certain I'd find him in the end. I simply mustn't give up. But as the days passed, it became harder to believe. The further down I got on the list, the more uneasy I became. Because I still hadn't found Wei-Wen, no trace of him. And the money had disappeared more quickly than I had planned; the tin box had become far too light. I didn't have more than 7,000 yuan left. It could still be enough, if we were really thrifty during the last two years before the age limit. But I still hadn't bought the train ticket home.

"It's been a long time since I've heard anything from that area," the receptionist said quietly. "Perhaps it's completely deserted now. Regardless, we have been advised to stay away."

"But the hospital?"

"It's on the border." She pointed. "The uncontrolled areas start here. Further south you can still travel. But are you certain that you have to go there?"

I nodded.

She held my gaze and understood. She knew I was searching for my son, but I hadn't told her more than that. Although, that was probably enough. Everyone who has children of their own understands that it's enough, enough so any danger to which you might potentially expose yourself comes second.

I craned my neck to look at the roof. Red tiles, worn by the wind and the weather, at one time they had no doubt been shiny, glazed, like the roof of a temple. The walls were gray, and the paint was peeling off. A faint buzzing noise in the sky got my attention, there was something moving through the air. I squinted to look at it more closely, but it disappeared behind the roof.

Above me lay an impenetrable gray sky. The sun had been out when I left the hotel, but here it was foggy. As if it were already getting dark.

The trip had taken four hours. It involved three changes and was a long detour, but went through what the receptionist had called secure areas. Still, everything was so quiet and run-down that I repeatedly caught myself being suspicious of the few travelers I met, and threw anxious glances over my shoulder.

I had tried to contact this hospital several times, but the answer was the same as everywhere else. They had never heard Wei-

Wen's name, couldn't help me. And the last times I had called them they hadn't answered. Only an automatic message greeted me on the other end, a voice-mail system that never led anywhere.

A centerpiece of dead plants was the first thing I saw. A dim light from a lamp confirmed that the hospital still had electricity. The huge lobby was empty. A counter of dark wood loomed before me. I found an old check-in machine for family members, it had to be from the time before The Collapse. It flickered beneath my fingers, but soon went black.

Aimlessly I started walking. First to the right, but I met a locked door.

To the left I found a lift. I tried the different buttons, but nothing happened. I kept going. Endless, dark corridors lay in front of me.

I tried several doors, but they were all locked.

Finally I found one that led to a dark stairway. I walked up a flight. The door there was locked. I tried another one. It, too, was locked. It wasn't until the third floor I found an open door. It led into a corridor, just as deserted as the others. I walked a few meters. My steps sounded like dull thuds against the stone floor.

I stopped by a window. That's when I discovered it. In one of the hospital's side wings there were lights on. I continued in that direction, hoping the corridor I was walking down connected the wings so I could go there directly.

Suddenly I heard a sound in front of me, of hollow metal being dragged across linoleum.

"Hello?" I said softly.

A door was open ahead of me, a double glass door.

I became abruptly aware of my heart, it was pounding hard. Something was wrong. Perhaps I should get out of there, get to the light way over there in the side wing. But I had to get past the doors. I began walking faster.

Yet another sound. Tottering steps.

Then a figure came into view in front of me. The first thing I saw was the bare feet. Unclipped toenails on wrinkled toes. She — because it had to be a woman — barely managed to make her way forward, supporting herself on a walker with a bag of intravenous medicine. It was the walker that made the sound. But the bag was empty. Her gray hair was growing in clumps, her scalp peeling off in large flakes. All she was wearing was a hospital gown. It was stained;

under it I could see the outline of a diaper and it was only then that I noticed the smell.

She stared at me, as if unable to recall any words.

I backed up, wanted to get away.

She hissed, tried again, wanted to say something.

I pulled myself together, took a breath, I couldn't abandon her.

I took a few steps towards her. She swayed a bit, looked as if she were about to collapse.

"Ll . . . loo . . . ," she said faintly. "Look." She swayed. I grabbed her by the elbow to support her. The stench stung in my nose; her arm was as thin as a child's. She wanted to bring me back to the room she had come from.

I pushed at the door. It slid open silently and we went in. I tried to support her the whole time. Nausea churned inside me, the stench was like a thick mass, impenetrable. It hit me and sucked the air out of me.

A room. Along the walls there were beds, shiny hospital beds of steel rods, side by side, all made up with bedding that had once been white. I didn't have time to count them, but there must have been more than a hundred.

There were people lying in the beds. Some

of them were elderly, many quite old, a few extremely old people. Awake, whimpering, clamoring, moaning, hands waving in the air. And a few lay with their eyes shut, as if they were sleeping.

My arrival caused several of them to get out of bed. They were skinny, so dreadfully skinny and just as unkempt as the woman I'd entered with. Now they clambered onto their feet and started coming towards me.

Twenty or so old people fought against their own bodies, fought against gravity and made their way forward, some so unstable that they had to crawl. All of them repeated the same words. *Help. Help me. Help us.* Over and over again.

But those who were sleeping just lay there, despite the noise, despite the cries of the others. It was only then I understood that it wasn't sleep that chained them to the beds. It was death.

I turned around then and ran.

I shouted. Screamed without words. Tried to summon somebody's attention, but nobody answered.

I continued in the darkness. To the other wing, where there were lights.

The only sound was of my footsteps against the linoleum, my own breathing.

I rounded a corner and finally saw the

rooms with the lights on. I ran towards the door. Threw it open with a bang. A woman dressed in white, a doctor or a nurse, looked at me in surprise. She was in the process of packing bedding in a box.

"Who are you?"

Only then did I notice I was crying.

I rubbed my eyes, tried to explain, but the words got all mixed up.

"Look here, sit down." She wanted to help me down onto a chair.

"No, no. The old people . . . they need help."

She looked away. Resumed folding the sheets.

I pulled at her arm.

"I have to show you. Come!"

She squirmed carefully out of my grasp. Didn't look at me.

"We know about them," she said calmly.

I put my hand on her again. "But they're sick. Some of them . . . I think they're dead."

She jerked away.

"We can't take them with us."

"What do you mean?"

"We're evacuating the hospital. It's not safe here. We're taking the patients to a hospital further south, in Fangshan. There are so few of us, we can't manage any longer. The supplies don't make it here, nobody wants to work here."

"But the old people?"

"They're dead."

"No. I saw them. They're alive!"

"They'll die soon." She met my gaze, straightened her neck, as if she wanted to harden herself.

I stood there. "No!"

She put a hand on my arm.

"Sit down."

She went over to the sink, was going to fill a glass with water, but the faucet coughed. She gave up and walked towards the hallway.

"Wait here."

Shortly afterwards she returned with a glass of lukewarm water.

I accepted it. The glass was something to hold on to. I clung to it.

She sat down with me.

"Are you a family member?" she asked mildly.

"Yes. No. I don't know. I mean . . . Not of anybody here."

She looked at me in astonishment.

"I'm looking for my son," I said.

She nodded. "You're right. He's not here. The last patients were moved earlier today. Now all that's left is equipment."

"And the old people?"

She didn't reply, just stood up abruptly.

"The old people?" I said again.

"We can't help them." Her voice was flat, and she took hold of the trolley without looking at me. "I must ask you to leave."

Nausea surged up inside of me.

"Are they just going to stay here?"

She turned her head away.

"Leave now."

"No!"

Finally she lifted her gaze. Her eyes were pleading.

"Go. And forget what you've seen."

I wanted to hold back the trolley, hold her back, but she tore it away from me. It hit the doorframe with a bang, she missed the opening, had to try again. She finally managed to tug the trolley with her out the door. The wheels vibrated against the floor as it disappeared down the hallway. The sound grated in my ears.

I stood on the street, didn't know how I got there. I'd walked away from them, left them like everyone else had, I was a part of it. This was our world. We sacrificed our old people. Was this what had happened to my own mother, too? She was sent away. Everything had happened so quickly. She'd disappeared. And I hadn't done a single thing to help. Just let it happen.

Mom.

I bent forward, sank down onto my knees. My diaphragm contracted, my stomach convulsed.

I threw up until there was nothing left. Then I stood there. I should go back. Give them food and water. Get them out of there. Or find someone who could help. I should act like a human being. Somebody had to do something. I was perhaps that person. Perhaps management didn't even know about the decision to leave them behind. Perhaps they didn't know.

But that wasn't why I was here.

Wei-Wen.

The people there weren't my responsibility. They were the hospital's responsibility. And their families'. Somebody had left them there. Not me, not this time.

Mom. I had failed her. I would not fail Wei-Wen. And the people in there . . . There was nothing I could do. I had to focus on my child. I threw up again, as if my body were protesting against my thoughts, threads of slime stuck to my lips. It tasted sour; there was an intense stinging in my nose and throat. I deserved it.

I sat there, dizzy and faint. Then I slowly got to my feet and started walking. I didn't have any idea where I was headed, just knew that I had to get as far away as possible.

My mouth was dry. I tried breathing through my nose, moistened my tongue with saliva. It didn't help. I stuck my hand in my purse, there was a bottle of water there. I took it out; it was half full, and I emptied it in huge gulps.

Then I walked on. Lost contact with time. A part of the sky was lighter. I was drawn towards it. Perhaps there was sunshine there, perhaps I could get away from all of this gray. But the point in the sky grew smaller and smaller, the light veil in front of the sun thickened into a wall.

It was only when it was too late that I realized I had lost my way.

GEORGE

The hives were back in the field, in the grove and on the edges of the ditch where Tom clearly wanted them to be. Strictly speaking, he didn't really want anything to do with them out here, either.

It was early morning and I was out in the field by the Alabast River. The sun was beating down on my white hat, my coveralls and net. I wore nothing underneath. Drops of sweat ran down my back, tickling until they reached the edge of my boxer shorts. Florida must be sheer hell now. God, how happy I was that we hadn't decided on *that.*

Because the summer up here was plenty warm enough. The weather had been sensational during the past few weeks. Not a lot of rain. The bees flying in and out, in and out. Gathering nectar from the moment the sun came up until it disappeared in the field in the evening, right behind Gareth's farm.

This was the best time. I was out with the

bees a lot now. Took my time. Sometimes I just stood there studying how they danced. The movements back and forth, in which I wasn't exactly able to discern any system, but I knew it was their way of telling one another about where the best nectar was: *Now I'm fluttering my wings a little, moving to the right, then two steps to the left, and then a spin around and that means you have to fly past the big oak, up the small slope, over the stream, and there, my friends, there you'll find the best patch of wild raspberries you could imagine!*

That's how they carried on. In and out, dancing for the others, searching, finding, bringing. And the hives grew heavier and heavier. Sometimes I tried to lift them, testing, assessing their weight, the honey that was already dripping inside. Golden, liquid money. Money for the down payment, money for the loan.

The hives had long since been expanded with honey supers. And now the task at hand was to prevent swarming, prevent the old queen from taking parts of the colony away with her to make room for a new queen and her offspring.

The field by the Alabast River was located far away from people, but I had nonetheless been summoned more than once to remove

a swarm in a fruit tree, by angry fussbud-
gets with frightened children, who stood
trembling inside with their noses pressed
flat against the windows, while I shook and
coaxed the swarm into a new hive. This kind
of thing gave us a bad reputation, so I
worked hard to avoid it. And the bees had a
curious ability to find trees in people's gardens, not just in God's open nature, when
they were taking a break while the scout
bees were searching for a new home.

That's why my head was down in the hives
all the time, searching for swarm cells. If I
detected the smallest sign, I squeezed them
flat. And if I discovered larvae, there was
nothing more to think about. The bee
colony had to be divided up.

In some hives the urge to swarm was
strong. I never found out why. It was a matter of replacing the queen, breeding from
one of the best. Resisting the temptation to
continue with the offspring of the swarming
bees.

I'd already replaced most of the queens
this year, but a few were allowed to live.
Some faithful queens that continued to lay
eggs for up to three years. Ideal queens.
These were the ones I preferred to breed
from.

I was standing beside one of them now. A

pink hive, a conscientious bee colony. One of those that brought in the most nectar. Bees I could count on, that produced like crazy; the hive had already been expanded by two boxes this year. Two heavy boxes full of honey. I hadn't been here for a week, had concentrated on hives in other places.

Tom was buzzing in my head. I didn't look any closer at the flight board before removing the outer cover. We hadn't heard from him. Nothing about the scholarship, nothing about what he was thinking in terms of his future. Or maybe he'd called and talked to Emma while I was out, without her mentioning it afterwards. I just waited. Maybe he was thinking through his options. No news was good news in a way. And he knew where to find me, it wasn't as if the farm had grown wings and flown away.

Had I lost him?

I put the outer cover on the ground and only then did I come to and focus. Because the sound wasn't the way it normally was, the way it should be. It was far too quiet.

I removed the insulation lining. Now I would definitely hear them soon.

I looked at the flight board, the opening. No bees.

Then I looked down into the upper box. The food stores were fine. A lot of honey.

But where were they?

Maybe in the next box. Yes. They had to be there.

I removed the top one. My back complained. *Remember to lift with your legs.* I tried to take it easy. Put it carefully down on the grass, straightened up and looked down into the next box.

No. The brood box. They had to be in the brood box.

I quickly removed the queen excluder. The sun was directly above my head, illuminating the box below me.

Empty. It was empty.

There was plenty of brood, but that was it. Just a few recently hatched bees crawling around, without anyone to take care of them. Orphans.

At the very bottom I found the queen; she was marked, like all the queens, with a spot of turquoise paint on her back. Around her several young bees were gathered, the children. They weren't dancing, were lethargic. Alone. Abandoned. Mother and children abandoned by the workforce. Abandoned by those who were supposed to take care of them. Abandoned to die.

I scanned the ground around the hive. But there were none there, either. They were simply gone.

I carefully put the queen excluder and boxes back in place. Noticed I was blinking rapidly. My hands shook, suddenly as cold as on a rainy autumn day.

I turned towards the hive next to this one. The flight board, the entrance to the hive, faced in the other direction, so I couldn't see it, but I didn't have to look to know what was waiting for me; it was way too quiet.

Not a trace of mites. No disease. No graveyard, no massacre, no corpses.

Just abandoned.

And the queen virtually alone down there, too.

My chest tightened. I hurried to replace the cover.

Opened the next one.

There was hope in my hands when they quickly removed the outer cover.

But no. The same thing.

Opened the next one.

The same.

The next one.

The next one.

The next one.

I looked up.

I looked at all of them, scattered out at varying distances. My hives. My bees.

Twenty-six hives. Twenty-six bee colonies. Gone.

WILLIAM

While Edmund was sleeping his way back to good health, I worked on the hive. The sun was shining again, out here my state of mind became more positive. Of course he wasn't sick, he was just tired, Thilda was surely right. One day more or less made no difference, and when he had the chance to see what I had accomplished, his eyes would really be opened.

The conditions for observation were excellent. I had put the hive high up, so I didn't even have to bend my back to see. The bees had settled in surprisingly quickly, they now brought in pollen and nectar and were breeding continuously. Everything was as it should be. But one thing amazed me: their incessant need to attach the board with beeswax to something. I had attempted several different strategies, but if the boards were too close to the sides of the hive, the bees produced a mixture of wax and propolis, the viscous material they made from resin, and if they were too far apart, the bees expanded with brace comb, combs running across. This tendency they had, to always attach the comb to something, would in the long run make it difficult to harvest. There was something there, something I had to continue working on.

He arrived while I was standing there. I noticed him before he saw me. The sight of him caused a quivering inside of me; his hat at a slant that cast a shadow over his face, a loose shirt over the sinewy body, the bag, the same worn sailcloth bag that always hung over his shoulder, full of glass containers, tweezers, scalpels and living creatures.

I bent down over the hive. This could be the opportunity I had been waiting for, but I mustn't show him how much was at stake for me. I kept my hands busy, although I was not fully paying attention to what I was doing. With my back facing the road I pretended I was completely absorbed, absorbed in this great undertaking, which was mine alone, the first that was fully my own.

His steps approached, slowed down. Stopped.

Then he cleared his throat.

"What do you know."

I turned around. Put a surprised expression on my face.

"Rahm."

He smiled briefly.

"So what they're saying is true?"

"It is?"

"You're back on your feet."

I straightened up.

"Not just on my feet. I feel better than ever." It sounded childish.

"I'm happy to hear it," he said without smiling.

I hoped he would follow up with more questions, want to know why I chose to use such dramatic turns of phrase, but he said nothing, stood half turned away, as if he would be leaving me shortly.

I walked towards the fence, removed my hat and veil. I wanted to keep him here, extend a hand in greeting and feel his hand in my own. At the same time I became aware of my perspiring face, probably glistening and red. I discretely wiped off my forehead, but he had already noticed.

"It's hot in there," he said.

I nodded.

"But it's probably sensible to cover oneself up."

"Yes," I answered, not really understanding what he was getting at.

"There can be really awful consequences if one doesn't cover oneself up."

He spoke in that familiar, instructive tone, as if this were news to me.

"I'm aware of that," I said simply and wished I could have said something crafty and wise, something that made him smile, but the only thing I had to offer apparently went without saying.

"That's why I've never been very enthusiastic about bees. One doesn't get any direct contact," he said.

"No. It depends a bit on how secure one becomes."

He ignored me, picked up where he'd left off. "Unless one is a Wildman." That brief smile of his slid across his lips.

"Wildman?"

Like so many times before, he produced an unknown name for me. His knowledge seemed inexhaustible.

"So. We have not read about Wildman?"

"No. I don't know. The name sounds familiar."

"A circus artist, a charlatan. And a fool. He let the bees climb on him, without protection. He was famous for his beard of bees." He stroked his face with his hands to demonstrate. "He had bees all over his cheeks, chin and throat. Even performed for King George III. Could it have been in 1772?" He looked at me as if I had the answer.

"Anyway. His name suited him, this Wildman. What he was doing was like Russian roulette, putting all the bees on him like that and pretending he had complete control over them, a kind of magic. While the only thing he actually did was conjure up an artificial swarming. Overfed them with syrup and took out the queen. And wherever the queen is, the bees are, too."

Rahm's condescending tone gave no indication that he was aware that this information was not news to me.

"His father worked with something similar, by the way. Thomas Wildman. But in time he became a respectable beekeeper, among other things, for the nobility. He came to his senses. The son, on the other hand, carried on with that madness for the rest of his life. I wonder what he was trying to prove?"

"Yes, I wonder," I said.

"Well, then," Rahm said and gave a salute. "You are absolutely no Wildman, Mr. Savage. We both know that very well. But be careful all the same." He swatted away a bee with his hand. "They sting." Then he started to leave.

"Rahm." I took a step towards him.

"Yes?" He turned around.

"If you have time, I have something I would very much like to show you."

He didn't say a word while I presented the hive. As he was dressed in Charlotte's hat and veil it was impossible to see his eyes. I spoke ever more quickly, carried away by enthusiasm, because I was presenting something of my own now, for the first time. And there was so much to say, so much to explain. I showed him how easy it would be to harvest honey, how smoothly the boards could be removed, explained to him how simple it was to clean the hive. Held forth about the thinking behind it, that my hive was inspired by Huber's movable-frame hive, but that this model was infinitely simpler in its function and also safeguarded a far better temperature for the bees. And not least, I showed him how the access provided ideal conditions for monitoring, the opportunities it provided for further studies of bees.

Until in the end there was apparently nothing more to be said and I noticed how short of breath I was from my uninterrupted flood of speech.

Finally.

I waited for his answer, but it didn't come.

As the silence grew between us, my anxiety also increased.

"It would please me to hear your thoughts," I said finally.

He walked around the hive. Studied it from all sides. Opened it. Closed it.

I held my hands behind my back. The gloves were more clammy than ever.

Then the inevitable.

"You've built a Dzierzon hive."

I stared at Rahm, didn't understand what he meant. He repeated the words slowly:

"You've built a DZIERZON HIVE."

"What?"

"Johann Dzierzon. Vicar and beekeeper. Polish, but for the time being he resides in Germany. It's his hive you've built."

"No. This is mine. I mean, I've never even heard of this . . . Tzi . . ."

"Dzierzon."

Rahm turned his back on the hive. Walked a few steps away, took off his hat. His face was red. Was he angry?

"I read about his hive for the first time more than ten years ago. He has published a series of articles about it in *Bienen-Zeitung.*"

He sized me up with his gaze; it was expressionless.

"I know that you don't read this publication and the articles haven't been in circulation outside of research communities. So I understand of course that you haven't heard of them." His tone was overbearing. "But this hive you've made gives you good access for observation, as you so correctly point out. It would be easy for you to study the bees in vivo. Perhaps something could come out of the work all the same."

Now he smiled and I understood that the red color of his face was not due to anger, but rather amusement; pent-up laughter, the curt, small laugh without joy, because once again I'd disappointed him and he just wanted to laugh.

But he didn't release it, just stood that way looking at me, clearly waiting for an answer. I was unable to say anything. This couldn't be true. Was all my work in vain? I felt a tightening around my throat, the blood rushed to my face. And when I was unable to say anything, he continued:

"I would recommend that you inform yourself better in the field before you get started on your next project. Great advances have been made in the field in recent years. Dzierzon claims, for example, that queen bees and worker bees are both products of fertilization, while drones for their part develop from unfertilized eggs. A controversial theory, but of great current interest and much discussed. He has apparently also inspired a young monk named Gregor Mendel to start up a research project on heritability, the likes of which nobody has seen. There is lot to delve into here, as you can see."

He handed me the hat.

"Nonetheless, it was good to see that you're on your feet again. And thank you for wanting to show me your little hobby."

I stood there with the hat in my hands, so it was unnatural to reach out my hand. Neither did I manage to say anything, fearing that a good-bye would be accompanied by a sob.

Rahm put his own hat on his head with a practiced movement, said good-bye with a nod and a touch of his hand to the brim of his hat and then he turned around and left.

I was left alone, a young boy with his little hobby.

GEORGE

I walked quickly across the field, towards the river. Past the oak tree. There was a knot in my stomach. They had to be somewhere.

I took out my cell phone, checked to see if anybody had called, maybe somebody had a swarm in their garden? But no. I would have heard it.

Because this wasn't swarming. Of course not. I knew that much. No hive looked like this after a swarm. No swarm abandoned the old queen.

I went through the landscape with a fine-toothed comb, back and forth.

Nothing.

I took out my cell phone again. Had to straighten this out, get it under control, and I needed help.

I punched Rick's number. He answered immediately; there was noise in the background, he was at the pub.

"Rick at your service!" He said it with a laugh.

I couldn't answer, the words got stuck in my chest.

"Hello? George?"

"Yes. Hi. Sorry."

"Is there something wrong? Wait a minute."

It got quieter around him; he had probably walked out of the pub.

"Hi. Now I can hear you."

"Yeah. Rick, I was just wondering if you could come over. To the field by the river."

The laughter disappeared from his voice; he heard from my own that it was serious.

"What do you mean? Now?"

"Yeah."

"George? What is it?"

My voice broke. "There's stuff, a lot of stuff to clean up."

Emma was crying. She was standing out in the middle of the field, under a tree, crying. The leaves threw shadows over her face, moving across her glistening cheeks. Maybe she'd tried to hide under the tree, hide that she'd broken down. But I found her, put my arms around her and held on tight, like I always did when she burst into tears. It helped, she calmed down. And I calmed down, too.

Around us lay hives I'd turned upside down, the candy colors garish in the sunlight. They were tiny houses, razed by a giant. And the giant was me. I hadn't bothered to clean up. Had rushed across the field, checking one after the other, while the blood raged in my body and my breathing wailed in my ears.

I hadn't lost all of them. A hive or two were just like before; the bees buzzed around and worked down there, as if nothing had happened, but there were far too few healthy hives. I couldn't bear to count. Just kept going. On and on.

Rick and Jimmy had both arrived. They were working a short distance away from us. Rick walked slowly back and forth; for once he kept his mouth shut, his body swaying slightly, like he didn't know where to begin. Jimmy had already started working. He lifted empty hives and stacked them together neatly.

"Something like this can't just happen." Emma sobbed into my sweater.

I didn't have an answer.

"There must be something that's been done wrong."

I released her. "You think this is because of operational errors?"

"No, no." Her crying abated. "But what about the feed?" She straightened up, her face was concealed by shadow, her eyes didn't meet mine.

"Fine — good Lord, look at the calendar, you know this isn't when they run out of feed!"

"No, of course not."

She wiped her face. I stood there, my hands idle; I didn't know what to do with them.

She looked out of the shadow under the tree, towards the field and the light.

"It's very warm. Many of them are out in the sunshine all day."

"They've done that every single summer for generations."

"Yes. Sorry, but I can't bring myself to believe they can disappear. For no reason."

I clenched my teeth and turned my back on her.

"You can't believe it. But that doesn't make any difference now, does it."

A lone bee buzzed past us.

"Sorry," she said softly. "Come here."

She lifted her arms again. Stood there, soft and safe. I let her hold me, buried my face in her sweater. Would have liked to cry like her, but my eyes were as dry as dust. I had trouble breathing. It was too suffocating, her sweater smothered me, the warm skin radiating through the fabric.

I pulled away. Began stacking some boards, but had nowhere to put them so I ended up piling them up on the ground. Tidying up aimlessly, haphazardly.

She came towards me, held out her arms. "Hey . . ."

I had been betrayed, like Cupid by his mother. But I had no mother to cry to. No mother to blame, either, because I didn't know who had betrayed me.

And I couldn't bawl like a child swollen with bee stings.

I shook my head severely at Emma's open arms. "Have to work."

I took a few more boards and put them on top of the last, a tottering tower.

"Fine." Her arms dropped to her sides. "I'll go fix you guys something to eat."

She turned around and left.

The evening sun was a fiery red hole in the sky. Hard rays and long shadows.

My body ached, but I just kept going. I had hives in seven different locations, and the same sight greeted me everywhere.

We'd come to the last place, the forest behind the McKenzie farm. A little grove in between the fields. The hives were half in the shade. Normally, they buzzed along with the birds in the trees and the flies swerving left and right. But now everything was silent.

All of a sudden Jimmy was there with three lawn chairs.

"We have to sit down now," he said.

He found a spot a bit away from the hives. Rick and I plodded behind him. Rick hadn't said a word all afternoon, I found myself wanting a story. Every time I looked at him, he turned away; maybe he wanted to hide his shiny eyes.

Jimmy pulled out a thermos and a package of cookies. Had he brought them? Or gotten them from Emma? I didn't know. He pulled the plastic off the cookies and put the package between us. Then he poured coffee. We each took our cup. No toast this time.

The lawn chair squeaked. I tried to sit still, not move at all, the sound was wrong. It belonged to another time. Jimmy took a sip of coffee, slurped. That sound was wrong, too. An everyday sound. The cup securely in his hand, I suddenly had the urge to grab that sturdy fist and fling the coffee in his face so there would be silence. What was I thinking . . . Poor Jimmy. It wasn't his fault.

We could talk about a lot, the three of us.

About beekeeping. About farming, about tools, workmanship, carpentry. And about the village, gossip, people. Gareth, we could talk about him for a long time. Women, too, at least Rick and I could. Usually the conversation flowed freely. We always found something to talk about and to laugh at. Jimmy and I took the lead; the talk between us was like Ping-Pong, while Rick delivered the longest monologues.

But today we had no words. Every time I tried to say something, it got stuck. And I think the others felt the same way, because Jimmy kept clearing his throat and Rick looked back and forth between us and kept drawing his breath. But nothing came out.

So we drank the coffee and ate cookies. And tried to sit completely still, so the creaking of the chairs wouldn't remind us that it was way too quiet. The coffee was tepid, had no flavor. The cookies went down, provided a little relief; only now did I realize that the craving in my stomach was hunger.

So we sat like that, while the darkness descended upon us, around us.

Into our bones.

TAO

I couldn't find any street signs, the map was no help. And I didn't meet anyone I could ask. But the certainty that I was somewhere I shouldn't be increased within me. I was in the areas the receptionist had pointed out, those over which the authorities no longer had any control. Only those who had refused to move remained here. Those who were abandoned. Those who were hiding.

I turned a corner. In front of me was yet another deserted street. It was getting increasingly dark, the shadows longer, and it was too quiet. A movement caught my attention out of the corner of my eye. I spun around. A gate revealed a courtyard. Was there somebody in there?

I kept walking forward and passed the gate. Until now I hadn't thought about being afraid, only about getting away. But suddenly I noticed how all of the muscles in my body tensed. Should I turn around?

I took a few more steps. A little slower now. Nothing else happened. Perhaps it had just been my imagination. Or maybe it was an animal. A cat, a rat. Something which tried in vain to continue its life in this abandoned place, where there was no food, barely weeds, just a few frail shoots that forced their way up through cracks in the pavement.

I lifted my head. At the end of the street I glimpsed something blue and white. I walked faster. It became clearer, the white icon against the blue background. It blinked; the power supply was perhaps not stable. But there was no doubt: at the end of the street was the subway.

I was jogging now. It was doubtful that the station was open, but there would presumably be a map there. And maybe I could follow the tracks from there and find my way to settled areas. Out here the subway was still beneath the open sky, not in a tunnel like in the city center.

But I wasn't quick enough. Somebody came out through the gate behind me. I caught sight of a tall, gawky body moving towards me. A short whistling signal cut through the air. All of a sudden I became aware of two more people who had popped up behind me, one on either side, without any idea of where they'd been hiding.

They were perhaps twenty meters away, but they were fast. They ran towards me, and were gaining ground quickly. A tall, skinny girl and two boys. Not children, not adults. With smooth skin and elderly eyes. They were all skinny, on the verge of obliteration. But it seemed as if the sight of me gave them far more strength than their body weights would imply.

I didn't wait, I knew what they wanted. Their eyes told me they were willing to do anything, as long as it alleviated their hunger. It was as if they were carrying all the desperation of the old people in the hospital, but had the energy and physique to act in response to their distress.

Again I ran. But differently this time. When I left the old people I'd run away from my own disgust. This time I was running for my life.

And they were catching up with me. I didn't dare turn around, but I heard them. The steps against the pavement. The six feet hitting the ground in an irregular rhythm. The sound grew louder and louder.

In front of me the blue sign grew. If I made it there, if I made it into the station, if a subway came.

But I understood that I was deluding myself. No train would come, not here. There was nobody here but me. And them. Three desperately hungry young people, without any hope for a life. But nonetheless compelled by the innate human drive for self-preservation. Compelled by instinct. *They* were also our world.

They were only a few meters away now. I could hear their breathing. Soon they would be on top of me. Grab my back, throw me to the ground.

I had no choice.

Suddenly I turned around and without a word I raised my hands over my head to demonstrate surrender.

All three of them stopped. Looks of astonishment spread across their faces, momentarily replacing the wildness. I focused my gaze on the girl. Why her? Perhaps because she was female, like me. Perhaps she would be the easiest to convince. I tried to express all of my ideas about human compassion through my gaze. Stared, forced her eyes to stay focused on my own. Had it happened later, she might never have looked me in the eyes. But two quick blinks told me I'd caught her by surprise. Because she stopped, looked back and forth, at me and then the two others. We stood there like that, all four of us. I dared to move my gaze now. From the one to the other, letting my eyes rest for a moment on each of them, wanted them to see me, really see me, have time to think. So I became something more than a fleeing back, prey. So I became human.

"Are you alone here?" I asked softly.

Nobody answered. I took a step forward.

"Do you need help?"

A tiny sound escaped from the girl, a whimper, a "Yes." She hastened to look at the one boy, the tallest. Perhaps he was the leader.

I took a chance and addressed him.

"I can help you. We can get out of here. Together."

A slanting grin slid across his face.

"You're afraid." His voice was loud, higher than I'd imagined.

I nodded slowly, kept looking him in the eyes.

"You're right. I'm afraid."

"When people are afraid they'll say anything," he said.

I didn't answer.

"Is the subway running?" I asked instead.

"What do you think?"

"Have you tried going to another neighborhood?"

He laughed. A sharp laugh. "We've tried

most everything."

I took a step towards him. "Where I live, there's food. I can buy some for you."

"What kind of food?"

"What kind?" The question caused me to hesitate. "The usual things. Rice."

"The usual things," he mimicked. "Do you want us to leave our home for a serving of rice?"

I looked down the street behind him. Deserted. Dusty. Nothing resembling a home.

He nodded at the other boy and the girl. They took a step towards me. Were they getting ready to attack me?

"No. Wait." I put my hand in my purse. "I have money!"

I rummaged around. My fingers came across crackling paper.

"And food. Biscuits."

I took out a package and held it towards them.

The girl was immediately at my side. She snatched the package out of my hand and started to tear off the paper. I moved a few meters away.

"Hey!" The tall boy leapt forward. The girl clenched her fist and I heard how the biscuits were crushed into crumbs in the package.

She was about to dash off, but the boy

was on top of her. He forced her fingers open and took the package of biscuits. She said nothing, but her eyes filled with tears. The boy stood with the package in his hands. The logo was simple, in black and white. The print was smeared a little, perhaps from the sweat on the girl's hands.

"We have to share," the boy said and looked at the girl. "We have to share."

The three of them were busy with one another now.

Should I try to run? No. I had to give them everything I had, be generous. Not flee. Then they'd be on top of me. I had no choice.

I stuck my hand into my purse again. Swallowed, hesitated, but had to.

"Look here. Money."

I didn't dare move any closer to them and left a few worn bills on the ground, the last. Only small change was left in the tin box in the hotel room.

The boy stared at them.

I took a step backwards. Tears welled up in my eyes. "Now you have everything I've got."

He continued looking at the money.

"And now I'm leaving." I took another step. Then I turned around. Calmly I walked away, in the direction of the subway.

One step.

Two. Three.

My legs wanted to run, but I forced myself to walk slowly. To continue to be a human being for them, not start the chase again, not become their prey. Hold my head high, not turn around.

I heard that they were moving a little behind me. The material of a jacket being twisted, the soft clearing of a throat. Every tiny sound stood out in the silence. But no feet against the pavement.

Seven. Eight. Nine. Ten.

It was still quiet.

Eleven. Twelve. Thirteen.

I dared to speed up my pace as I approached the station, which was closed with a chain and padlock. Only then did I turn around.

They were still standing there, in the same place and looking at me. All three of them equally expressionless. No sign of movement.

I walked towards the corner, keeping my eyes on them at all times. Then I walked around the corner of the house. I could no longer hear them. In front of me was yet another deserted street. I had the subway track on my right-hand side, a dead row of houses on the left. There was not a soul in sight.

I ran.

WILLIAM

The package arrived in the mail ten days later. The writings of Dzierzon. I brought it upstairs with me and closed the door to the room on the second floor, which was now wholly and fully mine. Thilda didn't sleep there anymore, not even now that my health was restored. Perhaps she wanted me to ask her to return to the conjugal bed, maybe she wouldn't come until I begged and so it would never happen.

The bed loomed, soft and safe before me. How easy it was, just to go to bed, let the blankets swaddle me, make everything dark and warm.

No.

Instead I sat down by the window with the package in my lap. I caught a glimpse of Charlotte's white-clad back at the bottom of the garden, bent over the hive. She spent hours down there. She had carried down a table and a chair for herself, sat with papers and an inkwell. I saw her constantly observing and taking notes in a little leather-bound book, with enthusiasm and lightness in her movements. She was like me, worked the way *I* had previously worked, though it felt like a long time ago now. I hadn't been to the hive myself since my conversation with Rahm. I had turned my back on it, wanted mostly to break it into pieces, jump on it, to see the pieces of board fly in all directions, splintered and destroyed. But I couldn't bring myself to do it — the bees prevented me; the thought that thousands of desperate and homeless bees would rise up and attack me.

I undid the twine, broke the seals and folded the paper to one side, and with a German dictionary at my side I started reading. Until the end I kept hoping that Rahm's claims were wrong, that he had misunderstood something, that Dzierzon had absolutely not produced such an advanced hive. But even though my German was shaky and I only understood a fraction of the texts, one thing was clear: his hive was very much like mine; the doors were positioned somewhat differently and the roof pitch was at less of a slant, but the principles were identical and the method of use the same. Furthermore, he had carried out a series of in-depth observational studies of the bees in their hives and a lot of the research entailed precisely this. The underlying philosophy was rock solid and testified to an infinite patience; everything was scrupulously documented and with an exemplary presentation of the argument. Dzierzon's work was world class.

I put the writings away and once again turned my attention towards the window. Charlotte put the lid on the hive out there, walked a few steps away and took off her hat. She smiled to herself before setting out towards the house.

I opened the door. I could hear her footsteps below. I moved over to the landing. From here I could see her. She walked into the hall. There she sat down by the sideboard, took out her notebook and opened it in front of her. She reconsidered, her gaze suspended for a second in space, before she bowed her head and wrote. I walked down the stairs. She lifted her head and smiled when she saw me.

"Father. How nice that you've come," she said. "Here — you have to see this."

She wanted to show me the book, held it out to me.

But I didn't look at it, simply walked to the coat stand, found my hat and jacket and quickly dressed.

"Father?"

She beamed at me. I looked away.

"Not now," I said.

The passionate enthusiasm in her eyes, I couldn't bear to be in the same room with her. I walked quickly towards the door.

"But it won't take long. You have to see what I've been thinking."

"Later."

She didn't say anything more, just had this gaze, so determined and assertive, as if she didn't accept the rejection.

I didn't even have the energy to be curious. She hadn't found out or thought of anything that had not already been thought and I couldn't bear to explain this to her, disappoint her, tell her that all the time she'd spent down there by the hive only resulted in things that were obvious, that all of her thoughts had already been thought a thousand times before. I opened the door slowly, registered how something indolent had once again descended upon my body and a sigh was released from my diaphragm. I prepared myself for many more in the time ahead. In my hand I squeezed the key to the shop, to my simple, country seed shop. That's where I belonged.

The Swammer pie left behind a coating of

grease on the roof of my mouth, but I was still unable to refrain from eating. I had already shoved two down in the course of the morning hours. The scent of them poured out of the bakery and was intrusively present also in my shop. It penetrated through all the cracks, even when I closed the door, a constant reminder of how simple it would be to buy one more, or several. The baker even gave me a discount; he thought I was too thin, but that wouldn't last for long. It felt as if my body had already begun to expand, as if it were in the process of recovering its former sloppy constitution.

No near-gale howled any longer through the streets driving customers to the shop. The novelty had definitively worn off and half the day had already passed without anyone coming by. The large orders of seed corn were long since completed, now it was mostly spices and seeds for fast-growing plants, such as lettuce and radishes.

I ate a few more bites, although the pie was too salty. I drank lukewarm water from a dipper to alleviate it, but it didn't help much.

Then I walked to the door. The afternoon carriage from the capital drove down the street. The diligence stopped at the end and people streamed outside, but nobody came in my direction.

I nodded to the saddler who was standing outside in the sun greasing a saddle, smiled politely at the wheelwright who rolled a new wheel out of the workshop, briefly greeted my former employee Alberta, who was carrying two large rolls of cloth into the dry-goods shop, all of them hardworking ants, with their hands full. Even Alberta was clearly managing to make herself a little useful, with rolling hips and rapid feet, saying hello right and left, while she stepped lightly up the stairway.

"Mr. Savage." She smiled in my direction.

Then she hesitated for a second; evidently something had occurred to her. "I have something you have to taste! Wait a minute."

She disappeared quickly into the shop with the rolls of fabric. Shortly afterwards she came out again with a bundle in one hand.

She stood in front of me. I could smell the scent of her. It made me unwell.

"What's this about? I have a great deal to do."

"I hear that you've begun with bees," she said and smiled with crooked teeth behind lips a little too moist.

I was suddenly reminded of Swammerdam's sea monster, but pushed the thought away.

"My father also keeps bees. He has five hives. Look here." She held up the bundle. "You can have a taste. It's the very best."

Without waiting for an invitation she walked into the shop. She laid the bundle down on the counter and undid the knot. It contained a loaf of bread and a small pot of honey. She held it up, looked at it and smacked her lips loudly. "Come." She waved for me to come closer.

Her skin was rough, spotty, on her chin two pimples were pushing their way to the surface. How old was she now? Well over twenty at least. Both her hands and face showed that she had already spent too many working hours in the sun.

She gave me a piece of bread. The honey, not translucent, but rather a cloudy color, coiled over the slice, oozed out and down into the bread.

"Taste it!"

She took a large bite herself.

The smell of honey, of her and of a half-eaten Swammer pie on the counter turned my stomach. Nonetheless, compelled by my upbringing, out of foolish courtesy, I took a bite.

I nodded as it swelled in my mouth.

"Very good."

I chewed while I tried not to think about the brood and larvae that were in the honey, crudely pressed out of the straw hive.

She kept her eyes on me at all times while she ate. Finally she licked the honey off her fingers, excessively, with a self-assurance verging on the ridiculous. "Lovely. Now it's time to do a bit of work."

At long last she walked out, although *walked* . . . Her hips undulated out the door, I was unable to refrain from looking at them and ended up just standing there, in the middle of the floor.

Then she was finally gone. I took two steps around myself, breathing rapidly. A drop of honey remained on the counter. I wiped it away quickly, trying to erase it from my mind, along with her, the moist lips, the pimples, the almost obscene movement her midsection performed with every tiny gesture she made. Hips I could pound up against, as if she were earth. But I restrained myself. I took control. Even if it would require all the strength I had.

The only chair in the shop beckoned me. I stumbled over to it, placed my expanded backside on the seat. I crossed my hands over my abdomen as if to hold myself in place.

I just sat there and breathed deeply. Several minutes passed, the fever in me cooled down, the nausea subsided. Yes, I was able to control myself.

It was hot, a strip of sunlight revealed dust particles in the air right in front of me. They moved calmly, suspended weightlessly in the air. I pursed my lips and blew at them. They leapt away, but stabilized again with surprising quickness.

I blew again, harder this time. They flew away this time, too, before quickly reverting to their former shapeless existence, so light that nothing could fetter them. I tried focusing on them one by one. But my eyes stung. There were too many.

So I shifted my attention to the entirety. But there was no whole, just infinite amounts of uncontrollable dust particles.

It was no use. Not even that. They defeated me. Not even this was something I could control.

And so I sat, completely overpowered. An impotent child once again.

I was ten years old. Streaks of sunlight shone through the foliage in the forest, spreading a golden tint over it all, everything was yellow. I sat on the ground. The soil that throbbed up from beneath me was warm and damp through my trousers. Motionless, with intense concentration I sat there, in front of the anthill: at first glance, a blessed chaos. Every single creature so tiny and insignificant, it was inconceivable how they could have built a hill that almost towered over me. But with time I understood more and more. Because I never grew weary, I could sit for hours and watch them. They moved in clear patterns. Carried, put down and retrieved. It was meticulous and peaceful work, systematic, instinctive, hereditary. And work that was not about each individual, but about the community. Individually they were nothing, but together they were the anthill, as if *it* were a single, living creature.

Something was awakened in me when I understood this, a warmth unlike any other, a fervor. Every day I tried to get my father to come with me, in here, in the yellow wood. I wanted so much to show him what they had accomplished, what such small creatures could manage together. But he just laughed. *An anthill? Leave it in peace. Do something useful, lend a hand, let's see what you're made of.*

That's how it had been on this day, too. He had mocked me, and again I was here alone.

All of a sudden I discovered something, a

breach in the system. A beetle had crept up on the outside of the hill, where the sun was shining. It was of monstrous proportions compared to the ants. The sunlight reached down between the trees and a ray hit the beetle's back. It stood completely still now. A space opened up around it, none of the ants walked past, they left it alone, they continued with their purposeful work. Nothing more happened.

But then I became aware of an ant on its way towards the beetle; it broke away from the customary patterns, was no longer a part of the whole.

And it was carrying something.

I squinted. What was it? What was it carrying?

Larvae. Ant larvae. Now more of them were coming, more of them broke the pattern and they all brought the same thing. They were all carrying their own children.

I leaned closer to look. The ants dropped the larvae in front of the beetle. It stood still for a moment, rubbing its front legs against each other. Then it started to eat.

The beetle's jaws worked furiously. I leaned over as closely as I could. The larvae disappeared into its mouth, one after the next. The ants stood in a long row, ready to serve the beetle their own offspring. I wished I could look away, but was unable to keep myself from watching.

Another larva, down into its mouth. And the ants waited, they had interrupted their usual patterns, liberated themselves from the whole to carry out this atrocity.

They crawled on me, within me. My cheeks became red hot, the blush spread through my whole body, the blood reached every part of me. I didn't want to see, became unwell, but was unable to stop myself. To my astonishment I felt a pumping sensation beneath the fly of my trousers. A sensation I had only barely discerned previously, but which was suddenly all-consuming. I squeezed my thighs together, squeezed around what had grown hard. Another larva was crushed between the jaws of the beetle. The wide-set eyes glistened, the antennae moved. I lay down on my stomach, flat on the ground, striking against the earth, thought my trousers would be soiled and ruined, but was unable to stop. At the same time, there were waves of nausea inside me, because the larvae were killed. They disappeared into the beetle's bowels. It was unlike anything I had ever seen before. And it aroused me.

While I was lying there and pounding hard against the earth, I heard footsteps behind me, my father's steps. He'd come after all, he stopped and he observed, but didn't see anything of what I wanted to show him. He just saw me, the child I was and my infinitely great shame.

This moment, me on the ground. My father's initial astonishment, subsequently his laughter, short and cold, was without joy and full of loathing, of scorn.

Look at you. You are pathetic. Shameful. Primitive.

It was worse than everything else, even worse than the belt I had a taste of when evening came and the glaring pain across my back all through the night. I just wanted to show him, explain to him and share my enthusiasm, but all he could see was my shame.

GEORGE

I drove down to the center of Autumn. Well, *center* is a bit of an overstatement. Autumn was actually just a single intersection. A northbound highway met another heading east, and there were a few houses gathered there. I didn't have a lot of gas left, but didn't fill up. Never more than half a tank. It was a new gimmick I'd come up with. And I drove until the tank was empty. As if it cost less to fill up an empty tank halfway than a half-full tank all the way.

The disappearances had been given a name now. Colony Collapse Disorder. It was on everyone's lips. I tried it out. The words rotated through my head. There was a rhythm to them, and the same letters. The *C*s and the *O*s and the *L*s and the *S*s. A little rhyme, Colony Collapse Disorder. Dilony Collapse Collorder, Cillono Dollips Cylarder, and something medical about the whole thing, as if it belonged in a room with white coats and intensive care equipment, not out in my field with the bees. Still, I never used those words. They weren't mine. Instead, I said *the disappearances,* or *the problems,* or — if I was in a bad mood, and quite often I was — *the damn trouble.*

There was a narrow space between a green pickup and a black SUV in front of the bank. I looked around — no other spaces on the rest of the street. I pulled the car up right against the green pickup and tried backing in. I've never liked parallel parking; I'm not much of a man when it comes to that, so I avoid it as much as possible. Don't think Emma knows how terrible I am at it, even. But I had to go to the bank. Today. Had put it off for too long already. Lost money with each passing day, every day without hives out there in the sun among the flowers.

I pulled the wheel all the way to the side, backed up until the car was halfway past the pickup. Then I pulled the wheel back and kept backing up.

Completely crooked. Almost on the sidewalk.

Out again.

A lady walked past, staring at me. Suddenly I felt like a teenager, a greenhorn behind the wheel.

I tried one more time, took a deep breath. Took it easy, twisted the wheel all the way, backed up slowly, halfway, and straightened out.

Shit!

The space was too small, that was the problem. I pulled out, drove into the middle of the street and set out for the parking lot a little down the road. Parking like this right in front of the bank was just laziness, we were too lazy in this country. I was perfectly capable of walking.

In the rearview mirror I saw a huge Chevrolet come rolling up. It slid into place in the too-narrow space in a single movement.

The air-conditioning was like a wall I had to break through when I opened the door to the bank. I was still shaking a little from the parallel parking crisis, but shoved my hands into my pockets.

Allison sat behind her desk, tapping on the computer, as usual. She had the sense to dress like a lady, flowery blouse, freshly ironed, against freckled, young skin, perfectly green eyes. She looked clean, smelled clean, too. She looked up and smiled with toothpaste-white teeth.

"George. Hi, how are you?"

She always made me feel a little special, Allison. As if I were her absolute favorite bank customer. She was good at her job, in other words.

I settled into the chair in front of her desk. Sat on my hands, wanted to hide the shaking, but the wool fabric of the chair made my palms itch. I took them out again. Put them in my lap, where I managed to keep them still.

"Been a long time." Her teeth sparkled at me.

"Yeah. Been a while."

"Everything fine with you guys?"

"Not as fine as it should be."

"Oh dear, no. Sorry. I've heard."

The row of pearls disappeared suddenly behind her soft, young lips.

"But I hope you can help us out of the worst of the trouble," I said and smiled.

No sign of her showing more of those pretty teeth, unfortunately. She just looked at me gravely.

"I will of course do my very best."

"Your best. Can't ask for more than that." I laughed. Suddenly noticed I was showing off a little, stuck my hands under my thighs again.

"OK." She turned towards the screen. "Let's see. Here you are."

She was quiet. Looked over the account. The sight didn't exactly make her jump into the air with enthusiasm.

"What did you have in mind?" she said.

"Well. It would have to be a loan."

"Yes. How much?"

I told her the amount.

The freckles on her nose jumped. The answer came without a trace of consideration.

"I can't do it, George."

"Golly. Can you at least do the calculations?"

"No. I can tell you right away that I can't do it."

"OK. Can you talk to Martin, then?"

Martin was her boss. The type who shied away from conflicts, not one to end up in a bar brawl, to put it that way. Mostly stayed in his office. Just came out every once in a great while, when large sums of money were to be assessed and signed for — I knew that from Jimmy, who had just taken out a mortgage on a house. Martin had less hair every time I saw him. I glanced towards him, where he was seated behind his glass wall. The bald spot shone in the glare of the ceiling light.

"There's no point. Trust me," she said.

A lump rose insistently in my throat. Should I sit here and beg? Was that what she wanted? She was almost twenty years younger than me. Emma used to babysit for her once upon a time. Delicate as a little fairy, who'd believe that she'd grow up to become a ball-breaker?

"Honestly, Allison."

"But George. Do you really need that much?"

I couldn't bring myself to meet her green eyes from across the desk.

"The entire operation is down," I said quietly to the floor.

"But . . ." She was quiet for a while, thinking. "Can't we look at how we can get it up and running again without your needing to make such big investments?"

I had the urge to roar, but didn't answer. She didn't know shit about beekeeping.

"Where are the majority of your expenses, would you say?"

"Manpower, of course. I have two men working for me, you know that?"

"Yes."

"And then there's running costs. Feed. Gas, that kind of thing."

"But now? Investments you *must* make?"

"New hives. We had to burn a lot."

She chewed on a ballpoint pen.

"OK. And what does a hive cost?"

"Materials. Hard to say. They have to be built."

"Built?"

"Yes. I build them from scratch. Every single one. Except for the queen excluder, that is."

"The queen excluder?"

"Yes. The part that's put between . . . Never mind."

She took the pen out. Her teeth had left marks on the top. If she chewed harder, she'd crack the plastic, get ink on those white teeth of hers. That would be something. Blue ink on white teeth, on the freshly ironed blouse, on soft lips, like clumsy Halloween makeup.

"But . . ." She reconsidered. "I've seen Gareth Green have hives delivered. I mean, I've seen them arrive, on a truck. Ready to go."

"That's because Gareth orders them," I said clearly, as if I were talking to a child.

"Is that more expensive than building them?"

She put the pen down. Apparently she wasn't going to give me the pleasure of soiling her clean appearance.

The lump pushed its way upwards. Soon it would reach the point where it was no longer possible to hide it.

"I just mean," she continued and revealed once again the white teeth, as if this were just so amusing, "that perhaps you can save

401

some money by ordering them. And time. Time is money, too. Don't build them yourself any longer."

"I understood that," I said quietly. "I understood that's what you meant."

WILLIAM

When I finally managed to move again, it was completely dark. The street outside was quiet, with the exception of yelling from the tavern a little way down the street. A sad place, cramped and oppressive, where the village tosspots met night after night and drank themselves senseless. Some ran past, on the way out of there, shadows across the window, howling and singing, rude laughter, which became gradually fainter the further away they got.

I was cold. The room had grown chilly, the evening air flooded through the door, which I hadn't gotten around to closing before falling asleep. My neck was stiff, my head had toppled towards my chest and my shirtfront was damp with saliva.

I stood up, stiff and sore, hurried to the door and quickly closed it.

Imagine if someone had discovered me, imagine if customers had looked in and seen me sleeping in the shop, right in the middle of opening hours. Even more stories could arise from such things, yet again I could put myself on the map as the village fool. But maybe, hopefully, the afternoon had been just as bloody quiet, or should I say as blessedly quiet, as the morning.

My stomach clamored for nourishment and wrapped in paper was a last piece of the pie. Dry and cold, the grease had congealed into a wormlike ridge around the edge. I ate it all the same and simultaneously swore I would never again allow myself be tempted into eating this dish. Perhaps not even pie at all. Although, what difference did it make?

I closed up, locked the door and set out for home.

The voices from the tavern grew louder.

The windows were warm yellow squares in the darkness. For the first time in my life, I felt drawn to them. A goblet of cheap wine, merely. It couldn't do any harm. I stopped. If someone saw me in there, that I'd become one of them, would it really change anything?

Everything was as usual outside the tavern. The same scenes played themselves out this evening as on every other evening; two rough workmen were arguing loudly, one of them bumped into the other, shoved him, soon they would fight. A stout tramp gurgled to himself as he lurched down the street; at the same time a tall lout came staggering out the door, brushed against the corner and spewed twice where nobody could see, but the sounds of the day's supper and the excessively large amounts of alcohol he had consumed, which found its way back out into the fresh air, were not to be mistaken.

No. I headed home. I had not sunk that low. When I passed the building, I noticed that even more people were outside on this bright summer evening.

A young girl's vulgar squealing. "Stop it! Don't!"

It was a no that said yes. Followed by intense giggling.

It was only now that I recognized the voice. It was Alberta. I didn't even need to see her to know how her large breasts were most certainly on the verge of swelling out of her dress, I could literally feel the penetrating odor of the cleavage between them all the way here.

Somebody was pressing against her and digging with his hands at all of her curves, slurring drunken incoherence against her throat, absorbed in his own lust, own intoxication, own desire, pounding against this wind-fallen fruit, this rotting fruit, that would soon bulge into something unrecognizable, swell up, for nine whole months. A young boy, judging by his ungainly figure, perhaps no more than fifteen or sixteen years old, the voice still hoarse and fresh, recently changed. He was far younger than she was, should have been at home, in bed, sleeping or perhaps reading, studying, planning for the future, to make somebody proud, to make a name for himself. A door opened, the light fell through, disclosing with whom Alberta was having vertical intercourse, who the young figure was, who far too soon had commenced his own process of putrefaction, consumed by what he believed was passion, who at exactly this moment was in the process of putting his entire existence at risk, and who didn't see me, see his father, his father who believed that life had long since hit rock bottom, but who at this moment truly had the rug pulled out from under his feet.

Edmund.

Tao

I continued along the subway track, passed several stations, but didn't see any people, saw no sign of any kind of life. Mile after mile, still running, with lungs that burned and the taste of blood in my mouth. Every station I caught sight of awakened a hope. But every attempt to open a door, to come out onto the platform was the same slap in the face. Because they weren't in operation. I was still in no-man's-land.

I had no idea my legs could carry me this far, that I could push myself this hard. But now there was nothing left.

I sank down against the wall of a house. There was a tearing in my chest due to lack of oxygen. The darkness closed in around me, around the city, around what had once been a city. Directly across from me lay a collapsed building, destroyed beyond recognition, perhaps the last thing they'd done, those who'd moved away from here. As if they didn't want there to be anything left. But everywhere there were traces of people. Old adverts posted, a broken bicycle, threadbare curtains bearing marks of the wind and weather behind a broken window, nameplates on entrance doors, some playful, handwritten, others formal and manufactured. Where were they now, all those who had lived their lives here?

I hadn't thought about it before, but the rubbish had been removed. The bins were empty, lined up along the sidewalk, neatly in a row, down the whole street. Perhaps *that* was actually the last thing that had happened here. A garbage truck had rumbled through the deserted streets and cleaned up to prevent rats. Or perhaps to gather up the final remnants of nourishment, of organic waste that could be scavenged, scraped out and served again. Preferably as animal feed, or also for us, as food for humans, camouflaged, disguised, mixed into forcemeat and sausages, as canned food — with additives of all the different artificial components of flavors and chemicals that made our food edible.

My mouth watered. I'd been saving the package of biscuits for the way home. Now I had nothing.

I tried getting on my feet, but they gave

out from under me. My muscles burned. I tried again, supporting myself against the wall, and this time I succeeded.

Step by step I walked over to the closest gate, pushed at it carefully. The movement produced a thunderous sound in the metal.

Inside there was an empty courtyard. Leaves had been blown into small piles in the corners. On both of the long sides there was a door. I tried one of them.

It led to an entrance, a cramped, narrow stairway. The day was sliding away out there, just a few small cracks in the wall admitted the dwindling twilight onto the steps.

I limped up the stairs. Every step hurt, but my breathing was no longer as heavy. I came up to the second floor. A door on either side. I tried the closest one. It was locked. I continued across the landing and stopped. Then I tried again, pushed the handle down. The expectation of meeting the same resistance was in my hand, so I jumped when the door slid open.

I stood there. The odor of the flat spread out into the staircase, hitting me. There was nothing special about it, but all homes have their own smell. The smell of the people who live there. The food they have eaten, the clothes they have washed, the shoes they have worn, the sweat they have secreted, the breath they have exhaled during the late-night hours — the rank smell from sleeping people's mouths — bedding that perhaps should have been changed, a frying pan that should have been washed, but left for the next day, so the food residue had congealed and started to decay.

But now only the shadow of all the smells remained, almost hidden by the massive stuffiness.

I stepped across the doorway. The flat was small, just two rooms. Like our flat, Kuan's and mine. Perhaps this had also housed a small family of three. A bedroom towards the courtyard, a combined sitting room and kitchen facing the street.

I closed the door behind me and walked into the sitting room. It was virtually empty, vacated, although the largest furnishings had clearly been left behind. A frayed corner sofa that was a little too big and covered with gray fabric loomed, taking up almost half the floor. An old, warped chest of drawers painted black stood against the opposite wall.

I searched quickly through the kitchen cupboards. I couldn't stop myself, even though I knew they would be empty. Just a large, worn pot was placed at the bottom of a cupboard. Otherwise nothing.

The chest of drawers was also empty, except for some old cables and a telephone with a cracked dial pad in the bottom drawer.

Then I walked into the bedroom. The closets gaped, the doors seemed to have been opened randomly, as if somebody hadn't had time to close them after they were emptied. On the walls were some empty nails, and the shadow of the pictures that had once hung there.

A narrow double bed was placed along one of the bedroom walls. Just a mattress, the blankets and pillows were gone. They had slept there, read, argued, laughed, made love. Where were they now? Still together?

Along the other wall was a child's bed. It could have belonged to a child of preschool age, was longer than a cot, shorter than an adult bed. It could have belonged to Wei-Wen. A small pillow was left behind. There was a dent in the middle, where a head had rested.

Suddenly my legs gave out from under me. I collapsed onto the child's bed, remained seated for a few seconds. Not a soul, just me, for miles around. Everything was abandoned. Empty. And I was just as abandoned as this flat.

No.

A craving in my chest. Was it yearning? I'd barely thought about Kuan, avoided it, held him at a distance, every time his face popped up in my brain, I forced it away. Forced myself to think just about Wei-Wen, about finding my child.

I stood up, went back to the sitting room, pulled the telephone out of the cupboard and looked around me quickly. There, beside the sofa, was a telephone jack. It couldn't be connected, not here, so far away from everything.

I rushed over and shoved in the plug. Then I lifted the receiver.

A faint dial tone could be heard.

Quickly I dialed my home number on the cracked dial pad.

At first all I could hear was a crackling sound, noiseless signals being sent mile after mile through old, virtually crumbling cables.

And then it rang.

Once.

Soon a voice would fill me, Kuan's voice. I had no plan for what I would say, just had to hear him.

Twice.

Because perhaps there still was an "us." Perhaps there could be, now that there was such a great distance between us.

Three times.

Wasn't he there?

The seconds passed.

Four times.

But then.

"Hello?"

His voice in my ear.

I gasped with relief. "Hi."

"Tao!"

I couldn't answer, tried to hold back my sobs, but they forced their way out.

"What is it? Has something happened?"

"I'm . . . I don't know where I am."

"What do you mean?"

"There's nobody here."

The sound became scratchy, the signals disappeared.

"Kuan? No!"

The telephone hummed faintly. Then the line went dead.

I tried again, dialed his number. Waited.

Nothing.

I took out the plug, put it in again.

The telephone remained silent.

I put the receiver in place, put it down on the floor. I stood up and looked down at it.

Suddenly my foot jerked out and kicked with all of its might. Again and again. The old electronics flew in all directions, along with cracked pieces of plastic.

Then I went into the bedroom, and over to the child's bed.

I remained sitting there, while the room grew dark. The feeling of loneliness hit me so hard that I gasped. The moment became everything, the moment was an eternity. Me, alone in an abandoned flat. There was nothing else. I had lost everything. Even the money was gone.

Our second child. Who would it have been? Another boy? A girl? Like me? Awkward, calm, one of the outsiders. I would never get to know this child. I had sacrificed it, and nothing was left. Life stopped here.

I lay down on my side, pulling my legs up beneath me. Blindly I found the little pillow, grasped it, pulled it against me, embraced it, pressed it against my body, against my breast.

That's how I fell asleep.

Wei-Wen's hair smelled of a child's sweat and something dry, like sand. I pressed my lips against it, captured a few strands of hair with them and tugged a little.

"Ouch, Mommy. You're eating my hair!" I released the strands and laughed. Found his cheek and put my mouth against it instead. So soft, surprisingly soft, such soft cheeks children can have. It was as if I could press my lips against them and never, no matter how hard I pressed, encounter resistance. Just lie like this and have all the time in the world.

"My baby. You're so sweet."

He sniffled vigorously in response. Stared at the ceiling, where some fluorescent star stickers made up the solar system. I'd had them myself when I was a little girl, had begged for them, when my parents actually wanted to buy a doll. So when I grew up and moved out on my own, I carefully picked them off the ceiling of my childhood bedroom. I put them in a bag, packed them in the very bottom of a suitcase of childhood memorabilia, and when Wei-Wen was finally born, stuck them up again. It was as if I'd created a bond between my own childhood and his, between us and the world, between the world and the universe.

I'd helped him to learn the names of all the planets by heart, so he would understand how small we were — that we were also a part of something larger even though he was still much too young to take it in. The stars and the planets were still just stickers up there on the ceiling. He could only understand that the moon and the sun really existed because he saw them in the sky with his own eyes. But that the moon didn't even have its own sticker, hadn't been worthy of it, up there on the ceiling, that he couldn't understand. It was almost as big as the sun.

"There's Jupiter." He pointed.

"Mm."

I sniffed his hair, couldn't restrain myself. But he didn't seem to notice.

"It's the very biggest."

"Yes. It's the biggest."

"And Satum. That's the one with the rings."

"Saturn," I said.

"Satum."

"Yes. That's the one with the rings."

"That's the nicest one."

He thought for a little bit.

"Why doesn't the earth have rings?"

"Well, I don't know."

"I think it should have some. That's the nicest."

I buried my nose in his cheek. He twisted a little, turned his face away from mine.

"You can go now, Mom."

"I can lie here a little longer."

"No."

"Till you've fallen asleep?"

"No. You can go now."

He was ready, the bed had been made safe for the night. My job as mother had been

416

carried out.

I kissed him on the cheek, one last time. He didn't even have the patience to wait, pulled the duvet over himself hard.

"Go on. I'm going to sleep."

"Yes. I'm leaving now. Nighty-night. See you tomorrow."

"Nighty-nightseeyoutomorrow."

I wanted to stay there, underneath the solar system, underneath Saturn's fluorescent, neon-green plastic rings, but woke up at the first hint of daylight. The window had no curtains and the light of dawn spread slowly across the room. I lay in the same position, tried to find my way back, to the other room, the other child's bed, but didn't manage.

This morning, in this strange bed, the first thing I thought of was the same as all the other mornings: his name.

Wei-Wen. Wei-Wen.

My child.

The softness. His face.

I didn't want anything else except to hold it tightly. But another face forced its way to the surface. A face from this world. The boy, the tall, gawky boy, with the package of biscuits in his hands. His eyes on me, ready to attack.

And the old people. Many of them incapable of understanding the situation, incapable of understanding that they'd been left behind to die. But the woman who'd come towards me — it must have been a woman — she knew. My arrival had awakened her. Awakened hope.

What would happen to her?

What would happen to the gawky boy?

And what about the waiter at the café?

His father?

What had happened to Wei-Wen? What had happened to him?

Something that involved all of the others.

The closing off of the forest, the military, the fence, the secrecy.

Something that involved all of us.

I sat up quickly.

I understood it now.

I'd started in the wrong end. I'd started by wanting to find him. But I'd never find him, as long as I didn't know what he'd been afflicted by. What it meant.

Wei-Wen's face emerged again. But not his usual, soft child's face. His face from that day. Wei-Wen in Kuan's arms. The skin that grew whiter with every passing second. The breathing that was heavy. The images became clearer now. The images I'd tried not to think about, couldn't bear to confront. I slid down onto the floor, pulled my legs up beneath me, stared straight ahead.

There he was. The pale, clammy face. The drops of sweat that trickled over the bridge of his nose. His eyes. He was conscious when Kuan came running with him. The whole tiny body struggling to breathe, breathing that tore in his chest, rasping. And the eyes scared to death. He stared right at me, couldn't even ask for help.

Then, halfway between the hill and the complexes, his head fell backwards. He was unconscious. I saw it happen, how his gaze slid away, he disappeared.

When we arrived his breathing was just a thin thread connecting him to the world.

I leaned my head against my knees. Forced myself to relive the minutes out there. Look at his face, look at it. What had stopped his breathing? What had happened?

The paleness, the clammy skin. It resembled something I'd seen before. Suddenly another image emerged. Yet another face. Daiyu. The garden party. Daiyu lay on the ground in her light blue jumpsuit. The black shoes gleamed in the sunlight. She was clammy, too, her forehead sweaty. She tried to fill her lungs with air, the same rasping breath and the same pleading eyes. *Help me,* her eyes said. We stood in a circle around her. We'd been playing at the very edge of the garden, the adults sat at a table a short distance away. Daiyu's hand was lying beside her. She was holding something. A piece of cake. The cake she'd helped herself to a little while ago. She'd just eaten it, lifted the piece off the plate, walked around eating while we played.

"Daiyu can't breathe! She's not breathing!" we screamed.

Suddenly her mother was there. We let her through; the mother shouted.

"My purse, bring it here. My purse!" Then she opened Daiyu's hand and removed the piece of cake before turning to face us.

"Are there nuts in it?"

Nuts? None of us knew. Her expression was so insistent that I felt responsible. As if *I* should have known whether there were nuts in the cake.

Someone came running up with her purse. Daiyu's mother dug around in it, didn't find what she was looking for, turned it upside down. The contents fell out onto the ground. I saw a lipstick, Handi Wipes, a hairbrush. She grabbed hold of something, a little white package bearing green letters. She tore it open and took out a syringe.

Then my own mother was there. She pulled my head against her, didn't want me to see any more. She led me gently away.

"What is it? What's wrong with Daiyu?" I asked. "What's wrong with her?"

WILLIAM

It was morning. The leaves filtered the light.
Everything moved above me, the trees in
the wind, the clouds that slid across the sky,
nothing stood still. I grew dizzy and closed
my eyes. Just lay there and let the yellowness enshroud me, on my back without
moving, against raw, damp soil. Because
there was nothing else, there was no longer
anything that could keep me away. Not the
research — my passion. Not Edmund, he
was lost, he'd been lost all along. Not even
desire. It had disappeared. I no longer
wanted to pound against the earth, eu-
phoric, towards a climax. I wanted to let it
swallow me, until I became soil myself.

I hadn't eaten, but it made no difference.
The pie continued to turn over in my stomach, stuck in my throat, dried out my
mouth.

The village, the work in and around it, my
own home, it could have been a thousand

miles away, I had walked in the darkness until my feet ached, until no sounds slipped through any longer. The forest was trampled down in some places, I followed a path but strayed off it, wanted to get away from everything that reminded me of human beings. In the end I just collapsed on the grass.

Did they miss me? Were they looking for me? Perhaps I would hear something soon, hear their cries, all the little girls' voices at different pitches, from Georgiana's thin, squeaky voice, the highest on the scale, to the deepest of them, Thilda herself, whose voice jarred rudely.

Or perhaps none of them had missed me. Perhaps they were accustomed to my leaving, disappearing, perhaps they didn't even notice I was missing.

Or were they busy with Edmund? He was ill today, he had to be, today like so many other days. He slept, presumably, until the sun had passed its zenith, was as pale as a ghost from never showing his face outdoors. But it was not illness. All the things I hadn't understood. And no, they weren't concerned about his illness. The day *was* like all others, because it was absolutely not the first time he stayed in bed like that. All the days he had dawdled away, sleeping in his bedroom, while the alcohol slowly left his body. No hereditary melancholy, only self-inflicted lethargy and damage. He was no better than the vulgar manual workers who let life slip away into pints of ale. A drunkard.

I followed the sun's progress in the sky. Soon it was directly above me, dried out every single remnant of fluid inside me. The perspiration settled onto my skin. I breathed with my mouth open. My tongue was like dried moss. I wanted to lift my hand, wipe away the drops of sweat, but my arm was far too heavy.

The day passed. The sun disappeared behind the trees again, the shadows grew longer, everything colder. My body temperature became the same as that of the earth beneath me. Behind my eyelids darkness awaited. Had I already been swallowed up?

"Father?"

Another shout. A clear pitch. At the middle of the scale.

"Father?"

The voice was louder now and soon I heard solid footsteps on heather and moss.

I opened my eyes and looked straight into Charlotte's clear eyes.

"Good afternoon," she said. There wasn't a trace of surprise in her. She just stood there and looked at me, studied me, as if I were an insect, as I lay there completely stretched out. Suddenly I felt the blood flowing to my cheeks.

"Yes. Here I am."

I sat up quickly, brushed the dirt off of my shirt, pulled my hand through my hair and shook off leaves and pine needles.

"Was it difficult to find me?"

"What do you mean?"

"Have you been searching a long time?"

"No, not very long. The path is there." She pointed behind her, and then I discovered it, the path towards the house, and then I couldn't help but notice some very familiar trees. I had in no way disappeared far into the depths of the forest. In my delusion I hadn't made it very far at all. I was right nearby my own home.

She sat down beside me, and it was only then I noticed that she had something in her hand. The notebook, the one she always had with her, where she eagerly filled up the pages with her pen.

"I'd like to show you something. May I?"

She opened it without waiting for an answer.

"It's something I've been working on for a long time."

I tried to focus, but the ink marks crawled like worms on the paper.

"Wait." She took off my glasses, polished them quickly with the fabric of her dress and put them back on my nose. They were cleaner, but that wasn't the main reason why I straightened up my back and tried to take in what she wanted to show me. The small gesture had given me a lump in my throat. I was so grateful that it had been she who had come, that she in particular had found me, seen me like this, and nobody else. I swallowed and directed my attention towards what she wanted to show me.

A drawing. A hive. But completely different from mine.

"I thought that if we turn it upside down, it will all be completely different," she said. "If we insert the boards downwards from above, instead of hanging them from the ceiling, we'll have much better control."

I stared at the drawings she showed me. They slowly came into focus on the page.

"No," I said and cleared my throat. "No. It won't work." I searched for the words. "They will get stuck on the sides of the box." I straightened up. I was, after all, an authority. "The bees will attach them with propolis and wax, it will be impossible to get them out."

Then she smiled.

"If they're too close together, yes. Five

426

millimeters or less."

"And if they are too far apart, the bees will build brace comb," I said. "Regardless, it doesn't work from above. I've already considered the possibility." I spoke the last words with an indulgent smile.

"I know, but you haven't tried different alternatives. It's just a matter of finding the right dimensions."

"I don't understand."

She pointed at the drawings again. "There must be an inbetween point, Father. A point where they will stop producing wax and propolis, and start producing brace comb. What if we find the inbetween point? If we determine exactly the right distance between the outer edge on the molding and the inner wall, they will produce neither wax nor brace comb."

I just had to look at her. Look at her properly. She sat with complete calm, but her eyes were shining, revealing her enthusiasm. What was it she said? Wax. Brace comb. Was there something in between?

My energy returned, I got on my feet.

The inbetween point!

GEORGE

After the meeting at the stupid bank, I went out to the field by the Alabast River. It was empty now. Just a few hives were left in one corner near the end. There was still life in them, but I didn't know for how long. There was nothing to set them apart from the others. There was no explanation for why they should survive.

I walked in a circle. The hives had left marks behind all over the grass. Flattened, dead grass. But between the dead blades of grass there were new shoots. Soon the marks would be gone and there would no longer be any trace of all the bee colonies that had lived here.

I walked closer to the buzzing. Suddenly I yearned to be stung. For the stinging pain. The swelling. An excuse to curse loudly and with a vengeance.

Once, just once, I'd been severely stung. I was eight years old. I remember I was sitting in the kitchen. My mother came home from the store. I don't know why, but on this particular day she'd brought me something. Yes, actually, it was to cheer me up because I was going to be a big brother for the third time, and she obviously knew the news wouldn't sit well with me. I never got toys except on my birthday and Christmas, but today she had nonetheless bought me something. A toy car. But not just any toy car. Hot Wheels. I had wanted one for ages. I was so happy it felt like my head would burst into flames. And I picked up the car and ran out to the field before she even had a chance to tell me about her tummy.

My dad was there. With his head in a hive. I didn't think twice. Ran straight towards him. *Look! Look what I got! Look, Daddy!* Then I noticed his eyes behind the veil. *Stay away from here! Turn back!* But it was too late to stop.

I was bedridden for several days. Nobody counted, but there must have been more than a hundred bee stings. I developed a high fever. The doctor came. He gave me some pills that were so strong they could have knocked out a bear. And I didn't learn about the child in Mom's tummy until much later.

After that I avoided bee stings at all costs.

I used to think of bee stings as punishment. Like a sign that I hadn't done my job properly. Hadn't protected myself. Hadn't been careful enough. A season without a bee sting was the goal, but there were always a few, no beekeeper manages to avoid stings for an entire summer. Except for this year. So far I hadn't had a single sting, but for reasons completely different from those I would have liked. I walked in a circle. Close and closer. They droned listlessly. I stopped and did a count of the density. Not enough. And at the very least not 2.5 per square yard.

I stomped hard on the ground. A single bee flew up.

Sting me. Sting me!

It sailed through the air, swerved away from me. Wouldn't do me the favor.

I turned and walked towards the barn.

I hadn't bought new materials. The spring's last order still lay in a fresh-smelling pile in a corner. It frightened me. Time stood between me and that pile. Hours and hours, all the work that would be required to build all the hives. And after that, even more. It was just a matter of getting around to ordering more planks. Because I was gonna build them myself. As long as I was working with bees, I was gonna build the hives myself.

I picked up a two-by-four, testing the weight in my hand. Felt the wood against my bare skin. Still damp. Suitably pliant. Alive.

Then I put on my gloves. Through them the wood was nothing but dead material. I took out the safety earmuffs. Turned on the saw.

Then light fell in across the floor through the doorway. The strip grew larger, a shadow filled it. Then it disappeared.

I turned around.

It was Emma.

She looked at the woodpile and then at me. Shook her head gently.

"What are you up to?"

She asked, even though she knew the answer.

She took a few steps towards me.

"This is madness."

She nodded at the planks.

"You have to build so many. We need so many."

As if I didn't know. As if I wasn't completely aware of it.

I shrugged my shoulders, was about to put the earmuffs back on, when something in her eyes stopped me.

"We could have sold," she said.

I dropped the earmuffs. They fell to the floor with a loud bang.

"We could have sold last winter. Moved. Already been down there."

She didn't say another word, not a word of what she was thinking. *While we'd had the chance. While the farm was still worth something.*

I bent over, picked up the safety earmuffs, lifting them with both hands, as if *one* hand wasn't enough, as if I were a child.

Then I put them on my head and turned away.

I didn't hear her leave. Just saw the strip of light on the floor, how it grew larger, how her shadow filled it, then it grew smaller, and disappeared.

We didn't speak of it again. She didn't say anything else. The days passed. I kept building until I got blisters, till my back hurt and my fingers were bleeding with cuts. I don't know what Emma was doing. But at least she didn't talk about it anymore. Just looked at me from time to time, with watery eyes, a gaze that said: *It's your fault.*

We tried to live like before. Do the same things. Dinner together every day. TV in the evening. She followed many shows. Laughed and wept in front of the TV. Gasped. Talked about them with me. *Have you ever! No, it isn't possible. But he doesn't deserve it. And* her, *she's so sweet. No, no, good heavens.*

And we sat together on the couch, never in separate chairs. She liked it when I stroked her hair. Ruffled it. But now my hands mostly rested in my lap. They hurt too much, were too sore.

One evening while we were sitting like that, the telephone rang. She made no sign of moving. Neither did I.

"You answer it," she said. Her eyes were on the TV, waiting for some vote or other, the tension was building, would the blonde or the brunette be voted out? Extremely exciting, apparently.

"Maybe it's Tom," I said.

"Yeah, so?"

"It's better if you talk to him."

She looked at me in surprise.

"Honestly, George."

"What?"

"You can't very well just stop talking to him."

I didn't respond.

The telephone kept ringing.

"I'm not answering it," she said and lifted her nose in the air.

"Fine. Then we won't answer it," I said. But of course she won. I went out into the hallway and lifted the receiver.

It was Lee. He was calling to tell me how the crop was doing.

"I'm out there every day," he said happily. "And it's growing. Heaps of unripe berries."

"Wow," I said. "In spite of the rain?"

"They must have been busy when the sun was out. It's gonna be a decent year after all. Better than I feared."

"Not bad."

"Not bad at all. Just wanted you to know. Great bees you have there."

"Had," I said.

"What?"

"Had. Great bees I had."

He was silent on the other end. It was sinking in, probably. "Don't tell me — did it happen at your place, too? Are they gone?"

"Yes."

"But I didn't think it had hit this far north. That it was just in Florida. And California."

"Evidently not." I tried to keep my voice steady, but it cracked.

"Oh, George. Good God. What can I say?"

"Not much to say."

"No. Are you insured?"

"Not against something like this."

"But what are you gonna do now?"

I wound the telephone cord around my index finger. It tightened against a cut I had gotten earlier in the day. Didn't know what to say.

"No."

"George." His voice was louder now. "Let me know if there's anything I can do."

"Thank you."

"I mean it."

"I know."

"Wish I could have lent you the money."

"No you don't." I snickered.

He laughed back, probably thinking it was all right to joke.

"Don't have anything, either. The crop isn't *that* good."

"Even though you got a discount?"

"Even though I got a discount."

He fell silent.

"I shouldn't have agreed to it."

"What do you mean?"

"To the discount."

"Lee."

"Had I known . . ."

"Lee. Forget it."

I unwound my index finger from the cord. It had made spiraling marks all the way down to my palm.

"You know what," he said, suddenly cheerful. "In fact, I am calling to tell you the opposite. The crop went down the toilet. What terrible bees they were."

I had to laugh.

"That was good to hear."

"Good thing they disappeared," he said.

"Yeah. Good thing they disappeared."

There was silence on the line.

"But George, honestly. What are you going to do?"

"I don't know. Maybe I have to switch to ordering hives."

"Ordering? No. That's your legacy. The hives are your legacy."

"It's not worth much these days."

"No."

I heard him swallow.

"But listen, anyway, don't give up."

"Right . . . no."

I was unable to say anything else. The warmth in his voice made it impossible to talk.

"George? Are you there?"

"Yeah."

I took a deep breath, pulled myself together.

"Yeah. I'm here. I'm not going anywhere."

Tao

A couple of kilometers away from the flat where I'd spent the night, I finally found a subway station that was open. I'd been close the night before, already headed towards the populated part of the city, but without being aware of it. Two other people waited with me, a shaky old woman, skinny, virtually emaciated, who dragged herself over to a bench, and a man in his fifties, with vigilant eyes, carrying a heavy, lumpy string bag. Perhaps he'd robbed abandoned houses.

We had to wait for half an hour before a subway finally lurched into the station. It took too long. I had to get back now, had to find a library, find answers. I snuck on without a ticket, scarcely noticing that the old woman was struggling to board. When it was almost too late I saw her eyes and hurried over to help. She said thank you many times and clearly wanted to start a conversation, but I didn't have the strength.

Inside the car I sat by myself. I would have preferred to stand, couldn't sit still, but the train shook so much that I didn't dare. It had been neither upgraded nor cleaned in a long time, perhaps decades. The smell was putrid, the windows covered with a thick layer of grease, the accumulation of thousands of fingers that had opened them when the hot sun beat down or closed them on cold days. On the outside they were discolored by dust and dirt. The deafening din when the train shuddered through the urban landscape made it almost impossible to think. All the same I felt like an animal on the trail of something — dogged, full of purpose. The same two faces revolved through my head. Wei-Wen and Daiyu. The same pallor. The same rasping breathing.

I had to change trains. First once. Then twice more. The timetable had been torn down, the electronic system had stopped working long ago. I just had to wait, the first time for exactly twenty-three minutes, then fourteen and then twenty-six. I timed it each time.

After three changes I finally arrived. It felt almost like coming home, at long last the surroundings felt familiar, as if I had been gone for much longer than twenty-four hours. My entire body clamored with hunger, but I didn't have time to sit down and eat, just shoved down a package of biscuits I had left — yet another package of biscuits — and asked the receptionist where I could find the closest library.

There was only one. One single open library left in all of Beijing. It was located in Xicheng, near a direct train line from the hotel. I passed the old zoo on my way. The decorations on the entryway were almost eroded away by the wind and weather. The plant life inside was threatening to take over, to burst through the fence. What had happened to all the animals? The species on the verge of extinction? The last koala bear? Perhaps they were walking around loose in the streets now, had found homes in vacated houses. It was a comforting thought, that they could still continue their life here on earth, even though there were so few people left.

The square in front of the library was deserted. I hurried across it, didn't have time to be frightened. The entrance door was so heavy I feared it was locked, but when I used all of my strength, I managed to open it.

The room was enormous, divided into levels, like a stairway. The walls were covered with books, thousands of them. On the floor, lined up in straight rows, were more tables and chairs than I could count. The room was in semidarkness, there was only light from the windows in the ceiling, all of the lights were out, and there wasn't a soul here, as if the library were actually closed.

I took a few steps inside.

"Hello?"

Nobody answered.

I raised my voice. "Hello!"

Finally steps could be heard from the other end of the premises. A young security guard stepped into view. "Hello?"

She was wearing a uniform that once upon a time must have been black, but was now a faded gray from laundering and wear. She looked at me in astonishment. Perhaps I was the first person to stop by in a long time.

Then she pulled herself together and held out her hand, indicating the sea of books. "I assume you want to take out books? Just help yourself."

"Don't I need to register? Don't you want my name?"

She looked at me in surprise, as if that was something she hadn't considered. Then she smiled. "It will be fine."

After that I was left in peace.

For the first time in many years I allowed

myself to be absorbed by books, by words. I could have spent my whole life here. Tao with the red scarf. The one who stood out. But *that* was another lifetime.

I started in the section for the natural sciences. Something Wei-Wen had no tolerance for had made him ill, he'd gone into an allergic shock out there in the fields. Maybe a snakebite? I found an old book about snakes in China. It was big and heavy. I put it on the table in front of me and searched randomly through the text. I knew there had been cobras in the area previously, but they no longer existed, at least that was what we'd been told. They'd eaten frogs, which in turn had eaten insects — and when many of the insects were wiped out, the cobra's basis for survival also disappeared. I turned the pages until I found a picture — a dark snake with flesh around its neck that opened up like a hood, with it's characteristic chalky-colored pattern, alert, ready to attack. Could there still be some of them left out there after all?

I read about the snakebite, about the symptoms. Numbness, blisters, pains, discomfort in the chest, fever, a sore throat, problems breathing. Not unlike Wei-Wen's reactions.

Necrosis, I read, an attack by a Chinese

441

cobra will always lead to necrosis, the death of cells, not unlike gangrene, around the area of the bite.

We hadn't seen a bite. Wouldn't we have noticed it?

And even if we hadn't noticed it, even if it was a snake, a cobra, that had attacked Wei-Wen, that didn't explain the secrecy, the tent and the fence, his being taken away from us.

I kept searching. If it wasn't a bite, what could it be? As I turned the pages of medical encyclopedias and doctors' manuals, the realization surfaced. Perhaps I had known it all along, but couldn't bear to take it in, because it was too big, too important.

It rang just once, and suddenly he was there.

"Tao, what happened? We were cut off. Where were you?"

I'd asked the guard if I might borrow the telephone; it was located in a separate office deep inside the library. The receiver was dusty, hadn't been used in months.

"It was nothing," I said. I'd almost forgotten our conversation in the flat the night before. "It all turned out fine."

"But what had happened? You seemed so . . ." In his voice there was a nurturing tone he usually reserved for Wei-Wen.

"I got lost. But I found my way again," I said quickly. I had to give him an explanation so I could move on.

"I've been thinking about you all day."

His worrying. I couldn't bear it. That wasn't why I was calling. Yesterday I would have embraced it, now it was just in the way.

"Forget about it," I said. "I think I've found out what happened to Wei-Wen."

"What?"

"Anaphylactic shock."

"Anaph . . ."

"It means allergic reaction," I said, and heard how slow and pedantic it sounded. I tried changing my tone of voice, not wanting to lecture him. "Wei-Wen went into an allergic shock. A reaction to something out there."

"Why . . . what makes you think so?" he asked.

"Listen," I said. Then I quickly read a text about symptoms and treatment. Rattled off terms like *respiratory distress, a drop in blood pressure, coma, adrenaline.*

"It all fits." I said. "That was exactly how he reacted."

"Did they give him adrenaline?" he asked.

"What do you mean?"

"When they came, was he given adrenaline? You said that one is supposed to ad-

443

minister adrenaline if it's life-threatening."

"I don't know. I didn't see them give him anything."

"Me neither."

"But they may have done it in the ambulance."

He was silent, all I could hear was the soft sound of his breathing.

"That sounds right," he said finally.

"It is right. It has to be," I said.

He didn't answer. Thinking. I knew about what. The same thing that I'd been thinking since I woke up in the abandoned flat. Finally he came out with it.

"But what? What was he allergic to?"

"It could have been something he ate," I said.

"Yes . . . But what, then? The plums? Or something he found in the woods?"

"I think it was something he found in the woods, but not something he ate."

He was quiet, perhaps he didn't understand.

"I don't think it was food," I continued. "I think it came from something outside."

"Yes?"

"At first I thought it was a snakebite. But that doesn't fit, not with the symptom."

He didn't answer; the sound of his breathing from the receiver was more rapid now. "I don't think it was a bite, but a sting."

WILLIAM

Hertfordshire, 4 August 1852

Honorable Dzierzon,
I write to you as my peer, although quite possibly you do not know my name. All the same, the two of us have a great deal in common and therefore I viewed it as an absolute necessity to establish contact. I, the undersigned, have been following your work for some time and in particular your development of a new standard for beehives has attracted my attention. I cannot but express my boundless admiration for your eminent work, the evaluations you have made and finally, the hive in itself, as it is presented in *Eichstädt Bienen-Zeitung*.
I, the undersigned, have also developed a hive, in part based on the same principles as yours, which I now, in all modesty, would like to share with you, in

446

hopes that you will perhaps be able to devote some of your valuable time to sharing your thoughts about my work with me.

Huber's hive convinced me at an early stage that it should be possible to develop a hive that made the removal of boards possible, without having to kill the bees, yes, without even causing them distress. After reading his notes I also realized that we are capable of taming these fabulous creatures to a much greater extent than was previously believed. This understanding was quite essential for the continuation of my work.

First I developed a hive that resembled your own, with an entrance from the side and removable top-bars. However, this design did not give me the solution to all of the challenges I perceived. As you have certainly experienced yourself, removal of the boards is not a simple operation on this model, but rather both time-consuming and cumbersome, and furthermore, it must be done, most regrettably, at the cost of both the bees and their offspring.

But once in a great while one is struck by an epiphany that changes everything. For me, it occurred on a late-summer afternoon, while lying on the floor of the forest, in intellectual contemplation. I had at all times envisioned the hive as a house, with windows and doors, such as your hive. A home. But why not consider it completely differently? Because the bees are not to become like us, like humans — they are to be tamed by us, become our subjects. The way the sky now looked down upon me, and perhaps also God the Father, yes, I believe in truth He must have had a hand in this, on that summer afternoon, because this is how we shall look down upon the bees. Our contact with them shall of course take place from above.

Everything changed when I turned all of it upside down, when I started thinking about creating an entrance to the hive from above. This led me to the idea that is also the reason behind my writing to you: my soon to be patented *movable frames*. The boards are attached to these so that they are not in contact with the hive itself, neither on the top, on the bottom nor on the sides. Through this design I am able to take out or remove the boards at my own discretion, without having to cut them down or hurt the bees. I am thus also free to move the bees over to other hives and have control over them to a far greater degree than previously.

And how, you will certainly ask, does one prevent the bees from attaching the boards to the sides or to other boards with wax and propolis, or from building brace comb? Well, I shall give an account of this. Throughout a long period of calculations and experiments I arrived at the critical dimension. And that, my good friend, if you will permit me to address you as such, is <u>nine</u>. There must be a nine-millimeter space between the boards. There must be a nine-millimeter space between the boards and the side, between the boards and the bottom, between the boards and the top, neither more nor less.

I hope and believe that "Savage's Standard Hive" will soon be available all over Europe, yes, perhaps it will even reach beyond the borders of the continent. In the course of my work I have cultivated simplicity as a principle and the practical aspect has been essential, so that the hive can be used by everyone, from the most novice of beekeepers to the most experienced with hundreds of hives. But most importantly, I hope the hive might contribute to simplified observation conditions for naturalists like ourselves, so that we can continue to study in depth and make new discoveries related to this creature that is so infinitely fascinating, and not least, important for human beings.

I have already applied for a patent for my invention, but as you are most certainly aware, the processing of these applications can take time. In the meantime I am eager to hear your response to my work. Yes, perhaps you will personally also attempt to develop a hive based on my principles. In the event you should be so inclined, I would feel more honored than you could imagine.

With the greatest humility,
William Atticus Savage

The first carriage drove into the yard. My heart leapt, because it was beginning now. I had dressed in my best clothes, neatly ironed and laundered, and my face was freshly shaven, I had even brushed the dust off of my top hat. The guests were arriving and I was ready.

The hives were lined up in two rows on the lowest part of the property. Yes, there were many of them now; Conolly had really had his hands full. The accumulated sound of thousands of bees was so loud that we could hear them from all the way in the house. My bees: tamed by me, my subjects, subjects which in truth also obeyed the smallest of my hand gestures as day after day, each and every one with its tiny offering contributed to filling the hive with shining, amber honey, and not least, did their part for the hive's growth and development — for even more subjects.

During the past few weeks I had sent out a number of invitations to my very first presentation of "Savage's Standard Hive." The invitations had been delivered to local farmers, but also sent to natural scientists from the capital. And to Rahm. I had heard from many, but not from him. But he would no doubt come. He had to come.

Edmund, too, was ready. It was my impression that he had understood that this was serious. Yes, Thilda herself had apparently talked to him. Because it was still not too late, he was young, in that phase of life it was easy to be led astray, seduced by simple pleasures. Follow his passion, he'd called it, an argument I had the very greatest respect for, now it was just a matter of ensuring that he discovered a passion of *distinction.* My hope for him was that in his encounter with the research, in direct contact with nature, he would be inspired. That the sense of pride I would awaken in him, the pride over being a part of this family, carrying on our name, would lead him back to the straight and narrow path.

Together the women of the family had moved chairs and benches down to the hives. The public would sit there while I gave my presentation. The girls and Thilda had chopped, roasted, boiled and sautéed away in the kitchen for several days. There would be refreshments, of course there would, although the very last of our money, yes, even the tuition money, had been spent. Because it was just a matter of a short-term investment, after this day everything would be resolved, I was convinced of that.

Charlotte had been at my side the entire time. Since that day in the forest we had done everything together. Her serenity infected me, her enthusiasm became my own. This was also her day, but all the same there was a silent agreement that her white beekeeper's suit was to remain in the clothes chest in the girls' bedroom. She belonged among the other women, and appeared to have found her place there, with a serving dish in her hand and her cheeks blushing like tea roses. But once in a while she sent me a happy, excited smile, which told me she was looking forward to this with at least as much excitement as I was.

The first carriage stopped in front of me. I prepared myself for a greeting. But then I saw who it was. Conolly, it was only Conolly.

I stuck out my hand, but he didn't take it, just pounded me on the shoulder.

"Been looking forward to this all week," he said and smiled. "Never been a part of something like this before."

I smiled back, tentatively indulgent, didn't want to say that neither had I, but he jabbed me with his elbow.

"You're looking forward to it yourself. I can see it."

So we stood there, jiggling impatiently like two young boys on our first day of school.

First the local farmers arrived — two who already kept bees and one who was thinking about starting up. They walked down to the hives while we waited.

A little later two gentlemen whom I didn't know arrived on horseback. Both were wearing top hats and riding clothes, and were covered with dust, as if they had traveled a long distance. They dismounted, came towards me and it was only then that I recognized my former fellow students, both with receding hairlines, potbellies and coarse pores on faces full of wrinkles. How old they had become. No, not them, we, how old *we* had become.

They greeted me, thanked me for the invitation, looked around and nodded in appreciation. They commented upon the types of opportunities found in living like this, at one with nature, instead of the existence they themselves had chosen, in the urban forest where the trees were buildings of brick, the fertile soil was cobblestone and all one saw when one looked up towards the sky were rooftops and chimney pots.

The people streamed in; more farmers, some merely for curiosity's sake, and even three zoologists from the capital, who came with the morning coach and were dropped off on the road below the property.

But no Rahm.

I hurried inside, checked the clock on the mantelpiece.

I had hoped to start at one o'clock on the dot. Only then, when everyone was in their seat, would I walk down and take my position in front of them. And Edmund, my firstborn, would be there in the audience — *he* would see me standing in front of everyone.

The time was now one thirty. People were becoming a little impatient. Some discretely fished their pocket watches out of their vests and glanced at them quickly. They had helped themselves to the food and drink that Thilda and the girls had brought around and were presumably quite full. It was hot; several people lifted their hats, took out handkerchiefs and wiped them over damp necks. My own hat was a scorching black ceiling that pressed down upon my head, and made it difficult to think. I regretted my outfit. More and more people looked towards the hives, and subsequently, at me, inquisitively. The conversation, and my own in particular, dried up. I was unable to stay focused on the person listening to me, as my gaze was again and again drawn towards the gate. Still no Rahm. Why didn't he come?

I'd have to begin nonetheless. I *had to* begin.

"Get the children," I said to Thilda.

She nodded. In a low voice she began gathering the girls around her, while Charlotte was sent inside to get Edmund.

I started walking calmly down towards the hives. My audience became aware that something was finally happening. The scattered conversations dissipated and everyone followed me.

"Gentlemen, kindly take your places," I

455

said and gestured with my arm towards the chairs we had placed down there.

They didn't need convincing. The benches were in the shade, they had no doubt already been longing to move down there.

When all those present had taken their seats, I saw that we had exaggerated. There were not nearly as many people as expected. But then the girls came, and Edmund also. They did a good job of filling up, spread out haphazardly, as only children can, and closed up the largest gaps.

"So. It looks as if everyone has found a seat," I said. But I wanted more than anything to scream out the opposite. Because he wasn't here, without him the day was meaningless. Then I caught Edmund's eye down there. No, not meaningless. It was, after all, for Edmund I was doing this.

"Then you must just excuse me for one moment while I put on my protective suit." I attempted a smile. "One is not, after all, a Wildman." Everyone, even the farmers, laughed, both loud and long. And here I thought that I had served up a witticism for the initiated few, something that would set *us* apart from *them.* But it didn't matter. What mattered now was the hive, and I knew that they had never seen anything like it.

I hurried inside and changed, squirmed out of the heavy wool garments and into the white suit. The thin fabric was cool against my body and it was a relief to take off the black top hat and instead put on the white, lightweight beekeeper's hat with the gauzy veil in front of my face.

I looked out the window. They were sitting quietly on the chairs and benches. Now. I had to do it now. With or without him. To the devil with Rahm, of course I would manage without the droning of his superior knowledge!

I went outside and down the path to the hives. It had become wider, with wheel ruts from Conolly's battered-up old wagon, in some places deep holes. I had driven all the way down with the hives, as Conolly did not dare to approach them and I barely managed to get the vehicle up the hill again.

Faces smiled at me, everyone in friendly expectation. It made me feel confident.

And then I stood before them and spoke to them. Finally, for the first time, I could share my invention with the world, finally I could tell them about Savage's Standard Hive.

Afterwards they all came over, shook my hand, one after the next; *fascinating, astonishing, impressive,* words of praise were showered on me, I could not distinguish who said what, it was all a blur. But I did pick up on the most important thing: Edmund was there and he saw everything. His gaze was alert and clear, for once his body was neither restless nor lethargic, simply present. His attention was on me, at all times.

He saw everything, all the hands, even the very last hand that was extended towards me.

I had taken off my glove and the cool fingers met mine. A shock went through my entire body.

"Congratulations, William Savage."

He smiled, not a flash of a smile, but a smile that lingered, that rested on his face, yes, that actually belonged there.

"Rahm."

He held my hand and nodded towards the hives.

"This was something else altogether."

I barely managed to speak.

"But when did you come?"

"In time to hear the most important part."

"I . . . I didn't see you."

"But I saw *you,* William. And besides . . ." He stroked the sleeve of my suit with his left hand; I could feel the hairs on my arm underneath stand on end in a marvelous shudder.

"You know I don't dare to come close to the bees without being properly dressed. That's why I stayed here, in the back."

"I didn't think . . ."

"No. But here I am."

He took my hand between both of his own. The warmth from them flowed through me, pumped by my blood out into every single component of me. And out of the corner of my eye I glimpsed Edmund. He was still there, still had his eyes on us, on me, was still just as attentive and alert. He saw.

Tao

I stayed at the library all day. Read books, old research articles, watched films on a clattering old projector on the ground floor. I had to be completely sure.

A lot of it was primary school curriculum. I felt myself transported back to sluggish classes in natural science history, where the teacher lectured on our history with the voice of doom, an intoning drone that led to our renaming the classes the History of Sleep. We were too young to understand the scope of what she was trying to communicate. When the teacher bored her wrinkle-framed eyes into us, we turned towards the sunlight from the window and conjured up shapes in suitable fine-weather clouds or checked the clock on the wall to see how long it was until the next recess.

Now I discovered anew all the facts the teacher had tried to drill into us back then. Some dates still remained in my memory.

2007. That was the year The Collapse was given a name. CCD — Colony Collapse Disorder.

But it had started long before that. I found a video about the development of beekeeping throughout the past century. After the Second World War, apiculture was a worldwide, flourishing economy. In the US alone there were 5.9 million colonies. But the figures dropped, both there and in the rest of the world. In 1988 the number of hives had been halved. Bee death had afflicted many places, in Sichuan as early as in the 1980s. But only when it struck in the US — and as dramatically as it did precisely in 2006 and 2007, farmers with several thousand hives suffered mass disappearances in the course of a few weeks — only then did The Collapse receive a name. Perhaps because it happened in the US, nothing was really important at that time until it happened in the US: mass death in China didn't merit a worldwide diagnosis. That's how it was back then. Later everything was turned around.

A good number of books were written about CCD. I leafed through them, but found no straightforward answer. Nobody agreed about the cause of The Collapse, because there was no one specific cause. There were many. Poisonous insecticides were the first thing considered. In Europe certain forms of pesticides were temporarily banned in 2013 and with time, also in the rest of the world. Only the US held back. Some scientists maintained that the poisons had an impact on the bees' internal navigation system and prevented them from finding their way back to the hive. The toxins affected the nervous systems of small insects and many people were adamant in their belief that several of the causes of bee death stemmed from these toxins. The ban stemmed from a better-safe-than-sorry principle, it was said. But the research findings weren't conclusive enough. The consequences of banning the toxins were too great. Entire crops were destroyed by vermin, with subsequent food shortages. It was impossible to carry out modern agriculture without the pesticides. And the overall impact of the ban was too negligible; the bees disappeared all the same. In 2014 it was established that Europe had lost 7 billion bees. Because the poison was in the soil, some claimed, the bees died because it still affected them. But there were few who listened. After a trial period the ban was lifted.

Not only pesticides were to blame. *Varroa destructor* — a tiny parasite that attacked the bees — was also a cause. The parasitic mite attached itself to the body of the bee like a large ball, sucked the hemolymph out of it and spread a virus which was often not detected until much later.

Then there was the extreme weather. The world gradually acquired a new climate. Starting in the year 2000 and onwards, it evolved faster and faster. Dry, hot summers without flowers and nectar killed the bees. Hard winters killed the bees. And rain. The bees stayed inside when it rained, like people. Wet summers meant slow death.

Single-crop agriculture was a third factor. For the bees, the world was a green desert: mile after mile of fields where the same plant was cultivated, along with a lack of uncultivated areas. Man's development took off, the bees didn't keep up. And they disappeared.

Without bees thousands of acres of cultivated fields suddenly lay fallow. Flowering fields without berries, trees without fruit. Suddenly farm produce which formerly had been everyday food became scarce: apples, almonds, oranges, onions, broccoli, carrots, blueberries, nuts and coffee beans.

Meat production declined over the course of the 2030s, in that it was no longer possible to produce some of the formerly most important types of feed for domestic animals. Human beings likewise had to do without milk and cheese, because the animals no longer produced enough. And the production of biofuel, such as sunflower oil, which had been invested in heavily as an oil substitute, was suddenly out of the question, because it was dependent upon pollination. Once again there was a return to nonrenewable energy, which in turn accelerated global warming.

At the same time, population growth stagnated. First it stopped, and then the curve began to descend. For the first time in the history of mankind, the human population was no longer on the increase. Our species was in decline.

The disappearance of the bees affected the continents differently. American agriculture was the first in crisis. The Americans couldn't manage, like the Chinese, to pollinate by hand. They didn't have the workforce. People wouldn't work cheaply enough, long enough, hard enough. An imported labor supply didn't solve the problem, either. The workers also had to be fed, and although they were hardworking and persevering, the food they produced was not much more than what they consumed themselves.

The collapse in the US led to a worldwide

food crisis. Simultaneously, the bees died in Europe and Asia, too.

Australia was the last nation to be affected. A documentary from 2028 explained how. Australia had been everyone's hope, here the *Varroa destructor* mite was still not found, here it seemed as if the bees didn't react to the contaminants to the same extent as elsewhere. Healthy bees came from Australia and with time apiculture grew into a large economy. Australia also developed into a leading research nation for bees, pollination and apiculture.

Nobody knew how it happened, but on a spring day in 2027 a beekeeper in Avon Valley noticed that there were defects in one of his hives. Mark Arkadieff ran an organic honey farm. He did everything right. Pollination on a small scale, only a small number of hives were ever moved at a time, gently and carefully, and only to farms that could guarantee that they didn't use pesticides. He took good care of his bees, changed the bottom boards when they were dirty, ensured that they always had enough to eat. Arkadieff himself said that the bees owned him, not the other way around. He was their humble servant, they controlled his life, his annual rhythm, when he got up and when he went to bed. He had proposed to his wife, Iris, while they were carefully trying to lead a swarming bee colony to a new hive.

That Arkadieff's farm, Happy Bees Honey Farm, would be the first place on the Australian continent to be affected by mites was a fate they didn't deserve. Presumably it was the sister's fault. She lived in California, and had recently spent two weeks on the farm. She must have carried the infection with her in her luggage. Or it could have been the work clothes they had ordered from South Korea. Nobody noticed anything when they opened the innocent-looking, gray-paper package and took out sensible overalls for use on the farm. Or could there have been something in the fertilizer the neighboring farm had just had delivered, large sacks of it, produced in Norway?

Mark didn't know, his wife didn't know. All they knew was that that spring their bees became ill, and they didn't discover it until it was too late.

He showed the news team around the farm while he told his story. He couldn't hide the tears when he opened empty hives, with just a few dying bees on the bottom. Now there were no longer any safe countries. The world was facing the greatest challenge in the history of the human race. A final all-out effort was made. The *Varroa destructor* mite was fought off to a degree. In some places attempts were made to diversify single-crop farming. Flower borders were planted between the fields. Pesticides were once again banned. But because of this ban, entire crops were eaten by vermin.

English scientists had experimented with the creation of genetically modified plants, plants that carried the pests' own pheromone, (E)-betafarnesene, a substance the insects secreted to signal to others that there was danger nearby. Now these genetically modified plants were used to a far-reaching extent. China was the first to implement this new standard, in desperation because of the food shortage. The pheromones wouldn't affect the bees, it was said, they wouldn't notice. The environmentalists protested loudly, held that the bees would react to the pheromones in the same way as the insect pests. But they weren't heard. It was a win-win situation, it was claimed. People could continue with their industrial farming — nobody knew of anything else — the bees would be spared the nerve poison in the pesticides.

So the fields were filled with genetically modified plants and the results were good

— so good that chances were taken all over the world. And the genetically modified plants spread like wildfire. They took over. But the bee death continued, and escalated. By 2029 China had lost 100 billion bees.

Whether the bees in fact reacted to the pheromone was never established. It was too late anyway. The plants were growing like crazy. On the edge of every ditch there were plants that scared away the insects.

The world came to a halt.

In the library I found interviews with beekeepers from every part of the world. There was no mistaking their fear. They had become spokespersons and representatives for the crisis. Some were furious, swore to keep fighting, but the later the interviews were done, the more evident was their resignation. Had I seen these films earlier, they wouldn't have made any impression on me. They were testimonies from another time. Worn-out men in worn-out work clothes, coarse facial features, sun-baked skin, banal language, they had nothing to do with me. But now every single person stood out, every single personal catastrophe meant my own.

GEORGE

One day he just showed up. Maybe Emma
had called him. I heard his voice when I
opened the front door. I'd been in the barn;
with my earmuffs on I couldn't hear anything, not whether cars came or went, no
voices in the yard, couldn't hear Emma calling.

A grown man's voice. At first I didn't understand who it was. Then I realized it was
him. That was what his voice was like now.

I jogged across the yard. He was here!
Emma had probably told him how things
stood. They talked to each other all the
time, I guess, and now he'd come to lend a
hand! With him here everything would be
easier. With him I could manage everything.
Do carpentry twenty hours a day. Work
harder than ever before.

But then I heard what he was talking
about. He was talking about his summer
job. Enthusiastically. I stopped, stood there,

couldn't bring myself to go inside.

"It was about tomatoes, but still," he said. "Everything is exciting in its own way when you learn more about it. I have never seen such big tomatoes before. Neither had the photographer. And the farmer who won the contest was so proud. The article was printed on the front page, imagine that! The very first article I wrote went straight onto the front page!"

I rested my hand on the door handle.

Emma laughed and praised him effusively, as if he were a five-year-old who had just learned how to ride a bicycle.

I pushed the handle down quickly and opened the door. They fell silent right away.

"Hi," I said. "Didn't know you were coming."

"There you are," Emma said to me.

"I wanted to surprise Mom," Tom said.

"He's made that whole long trip even though he has to go back on Sunday," Emma said.

"Was there any point?" I said.

"It's Mom's birthday," Tom said.

I'd forgotten about it. I calculated quickly and deduced to my relief that it wasn't until tomorrow.

"And I wanted to see how things are going," he said softly.

"What's the point of that?"

"George," Emma said sharply.

"Everything's fine here," I said to Tom. "But it's nice that you've come home for her birthday."

We celebrated with a fish meal the next day, hadn't had fish since the last time he was home. Tom told stories from the local newspaper where he was working. He didn't come right out and say it, but I understood that he received a lot of praise. The editor held that he had "a knack for it," whatever "it" actually was. Emma laughed the whole time. I'd almost forgotten how her laughter sounded.

I'd rushed into town and bought an expensive pair of pantyhose and some hand lotion as a present.

"Oh. I didn't need anything this year," she said when she opened the present.

"Of course you need a present," I said. "Besides, they're useful things, things you can use."

She nodded, mumbled thanks, but I could see that her eyes swept over the price tag that was half scraped off, probably wondering how much I'd spent of money we didn't have.

Tom gave her a thick book with a picture of a farm in the fog on the cover. She likes books that take a long time to read.

"Paid for out of my first paycheck," he said and smiled.

She gushed over the gift, all smiles. Then all of a sudden it was silent. Tom took a bite of fish. Chewed slowly. I noticed his eyes on me.

"Tell me about it, Dad," he said suddenly.

Did he mean about the bees? He probably just wanted to be polite.

"Well, let's see. Once upon a time . . . ," I said.

"George," Emma said.

Tom kept looking at me, the same open gaze.

"Mom and I have been talking a little, but she said you had to tell me properly, that you're the expert."

He asked questions like an adult. As if *he* were the adult. I squirmed, my behind was stiff, the chair pressed rudely against the small of my back.

"Well, somebody's sure taking a powerful interest all of a sudden," I said.

He put down his fork, wiped carefully around his mouth with the napkin.

"I've read quite a lot about CCD lately. But it's all just speculations. I thought maybe you, being out there, every single day, have some other thoughts about why . . ."

"I see, so it's the journalist who has come to call. Are you going to write an article about all this, then?"

He blinked, he made a wry face. That struck a nerve.

"No, Dad. No. That's not why."

Then he was silent.

Suddenly I couldn't bear the smell of fish anymore, it irritated my nose, settled into my hair and clothing. I stood up abruptly.

"Do we have anything else?"

"There's more fish," Emma said and put down the book that she'd been holding on to until now.

I walked towards the refrigerator, didn't look at either of them.

"I meant something other than fish."

"There's dessert." Her voice was still cheerful and light.

"Dessert won't fill me up."

I turned around and stared at her. Then I glanced at Tom. They were both looking at me, sitting there side by side at the table and just staring, sort of kindly, even though they probably thought I was an idiot.

Tom turned towards Emma.

"You didn't need to prepare fish for my sake. It's your birthday, after all. You should have made something you like instead."

"I like fish just fine," she said. It sounded like she was reading something aloud from a book.

"Tomorrow the two of you should go ahead and have what you usually have for dinner," Tom continued. Just as damned polite. Was there no end to all of this?

"Aren't you leaving tomorrow anyway?" I said.

"Supposed to," Tom said in a low voice.

"But he'll have time for an early dinner," Emma said. "Right, Tom?"

"Sure," he said.

"How early?" I said. "I'd like to get a decent stint of work in before I eat." My voice was rough and grating against their bright, cozy chatter.

"Around two, wasn't that what we'd talked about?" Emma said to Tom.

"I might be able to stay a little longer," Tom said.

I ignored him. "Around two? I call that lunch," I said to Emma.

"Don't go to any trouble for my sake," Tom said.

"A simple dinner is no trouble," Emma chirped.

"There's actually a lot to do around here these days, as you might have understood," I said. At least one of us could be honest.

"I'd be happy to help out while I'm here," Tom said quickly.

"Half a day of college muscles won't exactly do the trick."

Emma didn't even answer me, just kept talking to Tom in a sugary-sweet voice. "It would be great if you could help Dad a little."

"GREAT," I said.

Nobody responded to that. Luckily. I'd throw up if I heard any more of that sugary-sweet voice.

Tom picked up his knife and fork again, scraped at his food. Poked at some fish bones and glistening fish skin with his fork.

"I would have liked to have stayed a little longer."

Would have . . . As if it were something that had already happened. Something he couldn't do anything about.

"Maybe you could call and ask if you could stay a few more days?" Emma said.

"I was one of thirty-eight applicants for that job," Tom said softly.

I stepped towards the door. Couldn't stand to hear any more of his excuses.

I'd made it all the way to the yard when he caught up with me.

"Dad, wait."

I didn't turn around, just kept going towards the barn. "Have to work."

"Can I come along?"

"There's a lot to take in. No point for such a short time."

"But I want to. I want to."

Wow. This insistence was new. The words snuck their way in and coaxed out a bothersome lump in my throat. Did he mean it? I had to turn around and look at him.

"It'll just be a mess," I said.

"Dad. It's not because I'm a journalist. It's because . . . I care. Really."

He looked at me. Large, wide-open eyes. "It's my farm, too."

Then he was silent. Just stood there. Apparently wasn't going to say anything more. Just stare me down. I couldn't bear that gaze, the beautiful eyes, my child. Child and adult at the same time.

He meant it.

"Fine." I nodded, my voice gruff. "That's fine." I cleared my throat in an effort to purge my voice, but there was apparently nothing more to be said.

Then we walked in there together.

WILLIAM

The letter arrived with the afternoon coach. I was still flying after yesterday, when everything had gone as I'd wished, yes, perhaps even better, when my new life had begun. I could still feel the moment inside me, the moment between Edmund, Rahm and I, that period of time when everything was completely as it was meant to be, where the Idea about the moment and the Moment itself ascended to become a higher entity.

I started trembling when I saw the postmark. Karlowice. It was from him — an acknowledgment — it couldn't be anything else. It had been weeks since I'd sent my letter, his answer could have come on any other day, but imagine, it arrived just now, exactly today. I was shaking. It was too much. Was I Icarus? Would my wings catch fire? No, this wasn't hubris, this was the result of hard work. I had earned this.

I brought the letter into my room, where I

settled into my chair, and with just as much reverence as in meeting with St. Peter himself, I broke the seal.

Karlowice, 29 August 1852

Honorable William Savage,

It was with great enthusiasm that I received your letter. It is an incredibly interesting enterprise you have undertaken. I would imagine the local beekeepers in your district will benefit greatly from your hives.

Be that as it may: I assume a great deal has changed since you wrote me your letter, and that you have now learned about Reverend Lorenzo Langstroth's achievements. Perhaps you have even already received a denial on your patent application. Forgive me if I am now giving you information with which you are already familiar.

It appears to me as if you have had exactly the same thoughts as an apiarist on the other side of the Atlantic Ocean. I must say it was with surprise that I read the description of your hive, as it is very similar to the Reverend's. I have personally had the pleasure of corresponding with Reverend Langstroth during the past year and know with certainty that he has now received the patent on the frames, exactly the same as those described in your letter. He, too, has made calculations to arrive at the golden measurement for the distance between the hive's walls and frames and the mutual measurement between each individual frame, although the figure he has arrived at is 9.5 millimeters.

I hope you will continue with your extremely fruitful research, as I am wholly convinced that as regards knowledge about the life of bees, we have barely scratched the surface. I would enjoy hearing more from you and hope we can hereby commence a mutual correspondence as two peers within the field.

Yours sincerely,
Johann Dzierzon

I gripped the letter with both hands, but still it trembled, the letters shook, they were scarcely legible. Laughter reverberated in my ears.

Mutual correspondence. Peers within the field. I repeated the words to myself, but they had no meaning.

It was too late. I was nobody's peer.

I was the one who should be placed in a

box with a lid where I could be observed and controlled from above. I was tamed now, by life itself.

I dropped the letter and stood up. I had to knock something down, destroy something, tear something apart. Whatever it took to stop the hurricane inside me. Suddenly my hands flew out from my body and pulled down books, the inkwell and drawings from the desk. Everything fell to the floor, the ink gushed out, becoming a bottomless lake against the wooden floorboards, which could never be removed, and would remain there like a staring reminder of my defeat. As if that were necessary. All of me, my entire indistinct, inert body, was a reminder.

The bookshelves suffered the same fate as the inkwell, the desk chair followed. The wall charts were next, I tore them to pieces. Swammerdam's sea monsters were shredded, never again would I fix my gaze on them, see God in the tiniest of components of Creation.

Then the wallpaper, the blasted, yellow wallpaper. I tore it off the walls, strip by strip, till it hung in shreds and left behind large wounds upon the raw brick wall behind.

And then, finally I stood with them in my

hands, the drawings of the hive. Worthless. They had to be destroyed forever.

I flexed the muscles in my hands. I wanted to crumple them, tear them apart, but wasn't equal to it.

I wasn't equal to it.

Because I wasn't the one who should do it. They weren't mine to destroy, but rather his. Everything was his fault and therefore also his responsibility. I leapt out into the hallway.

"Edmund!"

I didn't knock, just stormed in; he hadn't gone to the trouble of locking the door.

He popped out of bed. His hair bristled, his eyes bloodshot. He stank of spirits. I turned away from the stench almost without thinking, as I had no doubt done before, deluding myself, pretending it didn't exist.

No. Not today and not ever again. He should receive a thrashing. A thrashing over his back with the belt buckle, until his skin was full of gashes and bleeding.

But first this. "Look here!" I threw the drawings onto his bed. "Here they are!"

"What?"

"You're the one who got me started. Here they are! What am I supposed to do with them?"

"Father, I was sleeping."

"They're worthless. Do you understand?"

His gaze became clear, he pulled himself together. Picked up one of them.

"What is this?"

"Not worth the paper they are drawn on! Worthless!"

He looked over the meaningless blotches of ink.

"Oh. The hive. It's the hive," he said softly.

I breathed heavily, tried to compose myself. "They're yours now. The drawings. You were the one who wanted me to begin this. You can do what you want with them."

"Wanted you to begin . . . what do you mean?"

"You started it all. Now you can destroy it. Burn them. Tear them to pieces, do what you want."

He stood up slowly and took a sip of water from a cup, with an astoundingly steady hand.

"I don't understand what you mean, Father."

"It is your work. I created them for you."

"But why?" He stared at me. I couldn't remember the last time I had met his gaze. Now his eyes were narrow. He looked older than his sixteen years.

"The book!" I cried.

"What book? What are you talking about?"

"Huber's book. François Huber! *New Observations on the Natural History of Bees!*"

"Father. I don't understand." He stared at me as if I were insane, as if I belonged in an asylum.

My body slumped. He didn't even remember. This moment that had meant so infinitely much to me. "The book you left with me after that Sunday, when the others were in church."

All of a sudden it was as if something dawned on him.

"That day, yes. In spring."

I nodded. "It is something I will never forget. That you, of your own free will, came to see me that day."

His eyes slipped away, his hands moved, as if he wanted to grasp something, but found nothing but dust particles in the air.

"It was Mother who asked me to go see you," he said finally. "She thought it would help."

Thilda. He was still hers, now and forever.

GEORGE

We kept building hives for the rest of the day. Until it got dark. He worked hard. But not with the same reluctance as before. He wanted to work now. He asked questions, probing away, learned quickly, was accurate and quick.

The sound of the hammer against nails, rhythmic. The whining saw, music. And at times, silence. The wind, the birds out there.

The sun beat down on the barn roof, the sweat poured off us. He held his head under the faucet to cool off, shook it like a dog and laughed. Thousands of cold drops of water hit me, cooled me off, and I was somehow unable to keep from laughing back at him.

Sunday went the same way. We worked, talked about little but beehives. It seemed as if he was enjoying himself. I hadn't seen him like this since he was a little boy. He ate well, too. Even had a piece of ham for lunch.

I looked at my watch. We were sitting outdoors, having a cup of coffee. It was almost two. The bus would be leaving soon. I didn't say anything. Maybe he'd forgotten about it. Maybe he'd changed his mind.

He looked at his watch as well.

Then he took it off. And put it in his pocket.

"Dad. What was it like, the first time?"

He looked at me; suddenly that profound gravity of his was back.

"What do you mean?"

"The first hive you opened?"

"What do you think? Completely awful."

"But what was different? How is this different?"

I took a sip of my coffee, and sloshed it around in my mouth, found it difficult to swallow.

"Oh, I don't know. They were just gone. Only a handful left at the very bottom. Just the queen and larvae. All alone."

I turned away, didn't want him to see my eyes tearing up. "And it happens so quickly, one day they're healthy, the next they're just gone."

"Not like winter death," he said.

I nodded. "Nothing like it. Winter death is the weather, it's food shortage, or both."

He remained silent, held the cup with both hands, thinking.

"But you're going to experience winter death again," he said finally.

I nodded. "Of course. There are hard winters from time to time."

"And they'll get even harder," he continued. "There will be storms, bad weather."

I should say something, contribute, but didn't know what.

"And summer death," he continued. "You'll have more summer death, too. Because the summers are getting more rainy, more unstable."

"Sure," I said. "But we don't really know."

He didn't look at me, just continued, his voice growing louder. "You'll have collapse again, too. It'll happen again." He was speaking loudly now. "The bees are dying, Dad. We're the only ones who can do anything about it."

I turned to face him. I'd never heard him talk like this before, and tried to smile, but it just turned into a lopsided grimace.

"We? You and I."

He didn't smile, but didn't seem angry, either. Just dead serious.

"Human beings. We have to implement changes. That's what I was talking about when we were in Maine, right? We mustn't be part of the system. We have to change operations before it's too late."

I swallowed. Where was this coming from? His enthusiasm? He'd never been like this before. I was suddenly so proud, just had to look at him. But he was suddenly preoccupied with his coffee cup.

"Want to get back to work?" he asked softly.

I nodded.

Evening came. Night fell.

We sat on the porch, all three of us. The sky was clear.

"Do you remember the snake?" I asked.

"And the bees," Tom said.

"The snake?" Emma asked.

Tom and I looked at each other and smiled.

I slept in the next day. And I woke up with a grin on my face. Ready for new hives. Emma was sitting at the table when I came into the kitchen. She had started reading that thick book.

There was a single plate in front of her. I looked around.

"Where is he?"

She put the book down. Turned down the corners of her mouth in a pout.

"Oh, George."

"Yes?"

"Tom left early. Before breakfast."

"Without saying good-bye?"

"He didn't want to wake you, he said."

"But I thought . . ."

"Yes. I know." She picked up the book again, sort of clung to it, but didn't say anything more.

I didn't have the strength to say anything, either. I had to turn away.

It felt as if God had been teasing me. Hung a ladder down from the sky and let me climb up to take a peek, let me see angels on candy floss wings before He suddenly pushed me off a cloud and let me fall back to earth. The earth on a rainy day. Gray. Slushy. Horrible.

Except the sun was shining just as doggedly. Scorching the planet to death.

I had lost the bees.

And I'd apparently lost Tom, too. A long time ago. I'd just been too thick in the head to realize it.

TAO

"Ma'am? We're closing."

The guard stood over me holding a heavy bunch of keys in her hand, which she rattled. "You are welcome to come back tomorrow. Or to borrow something."

I stood up. "Thank you."

In front of me was a long article about the death of bumblebees. The bumblebees and the wild bees disappeared at the same time as the honeybees, but their death wasn't as evident or ominous, the species were depleted without anyone actually sounding the alarm. Wild bees were responsible for two-thirds of the pollination in the world. In the US the honeybee did most of the work, but on the other continents wild bee species were the most important. Here, however, the continuous species decline made it more difficult to gauge population numbers. But mites, viruses and unstable weather also affected the wild bees. And pesticides. They were in the soil, enough to poison future generations, both bees and humans.

Intensive research was carried out on other insects that could be suitable for effective pollination. The first ones they tried were the wild bees, but it was useless. The farming of different types of pollinating flies was subsequently attempted for this purpose, *Ceriana conopsoides, Chrysotoxum octomaculatum* and *Cheilosia reniformis,* but without success. Simultaneously the climate changes made the world a more inhospitable place to be. The rising sea levels and extreme weather led to the emigration of human population groups and the food shortage became acute. Whereas previously people had started wars for reasons of power, wars were now being fought over food.

This article stopped at the year 2045. One hundred years after the end of the Second World War, the earth, as modern human beings had known it, was no longer a place that could be populated by billions. In 2045 there were no bees left on the planet.

I went over to the bookshelves where I'd found many of the most recent books about The Collapse, wanting to put some of them back. I was about to shove a book into the shelf when I noticed a green spine a little further down. It wasn't particularly thick or tall, not a big book, but my eyes were drawn to the green color all the same. And the yellow letters with the title: *The History of Bees.*

I grabbed it and tried to pull it out. But the book resisted; the plastic on the bookbinding was stuck to the books next to it and emitted a small sigh when I pulled them apart. I opened it; the covers were stiff, but the pages fell easily to the side, welcoming me in. The last time I had read this book was at my school's simple library, and at that time it had been a shabby printout, a copy. This time I was holding a pristine edition between my hands. I looked at the title page: 2037. A first edition.

Then I opened to the first chapter and my eyes were met once again by the same familiar pictures. The queen and her brood, which were just larvae in cells and all the golden honey they surrounded themselves with. Swarming bees on a frame in a beehive, crowded together, each identical to the next, impossible to distinguish from one another. Striped bodies, black eyes, rainbow-colored wings that shone.

I continued turning the pages until I came to the passages about knowledge, the same sentences I had read as a child, but now the words made an even greater impression: "In order to live in nature, with nature, we must detach ourselves from the nature in ourselves . . . Education means to defy ourselves, to defy nature, our instincts . . ."

I was interrupted by the sound of footsteps. The guard came around a bookshelf and walked towards me. She didn't say anything, but once again rattled the keys. Demonstratively now.

I nodded at her quickly to show that I was on my way out. "I would like to borrow this." I held up the book. She shrugged her shoulders.

"Help yourself."

When I got back to my room, still holding *The History of Bees* to my chest, I finally put it down on the bed along with a pile of other books. I'd borrowed as many as I could carry. Soon I'd continue reading. I just needed a shower first.

I peeled off my clothes while standing in the middle of the floor. I pulled off everything at once, my socks got stuck in the legs of my trousers. The clothes were left in a tangled heap on the floor.

I showered until the hot water ran out, washed my hair three times, scrubbed my scalp with my nails, to get out the dust from the dead city streets. Then I dried myself off for a long time. I couldn't remove the dampness from my skin; the bathroom was foggy. Finally I brushed my teeth for a long time, feeling how plaque and bacteria disappeared, wrapped the towel around me and walked into the room again.

The first thing I saw was that my clothes had been picked up. The floor was empty. I turned towards the bed. A woman was sitting there. She was younger than me. Her skin was soft, no dirt under her fingernails. Her clothes were clean and sleek, snug, like a uniform. This was a woman whose occupation was something completely different from working outdoors among the trees.

In her hand she held one of the books. I couldn't see which one.

She raised her head and looked at me, serious, dispassionate. I was unable to say anything, my brain was working intensely to make something fall into place. Should I know her?

She calmly stood up, put the book down, then handed me my clothes, which were now neatly folded and placed into a pile.

"I would ask that you please get dressed."

I didn't move. She behaved as if her presence here were a given. And maybe it was. I stared at her, searching her face to see if it stirred up any memories. But none emerged. I noticed that my towel was falling off, slipping down, about to leave me naked, and if possible, even more vulnerable. I pulled the towel up and squeezed my arms against it to hold it in place, feeling both awkward and exposed.

"How did you get in?" I asked and was surprised that my voice actually carried.

"I borrowed a key." She said it smiling a tiny smile at nothing at all, as if it were the most obvious thing in the world.

"What do you want? Who are you?" I stammered.

"You must get dressed and come with me."

It wasn't an answer, it was an order.

"Why? Who are you?"

"Here." Once again she held out the pile of clothing.

"Do you want money? I only have a little." I walked over to the bedside table where I still had a few coins in the drawer, turned around and held them out to her.

"I was sent by the Committee," she said. "You must come with me."

WILLIAM

The drawings lay in my lap. I sat on a bench in the garden, at a distance from the hives, close enough to see and hear them well, but far enough away to avoid being stung. I sat as motionless as an animal following a scent, a prey that would soon be attacked.

But the attack was already over. I was a carcass now.

The bee dies when its wings are worn out, frayed, driven too hard, like the sails of the *Flying Dutchman*. She dies midleap, as she is about to take flight, has a heavy load, perhaps she has taken on more than usual, is bulging with nectar and pollen, this time it is too much, the wings do not carry her any longer. She never returns to the hive, but plunges to the earth, with her entire burden. Had she had human feelings, she would have been happy at this moment, she would have entered the gates of heaven well aware she had lived up to the idea of herself, of the Bee, as Plato would have expressed it. The worn-out state of her wings, yes, her death in its entirety, is a clear sign that she has done what she was put on earth to do, accomplished an infinite amount, taking into consideration her tiny body.

I would never have such a death. There were no clear signs that I'd done what I was put on the earth to do. I had not accomplished anything at all. I would grow old, my body would swell, and subsequently fade away, without any trace of me left behind. Nothing would remain, except possibly a salty pie which left behind a greasy coating in the mouth. Nothing but a Swammer pie.

So it all might as well just come to an end right now. The mushrooms were still there, in the top drawer furthest to the left in the shop, carefully locked, with a key only I had access to. They would take effect rapidly; in just a few hours I would grow lethargic and listless, subsequently unconscious. A doctor would diagnose it as organ failure; nobody would know it was self-inflicted. And I would be free.

But I couldn't do it, because I couldn't move from the bench. I didn't even manage to destroy the drawings, my hands refused to perform that simple movement, the muscular impulse stopped in my fingertips, paralyzed me.

For how long I was alone, I didn't know.

She came without my noticing. Suddenly she sat down on the bench beside me. Without a sound, not even her breathing was audible. The close-set eyes, my own eyes, looked towards the bees that buzzed in front of us, or perhaps towards nothing.

In her hand she held the letter from Dzierzon. She must have found it among the chaos in the room, found it and read it, as she previously had also searched and gone through my things. Because it had been her all along, the tidy shop, the book on my desk. I just hadn't seen it, hadn't *wanted* to see it.

The proximity of another human being caused the paralysis to release its grasp. Or perhaps it released its grasp precisely because it was her. She was all I had now.

I laid the drawings on her lap.

"Destroy them for me," I said softly. "I can't do it."

She just sat there. I tried to meet her gaze, but she looked away.

"Help me," I begged.

She put a hand on the drawings. For a moment she was silent.

"No," she said.

"But they are rubbish, don't you understand?" My voice broke, but it didn't un-settle her.

She just shook her head slowly. "It's too soon, Father, perhaps they may still be of value."

I drew a breath, managed to speak calmly, tried to sound rational.

"They're useless. I really just want you to destroy them, because I'm incapable of do-ing it myself. Take them away, put them somewhere I can't see them and can't stop you. Burn them! A huge fire, flames reach-ing up to the heavens."

I wanted the words to provoke a reaction, get her to stand up and obey my earnest appeal, as she usually obeyed all my re-quests. But she just sat there, leafing through the pages, with one finger lightly tracing the lines I had done my best to draw straight, the details with which I had struggled so. "No, Father. No."

"But that's all that I want!" All of a sud-den there was again a tightening in my chest. I had my father's hand around my neck, his scornful laughter in my ears, dirt on my knees and a belt waiting. She was the adult and I was the child, ten years old again, with the heavy weight of shame on my shoulders, because yet again I had failed. "Burn them, please."

It was only then that I noticed the tears in her eyes. Her tears. When had I last seen them? Not when she sat beside me during all those hours last winter, not when she came home with a dead-drunk Edmund, not when she found me almost swallowed up by the earth.

And then I understood. These were her drawings, too, her work. She'd been there the entire time, but I'd only seen myself, my research, my drawings, my bees. Only now did I really absorb how there had been *two* of us from the first day. They were hers, too, the bees were hers, too.

"Charlotte." I swallowed. "Oh, Charlotte. Who have I really been for you?"

She looked up in astonishment. "What do you mean?"

"I mean . . . you should have had something more."

She drew her hand over her eyes; there was only amazement in her gaze now.

"Something more? No."

I wanted to say so many things to her, that she deserved a better father, one who also thought of her, that I'd been an idiot, only concerned about my own affairs, while her support was completely unshakable, regardless of the nature of my undertakings. But the words grew too large, I wasn't equal to the task.

All I could do was to take her hand. She let me do it, but hastened to lay the other one protectively over the drawings so the wind wouldn't take them.

We sat there in silence.

She inhaled several times, as if she wanted to say something, but no words came.

"You mustn't think like that," she said finally. Then she turned her head and looked at me with her clear, gray eyes. "I've received more than any girl could expect. More than any other girl I know. Everything you have shown me, told me, let me participate in. All the time we've spent together, all the conversations, everything you've taught me. For me you are . . . I . . ."

She didn't finish the sentence, just sat there, and finally she came out with it:

"I couldn't have had a better father."

A sob escaped from me. I stared out into space, focusing blindly on nothing, while fighting back the urge to cry.

We remained seated there; time passed, nature surrounded us with all of its sounds, the birdsong, the whistling of the wind, a frog croaking. And the bees. Their subdued buzzing calmed me.

Carefully Charlotte wriggled her hand out of mine and nodded gently.

"You won't have to see them anymore."

She stood up, took the drawings with her, carried them with both hands as if they were still something valuable and disappeared in the direction of the house.

A deep sigh escaped me, of thankfulness and relief, but also with a certainty that it was finally over. I remained seated, sitting and looking at the bees, at their perseverance, back and forth, never resting.

Not until their wings were torn.

GEORGE

Once again, I was unable to fall asleep. Everything was in place to ensure a good night's rest. The room was suitably cool, it was quiet. And dark. Why was it so dark lately? Much darker than before. Then I remembered the light. That was why. I'd never gotten around to repairing it. The cables were still crawling up there on the wall, like worms with heads of electrical tape. I passed by them every day, saw them every time, and they always put me in a bad mood. One of the many things I never got around to. It wasn't important, I knew that. I didn't need that light, none of us did. Emma didn't nag me about it, either. I don't even think she thought about it. But the crawling cables were a part of everything that wasn't the way it was supposed to be, everything that didn't work.

I needed seven hours of sleep. At least. I've always envied those who don't need much sleep. Those who wake up after five hours and are ready to perform at their best. They're the ones who really go far in life, I've heard.

I turned towards the alarm clock — 12:32 a.m. I'd been lying here since 11:08 p.m. Emma had fallen asleep right away and I dozed off, too, pretty quickly. But then I woke up again, my head clear, alert. And my body was running, unable to lie still, unable to make contact with the mattress. No matter what position I was in, it was wrong, lumpy, poking.

I had to get some sleep. I wouldn't be able to function tomorrow if I couldn't sleep now. Maybe a drink would help.

We didn't have any hard liquor, rarely drank it. But I found a beer in the refrigerator. And a glass in the cupboard. Then there was the opener. It wasn't hanging on the wall, in its place, a hook over the sink, the fourth hook from the right, between the scissors and a spatula. Where was it? I opened the silverware drawer. Found the corkscrew along with some rotten rubber bands in a separate part of the drawer furthest in. But the opener wasn't there. I opened another drawer. Nothing. Had she rearranged the system? Put things in new places? If so, it wouldn't be the first time.

I kept looking in drawer after drawer. Had to put down the beer, use both hands, couldn't be bothered to be quiet now. Since she'd gone and started rearranging everything, she'd have to put up with that much. Dammit, there were so many drawers in this kitchen and so much junk. So-called useful utensils gathering dust. An egg cooker, an electric pepper grinder, a gadget that divided an apple into six pieces. Things that had accumulated over the course of half a lifetime. Emma was the culprit behind the majority of the things. I got the urge to find a bag, start throwing things out, at long last. Clean up.

But then it appeared. It was lying in the big drawer with the ladles, scoops and whisks. In the very back. At the very bottom. Yup, had clearly been given a new place. I opened the beer quickly. Mostly I had the urge to go and wake her up, tell her she could give a damn about changing things. But instead I took a large swig of beer. The cool liquid ran down my throat.

My stomach rumbled, but I didn't feel like finding anything to eat. Nothing appealed to me. Beer was nutritious, too. I wasn't tired at all, just restless. I paced back and forth, went into the living room, grabbed the remote. But I froze midmovement, because suddenly I noticed something on the wall in the dining room.

I walked in and stood in front of them. The drawings. William Savage's Standard Hive. Which, strictly speaking, had not been a standard for anybody except the Savage family. On a wall never touched by sunlight. In thick gold frames, shiny, without a speck of dust, Emma made sure of that. Black ink on yellowed paper. Figures. Measurements. Simple descriptions. Nothing more. But behind it was a heritage that my family had taken care of ever since the drawings were made in 1852. The Standard Hive was supposed to be William Savage's great breakthrough; he was supposed to write himself into the history books. But he hadn't taken the clever American Lorenzo Langstroth into account. Langstroth won, he developed the hive measurements that later became the standard. And nobody paid any attention to Savage. He was, quite simply, too late. That was maybe how it had to be when they sat there in distant parts of the world, each of them working on the same thing, but without a telephone, fax or email.

Behind every great inventor are always a dozen crestfallen guys who were just a bit too late. And Savage was one of them. So there were neither riches nor honor for him or his family.

His wife apparently managed to marry off most of the daughters. But it was worse for the son, Edmund. He was a good-for-nothing, a restless guy, a dandy, had acquired a taste for liquor at an early age and eventually disappeared into the gutters of London.

Only one of the daughters had never married. Charlotte, the brightest. The first lady of our family. She purchased a one-way ticket across the pond. Her trunk was up in the attic. It was the one she traveled with, she and a baby. Who the father was, nobody knew. The two of them and the trunk came to America all alone. In it she had everything she owned. It smelled stuffy, old. We didn't use it for anything, but I didn't have the heart to throw it out. Charlotte had put her entire life into the trunk, including her father's drawings of the Standard Hive.

And that was where it started. Charlotte started beekeeping. Not full-time, on the side of her job as a teacher and headmistress. She only had three hives, but the three hives were all it took for the child, a little boy, to eventually take a shine to it, and he expanded with a few more hives. As did his son. And his son. And finally, my grandfather, who invested in full-scale operations and made a proper living out of it.

The damn drawings!

Suddenly I slammed my fist into the glass. It cracked; the pain radiated from my hand and through my entire body. The picture shook a bit, but hung there as before.

They had to come down. All three frames had to come down.

I lifted them off the hooks and took them with me out into the hallway. There I found my biggest shoes, heavy winter shoes with thick soles.

Shoes on, out into the yard.

I was about to put an end to them, land my boot on them, trample them hard, but at that moment I suddenly thought of Emma, of the noise it would make. I turned towards the bedroom window. The light wasn't on up there. She was still asleep.

I carried the frames outside, opened the door to the barn and put them down on the floor.

Of course I could have just opened the frames from the back and teased out the pictures, but it was the sound of glass I wanted to hear. The crunching under my boot.

I stomped away, again and again, jumped on them. The glass broke, the frames shattered. Exactly as I had imagined.

Then I plucked out the drawings. I had hoped the broken glass would destroy them, but they were as good as new. The paper was surprisingly stiff and resilient. I laid them one on top of the other, six in all, in a pile. Stood there with them. I could burn them, put a match to them and let the life-work of my ancestors go up in flames. No.

I put the pile down on the worktable, studied it for a while. Terrible drawings. They hadn't contributed to anything. Deserved a miserable fate. Not a fire, that was too dramatic, too dignified. Something else.

And then I knew.

I summoned my strength, took hold of the pile, my hands resisted, but I forced them. Then I started tearing. Long strips, I tried to make them as even as possible. But it was too thick trying to tear six all at once. I'd have to divide the pile in two. Three pages at a time. But that didn't take long enough. I wanted to carry on for a long while. So I did one page at a time.

I liked the sound. It was as if the paper were screaming. *Mercy. Mercy!*

It felt better than good. It felt sensational, doing something — accomplishing something substantial. I could keep this up all night.

But finally I had to stop. There was no

point tearing them up into too-small pieces, then they wouldn't serve the purpose I had in mind.

I gathered up the strips and took them with me. Couldn't be bothered to clean up the frames and the glass, I'd take care of it tomorrow. I just walked out into the night, across the yard and opened the back door.

Onto the porch and from there into the back hallway. There I opened the first door on the right and took two steps into the darkness. A gurgling sound informed me that as usual the flush valve was stuck. Probably needed to be replaced. I didn't bother to turn on the light and check now. I just put the drawings, the paper, down on the floor. Ready to be used. Where they belonged. In the john.

Tao

We were sitting in an old electric car. Many cars like this were built in the 2020s, when solar electricity really took off. The time I visited the city with my parents, the streets were full of them, most of them old and decrepit. This car was better taken care of than most, built for fastidious customers, large, black and shiny. I had never seen this type of vehicle owned by a private person, nor used by people below a certain rank. The cars we had at home always belonged to the police or health care personnel, like the one that had come to pick up Wei-Wen. They were simple boxes of lightweight material, created to consume the least possible amount of electricity. This car was larger, more grand. Only rarely did a car like this visit our little city; it glided through the streets with tinted windows and we always wondered what they were doing in our little corner of the world.

It was the first time in my life I set foot inside such a beautiful vehicle. I put my hand on the imitation leather seat. It had once been smooth, but was now full of cracks. Because the car was old. The seats gave it away, the smell gave it away, the cleaning products were merely camouflage for the stench of old age that had settled into the fittings and the car body.

The woman had directed me to a seat in the middle, while she sat in the front and read off an address to the autopilot, a place name that meant nothing to me. Then the trip started. I saw only her neck. She said nothing. For a moment I considered asking her to stop, so I could jump out, but I knew there was no point. She gave me no choice. And there was something in her eyes that told me that there would be consequences if I didn't do as she said.

Besides . . . perhaps she could lead me to Wei-Wen. That was all that mattered.

We drove for almost an hour, met a few cars while we were still in the city center, but after a while we were alone on the road. None of the traffic lights we passed was working, and we sailed through the streets without having to show consideration for anyone else. The sign on the highway indicated that we were on our way towards

Shunyi. I didn't know anything about the area, but the buildings told me that it must once have been inhabited by people who were well-off. Spacious, secluded houses, with just three or four floors, and enormous gardens. Now the houses were run-down and the gardens overgrown. We passed something that had once been a golf course. Now it was flatlands covered with weeds, where attempts at cultivation were being made on a few patches of earth in one corner. A lot of fertile land still lay fallow. It astonished me that nobody tried to make something grow there. But perhaps everyone had moved out.

Finally we stopped. The woman opened the door and got out, asked me to follow her.

We stood in a square, in the middle of which a once-handsome fountain was now rusting away. A statue of a bird, a crane, lay at the bottom of the pool, perhaps it had been knocked over by natural forces, or perhaps it had been vandalism. Not a single car could be heard, only the wind pounding against the buildings where roofing tiles and windows were loose, the sound of the earth's own muscles, which slowly and inevitably were in the process of getting the upper hand, which would wipe out civilization.

The sound of voices caused me to tilt my face upwards. There were two people standing on the roof of a tall building, I couldn't see anything but their silhouettes against the sky, and heard talking but not words. They had something in their hands, something they now dropped. Round shadows slipped through the air, away from us, in the direction of the city center. I had read about remote-controlled, flying computers before. Drones. Was this the same thing? Who were they following?

Suddenly it struck me that perhaps they had also followed me, and for longer than I had suspected. That they already knew a great deal.

"We're going in here," the woman said.

The building had no name, no sign informing me of what it concealed. The woman put her hand against a glass plate on the wall, each of her fingers against five points on the plate. Suddenly two large, sooty doors slid to the side. They ran on electricity, in spite of the fact that it seemed as if the surrounding area had long since been without power.

She led me into the large building. I jumped when we almost collided with a young man standing guard on the inside. I turned around and discovered more guards. They were wearing uniforms like hers and greeted her quickly. She nodded back and continued on hurriedly.

I followed her through a large hall and further on into an open office landscape. We passed people everywhere. It was unreal, after all of these weeks in the deserted city. Everyone was like the guard, soft, clean, not marked by manual labor or sun. They worked busily, many people sat in front of large screens, others in soft-spoken meetings on plush sofa suites or around conference tables. A transparent landscape. The walls were of glass, the rooms were open, but the sound did not travel far. It was muffled by thick carpets and heavy furniture. In several places I almost stumbled over flat, round vacuum cleaners whirring around the floor by themselves, and sucking up dirt that I couldn't see.

The deterioration had not made it here; it was as if I'd come to a world that belonged in the past.

Finally she stopped. We were at the end of a hallway, in front of us was a wall, the first one I saw that wasn't made of glass. This was of dark, shiny, polished wood. A tall, wide door that looked as if it were carved out of the woodwork. The woman knocked hard on the door. A few seconds passed; then it emitted a buzzing sound and a click, before it opened.

Wei-Wen. Was he here? Suddenly I was shaking.

"Please." She nodded towards the open door.

I hesitated for a moment, then walked inside.

The door closed behind me. I heard the sound of the door again — the buzzing sound and a click. She locked me in.

The room was large and bright, but had no windows. The floor was carpeted here, too. The walls were covered with fabrics, heavy draperies, from floor to ceiling. Were there walls behind them? Or did they hide something else? People, openings to other rooms? Was that a tiny movement I saw there to the right? I spun around. But no, the curtain hung just as motionless as before. The discreet soundscape on the outside was an ear-shattering racket compared to the silence in here. Perhaps it was a room where no sounds were supposed to enter. Or get out. The thought caused my pulse to start racing.

There was a rustling in the fabric to my right and all of a sudden they were pulled to one side. An older woman liberated herself from the curtains. She smiled kindly. There was something familiar, the way she held her head, the tight-fitting collar. The web of wrinkles around her eyes. I'd seen her before, many times, but never in real life, and I knew the cadence of her voice before she spoke.

Because she was Li Xiara. The voice on the radio, the leader of the Committee, our nation's executive body.

I took a step backwards in shock, but she kept smiling.

"I'm sorry we had to meet in this way," she said softly. Her voice was more familiar than my own mother's. "But we could no longer avoid having to speak with you."

She put her hand on the back of a soft armchair.

"Please take a seat."

She didn't wait, but sat down in an identical chair opposite me.

"I know you have many questions. I'm sorry I couldn't pick you up myself. I hope we'll get everything cleared up." She spoke with utter composure, as if reading from a script.

We sat facing each other with our heads at the same level.

I couldn't help staring at her. Without the

filter of media images her face was so na-ked. It was the unfamiliarity of having her so close, seeing her in real life.

My heart sunk. This woman . . . What choices had she made? What was she re-sponsible for? The death of the cities? The situation of the young boy in the restau-rant? The elderly people, left behind to die? The adolescents, no more than ghosts, so desperate that fellow human beings had be-come prey?

My own mother?

No. I mustn't think about it, mustn't let my questions, my criticism lash out, because she knew more than I did. I needed to breathe — and think carefully before I spoke.

"I would appreciate it if you could tell me why I'm here." I imitated her manner of speaking, spoke the words as softly and gen-tly as I could.

Her eyes came to rest on me.

"In the beginning we found you to be bothersome."

"What?"

"Especially when you came to Beijing." She paused. "But subsequently . . . We had really planned on contacting you, we didn't want you, the two of you, to live with so much uncertainty for so long. But we just had to be completely certain first. We didn't want any rumors circulating. At all."

"Certain of what?"

She leaned forward in her chair, as if to get closer to me. "Now we are."

I didn't answer. The singsongy, calm voice awakened rage inside of me, but I got nowhere with my questions.

"And it was perhaps for the best," she continued, "that you had to find your own way to the answers."

I struggled to breathe, tried to stay calm. "I don't understand what you mean."

"You will have an opportunity to play a part in the time ahead. And we hope that you will cooperate."

"What do you mean?!"

"I'll get to that. First, why don't you tell me about what you think has happened to your son? What have you found out?"

I forced myself to stay calm. She'd set the agenda, so I had no choice but to comply with it, to cooperate. What would happen if I failed?

"I believe that something has happened to Wei-Wen that has significance for many more people than myself," I said slowly. "Or him."

She nodded.

"And what else?"

"I believe that is why you have taken him. And that what has happened will potentially change everything."

She waited.

"Can't you just tell me where he is?" I was begging now. "That's all I know."

She was silent. Her gaze remained suspended in the air.

Suddenly it was as if everything inside me stopped, I could no longer take her calm, singsongy voice, the guessing games, the indifferent gaze and the little half-smile which was impossible to read.

"I don't know anything!" In one jump I was right in front of her.

She flinched in her chair.

I grabbed hold of her shoulders. For the first time her expression changed. A tiny glimmer of fear pressed its way through the wall of equanimity.

"Where is Wei-Wen?" I shouted. "Where is he? What has happened to him?"

I hauled her up out of the chair.

"I can't take any more! Don't you understand? He's my child!"

I held her up, shaking her. I was stronger, tougher after a life of manual labor. She didn't have a chance. I pushed her towards the door and slammed her against the woodwork. Her face twisted, finally I had shaken something inside of her. But I didn't let go; I held her tight and screamed.

"Where is Wei-Wen?! Where is he?!"

All of a sudden the guards were there, they came from behind, tore me loose, forced me down on the floor. Held me down. Deep sobs pushed their way up from my diaphragm.

"Wei-Wen . . . Wei-Wen . . . Wei-Wen . . ."

She stood over me. Once again she was calm, adjusting her clothes a bit, catching her breath.

"Let her go."

Hesitating, the guards let me go. I sat there leaning forward, no longer putting up a fight. There was no fight left in me. Slowly Li Xiara walked over to me, and put her hand on the back of my head. She let it rest there for a moment, then she stroked my cheek and took hold under my chin. She gently forced my face upwards, so that my gaze met hers.

Then she nodded.

They took me to him. He lay on a white sheet in a sharply illuminated room. He was sleeping. His body was hidden by a blanket. Only his head was visible. His face was soft, but thinner than before. His eye sockets stood out like clear shadows. I drew closer and then I discovered it — they'd shaved off all his hair on the one side of his head. I took another step, and understood why. A section behind his ear, by his hairline, was red. The sting. I resisted the urge to rush forward. I was alone, but knew they were watching. They were always watching me. But that wasn't why I remained standing there.

As long as I was here, two meters away, I could still believe he was sleeping.

I could believe he was sleeping and avoid noticing the ice crystals that were growing like vines from the floor and up along the legs of the bed.

I could believe he was sleeping and avoid noticing how my breath hung in the air in front of me, every time I let warmth escape from my lungs.

I could believe he was sleeping and avoid noticing that he emitted no corresponding white cloud, that above his bed, over the white sheet, the air was still, clear and cold.

GEORGE

Gareth's farm smelled of something burning. The sweet aroma of warm honey and gasoline. The smoke hit me the minute I opened the car door.

He was standing with his back to me and his face towards the bonfire. It was many feet tall. The beehives weren't stacked, but rather tossed in a pile. The bonfire roared, creaking and crackling. Merrily, was how it struck me. As if it had a life of its own, as if it were taking pleasure in destroying somebody's life's work. He held a gasoline can in his hand, his arm hung limply. Maybe he'd forgotten it was there.

He turned around and noticed me. He didn't look surprised.

"How many?" I asked and nodded towards the fire.

"Ninety percent."

Not the number of hives, not the number of bee colonies, but the percentage. As if it were all just math. But his eyes told a different story.

He walked a few steps, put the can down. But then he picked it up again, probably realized he couldn't leave it there, in the middle of the yard.

He was red, his skin was so dry that it was about to crack, a rash had spread upwards from his tanned throat.

"What about you?" He raised his head.

"Most of them."

He nodded. "Did you burn them?"

"Don't know if there's any point, but yeah."

"Isn't worth using the hives again. It's gotten into them."

He was right, they stank of death.

"I didn't think it was going to happen here," he said.

"I thought it was negligence," I said.

Gareth pulled up the corners of his mouth into something that was supposed to resemble a smile. "Me, too."

He wasn't so different from the little boy he had once been, the one who stood alone in the schoolyard, with his backpack emptied out on the ground in front of him, the books trampled to pieces, the pencils thrown away, everything full of mud. But he didn't give up then, never ran away, just crouched down, picked up the books, wiped the mud off with the sleeve of his sweater, gathered up the pencils, picked up his things, just as he had hundreds of times before.

I don't know why, but suddenly I reached out my hand, squeezed his upper arm.

Then he bowed his head, his face crumpled, dissolved in front of me.

Three gut-wrenching sobs escaped from him.

His body was in turmoil beneath my hand, straining, as if there were more inside that wanted to come out. I just kept holding on to him. But nothing more came out. The three sobs and no more.

Then he straightened up, drawing the back of his hand across his eyes without looking at me. At that exact moment a gust of wind hurled across the yard, the smoke from the fire surged towards us. And the tears flowed freely.

"Damn smoke," I said.

"Yeah," he said. "Damn smoke."

We stood still, he shook himself a little, pulling himself together. Then he produced his usual grin.

"Well, George, what can I do for you today?"

Gareth was right. The hives arrived right away. Allison approved the loan without blinking, and just two days later a gray truck pulled into my yard. A grouchy guy got out, asked me where I wanted them.

He dumped them on the field before I had time to get there myself. Didn't say a word, just held out a clipboard with a piece of paper on it and wanted me to sign for the delivery.

There they were. Stiff. Just as steely-gray as the truck they'd arrived on. They smelled of industrial paint. A long row of them. Every single one the spitting image of the next. I felt a cold shudder of distaste, turned away.

Just hoped the bees wouldn't notice the difference.

But of course they'd notice the difference.

They noticed everything.

TAO

The boy put the fried rice on the table in front of me. The last time there had been a few pieces of vegetables and a little egg mixed in. Today it was flavored only with artificial soy sauce. The scent burned in my nose. I almost had to lean away to keep from gagging. I'd barely eaten in the past few days, although Li Xiara had given me enough money. More than enough. But I didn't have the stomach for anything other than dry biscuits. Every nerve in my body was burning, my mouth was dry, the skin on my hands cracking. I was dehydrated, perhaps because I barely drank any fluids at all, or perhaps from all of the tears my body had released. I'd cried myself dry now, there were no tears left. I'd cried myself empty to the sound of Li Xiara's voice. She'd visited me every day, talked and talked, explaining and coaxing me. And slowly, as time passed, her words acquired meaning. I clung to them almost greedily. Maybe I *wanted* them to acquire meaning. Just to follow her lead, without having to think for myself.

"You have loved him too much," she said.

"Is it possible to love somebody too much?"

"You were like all parents. You wanted to give your child everything."

"Yes. I wanted to give him everything."

"Everything is far too much."

For fractions of time, seconds, minutes I thought I understood. But then I would encounter meaninglessness again, and what she said became just words, because all I was able to think about was Wei-Wen. Wei-Wen. My child.

Yesterday she came for the last time. We wouldn't be talking anymore, she said. I had to go home now, put my own grief aside. Duties awaited us. She wanted me to give speeches, talk about Wei-Wen. About the bees that had come back. About our goal, about her goal with them, to cultivate them like useful plants, in controlled surroundings, make every effort to ensure that they would once again reproduce, at such a rapid pace that everything would soon be as before. Wei-Wen was to become a symbol, she said. And I was to be the grieving mother who managed to see the bigger picture, putting aside her own needs for the community. *When I, who have lost everything, can, so can you.* She didn't give me any choice. Something inside me understood why. I understood that she, too, was doing what she had to, or thought she had to do. Even though I still didn't know if I would manage it, if I could cope with what she wanted from me. Because the only thing that had meaning was him. His face. I tried to hang on to it, his face between Kuan's and my own. He was looking up at us. *More. More. One, two, three — jump.* The red scarf lifted by the wind.

My departure was the next day. Wei-Wen had to stay behind. Later I might be allowed to give him a burial. But that wasn't important. The tiny, cold body covered with a layer of frost was not him. *That* face wasn't his, not the one I tried to remember all the time.

I pushed the bowl towards the boy.

"It's for you."

He gave me a questioning look.

"Aren't you going to eat anything at all?"

"No. I bought it for you."

He stood there jiggling one foot.

"Have a seat." I heard the pleading in my voice.

He quickly pulled out the chair and drew

the bowl towards him, looked at it for a moment with something like happiness, before he raised it to his mouth and started shoveling in rice.

It was good to see him eat. To see him keep himself alive. I just sat there studying him while he shoved the rice into his mouth, barely taking time to chew before the next mouthful was on its way.

When the worst of his wolfish hunger was sated, he calmed down, concentrated on guiding the chopsticks more slowly towards his lips, as if an inner etiquette teacher had suddenly reminded him of his manners.

"Thank you," he said softly.

I smiled in response.

"Do you know anything more?" I asked after allowing him to chew for a bit.

"About what?"

"About your family. Will you stay here?"

"I don't know." He looked down at the tabletop. "I just know that Dad has regrets every single day. We thought we were safe here, that this was where we should be, but then everything changed. We're just a nuisance now."

"Can't you leave?"

"Where to? We have no money, nowhere to go." The feeling of impotence crept through me again. Yet another thing I couldn't do anything about.

No. This was not insurmountable. This *was* something I could manage, somebody I could help.

I raised my head.

"Come with me."

"What do you mean?" He looked at me in astonishment.

"Come back with me."

"Are you going home?"

"Yes. Now I'm going home."

"But we aren't allowed — they'll refuse. And what about work? Is there work for us there?"

"I promise that I'll help you."

"What about food?"

"There is even less here."

"Yes." He put down his chopsticks. The bowl of rice was empty. Only a single grain of rice remained on the bottom. He noticed it, picked up the chopsticks to get hold of it, but quickly put them down again when he saw that I was observing him.

"You have to," I said softly. "If you stay here, you'll die."

"Maybe that's just as well."

There was something savage in his voice and he avoided my gaze.

"What do you mean?" I forced the words out, I couldn't take this. Not in him, someone so young.

"It doesn't make any difference what happens to us," he said with his head bowed. "To Dad and me. Where we live. Here. Together. Or alone. It's not important." His voice became hoarse suddenly. He cleared his throat, removing the huskiness. "Nothing matters anymore. Don't you see that?"

I couldn't muster a reply. His words were distortions of Li Xiara's. *Each and every one of us is not important.* But she was talking about community; he was talking about loneliness.

I stood up abruptly. I had to make him stop talking. The fragile hope I was clinging to was on the verge of being crushed. I looked in all directions except at him as I walked towards the door.

"You have to pack," I said in a low voice. "We leave tomorrow."

Back at my room, I quickly pulled out the bag. It didn't take long to gather up the few things I had with me. The clothes, some toiletries, an extra pair of shoes. I searched the entire room, wanting to be sure I hadn't forgotten anything. And then I discovered them. The books. They'd been there all along, but I hadn't seen them, they'd become a part of the room. They lay in a pile on the nightstand, I hadn't touched them since the guard came to get me, hadn't taken them out to read them, not once, knowing that the words would probably have as little meaning as everything else.

I had to return them, perhaps I could still make it to the library. But I just stood there holding them. I could feel the smooth protective plastic on the book cover at the bottom of the pile sticking to my hands.

I put them down on the bed and picked this one up. It was *The History of Bees*. I'd never had the chance to finish reading it. But I opened it now.

GEORGE

Emma was crying again. She stood with her back to me, peeling potatoes and crying. She let her tears flow freely, made no attempt to stop them, regularly releasing small sobs. The tears came often these days. She cried as if she were at a funeral, anywhere and at any time, over washtubs, while making dinner or brushing her teeth. Every time it happened, I just wanted to get away. I couldn't handle it, tried to find excuses to leave.

Luckily I wasn't inside very often. I worked from morning till night. I had hired Rick and Jimmy full-time. The money, the loan, poured out of the account. Eventually I couldn't be bothered to check. Couldn't bear to see the ever-diminishing bank balance. It was a matter of working now. Just working. Without work, no income. I could still save some of the harvest. Make enough money to service the loan.

The pounds melted off my body, ounce after ounce. Day after day. And night after night, because I was sleeping poorly. Emma looked after me, served me, decorating my food with cucumber slices and strips of carrots, but it didn't help. There was no taste to it; it hit my palate like sawdust. I ate only because I had to, to get the strength to go out again. I knew Emma would have liked to prepare steak every day, but she, too, was trying to save money. We didn't talk about it, but I'm sure I wasn't the only one observing the shrinking bank balance.

In fact we didn't say anything about anything these days. I didn't know what had happened to us. I missed my wife. She was there, but at the same time, she wasn't. Or maybe it was actually *me* who wasn't there.

She sniffled. I wanted to hold her, the way I always had. But my body resisted. All of her tears collected in this huge pond that separated us.

I backed out of the kitchen, hoped she wouldn't notice.

But she turned around. "You do see that I'm crying."

I didn't answer.

"Come here, won't you?" she said quietly.

It was the first time she'd asked me. I remained standing where I was all the same.

She waited, still holding the potato peeler in the one hand, a potato in the other. I waited, too. Hoping, I guess, that I could wait the whole thing out. But not this time.

She whimpered softly. "You don't care."

"Of course I care," I said, but couldn't bear to meet her gaze.

She raised her arms a little more.

"Crying doesn't help," I said.

"It doesn't help that we don't comfort each other, either."

She twisted my words around, as she often did.

"We won't get more hives by my standing here and comforting you," I said. "No more queens, no more bees. No more honey."

Her arms dropped. She turned around. "Go and work, then."

But I just stood there.

"Go and work!" she repeated.

I took a step towards her. And another. I could put a hand on her shoulder. I could. That would definitely help. Help both of us.

I reached out my hand, towards her back. She didn't see it, was busy peeling, took another potato out of the dirty water in the sink. Scraped off the peel with quick movements, as she had done hundreds of times before.

My hand was suspended in midair, but

didn't reach her.

At that moment the phone rang.

My arm fell. I turned around, went out into the hallway and answered it.

The voice was young, almost girlish, and was asking for me.

"I got your name from Lee," she said. "We went to school together."

"Right." In other words, she couldn't be as young as she sounded.

She talked quickly, was good with words. She worked for a television channel, they were making a movie, she explained.

"It's about CCD."

"Yes?"

"Colony Collapse Disorder." She pronounced the words slowly and with exaggerated clarity.

"I know what CCD is."

"We're making a documentary about the dying bees and the ramifications. I understand you've faced this issue on your farm."

"Did Lee tell you?"

"We'd like to make it personal," she said.

"Personal. Right," I said.

"Could we spend a day with you? Would you let us go out with you, so we could hear about your experience of the whole thing?"

"My experience. That can't be very interesting."

"Oh yes, to us it is. That's precisely what we want to show. How this has an impact on each and every one of us. How it can destroy people's livelihoods. Is that how you've experienced it? Has it been rough on you?"

"Well, it hasn't exactly destroyed my livelihood," I said. Suddenly I didn't like her tone. Like she was talking to an injured dog.

"No? Because my understanding was that you've lost almost all of your bees?"

"Yes. But now I've replaced many of them."

"Oh."

She fell silent.

"Worker bees only live for a few weeks in the summer," I said. "It doesn't take very long to get new hives up and running."

"Right. So is that what you're working on now, getting new hives up and running?"

"That's right."

"Great!" she said.

"Really?"

"We can use that. Terrific! Would it be convenient if we came next week?"

I hung up after we arranged a time. The receiver was all sweaty. I was going to be on TV. I'd become someone they "could use." It was apparently not possible to get out of it. I tried, but she'd talked me into it. Was

537

worse than Emma.

National television. The whole country would be able to see it. Geez Louise.

Emma had come into the room. She was drying her hands on a towel. Her eyes were red, but fortunately also dry.

"Who was that?"

I explained to her who had called.

"Interview us about the bees? Why do we have to?"

"Not we. They're just going to talk to me."

"But why did you say yes?"

"It can help influence things. Maybe the authorities will do something," I said and caught myself copying the words of the woman who had called.

"But why us?"

"Me," I said severely and turned away from her. Couldn't take any more questions, any more crying, any more nagging. All of a sudden it came over me again. The fatigue. I hadn't felt it through all of these weeks. Not since Tom was home last winter. But now it was back. I could have lain down and slept there and then, on the floor in the hallway. The worn wood floor looked tempting. I thought of the teddy bear thermometer, the peeping sound it made. I wished it would show a high temperature, a powerful fever. Then I could lie in bed. Soft pillow, warm quilt, like a lid covering me up. Take the temperature of a fever that never went down.

But I couldn't go to bed. Couldn't even sit down.

Because the hives were out there. Empty and gray. Way too light. They had to be filled. And there was nobody else who could do it. And now I was apparently going to be on television. I had to demonstrate that I was hard at work. That I hadn't allowed CCD to break me.

My coveralls hung limply from their hook. The veil and the hat were directly above them. Underneath were my boots. It looked like a flat man had hidden inside the wall. I took down the suit and started to change. I pulled up the zipper, made sure everything was closed up, battened down the hatches.

"It's almost dinnertime," Emma said. She stood there with her empty hands, her empty arms.

"I can eat later."

"But it's meat loaf. I've made meat loaf."

"We have a microwave."

Her bottom lip trembled, but she didn't say anything. Just stood there like that, completely silent, while I put on my hat, hung the veil in front of my face and went outside.

I went to the pasture by the Alabast River and stayed there the rest of the day. First I worked. The weather was annoyingly good. It shouldn't be this good. It didn't fit. The sun hung large in the sky to the west, above the blossoming field. As beautiful as a picture in a calendar.

But the work became cumbersome. My arms felt almost paralyzed, the fatigue took hold of me. I was unable to do anything but walk. In circles around the new hives. Empty. Gray, a giant mountain.

I stayed there until the bees began to come in. Nature fell silent.

It was only *then* that I walked across the field. To the other end. My legs just took me there. Towards the old, carnival-colored hives, the ones that still had life in them.

Why had these been spared? Who had decided that these particular bees should be allowed to live? I was breathing heavily and stopped beside a yellow hive. Every single time I was going to check a hive, I sort of cringed inside. Every time I expected to find the same thing. Could already picture the lethargic bees whirring around at the bottom of the hive, the emptiness, the queen alone with a small handful of young bees.

And there was something wrong with this one, too. It was way too quiet. There was something wrong, for sure. I checked the flight board. Just a few bees. Not enough.

I couldn't bear it.

I had to.

With my eyes closed I grasped the lid. Then I opened the hive. It rushed up at me immediately, the buzzing sound, the whirring. How could I not have heard it? That everything was normal. Completely normal, 100 percent as it should be. The bees buzzing around down there. Some were dancing. I caught a glimpse of the queen, the turquoise mark on her back. I saw the brood. Clear, golden honey. They were working, they were alive. And they were here.

My head spun. I was so tired. I sank down onto the ground and stayed there. The ground was warm, the grass was soft. My eyes slid shut.

But I didn't fall asleep. Because there was such a tightness in my chest. Emma's pond of tears had reached me. The water was rising. It splashed against my feet.

I swallowed and swallowed. Couldn't breathe. Drowning. But I fought back. Got to my feet again. Just stood there looking at the bees, who were also fighting down there. Fighting the ordinary, daily struggle for their offspring, for enough pollen, for honey.

They were going to die, too. It wasn't viable, what I was doing. Every single time I opened a hive, it would be like this. The same feeling, whether they were alive or gone. There was no point.

There was no point!

All the muscles in my body tensed. All my strength gathered in one of my legs, in my foot, and all of a sudden I kicked.

The hive fell to the ground with a crash and a swarm of bees rose up.

I shook the boards loose. The bees were everywhere now. Furious and terrified. They wanted to get me, to avenge themselves. I stomped on them, on the brood, on their babies. But the sound was muffled, barely audible. Not like broken glass. I continued all the same. Destroy them. Crush them. Tear their wings off. Because they had destroyed me.

And then it hit me. How simple it was.

We could destroy each other.

I was standing in the midst of a cloud of furious bees, raging around me.

It was so simple.

I lifted my hand to the zipper, to the veil.

All I had to do was lift it up.

Take off the hat.

Off with the gloves.

Pull down the zipper quickly — squirm

out of the suit.

Kick off the boots.

And just stand here and let them do the job.

They would sting me in self-defense. Pierce me, sacrificing their lives to take mine. And this time my father wouldn't be here to take me in his arms and run off with me, while the cloud of bees stormed above us and followed us all the way to the river, where he pulled us under and held us down until the attack was over.

This time I would fall down. Stay down. The poison would run through my veins. Let them keep stinging, and if they stopped, I'd kick them with bare toes, step on them so they continued, kept stinging until I was beyond recognition.

They should have their revenge. They deserved it.

And then everything would be over.

I'd do it now.

Now.

My fingers clutched the veil. The thin fabric against the heavy gloves.

Lifted it.

Now!

But then . . .

Footsteps crossing the field. Someone shouting.

Heading towards me.

At first calmly, and then stronger. Louder.

Wearing a white suit. Hat, veil. Fully dressed, ready to work. Once again he'd come without a warning. Or perhaps Emma had known.

He'd come. For good?

He was running now. Did he see me? What was happening?

The cries became louder, piercing through the air.

"Dad? Dad!"

TAO

The boy and his father stood behind me as I put the key into the lock and opened the door to an empty evening darkness.

Kuan's jacket wasn't hanging on the hook in the hallway. His shoes were gone.

I pushed down the handle on the bathroom door.

His shelf above the sink was empty. There was just a trace of soap where his razor had been.

He'd moved without saying anything. Because he wanted to? Because he thought I wanted him to? Because everything about me reminded him of Wei-Wen, the way everything about Kuan reminded me of him?

Because he blamed me?

Yet another one who'd disappeared. But this time I couldn't search for him. I couldn't ask, couldn't contact him. This was his decision, I had no right to ask. For I was still to blame.

The boy and his father had stayed in the hallway. They looked at me expectantly. I had to say something.

"You can take the bedroom."

I put my bag down in the middle of the living room floor and made up a bed for myself on the couch. I could hear the boy talking in there. His voice came in waves, eager, chattering about practical details with a newfound energy. He'd rediscovered a future. The darkness in him had disappeared. Or perhaps I'd put too much into the words the evening before. Loaded them with all of my own stuff.

I went over to the window. The fence was still there. In the air above it a helicopter was circling. The bees were contained, like in a cocoon, not a single one was supposed to slip out, not until there were many more of them and there was certain knowledge about how to control them. That was how Li Xiara wanted it to be.

She wanted to tame them. They were going to save us. She wanted to tame them, the way she had tamed me. And I'd allowed myself to be tamed. That was the easiest. Follow her, don't think.

The boy was laughing. It was the first time I'd heard him laugh. How young and bright his laughter was. I'd given them something.

The sound grew louder, made it easier to breathe. When was the last time somebody had laughed between these four walls? Behind me was the bag. Inside it was the book, I'd never returned it, but read all of it from beginning to end. I carried the words with me, but didn't know what to do with them. It was too enormous, I couldn't cope with it.

They were preparing the square, clearing away a space. A podium was being built, cameras rigged up. Several crews were working at once, because the speech was going to be broadcast to the entire world. An energetic producer bossed people around. In the background she stacked large baskets full of freshly picked pears. The symbolism felt exaggerated. But maybe that was what it would take.

I was given my own dressing room. A woman came in with some clothes to choose from. Nothing flashy, but all of the clothes were brand new. A simple design, it resembled the uniform from the Party's earliest phase, as if to remind viewers where I came from, that I was one of them, one of the people. They were a little stiff, with fold creases, but of a soft fabric.

"It's cotton," the woman said. "Recycled cotton."

I'd never before owned a cotton garment. Every meter cost a month's salary. I chose a blue suit, put it on. The fabric breathed, I could barely feel it against my skin. I turned to look in the mirror. It suited me. I looked like one of them. Like her, Li Xiara, not like a worker from the fruit fields, but like the person I was perhaps actually meant to be.

I was somebody else in this suit — the person she asked me to be. I turned around, looked in the mirror over my shoulder; the jacket hung nicely over the shoulders, the trousers fit around the hips. I tugged a little at the sleeves; they ended exactly where they should.

Then I met my own gaze. My eyes . . . they looked so much like his. But who was I? I looked down. Wei-Wen had never owned a cotton garment. And his short life had not had any meaning.

Again I forced myself to raise my head, to look at myself. A useful idiot stared back at me.

No. All of a sudden the fabric felt abrasive against my skin. I tore off the blouse. Stepped out of the trousers and left them lying on the floor.

It would have meaning. And I knew how.

I pulled my own threadbare sweater down

over my head, tugged on my old trousers, buttoned them quickly and put on my shoes.

Then I picked up my bag, which was lying on the floor, opened the door to the dressing room and quickly walked out. I found the producer and grabbed hold of her.

"Where is Li Xiara? I have to talk to Li Xiara." She was in the village Committee building, had received the largest office. Three men were chased out of there by a security guard when I arrived, even though it was absolutely clear that they had hadn't finished their conversation.

Li Xiara stood up quickly and walked over to greet me. She tried one of her gentle smiles, but I was done with this now.

"Here." I handed her the book.

She accepted it, but didn't open it, didn't even look at it.

"Tao, I'm looking forward to hearing you speak."

"You have to read the book," I said.

"If you like we can go over it one more time, I'd be happy to do so. The wording. Perhaps we should change some of the phrasing . . ."

"I just want you to read this," I said.

She finally shifted her gaze towards the book, stroked the title with one finger. "*The*

History of Bees?"

I nodded. "I won't do anything, I won't give any speeches until you've read it."

She looked up quickly. "What are you saying?"

"You people are doing everything wrong."

Her eyes narrowed. "We are doing everything we *can.*"

I leaned forward, held her gaze and said softly: "They're going to die. Again."

She looked at me. I waited for an answer, but it didn't come. Was she thinking? Did she take it in? Did my words mean anything to her at all? The anger rose inside me. Couldn't she say something?

I couldn't stand to be there any longer; I turned and walked towards the door. Then she finally reacted.

"Wait."

She opened the book and calmly turned the pages until she reached the title page.

"Thomas Savage." She glanced at the name of the author. "American?"

"It was the only book he wrote," I said quickly. "But that doesn't make it any less important."

She raised her head and looked at me again. Then she nodded towards a chair.

"Sit down. Tell me."

At first my words tumbled out in rush, as

I explained haphazardly, jumping back and forth. But then I understood that she was giving me time. Several times somebody knocked on the door; there were many people waiting, but she turned them all away and I slowly calmed down.

I told her about the author, Thomas Savage. The book was based on his experiences and his life. Savage's family had been beekeepers for generations. His father was one of the first to be affected by The Collapse and one of the last to give up. And Savage had worked with his father until the end. They had changed over to organic operations at an early stage, that was Savage's own requirement. He never forced the bees out onto the road, never took more honey than they needed to survive. But all the same they were not spared. The bees died. Again and again. Finally they were forced to sell the farm. Only then, as a fifty-year-old, did Savage sit down and write about all of his experiences, about the future. *The History of Bees* was visionary, but still real and concrete because it was based on a lifetime of practical experience.

The book was published in 2037, just eight years before The Collapse was a fact. It predicted the fate of the human race. And how we might, in turn, manage to rise from the ashes again.

When I was finished, Li Xiara sat in silence. She held the book calmly in her hands. Her gaze, impossible to read, rested on me.

"You can go now."

Was she throwing me out? If I refused, she would call security, give them orders to take me home. Demand that I stay there, in the flat, until it was time for the speech and then require me to give it and many more, against my own convictions.

But she did none of these things. Instead, she turned the pages until she reached the first chapter and leaned towards the text.

I stood there. Then she lifted her eyes again, nodded towards the door.

"Now I would like to be alone. Thank you."

"But . . ."

She put one hand on the book, as if to protect it. Then she said softly: "I have children, too."

WILLIAM

The wallpaper hung in tatters from the walls and its yellowness was still invasive. She was singing again, today like every day, a melodious humming of faint notes while she swept the floor with precise movements. I lay with my face towards the window; a few brown leaves fluttered past out there.

She swept the debris onto a tray and put it by the door. Then she turned to face me.

"Shall I shake out your blanket?"

Without waiting for an answer she quickly lifted it off me, picked it up in her arms and carried it towards the window. I lay there in my nightshirt only, feeling exposed, but she didn't look at me.

She opened the window, the air poured in. It had grown colder just since yesterday. I could feel the goose bumps rising on my legs and pulled my feet up under me.

She held the carpet outside the window and shook it with large movements. It stood straight up like a sail out there before she allowed it to drop. Just when it was almost hanging straight down, she gave it another yank and sent it up in front of the window.

When she was finished, she laid it over me. It was as cold as the air outside. Then she pulled up a chair beside the bed and stood there with her hand on its back.

"Shall I read for you?"

She didn't wait for an answer. She never waited for an answer, just went over to the bookshelf, which was again meticulously organized. Hesitated a bit, sliding her index finger quickly across the spines of the books. Then she stopped and pulled one out.

"We'll take this one."

I didn't see the title. She didn't read it to me, either, probably knew that it didn't make any difference. It wasn't what she read, but the *fact* that she read that was important.

"Charlotte," I said with the hoarse, old man's voice that wasn't mine. "Charlotte . . ."

She looked up. Shook her head gently. I didn't need to say it, shouldn't say it. Because I'd repeated it such a countless number of times already and she knew it very well. What I asked from her was to get away. Leave. Abandon me. Think about herself.

Live, not for me, but for herself.

But her answer was the same every time. Nonetheless I would keep on saying it again and again. I couldn't help myself. I owed her this, because she had granted me her entire life. But there were no words that would make her leave, no words could hold her back. She wanted only to be at my side.

Her voice filled the room along with the cool autumn air. But I wasn't cold. The words took me into an embrace. She would read for a long time now, never allowed disturbances.

I reached out a hand and knew she would take hold of it.

She sat like this, today like every other day, with her hand calmly in mine, and filled the silence with words. She wasted the words on me, was wasting her time, her life. That in itself was reason enough for me to get up. But I wasn't equal to it. I was stripped of — no, not stripped — I had *thrown away* both my will and my passion.

Then suddenly a sound rose up towards us from the ground floor. A sound I hadn't heard in many years. The crying of an infant. An infant? Not mine. Perhaps someone who was visiting? But who? Months had passed since I had heard voices down there other than those of my own family.

Charlotte stopped reading. She actually allowed herself to be disturbed and leaned forward a bit, as if she were about to take off at a run.

Someone was lulling a baby to sleep down there. Thilda?

The child whimpered, but allowed itself to be comforted. Gradually it became calmer.

Charlotte leaned back in the chair, picked up the book and resumed reading.

I closed my eyes. Could sense her hand against mine and the words rising and falling in the air between us. The minutes passed. She read, and I lay completely still, in a state of deep gratitude.

But then the baby's wailing started up again downstairs. Louder now. Charlotte stopped.

She withdrew her hand.

The crying intensified to despair, distress, tearing at the walls.

Then she stood up and put down the book. Quickly she walked towards the door. "I'm sorry, Father."

She opened the door. The crying filled the room.

"The infant . . . ," I said.

She stopped in the doorway.

I searched for the words. "Has somebody

come to visit?"

She shook her head quickly.

"No. The baby is ours now."

"But, how?"

"The mother died in childbirth. And the father, he's not able to take care of it."

"Who is he?" I asked. "Is he here?"

"No, Father." She hesitated. "He's in London."

Suddenly I understood. I sat up halfway in the bed, tried to look at her sternly, to make her tell me the truth. "It's his child, isn't it? Edmund's?"

She blinked rapidly. Didn't answer, but she didn't need to, either.

"I'm sorry," she said again.

Then she turned away from me and left.

The door was left standing ajar behind her. I heard her quick steps on the stairway, how she went downstairs and walked swiftly across the floor down there.

"I'm coming."

She stopped.

"I have him."

Her voice became lower.

"There . . . there, now . . . there, there . . . shhhh . . ."

And then.

The faint, humming song of hers.

But now she wasn't singing for me.

Finally she was no longer singing for me. She was singing for the baby she held in her arms, the baby she was slowly rocking.

GEORGE

The great shakes. They were in me. For days. Morning, noon, night. I struggled to hold a knife and fork. Emma saw it, but said nothing. Struggled to use tools, dropped the screwdriver on the floor, the saw swerved awkwardly.

I awoke with fear in my heart every single morning.

Woke up, went down and met him. He just glanced up at me and gave a little nod before diving down into his book again. But that was fine.

Because *he* wasn't shaking.

He didn't falter. Even when he was turning the pages of a book, it was done with confidence in his movements, calm and assured, the cup of coffee lifted with a steady hand. The footsteps towards the field, towards the hives, exactly the same length, his strides strong and solid against the ground.

And I followed behind him. At all times

with this trembling in me.

But as I witnessed these strides of his across the field, the lifting he did with his legs, not with his back, bend, lift, put down, again and again, as I watched these movements, I gradually stopped shaking. Every day it became easier to hold a fork.

And then, while we were extracting honey, while the autumn sun was low and gentle in the sky, just as yellow as the drops we shook off the frames, I suddenly noticed something. They were gone. The shakes were gone.

I worked with calm, stable hands. Like him. Beside him.

The two of us now completely in sync.

TAO

The hive was guarded, but the tent had been removed. The area was open all the way to the edge of the fields, right by the forest.

People had gathered at a proper distance, standing calmly and just looking at it. Nobody feared it, the bees weren't dangerous, Wei-Wen's allergy was an isolated case. Around us there were flowers on all sides, recently planted bushes, red, pink, orange, the same fairy-tale world I had seen in the tent, but which now extended across a large area, because the fruit trees had been chopped down and replaced by new plants.

The military had left. The fences were torn down. The cocoon had burst and the hive lived among us. The bees were allowed to fly where they wanted, completely free.

It was ten meters away from me, in the shadow of the trees, the sun shining on it through the leaves — not far from the place where the first wild hive had been found, not far from the place where Wei-Wen had been stung. Savage's Standard Hive, just as Thomas Savage had drawn it in *The History of Bees,* the hive that had been in his family since 1852, the drawings of which had disappeared at some point in history, but the measurements and appearance of which Savage had memorized and drawn again. The hive had been intended for honey production and observation — that's where he had wanted to tame the bees.

But bees cannot be tamed. They can only be tended, receive our care. Despite the original purpose of the hive, it was still a good home for the bees. In it everything was arranged to enable them to breed and reproduce. They kept the honey for themselves; nothing was to be harvested, never to be used by humans. It would be allowed to remain as nature had intended: food for the newborns.

The sound was unlike anything I'd ever heard before. In and out, in and out the bees flew. With them they brought nectar and pollen, nourishment for their offspring. But not just for the few that were their own; every single bee worked for the group, for all of the bees, for the organism they constituted together.

The buzzing pulsated through the air, made something vibrate inside me. A tone that calmed me, made it easier to breathe.

I just stood there like that. Tried to follow each individual bee with my eyes, see every individual bee's journey from the hive, out to the flowers, from flower to flower, and back again. But I kept losing sight of them. There were too many of them, their movement patterns impossible to understand.

So instead I let my gaze come to rest on the whole, on the hive and all the life it surrounded itself with, all of the life to which it attended.

While I was standing there, somebody appeared beside me. I turned. It was Kuan. He was concentrating on the hive, lifting his head to get a better view. But then he discovered me.

"Tao."

He came towards me. An unfamiliar gait, heavier, as if he were already old.

We stood facing one another. Kuan kept his eyes focused on me, didn't look down, the way he often used to do. There were dark circles under his eyes. He was drawn, pale.

I missed him. Missed the person he'd been. The cheerful lightness in him, the contentment, the joy over the child he'd had.

And the child he would have. I wished I could say something that would bring back this cheerfulness in him, but found no words.

We turned towards the hive, stood like that, side by side and looked at it. Our hands almost touched, but neither of us took hold of the other's hand, like two teenagers who didn't quite dare. The warmth between us. It was back.

A bee buzzed through the air past us, just a meter away, swerved to the right, a seemingly unplanned movement, then it flew between us — I could feel the tiny gust of air against my cheek — and then it disappeared into the flowers.

Then he took my hand.

I caught my breath. This time he was the one who dared.

Finally he touched me again. My hand grew small in meeting with his. He shared his warmth with me.

We just stood there, holding hands, while we looked at the hive.

And then.

Finally the words came that I had so yearned for.

Softly and clearly with a seriousness that was unlike him. Not something he said because he had to, but because he meant it:

"It wasn't your fault, Tao. It wasn't your fault."

Afterwards, after we'd said farewell, I walked alone down along the wheel ruts. The bees were still vibrating inside me. And his words released words in myself.

I walked on, more and more slowly, until finally I stopped and remained standing among the fruit trees. Everything was open, no trace of the fences and the military, everything as before, like last year at this time. It was snowing yellow leaves. The ground was covered, the trees would soon be bare. All the pears were harvested, each one carefully picked, packed in paper and carried away. Pears of gold.

But on the horizon I could glimpse change. The endless rows of fruit trees had been broken up. The laborers were hard at work digging up roots and getting the trees up out of the ground. Thomas Savage's vision had finally become a reality. We released our control and the forest would be allowed to spread. In the soil other plants would be sown, large areas would be allowed to remain uncultivated.

Yes. I wanted it now. To give a speech, as she wanted. Because I also wanted, for my own part, to speak about Wei-Wen. I was going to talk about who he was for all of us, who he would become — the picture of him that had been printed on large pennants in the square, on posters along the walls of the buildings, on banners above the doorways of public buildings.

It was one of the few photographs we owned of him. It had been fuzzy and washed out, taken against a neutral, gray backdrop, but on the posters the colors were clear, the contrasts defined, and his eyes had been given more light.

This bright, sharp picture was what the world saw and it was what I was going to talk about. Not about *him,* Wei-Wen, I would never give him to them. The people out there would never know his eagerness, his stubbornness, his defiance. They would never learn of how he sometimes woke up singing, off-key, but with enthusiasm. They would never hear about his eternal runny nose, about changing his trousers damp with pee, rubbing ice-cold feet, or having a body warm with sleep against me at night. For them he would never be any of this. That's why it didn't matter anymore. That's why the one he *was* didn't matter. A single person's life, a single person's flesh, blood, body fluids, nerve signals, thoughts, fears and dreams meant nothing. My dreams for him didn't mean anything, either, if I failed to put them into a context and see that the same dreams had to apply to all of us.

But Wei-Wen would nonetheless gain significance. The image of him. The boy wearing the red scarf, his face — that *was* the new era. For millions of people, his round cheeks, his large, shining eyes peering up at a bright blue sky were associated with a single word. A single, unifying feeling: hope.

ACKNOWLEDGMENTS

I would like to express my gratitude to all the many professionals who have taken the time to read the manuscript and answer my questions: historians Ragnhild Hutchison and Johanne Nygren; China expert Tone Helene Aarvik; zoologist Petter Bøckman; physician Siri Seterelv; senior advisor Bjørn Dahle at the Norwegian Beekeepers Association (Norges Birøkterlag); advisor Ragna Ribe Jørgensen at ByBi, the Urban Beekeepers' Association in Oslo; Roar Ree Kirkevold, who writes about beekeeping; beekeepers Ingar Tallakstad Lie and Per Sigmund Bøe and last but not least, Isaac Barnes at Honeyrun Farm in Ohio.

A special thanks also to all the committed people who have read, commented on and supported my work along the way: Hilde Rød-Larsen, Joakim Botten, Vibeke Saugestad, Guro Solberg, Jørgen Lunde Ronge, Mattis Øybø, Hilde Østby, Cathrine Movold, Gunn Østgård and Steinar Storløkken.

Finally, I would like to thank my wise editor, Nora Campbell, and all her accomplished colleagues at Aschehoug, who have demonstrated a warm enthusiasm for *The History of Bees* from the very first day.

I have drawn from a wide range of reference materials for the work on this novel. Among the most important are *The Hive* by Bee Wilson; *Ingar'sis birøkt* ("Beekeeping by Ingar") by Roar Ree Kirkevold; *Langstroth's Hive and the Honey-Bee* by Rev. Lorenzo Lorraine Langstroth; *A World Without Bees* by Allison Benjamin and Brian McCallum and *Det nye Kina* ("The New China") by Henning Kristoffersen, along with the documentaries *Vanishing of the Bees, More than Honey, Who Killed the Honey Bee?, Silence of the Bees* and *Queen of the Sun*.

Maja Lunde
Oslo, May 2015

570

ABOUT THE AUTHOR

Maja Lunde is a Norwegian author and screenwriter. Lunde has written ten books for children and young adults. She has also written scripts for Norwegian television. *The History of Bees* is her first novel for adults and the first debut to win the prestigious Norwegian Booksellers' Prize. She lives with her husband and three children in Oslo.